Maple & Moonlight

A Grumpy Maple Farmer Romance

The Maplewood Series
Book 2

Daphne Elliot

Published by Melody Publishing, LLC

Editing by Beth Lawton at VB Edits

Cover Design by Jenny Richardson at Classy Creeps

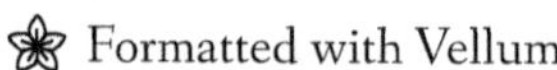 Formatted with Vellum

Content Warning

This book is a fun, contemporary romance with an HEA. However, it does contain some content that may be challenging to some readers. As always, I love you and want you to feel safe and comfortable reading my books.

This book contains content related to:
- Domestic violence (occurs off page)
- Child abuse (occurs off page)
- Anxiety and cPTSD
- Verbal and emotional abuse (occurs off page)
- Peril and danger
- Violence - Murder (off page)

This book also features a character with autism. Autism is a vast spectrum, and in the community we say, "If you've met one person with autism, you've met *one* person with autism." Julian's experience is not representative and is based on my own experiences raising my neurodiverse son.

Everyone's experiences with neurodiversity vary, and each individual has unique strengths and challenges. Thank you to my lovely sensitivity readers who shared their experiences and helped me portray this character as accurately and lovingly as possible.

Thank you and happy reading!

Chapter 1

CELINE

I'd come to Vermont for peace. A fresh start.

Not to burn down our new house on day one.

But my kids and I, we had a knack for creating catastrophe.

I'd survived the drive, the move, and my children's meltdowns, but standing alone on that porch was what finally made my knees shake and my throat tighten with a sensation dangerously close to relief.

With a heavy dose of exhaustion thrown in. By the time I waved off Chloe and Gus, I was running on fumes and borrowed hope.

While I was relieved to be moved in and thankful we'd driven up a day early to get things unpacked, I was anything but settled. I felt untethered. Hovering somewhere between escape and imprisonment. Between departure and arrival. Between the safety and peace I craved and the life I'd left behind.

I stood on the porch and waved as they drove away,

smiling even as my heart sank into my stomach. As the sound of Gus's tires on gravel faded, the late August haze settled around me. Vermont. It was warm and green, and the world here felt softer, like it hadn't yet learned how to hurt me.

It was beautiful. Fewer pine trees than I was used to, but I'd adjust. I could adjust to anything. I'd learned that lesson the hard way. The air smelled like wildflowers and river water. It was far preferable to the scent of fear and antiseptic and musty courtrooms I'd become far too familiar with lately.

In the front yard, relishing the peacefulness of the moment, I took what felt like my first deep breath in years.

This was the right choice.

I'd been repeating it to myself like a mantra all day.

We're safe now.

Maine didn't feel safe anymore.

My former home. Where I'd spent my entire life.

Every street corner held shadows of him. Every grocery aisle a familiar face. Even staying Downeast, far away from all of it, gave me no relief.

Turns out trauma can even ruin geography.

Chloe had offered us her giant lakefront house in Lovewell, but it was too close to where it all happened. We'd never move forward if we were constantly faced with pitying looks and the ghost of my kids' father lurking around every corner. Not to mention my ex-in-laws, who had vowed to make my life miserable while their son was too busy in prison to do the job properly.

We'd gone south, to Portland, last year. I'd gotten Julian a spot in a therapeutic kindergarten program at a specialty autism school.

It had been wonderful. And expensive.

But he'd thrived.

And he still was. The decision to leave was painful, but I needed a job and a fresh start. And given that he required far fewer supports than when he was younger, I was feeling good about a mainstream school. When we'd visited at the beginning of the summer, the kids had loved the area, especially the big park and coffee shop downtown. We'd ordered a dozen flavors of donuts and sampled them "for science" before taking selfies at the covered bridge. Maplewood was familiar, yet different. Small town New England, but with a quirky charm that I thought only existed in cheesy Netflix rom-coms.

The people here were friendly. Maybe even a little too friendly. Lots of hellos and several gifts of zucchini and maple syrup. I'd received welcome texts from the other teachers at my new school along with a surprising number of offers to help us move and get settled. It felt unnervingly like walking into a warm hug I wasn't sure I deserved.

I turned and surveyed the house. It was as advertised— quiet, rural, and secluded. Though it was nicer than I had anticipated. Far nicer than what we were used to. And the rent was laughably cheap. Callie, the school principal, surely had something to do with that part. When I'd told her I wasn't sure it was logical to uproot the kids and that I couldn't afford a big enough home for the four of us on my own, she'd laughed me off, insisting that she had the perfect place. And somehow, she was right. It was magically available at the right time and the rent was within my budget. I was still wary. I'd grown up in a small, tight-knit New England town in Maine. In Heartsborough, we were suspicious of outsiders; we weren't securing them prime real estate. Maplewood, on the other hand, went far above and beyond to welcome new arrivals.

This home was a gift from the universe. I'd rent from Satan himself if it meant access to a kitchen like this one and the fancy Wolf stove.

The poor landlord. Josh, I think? With his quiet voice, surly attitude, and giant shoulders, had probably rented to us under duress. From the interactions I'd had with townsfolk so far, they were all adamant that this was where I should live. So the idea that he really wasn't keen on having tenants made me feel bad. But not bad enough to find another rental. Hell no, this place was gorgeous. And it had a tub.

A freestanding, claw-foot tub in the primary suite. A tub like that wasn't a luxury; it was salvation. The farmer who owned this place might be grumpy, but his taste was impeccable.

I hadn't seen a woman around so far, but he must have a wife. Only someone familiar with the intricacies of motherhood and the stress that comes along with it—and probably some experience with witchcraft—would think to put a tub under a picture window, then hang a chandelier above it. A smart woman. One with kids, who understood the need for a really kick-ass tub. Or maybe broody, broad-shouldered Josh was secretly a romantic interior design savant trapped in the body of a bearded mountain man. Hard to tell.

Our first meeting had not gone as I'd planned, and it hadn't gone exceptionally well either. But I pivoted quickly. I'd gotten used to that. Julian had a tendency to upend even my best-laid plans. Our first interaction had been chaotic and somewhat mortifying. Especially since I hadn't been wearing a shirt. If first impressions mattered, then introducing myself while in a sports bra and Crocs said *unstable, sweaty mother of three who was flirting with a nervous breakdown.*

The interaction played over and over in my mind. One of the great gifts my anxiety had bestowed upon me was the ability to remember every detail of an embarrassing incident in a photographic way. So the replays were in HD with vivid detail.

Josh.

He was big. A little gruff.

Looked like he'd been carved out of the rock that made up the mountains of Vermont.

When I'd first caught sight of him, all my internal alarms had gone off.

But right away, he'd been respectful and kind to Julian. Gentle, even. It was a surprise, coming from a man who looked like he could bench press a tractor. And from the limited interaction we'd had so far, he seemed like he kept to himself, which was ideal in this scenario.

With any luck, he'd cash my checks and leave us alone. I certainly had no intention of spending more time with him than necessary.

Quiet landlord, quiet new life. That was the dream. But could that dream survive the chaos of my kids? That was yet to be determined.

Our arrival had been predictably intense. The kids had spilled out of the minivan like marbles and scattered. Ellie had complained about anything and everything while Maggie searched the property for horses and Julian vacillated between clinging to me and wandering off.

We were sweaty and cranky, but we'd gotten the moving pod—which had beat us here, miraculously—emptied and the furniture staged. Most of the unloading had been done by Gus, who'd proven himself to be my favorite brother-in-law. Never mind that he was my only brother-in-law. He'd quietly carried boxes and assembled furniture while Chloe barked instructions.

He'd put the girls' bunk beds together in record time and even had time to play a round of Uno with Julian before he left.

I owed them so much. My sister, who for far too many years had felt like a stranger, had shown up when I needed her and saved me. She'd been there on the worst day of my life and she hadn't stopped aggressively loving me and my kids since. I'd never felt so grateful, yet I'd never felt so alone.

My nervous system was still out of whack, making it difficult to wrap my mind around the events of the last few months. In quick succession, I'd finalized the protective order and the divorce decree and signed the rental agreement. During that time, I had one fresh start that turned out to be not so fresh. From there, I'd headed to Vermont. It was the farthest I'd ever been from him. It was safe. But the fear still hovered, like a shadow.

Yet beneath that fear, something else flickered. Possibility. Hope. That I could have a life that was my own, that didn't revolve around danger. A life where my kids could be curious and hopeful, and we could all just breathe.

Shaking off my ruminations, I kicked a large piece of gravel and steeled myself for the days ahead. I'd made it. I was fortunate, and my life would only get better from here. But part of me still wondered if I deserved good things.

Unsurprisingly, my kids had made themselves at home. Julian was already building a Lego masterpiece on the floor while Maggie buzzed around the kitchen, her blonde curls bouncing.

"Can we hive sleep tonight?" she asked.

With affection and a little defeat rolling through me, I nodded.

Someday I would sleep blissfully alone. Someday.

Donny had locked the door to keep the kids out of our room. And at the time, I hadn't argued.

But after all that had happened, we'd needed closeness. Comfort.

So Julian started sleeping with me.

And then, on occasion, Maggie and Ellie would join.

We'd nicknamed ourselves "the hive" because Julian had been super fixated on bees at the time. He'd read all the books about honeybees at the library and had begun teaching us about the incredible creatures. He'd declared me the queen and explained that in winter, a hive clusters around the queen, snuggling to keep her warm.

So on those nights when life got scary, they'd pile into my bed, and I'd read to them from the Shel Silverstein book my mom had given me as a kid.

"I'm hungry," Julian complained.

"I've got dino nuggets, microwave popcorn, and apples," I declared, thankful I'd popped into a small market on the way.

Ellie scoffed while Maggie declared "a feast!"

The kitchen was far from unpacked, but I'd work on it once the kids went to bed. Chloe and Gus had already helped with the big stuff, and for the most part, we traveled light these days.

That started when we packed up our family home almost three years ago. All the furniture went to storage, and I'd never been tempted to go through any of it. The last thing I wanted was to relive the memories made in that home.

But it wasn't necessary anyway. We had everything we needed.

And we'd moved so much in the past few years that we'd become pros.

Chloe had insisted on the storage pod and having furniture delivered. And, of course, she conveniently forgot to send me the bill so I could pay her back.

It shouldn't have surprised me. Our dynamic had always been like this.

She was an oldest daughter. And now that I had Ellie, I'd accepted that an oldest daughter is gonna oldest daughter.

"I think I like the farm," Maggie said. "There are some animals here." She pushed her glasses up her nose. "But I didn't see any horses."

Maggie was a horse girl. A budding horse girl, that is. Since she'd never actually ridden one.

She'd started showing interest not long after I left Donny. But horses freaked me out. And horseback riding was very expensive. I was a single mom of three and a teacher. My extracurricular dollars only stretched so far.

When I'd told the kids that we were renting a small house on a maple farm, Maggie had lit up with excitement, hoping and praying there would be horses.

"We can look around tomorrow," I suggested. "But it might not be that kind of farm."

Her smile wavered, the light in her eyes dimming.

"If there aren't any horses, I'm sure there are other cool things here," I told her.

"Like tractors," Julian added without looking away from the structure he was building. It was pink, not his usual choice, but he was quiet and happy.

Sighing, I turned to the oven. How the hell did it work? It was beautiful, but it looked like it had never been used before. I'd give it twenty-four hours before it was covered in fingerprints.

Once I'd figured it out, I went in search of a cookie sheet so I could bake the damn nuggets, rifling through the kitchen boxes before remembering that I'd seen baking stuff upstairs when I was changing.

"I'll be right back." I jogged up the narrow staircase, searching my mind for where I'd seen the box, wondering whether I really had or if the image in my head was just a figment of my crushing exhaustion.

Room by room I searched, and with every minute, I was more certain that I'd imagined it. But when I opened the box of winter gear and found the baking pans packed along with snow pants, hats, and gloves, I cried out. "Aha." Excellent.

Smiling, I headed for the hallway. At the doorway, a strange smell wafted over me, and before I could consider what it might be, a loud alarm blared.

The smoke detector above my head was flashing and screaming, yet there was no fire or smoke near me. This place must have had some kind of high-tech system where everything was wired together.

Shit. Heart lurching, I dropped the pans and ran downstairs.

It was a smoke alarm, not an air-raid signal, but my nervous system didn't know the difference. A switch in my brain flipped, and frazzled mom faded away. By the time I hit the bottom of the stairs, my body had prepared for mortal peril.

The sensation was a familiar one, filled with fear and paranoia and hypervigilance.

It wasn't him. It couldn't be.

But as I ran for my children, I expected the worst.

Chapter 2

JOSH

Most farmers wax poetic about sunrises, but for me, it's the sunsets. Dusk, when most of the work is done and the sun dips below the horizon, treating me to what has become my favorite show, as well as my favorite time of day.

The expanse above was filled with purple and orange and bursts of light, like the sky had been dipped in maple syrup. Details I never noticed as a kid and couldn't have even seen when I lived in the city. But now I relished it. Sunset signaled that the day was done. That I could put my feet up and just exist for a few hours.

I'd come home to Maplewood to be busy. So busy I could escape my thoughts.

Turns out trauma is a great motivator, and farmwork is cheaper than therapy.

Almost four years in, and I was still firing on all cylinders 365 days a year. The back pain I'd developed sitting at a desk? Gone.

The constant anxiety headaches caused by artificial deadlines? Gone.

The need to push myself beyond my limits to prove my worth? Sadly not gone.

But I was a work in progress.

Tipping to one side, I scratched Wayne's ears. He'd disappeared for a while this afternoon, probably to chase bunnies, but he was back for sunset, just like always.

I usually fed him at about this time, so that may have had something to do with it, but I liked to think it was because he enjoyed spending this moment with me.

The days were getting shorter, and the tug of autumn was getting more noticeable. But for right now, I soaked up as many moments of this Vermont summer as I could.

When a rude buzzing sound cut through my reverie, I yanked my phone out of my back pocket and checked the screen.

A notification from my security system.

My body tensed and panic flooded me, making me break into a cold sweat.

Smoke alarm. The cottage.

Aw, fuck. The new tenants.

I took off at a sprint, thankful I'd upgraded the system after Will's death so that it would call the fire department if the alarm wasn't disarmed in a certain amount of time.

The quick call was necessary this far outside town.

In the meantime, I'd stashed fire extinguishers in several spots.

Halfway there, Wayne passed me, darting straight for the cottage. He was a hundred and five pounds of heart, loyalty and questionable decision-making in a furry, cuddly package.

I bounded up the porch steps, where Wayne was circling, impatient, and threw the front door open, then followed the smell of smoke.

The alarm was no longer going off. Still, I expected flames. Maybe a small explosion. Or even wildlife. Given this farm's recent track record of bad luck, I was expecting all three at once.

Instead, I found my tenant, all five foot nothing of her, wielding a fire extinguisher with the kind of intensity usually reserved for hostage situations.

And she was spraying retardant at the brand-new Wolf oven I'd installed.

I stopped just over the threshold, and Wayne slammed into the back of my legs, almost knocking me over.

In the middle of the living area, three kids stared at me like startled deer—one hostile, one curious, and one ready to take off into the woods.

"You done?"

Celine turned, still aiming the fire extinguisher.

I put my hands up in surrender.

She eyed me, her chest heaving, then assessed her kids.

"Nothing's on fire anymore," the middle one said.

She had glasses and a ponytail and seemed the friend-liest. Which, I supposed, didn't say much since the older girl was looking at me with contempt and the little boy's eyes were still wide with panic.

"Mom took care of it."

"Just the oven?" I scanned the rest of the open area. The

oven was covered with flame retardant, but everything else looked untouched.

She nodded.

Focus drifting back to her, I confirmed. "Nothing anywhere else?"

"No."

I dug my phone from my pocket and dialed the fire department, who may have already been on their way.

"Marty it's Josh Lawrence. Yes. I'm at the house. Just the oven. No need to send a truck out. Yes, I'll make sure to turn off the gas. Thank you."

Head down, I hit the End button, then stashed my phone again. When I looked up, I was met by four curious faces.

"Could you hear the alarm all the way from your house?" Celine asked.

"Got an alert on my phone," I explained. "Security system."

Her eyes narrowed. "You're spying on us?"

I'd been prepared to stumble in on chaos. I'd braced for screaming, crying, or even smoke inhalation. Being accused of espionage came as a surprise.

"No. Not spying," I said gently. "I have systems and cameras installed all over the property. I'm happy to set up an account for you. That way you can have your own passwords and adjust settings so you're the one with access to the house."

Her expression remained stony, her mouth turned down in a frown.

Damn. What the hell had I done wrong?

"The system is set up for fires and break-ins," I added, my voice flattening with frustration. "Not... whatever it is you think I'm doing. Smoke alarm went off. I was worried." A sigh slipped out. How is it that I'd found myself having to justify my presence in a house I built and owned, on my fucking land? And that was before the annoyance that had begun to seep into me when I realized there was no danger. I kept that to myself.

"We're fine," the tallest child said, though her tone belied that sentiment. It sounded more like she was on the verge of calling the police on me.

"Are you?" I responded, genuinely curious, if not inconvenienced.

Celine placed the fire extinguisher on the table and shuffled to her kids.

"Guys," she said, "Mr. Lawrence is our landlord. Let's use our manners. Okay?"

The little boy skirted around her, hiding behind her legs.

"You've met Julian," she said as he wrapped his arms around her hips. "This is my daughter Ellie." She draped an arm over her the older girl's shoulders. "Only twelve and already taller than me."

The girl inspected me with the kind of scrutiny that gave me the sense she'd have a future in law enforcement. She was tall and lanky with short, choppy strawberry blond hair.

"And this is Maggie," she said, dipping her chin at the other girl.

"Nice to meet you." Maggie, the younger girl with blond hair, stuck out a hand.

Taken aback by her formality, I took it and returned her firm handshake.

She pushed her glasses up her nose and smiled. "Do you have horses? Can I meet them? Can I ride them?"

"Um—"

"Or goats? Mini goats? Do goats have jobs? Could I train one and take it to school with me?"

"Maggie." Celine sighed. "This isn't the time." She dropped her arm from her oldest daughter's shoulders and stepped toward the kitchen, the little boy moving with her. "Sorry. I turned the oven on to preheat, and when I opened it, black smoke filled the kitchen."

"Julian tried to cook his Legos," Maggie announced, as if it were a completely normal culinary experiment.

That's when the smell clicked. Melted plastic. Huh.

Julian reached out from behind his mother and shoved his sister, sending her staggering.

"It was an accident," Celine explained, wearing a compassionate expression. "I should have checked first. I didn't realize he'd made a cake for my birthday."

She leaned down and kissed his head.

He immediately swiped his hand over the spot, wiping it off.

Ellie was still staring at me, as if daring me to make some kind of comment.

Knowing better, I walked over to the oven. As I got close and assessed the mess, that irritation was back and growing.

"It's fine," I said a little too sharply. "I'll deal with it."

"We don't need help," Ellie snapped.

Teeth gritted, I surveyed the girl. She was so young, but she had an attitude that only came from carrying trauma around.

Her mother elbowed her. "Thanks, but we're okay."

"So about those horses," Maggie added.

"Dat's a horse." Julian pointed behind me to Wayne,

who sat patiently, puffing his doggie chest out like he appreciated the sentiment.

I choked out a laugh. "That isn't a horse, bud. It's my dog."

His little eyes widened and he shrunk a little farther behind his mom.

"It's okay," I added. "He's very gentle."

"He looks like a horse."

I snapped, and Wayne immediately padded over and sat in front of Julian, his eyes bright and his tail wagging.

"If you hold your hand out like this, he can smell you." I showed him. "That's how he gets to know people."

The boy did as I said, letting Wayne sniff him, only pulling back once before gaining confidence and sticking his hand out farther.

"You can pet him."

He looked up at his mom, his teeth sunken into his lip, searching for reassurance.

When she nodded and gave him an encouraging smile, he tentatively patted the top of Wayne's head.

Wayne, good boy that he was, stayed still, as if he could sense Julian's apprehension.

The little boy patted his head a few more times, then turned and smiled at his mother.

And if I wasn't mistaken, she let out a breath of relief.

"So do you have horses?" Maggie asked. The girl was persistent. "What about goats?"

"He only has tractors," Julian told her. "Giant ones."

"Gross," Maggie said.

"I saw apple trees," Celine said encouragingly.

Ellie grumbled. "What kind of farm doesn't have horses?"

"Guys," Celine said, her voice thin and accompanied by a fraying edge I recognized. It was the tone of a person who'd held it together all day and was two seconds from breaking.

It was familiar because I lived there most days. That tenuous spot right before my sanity and patience and hope in the damn world cracked.

Her small frame was coiled up like a snake about to strike.

Despite having other things to get done tonight, the urge to help overtook me. It was fully dark now, and judging by the boxes everywhere, she was still trying to move in.

"I was just about to order a pizza," I said casually. "You guys want some? Saves me from having to listen to the smoke detectors again."

"You have pizza out here in the sticks?" Ellie asked.

"Really good pizza." Nodding, I rocked back on my heels. "Tony uses local mozzarella."

Celine's eyes lit up.

Bingo.

I pretended not to notice. Getting attached was a bad habit. The need to witness that kind of relief was one I thought I'd quelled. It made me want to help more often. And this was a one-time offer of landlord assistance.

"I only like plain cheese," Maggie explained. "And Julian only eats crust."

"Crust is delicious." I eyed the boy. "I respect that."

Julian looked up from where he was gently stroking Wayne's fur. "Do they have fries?"

Nodding, I slid my phone out again.

"Fries are a safe food for him," Maggie explained.

I didn't know what a safe food was, but who didn't love a good french fry?

"Can we?" Julian asked, looking up at his mom, his eyes wide.

Celine nodded, though her focus was still fixed on me, her expression full of what I could only deduce was a mixture of relief and suspicion. Not that I blamed her.

"Do you always show up unannounced?" she asked.

"Only when my property is actively on fire," I replied.

Her mouth twitched. She didn't smile.

Tony did not let me down, and the minute the food hit the table, the kids descended like a pack of hungry foxes. Ellie tore into a slice like she had something to prove, Maggie narrated every bite, and Julian happily ate an order of french fries the size of his head.

While they were occupied, I headed for the kitchen to take care of tonight's real issue.

The oven.

The melted Lego structure had thankfully cooled into a rainbow-color geological formation, layers of the plastic fused to the bottom rack. I worked silently. There was no point in embarrassing the kid or his mom. Or opening the door to gratitude I didn't want or even know how to handle.

I'd seen a lot worse. This didn't even crack the top fifty of the shit I'd witnessed. Still, this appliance had cost a lot, and now it smelled like burnt childhood.

I snagged my work gloves from my back pocket, then removed the oven racks and the bottom tray and carried them to one of the equipment barns.

Wayne trotted after me, eyeing the art installation in my hands.

With a few good scrapes, I removed most of the mess. Then I hosed off the components, removing the last remnants of the fire retardant with dish soap.

They were scratched but not destroyed. I could live with that. Once I got it all reset, I'd turn the gas back on.

By the time I came back in, the kids had finished eating, and Celine was wiping down the table. Julian immediately zeroed in on Wayne, his attention flickering to me after a moment. I gave him a nod, making sure to relax my expression. I wasn't mad. He was a kid, after all.

While I reinstalled the bottom tray and racks, cleaned the exterior, and swept up the ash and debris from the floor, Celine watched me. Not judgmental, but not grateful either. Like she was bracing for the moment when help turned into leverage. Or like she wasn't sure how to stop me.

I washed my hands, dried them on my pants, and gave them a wave. "Good to go."

"Thank you." She shifted, not quite hiding a grimace. "I didn't expect you to do all that."

"I know." I shrugged. "But it's done."

"We still haven't discussed the animals," Maggie said, her head tipped back and her eyes expectant.

"Maybe tomorrow," Celine said. "You've got to go to bed."

"How about a tour?" I asked before I thought better of it. Why was I still here and not halfway back to my house by now? I should have left. I usually left. I'd already done way more peopling than I was used to.

It was late and I was tired. I needed to be alone to reset myself after this weird-ass night.

Julian homed in on me. "Can we see the tractors?"

"And the fruit trees?" Maggie's blond hair was wild around her inquisitive face.

I looked at Celine before answering, just to be sure, and when she gave a tiny nod, I agreed. "I'll give you all a tour tomorrow afternoon. Show you around your new home."

Home. That word reverberated through me, landing heavier than it should have.

Julian sat up a little taller and Maggie beamed at me.

An unfamiliar warmth gathered in my chest.

"Thanks again," Celine said, following Wayne and me to the front door.

"Don't mention it." I stepped outside, then turned around to face her. "Is it really your birthday?"

She squeezed her eyes shut, but not before a hint of pain flashed in them. "Tomorrow."

"Happy birthday," I said, stuffing my hands into my pockets.

She scoffed. "Thirty-five and starting over with three kids in Bumfuck, Vermont." Peering over her shoulder, she lowered her voice. "And I almost burned down the nicest house we've ever lived in on day one. Happy fucking birthday to me."

Anger seeped out of her, and there was no hiding the weariness she was carrying, or her general air of defiance.

"Yeah, that tracks," I said.

"You're kind of an ass," she said.

Taking a step back, I tipped my baseball cap at her. "I've been called worse."

Chapter 3

♥

CELINE

At five fifteen exactly, I opened my eyes. Julian was splayed across my legs, several of Maggie's stuffed animals crowded my head and shoulders, and her hardcover edition of *The Hunger Games*—the one she'd brought in when she couldn't sleep—was resting on my chest. *Excellent.*

Closing my eyes, I took a second to breathe in this moment. As I exhaled, I rubbed Julian's back. I picked up on the steady pounding of his heartbeat while I listened to the rhythm of the girls' breathing.

Mornings like this were rare. No alarm, no rushing, and no panic. Nothing but a moment of peace.

I would have loved to stay here and soak this in, but I hadn't run yesterday, and my anxiety would not let me skip again. So I slid out of bed, tucking Julian back in, and tiptoed to the bathroom to brush my teeth. Then I threw on shorts, a sports bra, and my sneakers.

My plan was to run the hill behind the house. From

there, I wouldn't lose sight of the structure. As I headed out, I relished the early morning chill on my skin. *I get to do this,* I told myself. *I choose to push myself. A strong mind requires a strong body.*

Quickly, I stretched, then I took off.

Rather than focusing on the run, I spent every second worried about the kids, so after thirty minutes, I headed back to the house, sweaty and panting but feeling slightly better.

The house was quiet as I flipped on the coffee maker and did my squats, lunges, and pushups. Thank God for Chloe. She'd insisted on buying a pound of fancy coffee for me from the café we stopped at on the way here. If not for her, I would have forgotten, and I would have been cursing myself this morning since I truly couldn't function without it.

The cup was halfway to my lips and I was milliseconds away from taking my first glorious sip when footsteps pounded down the stairs.

"Happy birthday, Mom," my kids shouted when they came into view. All at once, they threw their small arms around me and hugged me tight.

"Thank you." One at a time, I kissed them on the forehead. "I love you."

"Here." Maggie held out a handmade card. On the front was a portrait of the four of us wearing huge smiles. Inside it read "You are the best mom in the world. I love you so much. You're awesome and cool and pretty."

"Thank you," I said, my throat getting thick.

My sweet girl bounced on her toes, beaming.

Julian had disappeared, and when he returned, he held a new Lego cake. Pink, square, and decorated with green Lego icing. "I didn't bake it," he said proudly. "It's raw, but it should still taste good."

A laugh bubbled out of me as I ruffled his shaggy hair. "Thank you, baby," I said. "I love it." I pretended to take a big bite of the side, making him giggle the way I hoped he would.

"Here." Ellie held out another card. She'd drawn a huge bunch of balloons on the front. As I opened it, I expected to find a simple "happy birthday" and nothing else. The last few years had been hard for her, and she rarely made a show of affection anymore.

Instead I found three full sentences.

"Thanks for not giving up. On us or yourself. You're all we've got, but we're damn lucky."

I looked up at her, tears in my eyes. "Language," I laughed.

After a short, simple hug, she backed away. That was it.

The day couldn't have started any better. The celebration had been small, but it had been meaningful. Exactly our speed. Emotions pummeled me as I took in my kids. For years I'd gone without birthday cards or any real acknowledgment, yet here were these perfect little creatures making me feel more valued than I ever had.

"I'll be back in one sec." Skirting them, I headed for the stairs so I could put the cards and small cake in my mom's jewelry box right away. Not only so I could keep them forever but so I could give myself a minute.

Once I'd stashed them in the box, I darted into the bathroom, shut the door, and turned the sink on, just in case little ears were listening.

Then I let the tears fall. Sadness washed over me, along

with a sense of grief, but also hope, all mixed together into an emotionally exhausting cocktail.

I gave myself a few minutes to cry silently, then splashed cold water on my face and breathed deeply, composing myself. This day had started beautifully, and while we had endless unpacking to do, along with errands and apparently a farm tour to get to, I had hopes that it could be one of the best days I'd had in a while.

I was doing it. I was still here. And maybe we really would be okay.

Eventually, I got that cup of coffee and a shower, then we headed out. The hardware store was our first stop. I needed batteries, light bulbs, extra sliding locks for the exterior doors, and laundry detergent. I was repeating my list to myself when we entered the store, the bells jangling above us.

"My goodness." The man behind the counter perked up, his smile wide. "It's the new family in town! Emma is gonna be so jealous that I got to meet you first. She runs the grocery store, but if you'd already been over there, she'd be bragging and I would have heard about it."

He rushed around the counter, wiping his hands on his jeans before offering one to me.

"Walt Pierson." The man was in his sixties and spry, with a white mustache.

I forced a smile, even as a little wave of discomfort rolled through me. This kind of scrutiny was not something I was used to.

"Celine LeBlanc," I said, shaking his hand. "And these are my kids."

"Such a pleasure. What can I get for you today?"

Before I could explain myself, Maggie and Julian had taken off, exploring the store with glee, Maggie stopping nearby and sizing up an expensive-looking bird feeder.

"Don't worry about them," Walt said as if he could sense my anxiety. "You kids play sports?" he asked Ellie. "My daughter-in-law coaches the basketball team. A tall girl like you should play."

My moody tween stared at him for a minute, then turned and stalked in the direction Julian had gone.

I gave him a tense smile, my face heating. "She's getting used to a new town."

Walt collected all the items I'd come in for, then he gave me a 15 percent friends and family discount and told us about the upcoming fall festival.

"Just keep an eye out for the Maple Street Mafia." He held out a tape measure to Julian, insisting he keep it, which would probably make my son's year. "They mean well," he continued. "Most of the time."

"The... what?" My chest tightened.

Mafia?

I looked out the front windows, scanning the sleepy New England tourist town. Could this really be a hotbed of organized crime?

He shook his head and shuffled away, not the least bit concerned about the information he'd just given me.

I'd worry about that later, I supposed. With the kids in tow, I dropped our purchases off at the car. Then we cut through Market Street toward the grocery store, passing not one, but two cheese shops along the way.

Huh. I really liked cheese.

A truck passed us, the driver honking, and two cyclists waved from the road.

"Are these people okay?" Ellie asked, her lip curling with derision.

"I think people just wave here," I offered weakly, though I was equally confused by the hospitality.

The grocery store looked like a cottagecore film set. The flower boxes out front were overflowing with blooms, and there was a whimsical hand-painted sign featuring a smiling maple leaf waving hello.

"This place is strange." Scanning the storefront, Julian pulled his noise canceling headphones over his ears.

We had a well-established grocery store routine, and step one for my son was donning the headphones. Grocery stores were sensory overload for a neurotypical person, but for Julian, who was sensitive to noise, visual clutter, temperature changes, and bright lights, it was a battle.

I pulled a bright yellow shopping cart from the corral and wheeled it inside, instantly finding myself surrounded by twinkly string lights and overflowing baskets of produce.

"Welcome to Sugar & Sprout Market," a middle-aged woman wearing a headscarf chirped. "I'm Emma and I'm so pleased to meet you."

I gave her a tense smile. How was it that the kinder these people were, the more on edge I became?

"The new teacher?" she asked. "From Maine?"

I nodded. Did I really want to give this stranger details about my personal life?

"We are so grateful you're here." There were a few other shoppers around, though none of them were close, so I couldn't tell if she was using the royal *we* or if she was refer-ring to the voices in her head.

Julian pushed his headphones down, his focus fixed on the floor in front of him. "Do you have ice cream?"

His sweet voice interrupted my anxiety spiral, cutting through the concerns about all these unfamiliar people knowing who I was and what I did for a living.

I rested my hands on his shoulders and bent forward, reminding him to make eye contact.

"We sure do," Emma said. "We also have a reading nook and a little free library."

Maggie's eyes widened, and I swear hearts danced above her head.

"And what do you think about trying our newest black-berry jam?"

Eye twitching, I inhaled deeply. Was it too much to ask to buy milk, cereal, and a secret chocolate stash in peace?

But I kept my mouth shut because even Ellie had bright-ened a little and was now drooling over the display of fresh-baked bread.

Because carbs were one language even snarky tweens could understand.

"It's my mom's birfday," Julian explained, having found his favorite, raspberry sorbet, in the freezer section.

Emma beamed at him, then me. "Then you'll need a cake."

After spending way too much money on artisanal pret-zels, the best-looking strawberries I'd ever seen, a small chocolate cake, and several pints of ice cream, we hauled it all to the car.

As we walked, the kids happily chattered, discussing

which snacks they wanted to try first. I, on the other hand, scanned the area for threats.

Old habits died slowly.

But the sunny streets were filled with tourists taking photos and parents pushing strollers and wrangling young children. Maybe this place was as charming as advertised. Regardless, I wasn't ready to let my guard down.

On the way back to the farm, I found myself getting lost in the rolling green hills and the stacks of hay. Even if the place was safe, it wasn't quiet. I'd been waved at no less than half a dozen times before I turned off Main Street. Apparently everyone wanted to speak to me.

In the back seat, Julian hummed as he played with a Rubix cube, ignoring Maggie as she coached him on what to do next.

Beside me, Ellie stared out the window silently. It gutted me to think that she might also be scanning for threats. God, I wished she could just be a kid. That she could let loose once in a while. She was only twelve, yet she behaved like a battle-hardened general.

And it was my fault. Maybe if I'd been stronger, tougher, smarter, we could have avoided this.

"Mom, look!" Maggie rolled down her window and stuck her head out as far as her seat belt would let her.

Josh stood outside the big red barn, leaning over a piece of equipment while Wayne the horse dog sat beside him like a statue.

"*Hello,*" Maggie trilled, waving madly.

"The horse dog," Julian shouted. "Let's go see the horse dog."

Ellie slunk down in the front seat. "My God, can we not embarrass ourselves for five minutes?"

I slowed the car, deliberately ignoring the way Josh's T-shirt hugged his thick arms. Arms that had, if I wasn't mistaken, a small bit of ink? Not that I cared.

Josh straightened and lifted a hand in greeting.

"Can we have a tour now?" Maggie hollered out the window. "I wanna see the animals."

Josh's stoic face cracked into the tiniest smile. Then he focused on me. "Sure. Give me fifteen minutes."

Already annoyed by his presence, I huffed. But my kids were begging, and what would it hurt?

"Okay, fine," I said, hitting the gas pedal.

As I pulled up to the cottage, I discovered an unfamiliar woman standing on the porch with several Tupperware containers in her arms.

My muscles tensed up. Though she looked harmless enough, in her late sixties or early seventies, with long white hair, I'd learned firsthand that looks could be deceiving. My ex-mother-in-law looked like Betty White, but the woman would slit my throat if given half the chance.

"Hello, dear," the stranger said, her long hair swishing as she smiled brightly and waved. Her earrings were long enough to touch her shoulders, and she wore one of those long, flowy skirts that short girls like myself could never hope to pull off.

The kids, accustomed to my paranoia, stayed in the car as I approached her.

"I'm Gail. Emma at the grocer texted and mentioned that it's your birthday, so I brought some treats from the Maplewood welcome wagon."

"Thank you," I said, trying to be gracious even as unease threaded through me. We'd been at the grocery store less than thirty minutes ago. "I'm Celine LeBlanc." I nodded at the car. "And these are my children."

"So lovely to meet you. You're the talk of the town," she said as the kids finally clambered out of the vehicle. "Callie says you're a brilliant educator."

I wasn't sure how to respond, so I settled for bland pleasantries. "This is such a lovely town. Everyone has been so friendly."

"I'm glad. This is a wonderful place. America's Most Charming Small Town, you know." Her cheerful expression faded. "Despite recent ... events and the vicious rumors Birch Hollow is spreading."

Clearly there was a story there, but I didn't dare ask, hoping she'd leave quickly.

"But I won't keep you. Here." She thrust the stack of Tupperware at me. "That's from Bitsy, and Olive's famous snickerdoodles are on top."

I steadied them and gave her an awkward smile. "Thank you."

"There's more in the car." She shuffle-walked to her small sedan and pulled out two shopping bags. "Basil sent a loaf of sourdough and some Munster. There's a bouquet of flowers here from Lorraine, and Tony included a few coupons, since you have already enjoyed his pizza. Also, if you need school supplies for the kids, Bitsy has a whole selection at the general store."

I nodded, confused by this level of generosity. It was sweet but also concerning. How were so many people aware that we'd moved to town, and what did they know about me?

Anonymity was important to me. It was one of the reasons I'd chosen to relocate to rural Vermont. No matter how good that bread looked, I couldn't help but worry.

She drove off with a wave and a smile, and I was left stunned and shaken.

"Look at this cheese," Ellie said, holding up a block that looked very delicious and very expensive. "We're gonna have a feast."

"Can we tour the farm now?" Maggie pleaded. "Pretty please? I wanna see the animals."

I sighed. "Let me get this stuff inside."

And make a new birthday wish: that I'd survive this tour without crying, yelling, or spontaneously combusting.

Chapter 4

JOSH

Though I didn't want to delay my chores, I'd made a promise, and at least the chickens had been fed, and I'd checked on both greenhouses, even ordering new panels to replace the ones that were cracked. We didn't grow a lot here, but I maintained a half-acre garden, growing mainly fresh herbs and greens along with a bed of strawberries I'd planted with my mom when I was in kindergarten. Every summer, I ate the first fat, juicy strawberry and cried.

In a matter of weeks, I'd be knee-deep in winter prep. In the maple business, we called the fall "training camp." The autumn months were filled with prepping for winter's game time. I'd check miles of sap lines for cracks, squirrel damage, and weather wear. I'd replace tubing, clear brush, and inspect the tap holes from last season to make sure they closed properly.

The repetitive rhythm of the work soothed me. So did logging tree health and modeling out yield projections.

Documenting the weather and inspecting trees and estimating yardage for food-grade plastic tubing were all tasks that made sense to me. People, however, did not make sense.

Here and there I'd hear whispers about the Wall Street suit who freaked out and became a farmer. But life here wasn't all that different from what it'd been like there. Either way, I was under constant pressure. Except out here, Mother Nature fucked up my life, not the stock market. The repetitive nature of the work was comparable. So was the need for precision and strategy, and ultimately, the inevitable moment where one had to start over and do it all again.

And fall was my favorite. The weather was mild, giving me ample opportunity to work hard and run through the checklists. This year, especially, I was anticipating the way muscle memory and sweat would carry me through Thanksgiving, giving my brain a bit of downtime to recover from the shit show of the past year.

None of it made sense, but a young guy had confessed, and he'd been arrested. It was a terrible tragedy, but now that he was locked up, we didn't have to walk around paranoid about a murderer being on the loose. The hit to the business had been intense, but now that law enforcement wasn't crawling around, I had hope that I could get things back to normal. That is, if normal had ever even existed in Maplewood.

I pulled out my phone, intending to leave myself a note to call Gabe tonight to get the latest news, when screams floated through the air. My shoulders tightened on instinct. This was a workday. A real one. Not a petting zoo open house.

My heart took off at a gallop. Was this the fun kind of

screaming or the call 911 kind? I'd gotten good at distinguishing between the two when my nephews were little and running around this farm like wild animals.

And a moment later, when Celine and her kids came into view, I let myself believe that it was the fun kind.

Her children had not forgotten about my promise to give them a tour, and clearly, they were eager for it. It was sweet, but also annoying. When Callie had come to me asking if I'd be willing to rent out the cottage, she'd been insistent. So, wanting to get out from under her scrutiny, I hadn't asked as many questions as I should have. Not that it would have mattered. I'd never say no to a single mom with three kids needing a home to start over. Even without Callie's pressure and no doubt the full force of the Maple Street Mafia. My mom, God bless her, would haunt the shit out of me if I didn't do what I could to help her. And after what my sister Jess had been through as a single parent, I was even more committed to helping.

Callie had been light on details, but I'd read between the lines, and after last night, it was obvious to me that Celine had run from something. But I wasn't one to pry, so with any luck, I'd satisfy the kids' curiosity about the farm and then go back to work. I couldn't possibly rearrange my life around a tenant and her kids. This was a courtesy. Nothing more.

It wouldn't take more than twenty minutes, anyway. Thirty tops.

At my feet, Wayne snorted.

I peered down at him. "They'll probably have a lot of questions."

He barked once in agreement.

Celine and her kids headed down the hill toward the

barn, moving like three chaotic weather systems, each different from the last, anchored by one exhausted mother.

Her long red hair was tied up on top of her head and a halo of curls framed her face. She couldn't have been more than five feet tall, and she had the wiry muscles of a woman who had carried more than her share of burdens. She was tiny but fierce. A body made by survival, not the gym.

As they made their way to me, she lengthened her strides, stepping in front of them, instinctively forming a protective barrier. Despite the confidence with which she carried herself, fear and hesitation radiated from her. And my instinct told me it had nothing to do with me.

I lifted my hand in a brief acknowledgment. Friendly took energy I couldn't spare.

"Can we see the animals?" Maggie asked. She was wearing pink shorts and a T-shirt with a cat on it. Her hair was blond, and she eagerly smiled at me as she pushed her glasses up her nose.

"Depends," I said. "On whether you can follow directions." Clearing my throat, I put my hands on my hips and assessed them. "Which is still up for debate."

Ellie rolled her eyes. "Jeez, Maggie. Chill. There are no horses." She was all in black, and her strawberry blond hair was cut into a blunt, short style around her chin. Celine had mentioned last night that she was twelve, but she had the attitude of a jaded thirty-five-year-old and was already several inches taller than her mother. Behind the façade, though, there was a kid still in there. Maybe it was in the knobby knees and elbows or a flash here and there in her eyes.

"But why?" Maggie asked, scanning our surroundings.

"Seems like you've got room for horses. They are very versatile animals."

"This farm is illegit," Ellie grumbled.

Julian, who was staring intently at Wayne, with a pair of headphones worn around his neck like a scarf, looked at his sister. "I'm pretty sure you could ride this dog if you needed to."

Wayne sat up a little taller, preening.

Yeah, this would not be a quick and easy afternoon. Dammit. I supposed it wasn't the first time I'd lied to myself.

I took a breath and attempted to smile at Maggie. "Back in the old days, we had giant draft horses. My grandma loved them and cared for them every day of her life. We'd load the sap from the trees into large buckets on sleds, and the horses would pull them through the snow to the sugar house."

Maggie perked up, her face brightening. "I knew it. They are useful for everything."

"But now we drive ATVs and snowmobiles out through the maple stand."

Her mouth turned down thoughtfully. "What's a maple stand?"

"A stand is a big group of trees. We've got over ten thousand maple trees," I explained. "We use tubing and other equipment to gather the sap into massive plastic containers and then drive them on the ATV back to the barn."

"So you killed the horses?" she asked, panic flitting across her features.

"Of course not," I said, cringing. "They died of old age. They had wonderful retirements filled with treats and lots of brushing."

She hummed skeptically. "So what animals do you have?"

I looked at Wayne, who was watching me with a nonplussed look. "We have chickens," I offered.

She scoffed. "Chickens are boring."

"Untrue," I offered, rocking back on my heels. "They have complex social structures and do hilarious things. And some of them like to be picked up and cuddled."

Head tilted, she studied me, her face relaxing a little. "You should think about goats," she said. "They eat poison ivy."

I nodded. The last thing I needed was another animal to care for, but goats really were great at taking care of poison ivy, which seemed to have been winning its power struggle with me this year, and my nieces had been going on and on about goats all summer. But if Logan caught wind of that, I'd have a dozen of them by the time I woke up tomorrow.

"Let's walk up this way." I nodded toward the largest barn. "I'll show you around and point out potential dangers." I added the last part, figuring it would satisfy Celine.

"What does sap taste like?" Ellie asked.

"Like watery maple syrup." I slipped my phone back into my pocket and took off toward the barn. "The sap is mostly water, which is why it gets boiled down into syrup."

"Because the water evaporates." Ellie finished my thought.

"Exactly. It takes forty gallons of sap to make one gallon of maple syrup."

"What?" Maggie's eyes went round. "That's way too much."

I shrugged. "Take it up with the trees." I gestured up the

hill toward the tree line, where generations of my family's hard work towered over us.

I felt closest to them up there—Mom and Dad, and even my grandparents. This land was important. To me and to generations of my family. It had been easy to walk away from the money and the suits and the private clubs of New York. Because my heart was here, in these tree roots.

In the main barn, Julian immediately jumped on top of a backhoe, the machinery too tempting for him.

Celine was right behind him, pulling him off.

"Stop," I barked. "Don't climb on that. Ever."

He froze, his head lowering.

"There's a lot of stuff here that could hurt you. You should never come in here without me."

Maggie and Ellie both nodded. Julian continued staring at his feet.

Celine crossed her arms, her posture defensive, like a coiled snake about to strike. "I do watch my children."

"Good," I said flatly. "Because this place doesn't give second chances."

I finished the warning off with a nod. Dammit, when had a simple safety briefing turned into a standoff?

Part of me wanted to come out and ask "who hurt you?" But I killed that instinct quickly. It was none of my business. She was a tenant. We all had shit to deal with. Nothing good would come from getting curious about this woman.

The girls were unimpressed by the machinery, wandering aimlessly but sticking close. But Julian was in heaven.

Memories of following my dad and uncle around when I was his age assaulted me. By the time I was old enough to go to school, I was desperate to take apart an engine and prove myself. Dad never let me touch the "good" tools, but I had access to an older set, and he always left broken equipment lying around for me to practice on.

For a moment, I envisioned teaching Julian the way Dad had taught me. Giving him his first socket wrench as a coming-of-age moment. I closed my eyes and willed the thought away. It was stupid. He wasn't my son, and it didn't seem like Celine liked to let him out of her sight. Not that he wasn't a bit wily. The first time I'd met him, he'd gotten away from her. I'd add more cameras to the outside of this building and pray that he'd stay out.

She just continued to glare at me like I'd accused her of negligence.

I held her gaze. I wasn't backing down. Not when serious injury was a possibility. I'd been kind and accommodating thus far, but this was a working farm, and I couldn't wrap the kid in bubble wrap.

"This isn't personal," I said. "It's safety."

"Feels personal," she shot back.

"Not my problem."

Our staring competition was quickly interrupted by a clanging sound.

In the five seconds we'd locked eyes, Julian had wandered to the far side of the barn and pulled a huge coil of tubing off one of the hooks. What could happen next flashed in my mind. The entire thing coming down on him. Broken bones, head trauma. An ambulance too far away.

Celine shouted sharply, her voice filled with raw fear. The sound punched a hole in my chest. Not hysteria, but memory. The kind a person doesn't forget once they've heard it.

I sprinted over, pushed him aside, and grabbed the coil. It only weighed about fifty pounds, but if it had fallen on him, it could have done serious damage. Jaw clenched tight, I rewound it around the hook. Then I snagged a roll of duct tape from a nearby shelf and taped the end down so he couldn't pull it loose again.

Next to me, Julian hadn't moved, other than to lower his head. Rather than fight or flight, his instinct was to freeze. Shit. What a terrible place for that to kick in.

"Julian. You can't touch," Celine said, her voice shaking.

The kid didn't move. He was a complete statue, his lack of response tempting me to inspect him to make sure he was breathing.

I'd barely resisted the urge when he started to shake. Celine wrapped her arms around him, and then he was thrashing against her. His movements were stronger than I could have imagined, but she remained calm. Within seconds, he settled, burying his face in her neck.

She stroked his back. "I know you're curious. But you can't touch things in here."

I stood awkwardly close, at a loss for how to respond, willing my heart rate to slow down. Wayne trotted over and licked Julian's arm, and finally, the boy came back to life, taking his mom's hand and letting her lead him outside.

We hiked up the hill and to the garden, then the greenhouses, and the orchard. The kids loved the apple trees, so I refrained from complaining about them. They were a major pain in my ass. But these trees had been planted by my great-grandmother, and in the fall, we'd harvest them, and

Jenn would use them for baked goods at the café. We'd keep some too, and we'd make cider using the old press my grandpa had taught me to operate when I was a kid. And maybe that part was fun. Mostly because my nieces and nephews loved it.

The damn trees, though, were fussy as hell and required constant pruning and maintenance, otherwise they wouldn't produce.

As we continued on, the tension rolling off Celine eased a bit, allowing my own agitation to subside. I hated that I'd upset her, but I wasn't sure I could avoid it. During every interaction we'd had, she'd been suspicious and untrusting.

"We don't drive on this road," I explained, not sure any of them were listening. "So you can ride your bikes here. But stay off the paved road that cuts through the farm. Trucks come and go down it most days, and in the spring when the sap runs, they'll be here every few hours."

"My bike's broken," Maggie said. "The chain snapped."

"I can fix it." The moment the words left me, I regretted them. Dammit. Why was I getting involved?

Her little face lit up.

Celine shot me a glare, proving again that she was untrusting. The woman treated help like a threat.

But I didn't have the time to untangle that.

"I told you I'd get to it," she said to her little girl, still clutching Julian's hand. "I just need the right tools."

"Mom." Ellie turned around and walked backward up the hill. "This guy's got a whole barn full of tools. We just saw them."

As much as I resented being called "this guy," she wasn't wrong.

"It's no trouble," I said to Maggie. "Even got an air pump for your tires."

When no one responded, I exhaled and continued on, though I kept step with Celine.

"I'm sorry about back there," I said. "I hope I didn't scare him. I just don't want anybody to get hurt."

She slowly looked over at me, her eyes hard. "I'm capable of keeping my kids alive, thanks."

"Great." I scoffed. "Then we're on the same side. Stop treating me like the enemy."

"You implied it."

"I don't imply," I said, forcing a soft tone. "If something needs to be said. I say it."

"Sounds like a threat."

"Just a promise." Damn, she was getting under my skin. I didn't threaten, I prepared. And people who didn't know the difference were the ones who got hurt. I was usually more collected than this, but this woman had shown up and made me feel like a villain on my own farm.

I trudged ahead, catching up with the girls so I could direct them away from the tree line toward the back end of the property. The steepness of the hill made it a challenge to close the distance between us, but this was the fastest way up here, and I hadn't thought to take an ATV.

"This is important," I said as we stepped into a small pasture that flanked the massive rows of maple trees.

I pointed to one side, catching my breath. "See this long hedge?"

Ellie wandered over and studied the massive thicket of bushes. "Are those thorns?"

Maggie joined her. "And berries?"

"This is a blackberry hedge," I explained. "It's taken years to get it this large."

"Kind of looks like something out of a horror movie," Ellie mused, more light in her expression than I'd seen from her yet.

The branches were winding and twisted, the plantings growing into one another to form a complex maze of thorns, branches, and fruit.

"This is the western border of the property." I looked out over the land on the other side. "And I'm bringing you up here to show you that this area is off limits."

"Past these trees," I said, pointing to a towering row of pines separating the working farm from the wild forest that lay beyond. "You cannot go past here. I don't maintain the road and the woods get very thick. Do you understand?"

I made eye contact with each child as they nodded at me.

This area was completely wild save for the blackberry bramble I'd planted. I'd put it here for the sole purpose of distracting Betsy Ross and thus keeping her from visiting the farm. My bear defense system. I had cameras, of course, but this worked better than other deterrents I'd tried.

I'd been with them for close to an hour, but the inane questions had drained me far faster than any manual labor. And I was disturbingly sweaty. Maybe it was the end of summer heat or maybe it was the disquieting sensation of having Celine's eyes on me.

"Can we have a sleepover in one of the barns?" Maggie asked. "Not the scary one where Julian almost got hurt, but there are a bunch."

"You wanna have a sleepover with the chickens?" I teased.

"Um, that would be awesome," she replied.

"Do you have raccoons?" Ellie asked, eyes lighting up. "Do they have rabies?"

I took my hat off and ran my hands through my hair. I had absolutely no idea how to answer that question.

"Can we name the tractors?"

"When can we pick the apples?"

"Do the trees cry when you hammer the thingy into them?"

The questions were endless, and Julian had joined in as well, bringing tractors into the conversation.

A prickly unease took over. These kids had already eaten up a good chunk of my afternoon and too much of my attention. This wasn't like me. I finished my to-do lists. I stuck to my routines. I didn't get sidetracked. I didn't get attached. I didn't get... anything these days.

But here they were, worming their way in without shame. Suggesting cutesy names for farm equipment as Wayne trotted happily between them like an emotional support linebacker.

And their mom. Fierce eyes and wiry strength, but not a stitch of trust for me.

Once I'd left them at the cottage, a wave of relief hit me. But there was irritation there too.

Mostly because I was slightly intrigued by the little family.

Celine's walls were high and fortified for a reason, and that only sent my instincts to protect into high gear. Yet at the same time, I wanted to retreat to my house and stay there, because I was pretty sure it would take days to recover from this farm tour.

"Wayne," I hollered to my dog, who'd lagged behind, looking forlornly at the retreating kids. But when I called him a second time, he trotted over, head down. And with him at my side, I strode back to the barn to restart my workday.

"Don't get attached," I said to him. "They are tenants. Not friends."

He picked up his pace, leaving me in the dust, as if he didn't agree.

Chapter 5

CELINE

With my eyes closed, I took a deep breath, attempting to steady myself. I was a professional. I just needed to get my head together.

The kids were in the cafeteria with coloring pages, iPads, and enough snacks to last them several hours. Ellie could handle things while I got my classroom set up, and when we got here, Julian and I had walked back and forth to my room three times so he knew where to find me.

It took forty-five minutes to get them prepped and for me to set expectations, but I was finally ready to start my day. My classroom was at the end of a long hallway that had been decorated with cheery signs. A rainbow stripe cut down the middle of the linoleum floor, leading me to an old-school classroom with super high ceilings, giant industrial windows, and a few inches of dust on every surface.

The room was filled with out-of-date materials, and there were a few broken chairs, but on the far wall, the holy grail.

A brand-new smartboard.

I smiled. A work in progress didn't scare me. After years of desperately missing the classroom, every first day felt so special. By the time I was in first grade, I'd known I wanted to be a teacher. Ms. McDonald was the kindest, most patient woman, and she taught me to read and write my name and to love being at school.

I perused the classroom, inspecting the materials and equipment, letting excitement wash over me. Getting this place set up would take a while, but it already felt like home.

The tiny mismatched chairs never failed to make me smile, and the faded alphabet posters were familiar and comforting. The weather chart complete with Velcro icons and a big rug for circle time were bonuses.

The space came alive as I wandered, envisioning where I'd create the calm down corner and where I'd set up sensory bins and the rotating choice stations. There was even a dusty terrarium on an old industrial shelf. It had probably once housed a class pet, though now it was empty. I giggled as I passed it, remembering Julian's eager suggestion that I get a class tarantula.

I pulled a notebook from my bag and jotted down notes, making lists of supplies I'd need and wondering if there was a supply closet in the building I could raid.

"You made it!"

At the cheerful greeting, I turned finding Callie Mayhew-Beauregard, my new principal, bursting into the room, iced coffee in one hand, a clipboard in the other.

I smoothed down my navy shorts. They weren't the most professional, but my selection of clothing was limited, and it was unbearably hot this week. The end of August in Vermont was no joke.

"I'm so pleased you're here." With a warm smile, she approached and pulled me into a hug.

It took effort not to tense up in response. I wasn't much of a hugger. At one time, years ago, I had been, but now I struggled with physical touch.

My sleeveless blouse and shorts combo had looked cute this morning, but now I was feeling sticky and gross.

Callie, on the other hand, looked like a wilderness goddess. All long hair, a flowy maxi dress in a funky print, and a diamond stud in her nose.

She was unlike any principal I'd ever met. But her energy was calming, which I could imagine helped when dealing with parents and students.

"This room was used for storage for a long time." Hands on her hips, she assessed the space.

"This is the first time we've added a second kindergarten class. It's wild, really. It's the largest incoming class in town history. You came at a good time."

"Thanks for letting me bring my kids," I said, wiping off a dusty shelf.

She probably thought I was a weirdo when I'd asked if they could tag along today. But without friends or family to keep an eye on them, this was my only option. Because there was no way I could leave them home alone. It was hard enough that they were halfway across the building now.

"No problem. When I walked by the cafeteria, they were quiet and seemed content. I'm jealous, honestly. Mine are here too, though they're probably off setting small fires as we speak."

Though my first thought was that she was joking, the

way she took a drag from her iced coffee indicated that maybe she was serious.

"I have twin boys. They're ten, and they're feral. Yesterday one tried to skateboard off the school steps while the other one livestreamed it."

My stomach sank. "That sounds ... dangerous."

"It is. They are why I meditate. And why I drink green juice that tastes like lawn clippings. Oh, and why I'm on a first-name basis with every individual who works in the emergency room."

Though I was a little shocked by her admission and maybe the oversharing as well, her self-depreciating humor was disarming.

"I feel you," I said. "Three kids. One is neurodiverse. Divorced. Starting over in a new state."

Her lips tipped up in a genuine smile. "We're going to be friends, just so you know. It's nonnegotiable."

An unfamiliar warmth flickered in my chest, but I sighed and lowered my head. "I don't know if I have the time or the energy for friends."

"That's fine. We'll just stand next to each other at school events and laugh about all the weird stuff later."

A little chuckle worked its way out of me. "Okay, that I can do."

"You may not see it yet, but you picked a great place. I promise—" At the sound of a noise behind her, she spun. "Ooh. My reinforcements are here!"

Two women wandered into the room, both smiling. The younger of the two had a bouncy ponytail and the other was carrying a large bakery box.

"Celine LeBlanc, this," Callie said, holding out an arm, "is Stella Stone. She teaches first grade."

Dressed in paint-splattered cutoffs and a cheery yellow T-shirt that hung off one shoulder, the younger woman held out her hand.

"I am so excited to meet you," she squealed. "And I'm here to work. We want you ready for the first day."

"This is Ashley Wilton."

The other woman put the box down and scooped me into a hug. She looked to be in her early fifties and had a gray streak in her dark hair that looked natural but surprisingly fashionable.

"Callie has told us so much about you." She stepped back after the awkward embrace and grinned. "Fourth grade. I brought muffins and my toolbox. We're going to fix all these wobbly chairs for you." With a wave, she gestured to the bakery box. "I figured since you just got into town and don't have much time to get your classroom set up, you could use emotional support carbs."

I opened my mouth to thank them and to insist they didn't need to go out of their way, but before I could speak, my stomach rumbled. I hadn't eaten breakfast, and everyone was now aware, so I decided not to fight it.

"Maple walnut," Stella said. "The specialty at Bean There, Done That. You will not be disappointed."

Ashley opened the box, and as I stepped closer, my mouth watered. Okay, yes, those looked incredible. They were also the size of my head, but I had a lot of work to get done, so I could use the calories.

I handed one to Callie, who bit into it with an exaggerated sigh of relief, then snagged one for myself.

When the flavor registered, my eyes rolled to the back of my head. Damn, this muffin was heaven.

Ashley got right to work, inspecting every tiny table and chair and making adjustments. Stella jumped right into cleaning out the large storage closet and sorting the materials.

"We've got a supply closet down the hall you can raid," Callie said. "I'll let you check out the new shipment of crayons first."

Setup went a lot faster with help. I showed them the signs I'd made and explained how I wanted the cork boards decorated and the zones set up, and the three of them got to work without questioning my choices or adding their own opinions.

Pretty quickly, I found myself having fun. The girls gave me necessary information about the school and the students and explained the upcoming Harvest Festival. I soaked in as many details as I could.

They mentioned the local waterfall but didn't go into the legend that supposedly went with it. And they laughed about how everyone had thought a set of trash cans had been vandalized, only to find out they'd been raided by a bear.

This was the second time a citizen of Maplewood had mentioned bears. Internally, I grimaced. "Do we need to worry about bears a lot?"

Callie turned and smiled. "Worry, no? But you need to be aware."

"Bear aware." Stella giggled. "Sorry. It's an inside joke. Our mayor does this whole 'be bear aware' program every year and it's kind of hilarious."

I frowned, not following.

"Our mayor," Callie said. "He's very…"

"Hot," Stella blurted, her face flushing.

"But unintentionally hilarious," Ashley finished. "He's very earnest and serious. A total boy scout, and it's a treat, watching him demonstrate how to scare off a bear. You'll see. Are you coming to the town meeting next week?"

I pressed my lips together. "Town meeting?"

"Yup. First Tuesday of the month," she responded. "It's kind of a requirement here."

"I don't have a sitter," I said, turned off by the idea that people were forced to participate. I was not one for civic engagement. In fact, my plan when I made the decision to move here was to lie low.

Not that it was working at all so far.

"Kids are welcome," Callie said. "Trust me. It's educational."

With a forced smile, I nodded. I'd figure out how to avoid it later.

"Anyway, his name is Gabe," she went on waggling her brows, "or Mayor McHottie, as Stella likes to call him."

Stella rolled her eyes.

Callie cackled. "She's had a crush on him since middle school."

"Ooh. You'll probably see him at the farm," Ashley said. "He grew up on the farm next door. He's your landlord's cousin."

"Oh, that's right," Stella chirped. "You're renting from Josh Lawrence."

Shoulders tensing, I nodded and left it at that. The last thing I wanted was to discuss my confusing and somewhat infuriating landlord.

Stella hauled a messy stack of construction paper out and put it on a desk. "He's a quiet guy. Keeps to himself."

"Unlike his parents," Ashley said. "They were everywhere. Always volunteering, and they were at every town event. Such a lovely family."

I busied myself sorting folders into bins by color, ignoring the talk of Josh. So far, he'd been kind of a jerk. But as long as he was a decent landlord and left us alone, I could tolerate it. My goal was to be pleasantly distant, so there was no sense in learning more about him.

"He was a heartbreaker in high school." Stella sighed. "He graduated with my older sister Ruby. Literally every girl in town had a crush on him."

"I can see that," Ashley said. "He seems like the type that came out of the womb a full lumberjack—beard, axe, and all."

As they giggled, I headed for the other side of the room to move bookcases. That would give me something to do and also keep my face hidden.

"I'm married," Callie said. "But I get the appeal. He's all rugged protector on the outside and sweet softie underneath."

My cheeks heated immediately. Dammit. I was so damn weak.

"How do you know he's a softie?" Ashley asked.

"Because when I called him and asked if he'd rent his cottage to Celine, he agreed immediately. Reduced the rent to below market rate and everything. He was more than happy to help out. He may put on a grumpy front, but he's always the first to offer help and he does a lot for the town."

I stood with my back to them, listening, regardless of

how badly I wanted to ignore the topic of my landlord. Farmer Josh was a bit of a softie? That was news to me. So far, he seemed to spend most of his time judging me.

The arrangement was already a bit uncomfortable, but now that I knew he'd offered me a deal on rent, that was magnified.

After Callie offered me the job in July, I'd immediately started looking for housing, but most of the rentals in the area were cute apartments in town, and with three growing kids and Julian's hatred of noise, I wasn't sure any of them were right for us.

With this new information, guilt washed over me. Josh could make a lot more if he rented to anyone else. The cottage was gorgeous. And far nicer than what we were used to. The oven that Julian had nearly destroyed with his Lego birthday cake alone probably cost more than my minivan.

I squeezed my eyes shut and sighed. Dammit. I was softening to him already, and the last thing I needed was to let my guard down. As I pinched the bridge of my nose, I reminded myself to stick to my plan of polite distance and friendly indifference.

Needing a moment to reset, I took the box of muffins to the cafeteria to share with the kids. The three of them were happily coloring while Ellie played Julian's favorite songs from the tiny portable speaker Chloe had given her for her birthday. God, I had the best damn kids.

We worked for another hour, running back and forth to the supply closet, leaving items I wouldn't need and bringing others I would back to the classroom. Callie drifted off to attend a meeting, and not long after, Ashley headed to her own room to finalize some things.

The two of us had been silent for a while when Stella spoke again.

"I'm very excited to meet Julian," she said, wearing a genuine smile.

My heart stuttered. Often it was hard to draw the line between teacher and mom. And given Julian's history with educators, I usually had to brace myself for these conversations.

"We'll have the official IEP meeting soon, obviously. But I've read through his files already, and I'm working on plans to make sure he has a successful year."

The tightness in my chest loosened a little.

Stella kept shelving the books, seemingly unaware of how intensely this conversation was hitting me. "We have a quiet corner and alternative seating, and I keep a visual schedule and allow for frequent movement breaks."

I swallowed thickly, my eyes heating. "That's great."

"The file said he stims. That's not a problem. I won't prevent him from doing what he needs to feel comfortable."

Julian's stimming had been a major issue in the past. Not only at the preschool he'd been kicked out of, but at home. My ex-husband thought it was weird and hated that it drew attention to Julian's differences.

At the therapeutic school he'd attended last year, his stimming had tapered off, mostly because he was surrounded by qualified professionals and other neurodiverse kids, which allowed for a comfortable environment where his nervous system could relax. But even with all the progress he'd made, I was still terrified of how he'd be treated in a public school.

"He's safe in my classroom," Stella said.

An overwhelming desire to hug her washed over me, but I couldn't move, my feet glued to the spot.

"And," she added in a conspiratorial tone, "I have a drawer full of Lego sets I use for choice time. I'm counting on him to be my engineering expert."

"Thank you," I said. "There's a lot to figure out—"

She held up a hand. "Figuring it out is my favorite part. We're coworkers, but we're also partners in the journey to making sure he's happy and thriving."

With my lips pressed together, I nodded. Then I turned my back so she wouldn't see the way my eyes filled with tears.

Not long after, we finished up, and I took a moment to admire the progress. The cubbies and desks were labeled, the daily calendar station was set up, and our little library was bursting with books and beanbag chairs.

I was doing this. For so long, I'd dreamed of the day I'd have my own classroom in a lovely small-town school, where I could watch my kids grow while doing what I loved with my whole heart.

As I gathered the kids and headed for the car, the reality of the kindness I'd experienced today sank in. No, not just today, but since we'd arrived. This town was strange. Loud and maybe too nosy.

But maybe it was exactly what we needed.

Chapter 6

JOSH

"Reed, get me something stronger," Gabe said, raising his glass.

"Day drinking, Mister Mayor?" Logan lifted his own drink to his lips and chuckled.

The three of us sat at a high-top at Timberline Brewery, our usual summer Saturday tradition. We'd play hockey for a while and then grab lunch. The attendees varied, but my desire to leave the farm and feel like a normal person for a couple of hours did not.

We'd played pee wee hockey together as boys, eventually graduating to playing on any frozen pond we could find. None of us had ever been particularly good, though our high school team had mostly winning seasons. These days we just fucked around once a week to keep from feeling like we were over the hill.

The arena was shut down for the month in preparation of hockey season, so today we'd played street hockey in the high school parking lot. As fun as it was, falling hurt a hell of a lot more on the asphalt.

"Fuck off with your judgment. It's an IPA, not heroin."

"Just saying, as a medical professional." Logan chuckled.

"You deliver calves for a living, asshole. Why would I take medical advice from you?"

Logan sipped his beer and smiled lazily. "Undermining my accomplishments? Fine. I don't mind. And yes, I deliver calves and foal and sheep. I sleep just fine."

"Order up, assholes," Reed shouted. "Don't make me walk over there."

The three of us clambered off our high stools and headed to the bar.

Reed pushed one plate forward. "Turkey club and fries."

Gabe picked it up and snagged a ketchup bottle, then made a beeline back to our table.

"Veggie burger."

With his head held high, Logan took it.

It looked nice on the plate, but I wouldn't eat fake meat, even if someone offered me a hundred bucks to do it.

"And this can't be right." Reed scrutinized me, his expression full of judgment. "Greek salad with grilled chicken."

Without a word, I gave him the finger.

So what if I was trying to be a little healthier?

As I approached the table, Gabe was chuckling.

"Doing that annual thing where you try to locate your abs?" he asked.

I picked up a cherry tomato and pelted it at him. It hit him square in the chest, though it didn't faze him.

He only grinned and shoved a handful of fries into his mouth.

Gabe had always been lean and athletic, where I hovered more toward the chunky side. I'd given up on vanity a long time ago, but given that my dad died of a heart attack at far too young an age, it was important that I keep an eye on my health.

Watching my new neighbor run laps up the big hill every morning only brought my concerns to the forefront. That woman looked like she was training for the Olympics.

Not that I noticed.

Not at all.

Especially when she wore nothing but a sports bra and tiny shorts.

The farm was huge, with lots of beautiful scenery. Yet she kept running up and down the same hill. I didn't have a clue why, but who was I to question a person's fitness regimen?

"I even dug the rower out," I admitted.

Logan offered me a fist. "Good on you." He patted his own flat stomach. "It's not as easy as it was when we were in our twenties."

Wasn't that the truth. Nothing, in fact, was remotely like those days, least of all my metabolism.

I'd been talked into trying rowing during freshman orientation. It was the first time I'd even left Vermont, and I was attending a big university in Boston. The coach at the rowing team's booth took one look at me—six four with barn-door shoulders, even at eighteen—and convinced me to try it.

I rowed all four years of college and even traveled to a few international tournaments. And I was in the best shape of my life. I missed it sometimes, the early mornings on the river, the mental grind of the sport, the comradery of my boatmates.

So I'd dug out the old rower, tuned it up, and started rowing every morning. The first day, I made it four minutes before I felt like my heart would explode, not that I'd tell these guys that detail.

"Where's Jas?"

"Working," I said. My brother was a firefighter in town, but he worked with me on the farm on his off days as well.

For years he'd lived with me, sleeping in his childhood bedroom, working around the clock, and drinking away whatever spare time he had.

Then he'd had a baby. And then he'd fallen in love with his son's mom. Not long ago, he moved into town with them. With Evie and Vincent.

I wouldn't tell him to his face, but I missed him. Some nights we'd sit on the porch or around the fire and just talk. About our parents, the farm, our sisters, anything, really. I'd make extra dinner and set it aside for him. He'd come home from a twenty-four-hour shift at the firehouse starving, he'd go straight to the kitchen to eat and then pass out on the couch.

He was relatively easy to care for. Just needed to be fed and watered like Wayne, but Jasper talked a hell of a lot more.

The house was a hell of a lot quieter since he'd been gone.

Not that Wayne minded. He was a solitary dude like me.

"You fuckers should get girlfriends. You'd be less pathetic," Reed said, filling our water glasses.

"We can't all be as lucky as you and convince a woman far out of our league to marry us," Gabe quipped.

Reed beamed. "I know. I'm lucky. You sad sacks are not." His wife Faith ran the brewery with him and Gabe's brother—my cousin—Nate.

"I tried the apps," Logan groused, picking up his veggie burger. "It's a wasteland out there."

"It's because you look like a hippie sasquatch," Gabe said.

Face screwed up, Logan reeled back. "Try not to be too jealous of my lustrous locks," he said. "It's not my fault you couldn't grow a full beard if you tried."

Logan held out a fist, I bumped it. While my beard was full, Logan's veered into mountain man territory. Combined with his man bun and the cow placenta that often clung to his work boots, he was far from a pretty boy.

While Gabe was the clean-cut, collared-shirt guy, the two of us got more feral by the year. Gabe had tried to keep up with us and grow a beard in high school, but it never turned into anything more than a few errant hairs across his cheeks. We'd never let him live it down.

Gabe was only three months older than me. We'd shared a crib as babies and I'd been bigger than him our whole lives, but he'd always had this older brother energy.

It was no surprise to anyone when he ran for mayor, it felt like he'd been doing the job since grade school.

The guy had this way about him. People loved him. Listened to him. He was patient, friendly, and a great leader.

While I was acing AP calculus, he was winning debate competitions and homecoming king.

When a group of people walked in and passed us, he turned on his professional smile and waved at them.

"Doesn't it get exhausting?" I asked once they'd settled at the bar. "Smiling all the time and kissing babies and shit?"

He grimaced.

"He's a small-town mayor. It's not like he has any actual power," Logan teased. "What's he going to do? Issue parking tickets?"

"Nah." I shook my head. "He has no ticketing authority."

"What does he have authority over? Zoning ordinances?" Logan threw his head back and barked a laugh. "Guess he could zone us to death."

"Death by municipal ordinance." I brought a hand to my chest and leaned back like I'd just been stabbed. "My nightmare."

Gabe glared at us over his sandwich.

Elbows on the table, Logan angled forward, grinning. "When are you gonna make Lainey Mrs. Mayor?"

"We're not together," Gabe said around a mouthful of food. "It's been years."

Scoffing, I gave him a side-eye. "What about Paul's bachelor party last year?"

"That was a backslide," he grumbled. "A one-night thing."

"Tell her that. I'm pretty sure she's picking out china patterns," Logan mused.

"Are you five hundred years old?" Gabe snapped. "How do you even know what a china pattern is?"

Logan's lips tipped down thoughtfully. "I don't know. It's an expression."

"A weird-ass one."

Reed chuckled. "I'm just saying, you're youngish. You should get out there."

"I date." He shifted on his stool, grimacing. "Just not anyone in town. I've met people through committees and events in Montpelier and Burlington and Concord. Sometimes I go down to Boston."

"Concord? You date New Hampshire girls? Do they have teeth." Logan laughed at his own shitty joke.

"Asshole."

"You know I'm kidding." The rivalry between Vermont and New Hampshire had been going on since long before any of us were born, so we'd been talking shit about them all our lives.

"Good luck convincing a city girl to come up here," I warned.

That was an easy recipe for a crash-and-burn relationship.

"Yeah, I know that."

Reed wandered away, and the three of us settled in to eat.

We were quiet, all focused on our lunches, when I swore the front of Logan's hoodie wiggled. But both of his forearms were resting on the table.

"Did your hoodie just move?" I asked.

Glaring, he leaned to one side and snagged a piece of turkey from Gabe's plate. He hunched over, holding the turkey near his abdomen, his chin tucked, and a tiny head peeked out of the pocket of his sweatshirt and snatched the meat out of his hand.

"Is that a fucking kitten?" Gabe hissed. "Did you just steal my lunch and feed it to a pocket cat?"

"Shh." Logan frowned at my cousin, then gently eased the critter back into the pocket. "You know Reed gets weird about this kind of shit."

I cocked a brow, stabbing at my salad. "About health codes?"

Shrugging, he picked up his veggie burger. "She's a runt. I'm just keeping an eye on her."

I huffed a laugh. "I was wondering why you were wearing a hoodie in this weather."

"She'll be good in a few days." He took a big bite, chewing noisily. "Just keeping her warm and safe."

"God, he's a full-blown cat man now," I griped.

"It's a genuine mystery why women weren't swiping right constantly on those apps," Gabe joked.

"Laugh all you want, but my lady is out there." He gave us a dopey smile. "She's probably curled up on her couch reading and drinking iced coffee, considering leaving her house but ultimately deciding against it. She doesn't yet know I exist, and I love her for that."

I couldn't deny the fantasy wasn't a bad one. After what Allie had done, I went full on monk. The thought of dating made me sick to my stomach. And like Logan's, my perfect woman sure as hell wasn't on a dating app. She probably hated dating apps. Probably hated dating too, now that I was thinking about it.

"Besides, I've got bigger problems. I want to buy out

Marigold. She's been making noise about selling the land for a while."

Logan rented a small farm from Marigold Shaw, one of the older ladies in town. She moved into a condo near the town green a few years ago. He'd revitalized the property and turned it into his animal sanctuary, building and landscaping and taking care of all his animals while working fourteen hours a day seven days a week as one of very few vets in the county.

"Make her an offer," I told him. "Marigold's got plenty of cash, and it's not like Paul wants it." Her grandson Paul was an accountant who wanted nothing to do with the place. He lived in town with his wife and son and seemed content with his small yard and newer construction home.

Gabe dipped his chin. "Sounds like her granddaughter doesn't either."

"I don't have a lot of cash lying around." He smoothed his hand over his overgrown beard. "The student loans are killing me. I swear I'm gonna be paying for my degrees for the rest of my life."

I nodded. I understood that. None of our parents had had money when we headed off to college. I'd gotten my BA, but I'd paid it all off with my Wall Street money. Majoring in finance did have its perks.

But while I'd gone to work, Logan had headed to vet school and Gabe had gone to law school. The debt they accumulated had to be staggering.

"Start a nonprofit," I told him. Again. "Get tax exempt status and fundraise. I can set up a trust and manage it. We can grow a nest egg to take care of the place."

He nodded, his lips pressed together in uncertainty. "I gotta own it first."

He had plenty of options. And I'd happily talk tax strategy, secured investment funds, and indexed growth all day. But my friends would kill me. Besides, that wasn't who I was anymore.

I was a quiet farmer, living a quiet, solitary life.

Except recently, I'd been feeling more and more unsettled. And it wasn't only the murder this spring or the business or the fluctuating price of sap that had me waking up in a cold sweat at night.

It was my new tenant. A red-haired terror in Crocs.

Head down, I finished my salad. When I looked up again, the beer hall was a hell of a lot busier than it had been when we walked in, and several folks were staring over at Gabe and whispering.

"Does Josh need to worry?" Logan's words floated on the air, making me perk up.

Gabe rolled his eyes at me. He knew me well enough to know I'd been in my own world. "The lawyers say no," he said softly. "But there are some... complications. We're all trying our best to do this by the book."

"And Sugar Moon?" Logan asked.

"Lawyered up and they're not speaking to anyone. Or cooperating. Louisa has been on a rampage since Nolan arrested her."

"But they let her go," I argued.

"Yeah, but the woman has reach. She's the CEO of one of the largest maple syrup producers in the world, and she hasn't taken kindly to being perp-walked through the Founder's Festival."

That may have been how the Founder's Festival ended, but the events leading up to it had started back in April. At the annual Maple Festival.

I'd been attending the festival since birth. Hell, I was pretty certain every citizen of Maplewood had. It had been around longer than anyone here had been alive, and it was the only good part about the dreary spring in Vermont.

When the ceremonial sap barrel had been tapped at the sugar shack on the town green during the festival, they'd discovered a body inside.

The body of Will McManus, a kid who'd done a lot of seasonal work for most farmers in town, including me, and who'd been working as a delivery driver for Sugar Moon, the syrup conglomerate in town.

And on top of that, the barrel of sap where his body had been found had come from my farm.

His death had kicked off a shitstorm in town, one full of paranoia and suspicion.

Tourism numbers were down, and all my contracts were in jeopardy.

Plus, every person in Maplewood was reeling. This was "America's Most Charming Small Town," after all.

I leaned back and took a deep breath, then let it out slowly. I got upset every time I thought about it. It was a senseless tragedy, and to add salt to the wound, much of the scrutiny had been directed at me and the farm.

"The rumors are the worst part," I said.

"Don't even get me started." Gabe peered over one shoulder, then the other, then leaned in. "People have all kinds of ridiculous theories. Some crazy shit. Alien invasions, demonic possessions."

"I was at the coffee shop the other day," Logan added, "and Morty Fletcher was there, swearing it was Betsy Ross."

"Can't really blame him there. Betsy can be a real terror sometimes," Gabe said.

Logan, who had some kind of weirdly respectful relationship with the wild fucking bear, shook his head. "None of the Maplewood wildlife were accessories to this crime."

"Half the town thinks you did it," Gabe said, nodding at me.

My stomach sank. This fucking town. Caleb Dunne had confessed and he'd been arrested. But no one believed it was that cut-and-dry.

The entire town, me included, had been waiting for the other shoe to drop.

"Only half?" Logan marveled around another bite of his gross-ass veggie burger.

"The other half thinks he covered it up."

"Efficient," Logan remarked, still chewing.

I glared at him.

"And I've got people accusing me of hiding information too, saying I've helped Nolan tamper with evidence and threatening to recall him. Never mind that his position isn't an elected one. But they don't care about simple things like law or procedure." He reached over and plucked one of Logan's fries from his plate.

Gabe was an emotional eater. After we lost the state hockey tournament during our junior year of high school, he'd eaten an entire lasagna that my mom had frozen for an upcoming church potluck.

"The fucking state police," he murmured, "came in here,

stomped all over everything, got everyone riled up, and muddied the investigation." His face was red, sweat beading at his temples. My always put-together cousin was on the brink of losing it. "And everyone wants my head on a platter because tourism suffered this summer."

"Fall season's looking good," Logan said. "That's what I heard, at least." He was hardly plugged into the Maplewood scene, but his support was genuine.

"I'm fielding phone calls from crime bloggers left and right. One even had the audacity to pitch a 'Maple Murder Tour.'" He closed his eyes and blew out a loud breath. "I've had to issue a dozen statements, insisting people stop speculating and trying to monetize this tragedy."

I set my fork down. "Did it work?"

He glowered. "Of course not. This is fucking Maplewood. People can't keep themselves from being ridiculous."

Maybe that was true. I myself had felt out of sorts since that night. Will's death had put all my beliefs about this place and the life I'd built on shaky ground.

Last season had been a busy one. The weather had turned, making the late-season sap run longer than anticipated. We hadn't complained. Late-season sap was the darkest, and restaurants and kitchens were always eager to purchase it.

We'd been working around the clock, and the last time I'd seen Will, he had come to pick up the barrels from the night before.

Maple syrup was shelf stable. It could last for years. But fresh tree sap was not. It had to be collected daily and processed immediately or refrigerated. And since we sold most of our sap to Sugar Moon, they picked up daily and processed at their facility.

The process was more efficient and more lucrative for the farm. Sugaring our own syrup, as my grandparents had done, required working twenty-four seven in the sugarhouse during harvest time with a massive fire going constantly, boiling the sap to the right consistency, then bottling and labeling it. We'd pared back when I was a kid, and Dad had planted more trees and increased our farming operation.

"I've been sleeping with my phone on my chest," Gabe admitted. "Too afraid to miss something big. Everything is a mess."

"It's everywhere," Logan agreed. "Kids are asking questions they don't even understand and people no longer trust their neighbors." He roughed a hand over his pulled-back hair. "It's a coping mechanism. They're scared."

"I fucking know that," Gabe snapped. "But I'm doing the best I can."

Logan nodded once. We both knew that.

We finished up and paid the bill in silence, the heaviness of the whispers and stares getting to us.

We were two feet from the door, almost home free, when we were stopped.

"Joshua Lawrence." I pulled up short like I'd hit an invisible wall and closed my eyes, bracing for this interaction, then turned and plastered on a smile.

Bitsy Bramble, Olive Foster, and Gail McNamee sat in the corner booth, each with clean plates and half-full pint glasses in front of them.

The ladies around here sure did love craft beer.

Bitsy wore a cardigan and a judgmental scowl, as usual. Olive was all curls and bright red lipstick while Gail batted her eyelashes at Gabe like he was a movie star.

"Well." Bitsy clapped once. "If it's not the mountain man himself! Out and about in town."

Logan groaned behind me. That asshole was probably planning to take his pocket kitten and run. Not that I'd blame him.

"We hear you've got new tenants."

I nodded. "Yes, ma'am. Rented out the cottage. They moved in last weekend."

"Single mother," Olive said. "Three children."

"I visited her on behalf of the welcome wagon," Gail said, her voice breathy. "Lovely redhead, brave eyes, good manners." She lifted her chin, scrutinizing me, her friends following suit. "We like her."

Okay. I guess it was good to know my tenant was well-liked in town. Was that why they'd stopped me, to inform me of their reputation?

Before I could figure out a way to ask them to clarify, Gabe cleared his throat.

Thank fuck. I could always count on him to intervene. He'd had my back since we were kids.

"Ladies. We'll leave you to your lunch."

"Don't patronize us, Mister Mayor," Bitsy snapped. She leaned to one side and peered around him. "Logan Becker, is that you under all that hair?"

"That beard could house wildlife," Olive mused.

Logan opened his mouth to respond but then thought better of it and focused on his work boots.

"We want to make sure that Celine and her family are adequately taken care of," Bitsy said. "Your parents were pillars of our community. They showed up, they volunteered, they gave to the town."

"And you disappear," Gail muttered.

Olive joined in on the criticism, though she softened it with a wink. "And not in a mysterious, sexy way," she said. "Your vibe is more ..." She tapped her chin. "Grumpy sasquatch."

Logan snorted behind me.

I forced myself to smile. The move made my facial muscles ache. "I keep my head down. Lots of work to get done on the farm."

"And that," Bitsy said, "is why we're watching out for you."

"You are a treasure, Bitsy," Gabe said, using his professional tone. "Always watching out for everyone."

"Oh I'm not watching *out* for you, Mayor," she said, lifting her chin and giving us a better view of her ever-present pearls. "I'm watching you. There's a difference."

Gabe grimaced, but he wiped the expression away quickly.

"We want that kind woman and her kids to thrive here," Bitsy went on. "I've heard she's a wonderful teacher."

"What an asset to the community," Olive chirped.

"So don't scare her off with your grumpy bad moods."

"Not a problem," I said.

I'd already promised myself I'd stay far away from Celine and her kids. As long as they stayed away from my farm equipment, I'd probably never see them. I had almost two hundred acres across the two farms, so it should be easy to keep my distance, and as always, I had plenty of work to keep me busy.

"Okay, then." Olive clasped her hands in front of her chest. "I think he's been adequately warned, hasn't he, girls?"

With a final tense smile, I hightailed it for the door, desperate to get back to the farm and a sense of normalcy.

Chapter 7

CELINE

The day before the first day of school always filled me with jitters.

On top of that, I had so much to get done. Ellie was angstier than usual and headed to the combined junior high and high school across the street from the elementary where Julian and Maggie and I would be.

It hurt my heart, making her bounce around during what were really tough years to be a girl. In another universe, she would be painting her nails and chatting with friends about how the first day of seventh grade might go.

Instead, she was the new kid. *Again.*

The kid from a broken home. The kid whose dad was in jail.

With that thought bouncing around in my head, I emptied the dryer and carried the basket of fresh laundry up the stairs.

I felt much more at ease with where Maggie was at. She

loved school and was too busy finishing her summer reading list to really get anxious about starting in a new school.

Then there was Julian. Stella—Ms. Stone—had sent a detailed visual schedule, as promised, and we'd been reviewing it every day since.

She'd also sent photos of the school staff, and Julian had memorized all their names. And more than once, he'd counted the number of steps between his classroom and mine and knew exactly how long it would take to get to me.

In the past, his separation anxiety had gotten so intense that he couldn't bear not being in the same room as me. Sometimes he'd even have to sit close enough to touch me while building with Legos or looking at a book.

After we finally escaped his father, Julian's therapists said it would get better over time. After a few attempted escapes from class in kindergarten, he settled in and eventually found a lot of comfort in the routine that came with the school day.

Once I'd folded the clean clothes, I shuffled across the hall into Julian's room. "I have pants and PJs," I called out. "Can you put them in your drawers?" My little guy liked having tasks to complete and Ellie had used my fancy label maker to label his drawers. She'd even made a daily checklist and mounted it next to his door.

Inside the quiet room, I turned in a circle. "Julian?"

All I found was a half-built Lego car on the floor.

Terror rushed through my veins, fast and relentless.

"Girls," I shouted, dropping the clean laundry onto the floor. "Do you know where Julian is?"

I darted from room to room, wildly searching. Ellie joined me, sweeping through the house, calling his name.

"He's probably hiding," she said, though she was rigid with tension just like I was.

He wasn't on the second floor or anywhere downstairs, and he wasn't in the driveway.

After I'd checked the small back yard, muscle memory took over, and I ran down the hill, calling out his name.

Dread swamped me. Not again.

How could I have lost him again?

As I ran, my thoughts spiraled. Why did I think living here was a good idea? This place was a death trap. Nothing but machinery, water, and roads traveled by monstrous trucks. Not to mention the bear everyone kept talking about like it was the towns goddamn mascot.

Where the road forked, I headed toward the main barn. Julian liked to tinker, so odds were he'd go there first.

I picked up speed, jumping over a small fence and cutting through a field, rushing straight for the open door and the large dog happily trotting around just outside it.

"Julian." I launched myself over the threshold, braced to find an accident or disaster or injury.

Instead I found Julian sitting on a barrel, sorting wrenches by size and explaining *Sponge Bob Square Pants* to Josh, who was crouched nearby, fixing a grease-covered machine.

My eyes blurred and my heart pounded in my ears, my nervous system not quite caught up to my brain.

He was safe. He was perfectly safe.

Calm, focused, and engaged. Probably learning something, for Christ's sake.

I, on the other hand, was cracking into pieces, panting

and sweating. Wild with rage and frustration and, somehow, relief.

The worst hadn't happened.

Yet my body still hadn't received that message. No, its reaction only escalated. My fingertips prickled and my lungs burned as I gasped for breath.

"You couldn't bother to tell me he was here?" I shouted at Josh as I darted to Julian and gathered him in my arms.

"Mom," my little boy complained, fighting my hold, his focus drifting to the wrenches and their individual compartments in the tool chest.

"You can't leave without permission," I murmured to him. Then I zeroed in on Josh with such fury I was sure lasers were shooting from my eyes. "You have my number. You could have called."

"He's only been here a couple of minutes. I told him I'd walk him back to the cottage," Josh said, his nostrils flaring. "You'll have to excuse me for delaying three or four minutes. I've got my head in an engine."

The anger continued to roil inside me. Logically, I understood that this wasn't actually his fault, but I couldn't temper the emotions or control the words coming out of my mouth. "You know he's a flight risk," I said, my voice shaking slightly.

He stood to his full height. My first instinct was to take a step back. He was quite a large man. But I only lifted my chin.

"He wandered in here. I engaged him so he didn't take off again. As soon as I could safely complete my task, I'd have walked him home. He knew that and was waiting for me."

The words sounded rational coming out of his mouth, yet they only made me angrier.

"This place is a death trap," I growled, kicking a piece of wood lying near my foot.

"It's a working farm," he said, his tone low. "There are dangers, sure. But I do a damn good job minimizing any risk. A city girl like you might have some romantic idea of farming, but I guarantee it's nowhere close to the reality."

"I am not a city girl," I spat, my free hand on my hip—the other still on Julian. That was a low fucking blow. "I am from rural Maine, North Woods, sir. My father was a logger, and I learned how to dodge moose on the road while I still had my learner's permit. Do not patronize me."

He grunted. "Then understand the danger and parent appropriately."

A red curtain dropped over my vision. Did this man seriously just judge my parenting? On autopilot, my body ran through the self-defense training I'd taken. One swift kick in the balls, and I'd have him on the ground.

"Mom," Julian said softly.

His sweet voice brought me back to earth and immediately doused the aggression building inside me. I was not the type of person who got into fights, verbal or otherwise. We'd moved here for peace and tranquility. And the only way to achieve them was to get far away from Josh Lawrence.

"Julian." I kneeled next to him.

He bristled, but he didn't move or complain.

"TTG," I said softly.

His eyes widened and his little body stiffened.

It was our family code, when something was wrong or

we needed to exit an uncomfortable situation quickly, one of us uttered the code and we all moved.

Blinking, he stood and gave Josh a random thumbs-up. Then he scurried toward the exit.

I followed, refusing to look back at that asshole.

I trudged back up the hill while, at my side, Julian chattered happily about his new friend Wayne and how the beard guy let him help with tools.

This should have brought me nothing but joy. I'd waited so long for him to speak. He'd endured early intervention and therapy, and I'd endured so much worry. He was three years old the first time he said "Mama."

It was one of the happiest moments of my life.

Although it took him a long time to start talking, once he hit that milestone, the words didn't slow. His stream-of-consciousness observations were a normal part of our days.

Seeing the world through his eyes was a special gift, and I would always cherish it.

But I couldn't even bring myself to listen to his storytelling. My ears were ringing too loudly and anger, mostly at myself and the situation, simmered inside me.

Had I been kidding myself?

Maybe I couldn't do this.

Shit, I couldn't even fold laundry while keeping an eye on Julian.

I was a fucking failure.

With every step, my feet grew heavier.

"Can I have some cooking popcorn?" Julian asked as we climbed the porch steps. "I'm hungry." He loved popcorn and I'd bought a fancy machine and organic corn kernels, but he always preferred the microwave kind, which he called his cooking popcorn.

A long breath escaped me, my shoulders finally deflating. "Can we talk about what just happened first?"

Head lowered, he focused on his hands. I rubbed and squeezed his shoulders firmly. Light touches could make him uncomfortable, so when I needed his attention, I had to apply some pressure.

"You can't just leave the house, bud."

His shoulders sagged, but he didn't look up.

"This is a very cool place." I kept my tone even, willing myself to remain calm. "I know there are all kinds of exciting things to see. But you can't wander off and not tell me."

He nodded.

"I love you," I said, squeezing his shoulders again. "All I want is to keep you safe."

He threw his arms around my hips and squeezed me tight. "S-sorry." He sniffled. "I just wanted to see the dog. I really like him. I think we could be friends."

I nearly staggered back. That admission hit me square in the chest.

"He seems like a very nice dog. But I have to take you to see him."

"But you were busy. You were doing that thing where you argue with yourself."

For the first time since I stepped into his room, a thread of lightness wove through me. I almost let out a laugh. My kids loved to call me on my shortcomings, and they absolutely pointed out when I was having spirited debates in my own head.

"I've got a lot on my mind," I murmured.

He tilted his head back, his focus fixed on my shirt. "Are you worried about Dad?"

A wave of anguish hit me, and I kneeled and pulled him into my arms.

"No. I'm not worried about Dad at all. He's in jail, where he belongs. He's not a kind man. He's sick."

"Will jail make him better?"

"I don't know, bud." My lungs constricted. "But I know it's the best place for him right now."

I held him, tucking his head beneath my chin, until he wiggled out of my arms. Then I microwaved a bag of popcorn, sliced a cucumber, counted out eleven blueberries, and set him up in front of the TV while I recovered from this adventure.

Explaining to my kids that their dad was in jail and that I had put him there had been devastating. We'd had help from therapists, and I'd done a lot of my own research, learning special phrases to use in the hope of comforting them, but there was just no way to articulate to a six-year-old that his father was a piece of shit. That I hoped he rotted in prison for the rest of his miserable existence.

That he wasn't redeemable. Not because of what he'd done to me, but because of what he'd done to Julian. I couldn't close my eyes at the end of the day without reliving that night. The moment he struck my baby. Parts of me shattered right there and then. Along with the innocence that all three of my children still possessed. And we'd never get any of it back.

But we had to move on. It was up to me to rebuild their lives. I had to do better, be better. Give them all I could.

I settled Julian with his lunch in front of an episode of *Octonauts* and made sandwiches for the girls. All the while, waves of shame rolled over me. Lashing out at Josh was unfair. I'd taken out my fear and panic on him. Yet it wasn't his fault I carried so much trauma around with me and he didn't deserve to suffer because of it.

Each time our interaction replayed, I was even more certain I'd been wrong. Maybe he was an ass, but regardless, I'd lost the plot.

After giving the girls strict instructions to sit next to Julian and keep eyes on him until I returned, I picked up my phone and headed back to that barn. I was a big girl, and I'd take responsibility for my fuck-ups.

I'd just closed the door behind me when the sound of boots on gravel caught my attention. He strode toward the cottage, sweaty and looking annoyed in his damn hat.

At the sight, my stomach did a weird little flip that I refused to acknowledge.

"I was coming to apologize." I crossed my arms, setting a boundary between us.

He stopped a few feet from the porch, his lips turned down.

I eased down a few steps, putting us eye to eye.

"I was also coming to apologize." He gritted the words out like they tasted badly and dug the toe of one of his work boots into the dirt.

A flare of annoyance flashed inside me, he couldn't even let me apologize? But I forced the emotion away and steered back to my plan.

"I'm sorry," I told him. "I overreacted and took it out on you."

He nodded. Saying nothing, his eyes hidden beneath his hat.

"I'm struggling." I hated that I was spilling my guts to this grumpy stranger. I'd worked too hard for too long to be strong, to hide my vulnerabilities so no one could ever exploit them again. Yet I couldn't stop. "He's eloping again. Bolting. Regressing in some of his progress," I admitted, shaking my head. "It's the move and all the uncertainty. I thought I was prepared for it, but..." The weight I always carried on my shoulders grew.

He studied me intently, his head slightly tilted. It was unnerving, being the focus of his scrutiny. "I should have been watching more closely."

That was like a blow to the solar plexus. I did not need his help.

"If it helps at all," he went on, "he was very polite and curious."

Shrugging, I lied. "That kind of helps."

He continued surveying me. Not in a creepy way, but like he was cataloging every flaw and strategizing about how best to exploit my weaknesses.

He shoved his hands into his pockets. "I don't want to overstep. But do you have any help? Seems like you've got your hands full."

There wasn't a hint of judgment. No pity. Just logistics. This man seemed to speak only in practicalities.

And between one breath and the next, any charitable feelings I'd held for him crumbled into dust. Long-simmering rage bubbled up inside me again, its target the brick wall of a human standing in front of me.

"Excuse me?" I sneered. "That's rude."

He had the audacity to look ... confused? His brows lowered and his lips tugged down. Like he hadn't just insulted the core of my being.

"I work my ass off, thank you very much," I snapped. "My kids are well cared for. And yes, things have been a bit chaotic, but I've got it under control." The words poured out, years' worth of trauma unloaded on him.

He held his large, rough hands up in surrender. "I didn't mean to offend."

"Yes you did." I took a step forward, relishing the power that came with having this big, strong man on the defensive. "What's your problem? You hate women?"

He shook his head. "Of course not. I'm just." He took a step back and smoothed his hand over his beard, his eyes darting to one side. Even his dog was staring at him like he'd royally fucked up. "Um, I... Sorry. And well." He took his hat off and ran his hands through his dark hair.

He really had the rugged thing going, not that I cared at all.

"I don't have a problem," he finally said. "I've got a farm to run."

An annoyed huff escaped me. "I'm getting tired of this whole noble farmer bullshit," I said. "Just admit it, you're an ass."

He swallowed, his throat working, his focus still locked on my face. I hated it.

And then he smiled.

A smile.

A fucking smile. Big and wide and toothy. And was

that...? A dimple? Just one on the left side, barely visible through his beard.

My traitorous heart tripped over itself, and a warmth I hadn't experienced in years bloomed low in my belly.

Then he laughed. A deep laugh that in other circumstances would be annoyingly sexy, making my damn knees wobble.

"I live to please, Matchstick."

All the pleasant sensations vanished and my spine snapped straight. "What did you call me?"

He laughed again, motherfucker. "Matchstick. Small. Dangerous. One spark and you'll light the place up. A lot of power in a tiny package."

I scowled. Was that an insult? I couldn't wrap my head around it. Because I was kind of flattered. Not that I'd admit it. And I definitely didn't need this grumpy ass giving me a nickname.

"We're not friends," I groused, trying to fend off the little thrill that zipped through me.

"Oh, I know." The words were lighter than any he'd spoken to me since we met.

A giggle bubbled up inside me, but I choked it back. It was a miracle, really.

I was tired. It was a million degrees outside. And we both had better things to do than stare at each other in the driveway.

"I'd love to hate you," I told him, "but this house is unfairly beautiful. And the tub is magnificent. I'll give you that. You hired a great interior designer."

He crossed his arms, which only made him look beefier.

"Hate to burst your bubble, but I chose everything myself. Every single detail."

"Well," I huffed, possibly more annoyed by that than anything else he'd said to me. "Then I like it less now."

The corner of his lips twitched.

Shit. If I had to experience his damn dimple again, I was done.

So I nodded firmly, keeping my tone serious. "Yup. I hate that tub."

"You love the tub."

"Fuck off."

With his head tipped back, he barked out a laugh. "Gladly. Can I go back to my job now? Are you done with your rage apology yet?"

The absurdity of this situation nearly took me out at the knees. I needed to go do yoga or something. All the pressure must have been getting to me.

But instead, I continued to poke this bear. Because though I hated to admit it, it was fun. And the bear had that dimple.

"It's a wonder there's no Mrs. Maple Tree in this place. What with your sparkling personality."

His smile only grew.

"You must be fighting the ladies off with sticks, or ..." I trailed off. "Pine cones or whatever country shit you're into."

"You could not handle what I'm into."

A confusing mix of irritation and intrigue hit me. I cleared my throat. "Good. You should go now."

"Great. Keep your kids away from dangerous equipment please."

"Excellent," I gritted out. "Don't question my parenting again. Ever."

"Perfect. Distance works for me."

"I look forward to rarely interacting with you."

We stood face to face for a beat too long, neither of us moving. Like maybe we'd just agreed to the wrong solution, and we knew it. And then he tipped his hat and started walking away, the dog trailing after him.

Chapter 8

CELINE

eek two in Maplewood arrived like a bar brawl disguised as a Monday morning in September. We'd survived the first week of school—a three-day week only, but I still counted it as a major victory. So far, Ellie had forgotten to bring home all the forms she needed signed and Maggie had forgotten her glasses. But we'd made it.

I was doing it. Momming. Teaching. Living in a new place. And I was still standing.

When my alarm blared, I shut it off with a groan, then surveyed Julian, who was sitting on the floor, lining up his Lego mini figs by theme and color.

He looked calm. Too calm. That could only mean the storm was delayed. It typically took two weeks to get him into a new routine, so we were far from it, and this was his first five-day week of school.

Stella had reported that he'd been quiet and hesitant but

curious so far. Which was as good an outcome as I could ask for.

"Morning, Mama," he said, not looking up from his Legos.

"Why is Darth Vader hanging out with Iron Man?" I asked, pulling my hair back and stretching.

As much as I could use my morning run, I was too overwhelmed with getting this full school week started to take the time.

He looked up at me. "Because they both wear metal helmets," he explained like it was obvious. Of course.

I let out a light chuckle, blinking. Coffee. Good God, I needed coffee.

"I don't wanna go to school today," he murmured, his head down.

"Why not?"

"It's Monday. We have music class."

"I know that's not your favorite, bud, but your headphones are in your backpack."

He looked up, his little lips turned down. "It's loud, and I don't like the room. The windows are low and I can't see the sky."

I crouched and kissed the top of his head. "That's annoying." Knees popping, I stood, then headed into my bathroom to grab my toothbrush. "The good news is, the sky is still there, and music is only forty-five minutes long. And don't you have recess after?"

He muttered something unintelligible.

"And isn't Monday gaga day?" I stood in the doorway, toothbrush held aloft.

He picked his head up and smiled. "Yes. I forgot. First grade gets the gaga pit on Mondays."

"See? Lots to look forward to. Now go get dressed."

Down the hall, Maggie was already singing enthusiastically. Ellie was probably still asleep. Knowing I'd have to face her soon, I took a two-minute shower. Then I brushed my hair. A layer of tinted moisturizer and mascara completed my supersonic morning routine.

Julian, God bless him, had dressed and brushed his teeth. The visual calendar we'd hung on his wall was a game changer.

"I'll fill the water bottles," he chirped. "I'm not waking up Ellie."

With a fake pout, I agreed, but when his little feet pattered down the stairs, I couldn't help but smile.

While Julian was up at five thirty every day, Ellie was a tween and therefore believed that waking up before ten a.m. was a war crime.

"Mom, can you do a French braid today?" Maggie stepped out of her room wearing turquoise bike shorts, an oversized yellow T-shirt, at least four necklaces, and a big morning smile.

I pulled her in for a side hug. "Morning, luvie. We might have braiding time, but if you've already brushed your teeth, I need you to make the coffee."

"On it."

The door to the girls' room was wide open and the lights were on. Maggie's bed was already haphazardly made, but Ellie was buried under a mountain of blankets.

"Ellie belly," I singsonged. "Time to wake up."

"*Ughbsr*," she moaned.

"I know you're awake," I murmured. "How could you not be after twenty full minutes of Maggie's scream singing?"

"It's the worst," she grumbled.

"No. Mondays are the worst." I grasped the edge of the blankets and swiped them off her in one quick motion.

"*Mom*," she moaned, pawing at the air like an annoyed kitten.

"We've got twenty minutes. Move it, lady," I said, heading for the door.

Maggie had gotten the coffee maker going and had found the cereal, so that was a start.

I filled my mug and burned my tongue twice, though I counted it was a win, hoping it meant I could drink half of this cup before it got cold.

Somehow, through sheer force of will and mild bribery, I got all three kids fed and out the door with two minutes to spare. Yes, Maggie had one shoe on and the other in her hand, and I'd had to use Ellie's full name twice before she put her damn binder in her backpack, but it was progress.

We spilled into the driveway in a blur of backpacks and complaints as I took a sip of now tepid coffee.

As the kids were scrambling toward the van, a dark blur caught my eye. Just past the rear door, Wayne sat.

Julian saw him a second later, darting for him and burying his hand in his fur, the two of them staring at one another with deep mutual devotion.

"Wayne likes mornings," he's said. "He's an early owl like me. Not like Ellie. She's a night owl."

"I'm sure he does." Inhaling deeply, I scanned the property for Wayne's owner.

We'd managed to politely avoid each other for the past few days, and it had been blissful. It turned out living on this farm was lovely when one never had to see the grumpy farmer.

"Tell him goodbye," I said firmly. "Wayne would not want you to be late for school."

Wayne's tail thumped happily against the gravel drive.

Maggie hopped out of the van's sliding door and threw her arms around him. "You might not be a horse," she said into his fur, "but I still love you."

"Guys," I barked. "Car. Now."

Julian gave Wayne a forlorn look, then climbed in.

Rather than trotting off, Wayne stayed perfectly still, watching our vehicle. Unwilling to move an inch.

Sighing, I pulled out my phone and navigated to Josh's contact info.

CELINE

Come get your wolf dog, he's blocking my car and we'll be late for school.

The reply came faster than I expected.

Josh: Just go around him.

I stared at the response that came in unreasonably quickly. This fucking guy.

CELINE

I'm not playing chicken with a 150 pound dog.

JOSH

He only weighs 130 pounds. Please don't give him a complex. He's lovable at any size.

Huffing, I rolled my eyes.

JOSH

He probably just wants a proper goodbye.

Pinching the bridge of my nose, I resisted the urge to throw my phone.

"Ellie," I said, my tone a little too short, "say goodbye to the dog."

With far less arguing than I expected, Ellie hopped out of the passenger seat. But she took her sweet-ass time wandering over and scratching his ears.

"We've got to go to school," she told him, standard tween sarcasm dripping from each word, "but if you move, we can throw the tennis ball later. I don't want my mom to blow a gasket again."

In response, Wayne turned his head and looked at me.

With a shrug, Ellie got back in the car. But the dog remained where he was, attention still set on me.

"Oh fuck it." I scurried over and bent down, scratching his ears. "You're a good boy," I said. "Now get out of here so I can drive these animals to school."

I stood, half annoyed and half flattered that he was watching me with a dopey look on his face.

Then, instead of trotting off like I was certain he'd finally do, the damn dog jumped up on his hind legs, standing taller than I was, and licked my face.

I took a step back, screaming, while the kids burst into laughter.

Body tense and hands clenched, I surveyed myself. Dammit. I had a pawprint on my boob and my face was damp with dog drool.

Jesus Christ.

Wayne must have been satisfied after making it to second base because he trotted away happily.

We rolled slowly past the barn and the farmhouse, where, shocker, Josh was standing, beefy arms crossed, watching us, with Wayne sitting happily by his side, like he hadn't just licked off my mascara.

The joke was on him. I bought the cheap stuff.

My kids lowered their windows to wave, and I slowed further, lowering my own.

Josh's sleeves were rolled up, and he had that damn worn hat on backward. Bastard.

"Control you dog," I said.

"He's just friendly." His lips quirked a fraction.

I pulled my head back in and examined myself in the rearview mirror to make sure I didn't have any dog drool left on my face.

"That's what they say about serial killers," I quipped.

"He's easy," came his response. "Just bribe him with bacon."

"I'm sorry," I hissed. "I don't carry bacon on my person."

He gave me a solemn nod. "Rookie mistake, Matchstick."

As the kids laughed hysterically, I rolled up my window, sufficiently humbled for the morning.

As I hustled to my classroom, chugging the last of my now cold coffee, my phone buzzed.

JOSH

He likes Julian. Doesn't happen often.
Wayne's not a people person.

I hesitated, rereading the message, and then typed back.

CELINE

Could have fooled me. The damn dog jumped on me and licked my face. And that was after demanding hugs and kisses from all three of my kids.

JOSH

No way. I spent years training him. He never jumps on people.

CELINE

Wanna bet? I've got a paw print on my left boob to prove it.

CELINE

How's it feel to know your dog's getting more action than you are?

The second I hit Send, I regretted it. What the hell, Celine? I didn't know the first thing about Josh's *actions*, and it definitely wasn't my business. And if the teacher chatter and common goddamn sense were any indication, he did not struggle in that department.

JOSH

I'm man enough to admit I'm jealous. But I'm also impressed by Wayne's game. He's getting extra bacon today.

The bell rang, startling me, and I put my phone on silent and stashed it in my top drawer just as the screaming of far too many children echoed down the hallway.

I was annoyed by my landlord. But my body felt lighter. Something that had been happening little by little for the last several days.

Not because life was suddenly easy, but because things

were working. The four of us were almost thriving. And that felt like a small miracle.

Chapter 9

JOSH

I fucking hated meetings.

Whether they were in glass office towers or dusty gravel parking lots. Meetings were still meetings.

I thought I'd left them behind when I walked away from my corporate job. Should have known better. Today I was wearing clean jeans and driving into town to deal with the ongoing sap supply mess.

Same nonsense, different uniform.

I should have been fixing equipment, harvesting the kale that was growing into a jungle in the garden, and finalizing payroll. Instead I was wasting precious daylight hunting for a parking spot so I could at least properly caffeinate. If I had to be miserable, at least I could be alert.

The stop at the coffee shop should have been simple. Lately, though, it never was. The tourists had begun trickling back in, and while that was wonderful for the town, it set me on edge.

So did the unfamiliar questions murmured here and

there and the much more morbid interest than what visitors had shown in the past.

Despite the town's attempts to sweep the tragedy and all the drama that came with it under the rug, none of it was settled. Like a board that hadn't been nailed down properly. Solid until it's stepped on wrong.

The line at Bean There, Sipped That wasn't terrible, and despite the strangers wandering outside, my sister's coffee shop was filled with warmth and familiarity. Wood floor that creaked in the right places, chalkboard menus smudged from daily revisions, and the low hum of the voices of the locals. And to top it all off, the air smelled like my mother's maple scones. Jenn kept that recipe locked in her mind like a sacred text. Not even I was privy to the details.

As I settled in to wait my turn, she shot me a wink.

The tables were packed with locals and tourists, and the walls were covered with local artwork. Mel, Jenn's wife, was behind the counter too, adding a fresh batch of donuts to the pastry case.

Damn, they looked delicious.

But today was not a donut day. It was a black coffee and ass-kicking day.

Jenn grinned at me when it was finally my turn to order. "You look like shit."

"Always a delight to see you, big sis," I responded.

She turned and filled an extra-large mug, humming. "This is the rainforest blend you like. Breakfast?"

With a shake of my head, I dropped a few dollars into the tip cup. Jenn and Mel never let me pay, but I did a fair amount of repairs here, including maintenance on that monster Italian espresso machine more times than I could count, so I figured it usually evened out.

"Shouldn't you be climbing a tree right now?"

"Meeting," I grunted, the smell of the rich dark roast filling my nostrils.

She winced, wiping at the counter. "Good luck."

Carefully, so my coffee wouldn't spill, I wandered to the back rail, where I sipped from the large mug and mentally prepared for today. Here and there, I greeted folks, giving nods and waves to Father Coughlin, and Mrs. Woodson. People who'd known me since I was a kid with skinned knees and a crooked smile.

This morning's meeting was at Sugar Moon, the facility I hadn't been back to since the fire this summer. It had been arson, and it had taken out most of the corporate offices. My brother, a firefighter, had gone in and rescued his girlfriend and the mother of their infant son that night. It might have been the most traumatic day of my life. My chest tightened and it got hard to breathe when I remembered clasping my nephew to my chest as my brother ran into the burning building. One wrong turn, one delayed second, and the world never would have been the same again.

I shuddered, pushing away the images.

"Headed to the office?" Tony appeared, clapping me on the shoulder. He owned the pizzeria and was the high school football coach, and here and there, he'd helped me out during sugaring season. The man was the definition of a good guy.

I gave my friend a nod. "Yup."

"Have they rebuilt that quickly?"

"Not sure. I assume they've got trailers set up

temporarily or something. Manufacturing is still going strong."

"Calloway was complaining about insurance dragging their feet." He shook his head, stepping closer to me. "None of this smells right. Why the offices? And Caleb?"

I paused, my cup halfway to my lips, my stomach rolling.

Caleb Dunne had confessed to setting the fire and then eventually to the murder of Will McManus. The town had breathed a sigh of relief when he turned himself in, feeling a bit safer with a violent criminal behind bars. But relief didn't erase doubt; it just buried it.

Both Caleb and Will had done work for me over the years. Both were good kids. Young and a bit wild but good. And this mess had continued to snowball over the months. I'd just gotten the police off my farm when the FBI showed up. And then the CEO of Sugar Moon had been arrested in front of half the town, kicking off another round of speculation. Every answer we got created three more questions.

And I couldn't help but think that the timing and location of the fire were convenient. Years of files had been destroyed, erasing God knew how many potential answers. Truth reduced to ash.

It wasn't my business, of course, but since my farm was involved and folks had whispered bogus theories that I was involved, I couldn't help but take it all personally. I didn't like shadows on my land. I had too much work to do to be worrying about the implications of those crimes on the legacy my family had built.

Before I could respond, Marco, Tony's brother, sauntered up, wearing a huge smile.

"How you doing, bud?" I asked, opening my arms for a hug.

Marco lived with Tony and worked with him at the pizzeria. He had Down syndrome and was one of the funniest, friendliest people in town. No agenda. No bullshit.

"Good," he said, lifting his cup. "Jenn made me the best maple latte."

"She's awesome," I added. "When are you coming to visit the farm? Wayne misses you."

"*Soon*. This guy"—he shot a look at his brother, his lips flattening—"has been making me work nonstop."

Tony huffed. "Speaking of," he said. "We gotta head to the shop and prep dough. Call me if you need to talk." The look he gave me said he knew I was carrying more than I was willing to admit.

I waved them off and focused on my coffee, desperate to get the upcoming meeting over with.

At a nearby table, Kate Bowen was sitting with her toddler son, who was chugging chocolate milk with gusto while she desperately swiped at crumbs from the blueberry muffin he'd just destroyed.

The sight sent my mind shifting to Celine. The set of her jaw as she busted my balls in the driveway this morning. The way she held her ground. That shock of red hair piled on top of her head. And the way her face had heated when I'd called her "Matchstick."

Trading jabs via text message had been more fun than was appropriate. I hadn't smiled like that in months.

When she'd huffed about Wayne's antics, I couldn't help but be proud of my pup. And that was a problem.

There was no use feeling any sort of way about her. Emotions were inefficient. Distractions were a liability.

As if sensing my vulnerability with her older sibling spidey senses, my sister sauntered over, smiling. "How's the new tenant?"

"Fine." I took a long, slow sip of coffee, praying a customer would walk in and Jenn would have to leave me alone.

"Sounds like she's a great teacher. And the kids are sweet." With a brow arched, she studied me. I wouldn't give her an inch. "Town's adopted them already."

I nodded. "Great."

She took a step closer, head tilting, staring at me in that all knowing way. "Have a good day, little brother."

With that simple phrase, the one that sounded suspiciously like a warning, she waltzed away.

In the five years that he'd been my point of contact, Alex, the procurement manager at Sugar Moon, had done a lot to build their business while protecting the suppliers. Selling our sap, while not the way my grandparents had done business, was the most efficient and cost-effective way to keep the farm alive in a market that didn't care about tradition or nostalgia.

Directing all my focus to the trees, new plantings, stand management, and disease prevention, had allowed me to improve our yields, better manage our acreage, and build a more sustainable farming model. I didn't romanticize the work; I optimized it. The trees were assets, but living ones. When I treated them right, they paid me back.

For years, especially after Dad's first heart attack, the Lawrence Farm struggled. These days, though, we were routinely in the black, and when my aunt and uncle retired and I purchased their land, it allowed me the space to grow rather than just survive.

For the last five years, seven days per week, I'd used generations of maple knowledge and my background in financial strategy to get the farm to a good place. My siblings got their quarterly shares of the profits, ensuring all my nieces and nephews were cared for. And my parents legacy was safe.

But last spring, everything went to shit, and now the entire industry was scrambling. For the first time in a long time, our future felt shaky.

Sugar Moon's temporary conference room was housed in a shipping container in the parking lot. The manufacturing facility produced a steady sugary smell, but the lingering stench of fire persisted, even with the rebuilding efforts taking place, and folding tables and chairs replaced the formerly grand conference room.

This meeting was unlike others I'd attended at Sugar Moon. In addition to the CEO, Louisa Meyers, Ethan Calloway, the CFO was here. Leaning back in his seat like he didn't have a care in the world. He looked like he'd been born in a dress shirt and cuff links. While our paths crossed a fair amount in town, I generally stayed away. Too slick and too smart to trust.

We went through the usual overview of timelines and yields, then reviewed recent weather patterns and quality testing. Every word felt more measured than usual, the murder and the fire sitting between us like an elephant at the table.

"I have no plans to sell elsewhere." Sitting back, I crossed my arms.

Sure, I'd been approached by other manufacturers, but this partnership with Sugar Moon was necessary in order to secure financial stability for myself as well as other farmers in the area.

Ethan leaned forward and put his elbows on the table. "Joshua," he said slowly.

He was deliberately calling me by my full name as an intimidation tactic. It only had the opposite effect. I sat up a bit straighter and met his eye.

"It would be bad business not to consider other offers. And although you and I have had our differences, you've never been bad at business."

"The Fitzgeralds didn't sign the contract." Alex said, taking off his glasses and cleaning them with his shirt.

Interesting. The Fitzgerald Farm was on the south side of town and produced almost as much sap annually as we did. They'd fought off bankruptcy, lawsuits and developers to keep their farm from going corporate. Mary Fitzgerald was in her eighties and was known as a shrewd negotiator.

"And others are grumbling," Louisa added. She sat at the head of the table, back straight, suit immaculate, and expression cool. She hadn't joined a meeting with my farm in the last five years. Not until things caught fire. Literally.

The tension thickened as her words rang out. I didn't have patience for posturing.

"Once I'm paid for last season, I will sign next year's contract," I reminded them.

"Thank you for bearing with us through the payment delays," she said, clasping her manicured hands.

I only dipped my chin. While I understood that the murder, her arrest, and the fire had done a number on them, at the end of the day, I needed to be paid. That sap had already been sugared, bottled, and shipped across the country to be consumed. Sympathy wouldn't fund my payroll.

"We're working on it," Ethan said flatly, clearly bothered that he owed me and not the other way around.

"Accounting will reach out," Alex said, scribbling a note on the legal pad in front of him.

"But in the meantime, it would do us all good if you signed next year's exclusive distribution contract. So we're all on the same page," Ethan drawled, spinning his expensive pen in his fingers.

Irritation crawled through me, making me shift in my seat. "No."

The word landed hard. Alex grimaced while Ethan's eyes went hard.

I sat straighter. "I'm not signing a contract guaranteeing to sell you my sap at this lower price without payment for last season. And it's too early to make predictions about demand, weather, and yields. Locking in at this rate is not good business. I won't gamble my family's livelihood."

Louisa's lacquered red lips pursed in frustration.

"We're renewing our commitment to organics," Ethan said, his expression stony. "Maybe we should do another round of environmental audits."

There it was.

A threat.

An empty one, but it sent a ripple of anger through me anyway.

"My farm was federally certified two years ago," I said, trying to hide my smile. "Which means we're exempt from company audits. Only the department of agriculture has jurisdiction. And I'd welcome them. Our upgrades are best in class." Lacing my fingers on the tabletop, I shifted forward and looked at Alex. "Your compliance team has all my consultant reports and certification paperwork, correct?"

He nodded, keeping his eyes down.

I felt for the guy. He was in a tough spot. But strong-arming me into a shitty contract was not going to save their business.

"And it seems you rejected the suggested implementation of BGX-9 for this season," Ethan said, flipping through his phone as if he was already bored of this conversation.

"Don't need some untested fertilizer," I said. Those damn sales reps had been relentless, but we had our systems, and my root nutrition was already optimized. But they knew all of this because I filed annual reports with Alex and the state department of agriculture.

"It's not a fertilizer," he said. "It's a bioorganic enhancer. And we're seeing excellent results from other farms."

"My trees are my concern," I said with a grin. "You guys should be more worried about paying my invoices." I ran my hand through my hair. Five more minutes in this airless room and I'd lose my mind. "And I'm happy to involve my legal counsel," I added, "if you have more questions."

Louisa shot me a disgusted look and gathered up her files. "We just want to make sure next season is unaffected."

I nodded. "Things are stable on my end."

Without another word, she left the room. Ethan

followed, shooting me a smug look on his way out and leaving me with Alex, who looked defeated.

"What's really going on?" I asked Alex.

"Wish I could say." He sighed. "But I'm just trying to hold it all together."

I studied his face, noting the dark circles under his eyes, the restless energy. When systems broke down, good people always paid the price.

"Should I be looking for other buyers?" I asked point-blank.

"Not yet," he said softly. "Give me another month."

After we said goodbye, I walked back to my car, feeling the warmth of the sun on my face and cursing the time I'd lost to this bullshit meeting.

I was leaving with more questions than answers, and this wasn't the first time.

It was as if the world had stopped moving. Pausing to watch and wait.

For the sap to run.

For the bills to be paid.

Or for something else to break.

Chapter 10

♥

CELINE

"You've got to come." Callie begged, snagging a cookie from the tray Stella had baked and left on the table in the teacher's lounge.

I'd dropped the kids off at music, then come in to refill my water bottle. If I'd known she'd corner me, I would have used the filling station on the other side of the building.

"I don't have time to read."

"Doesn't matter," she said easily. "It's *No* Book Club. Reading isn't required. But you need to meet people. Trust me. It'll be good for you to take a night off."

Socialization wasn't in the cards for me. At least not anytime soon. "I have no childcare." And my kids weren't the type that I could leave with a random teenager recommended by a coworker.

"Sure you do." Stella waltzed into the room, bringing her sunshiny warmth with her.

"Stell, you have no idea how much I needed this," Callie

said, mouth full of cookie. "The twins clogged the sink with their homemade slime, and I've been craving sugar."

"I'll babysit," Stella said. "Julian is already comfortable with me, and I can bring over the new sight word games I picked up for my classroom. He can help me test them out."

A pit formed in my stomach in response. "I couldn't ask you to do that."

She shrugged. "Then good thing you're not asking."

"Don't you want to go to the club?" I asked her.

"I go sometimes." She picked up a cookie. "But I know everyone already, and I'm tired of answering questions about you. Trust me, the town would rather you go."

"But—"

"Looks like the problem is solved." Callie clapped once. "Good. There are so many people I want you to meet."

I had full confidence in Stella. She was an educator but also an all-around amazing person, and my kids were fully in love with her.

The problem was me. Was I ready to leave them? And what would I do at this No Book Club? I was the least interesting person in this town. An entire evening of awkward small talk was not my idea of fun.

But Stella left before I could turn her down, and if it wasn't clear she'd made up my mind for me then, it was when she showed up at six thirty, a wide smile on her face.

A teacher through and through, she arrived with a tote bag full of games, crafts, and ingredients for cookies.

Everyone, including Ellie, was smitten, not one of them looking my way when I said goodbye.

Was it weird to be jealous? And maybe a little hurt that they were so eager to get rid of me?

I started the engine, but rather than drive away, I closed my eyes, engulfed in panic. For so long, leaving hadn't been an option. A break from my duties would bring either punishment or danger.

With a deep breath in, I rested my head against the seat. We were safe now. The kids were in good hands, I was going out to meet people. It was what I should be doing. And exactly what I'd wanted when moving here. A fresh start. A normal life.

But my nervous system had not caught up. It took another two or three minutes to calm my racing heart. Then with shaky hands, I drove into town.

Parking was easier than I thought, and I found myself lingering outside the restaurant a few minutes before the meeting was set to start, looking down at the sundress I was wearing. It was a hand-me-down from Chloe. She'd given me a closet full of clothes after I'd left Donny. Since the time I hit puberty, she'd been smaller than me, but in recent years, I'd shrunk quite a bit. Stress was to blame for the most part, but the intense workouts played a part too, and I couldn't give them up. Running was the only thing that quieted my anxious brain.

The garment was pretty and had probably cost a fortune, but my face suddenly heated and I wished I'd worn something simpler. I couldn't pull this off. Who was I kidding? But I was here now, so I might as well get this over with.

I hadn't been to the Drip Line yet, so as I walked into the bar-slash-restaurant off Market Street, I surveyed the sights. The walls and floors were dark wood, and the lighting wasn't much brighter. The windows were fogged a little, and the interior was decorated with pumpkins, gourds, dried corn, and fairy lights.

The chalkboard menu was quirky and cute, highlighting several fall menu items. The place was intimate, the vibe easygoing. Like the kind of bar I would have enjoyed in a former life.

As I wandered deeper, a delicious fried scent filled my nostrils, making my stomach growl.

But that didn't distract me from locating all the exits, and it didn't temper the wave of shame that hit me when I registered what I was doing. My paranoia was dialed up tonight.

I wasn't hopeful that I'd do a great job acting human like I had promised myself. My plan was to stay for an hour. I would give myself one hour to interact with other adult humans.

I was repeating the mantra when Callie bustled my way. Her tall, willowy frame was hidden under an enormous tent of a dress in a bold red print, and she was wearing her familiar perfume.

If it weren't for Callie, I never would have moved to this town, so I was grateful for her. But while I adored her enthusiasm and support, I wasn't so keen on being physically pushed into a large group of people.

Yet that's exactly what happened.

"Everyone," she called, grasping my arm and leading me to a massive oak table at the back. "This is my dear friend and kindergarten teacher extraordinaire, Celine LeBlanc."

The table was loaded full, and every eye was on me. As I looked back at them, the desire to run straight to the emergency exit bubbled up inside me.

It didn't subside when they took turns greeting me. All the smiles, handshakes, and questions were flattering, but also a bit alarming.

From what I'd experienced so far, Maplewood adopted aggressively. With food and hugs and lots of noise.

I insisted on sitting at the end of the long table. Because I wanted to observe and also because being locked in made me uncomfortable. Knowing my potential exit routes and having access if necessary allowed me to breathe easier.

"It's so nice to meet you," a woman with jeweled glasses said, holding out her hand. "I'm Nora Hatch. I own the apothecary, though I'm a pharmacist by trade."

I returned the greeting, conjuring an image of the cute storefront with big windows in my mind.

"She's so much more than that. You need any kind of natural remedy, Nora is your woman," Ruby—whom I'd learned was Stella's sister—added, raising her wineglass high. "She's a witch."

"I'm a person who believes in holistic health," Nora said, her lips twitching a little. "If your kid has an ear infection, I'll fill the script for antibiotics, and I'll add some herbal tea to help him sleep."

Callie grumbled, her face pinching. "Except none of your vitamins or tea blends have calmed my twins down."

"That's because I'm not legally allowed to dispense elephant tranquilizers. Sweetie." Nora tutted into her martini glass.

I bit my tongue to keep from laughing, but Callie herself burst into laughter, with tears rolling down her face.

Amusement threaded through me as I watched her. If

there was one thing I loved about my principal, it was that she didn't take herself too seriously.

"How do you like living on the Lawrence farm?" Ruby asked.

"It's a lovely home," I replied, leaving it at that.

"You won the lottery with that landlord," she said, her eyes twinkling.

I frowned at her, not following.

"He's one of the good ones," an older lady wearing a sequined turban added. "If I were thirty years younger, I can't say I wouldn't be out chasing that man."

"Mrs. Fitzgerald. You're married," Ruby chided.

"Eh." She shrugged and stood. "I'm gonna get an order of onion rings."

"So there's no, um, Mrs. Lawrence?" I asked, my cheeks heating. I wasn't asking for any particular reason, just curiosity. And because I wanted to be a good neighbor. Of course.

"Oh God no," Callie said, straightening beside me.

"My future brother-in-law is *very* single." Evie leaned over, giving me a wink.

Head lowering, I studied my glass of soda water to hide what I was sure were bright red cheeks.

Evie was beautiful, with the perfect balance of stand-offish energy and blissful glow.

Her sleeveless silk blouse and colorful skirt looked professional and effortless, giving her an air that told the world she was put together. A state of being that I'd never been able to manage.

"I'm so glad I finally get to hang out with you." Ruby said. "I've been ridiculously jealous of Stella. She's been hogging you.."

"Ruby is brilliant," Evie said. "She's in charge of picking out all my outfits."

"You should come by my boutique," Ruby chirped. "We just got a shipment of thick sweaters in for winter. You'll need a few if you're new to Vermont."

"I'm actually from Maine." I cleared my throat. "Northern Maine."

"Then you get it." She picked up her glass and took a sip. "You've got ice in your veins like we do."

"This is Basil." She gestured to a middle-aged man with thick round glasses. "Cheesemonger and sourdough wizard."

He gave me a bashful grin. "How do you feel about Camembert?" he asked, swirling his glass of red wine.

I had no idea how to respond. Raising children on a teacher's salary meant I didn't have many occasions for fancy cheese.

"Good?" I said tentatively. "I feel good about it."

That appeared to be the right answer. "Excellent," he replied. He gestured out the dark window across the street. "Please stop by anytime. Have some samples. I'd love to introduce you to Taleggio." He let out a little sigh. "Life-changing."

At the other end of the table, a woman with pink hair and an eyebrow ring snorted.

"Leave her alone, Basil. Stop trying to recruit for your curd cult."

His head snapped her way, and his kindly face transformed into something sharp and defensive.

"Go peddle your pedestrian cheddar elsewhere, Lola," he snapped.

"Children," a voice shouted.

A petite woman stood behind the bar, eyeing us all expectantly, arms crossed. She had the kind of authority earned from decades of not taking any shit.

"The Drip Line is neutral territory," she said. "No cheese warfare allowed."

"Sorry, Dotty," Basil said sheepishly.

I made eye contact with Ruby. "Don't ask," she muttered.

The conversation shifted quickly, and as the people around me chatted, I found myself relaxing a bit. This wasn't terrible. I could socialize. Maybe I hadn't completely lost my ability to function as an adult. It was far easier here than in any other environment I'd been in during the last decade or more. I'd never felt like I belonged the way I did tonight. I'd never felt so instantly welcomed into the fold, and the relief that washed over me now made it easy to listen and laugh. And I found myself hoping that eventually I'd be in a place where I could enjoy this for more than the allocated sixty minutes.

"There's no reading required," Marty, who I'd learned owned the diner, explained.

"We started as a book club, but along the way, our gatherings became focused on drinking and eating instead. And once that happened, the group grew to this," a tall, elegant woman explained, holding out an arm to gesture at the good-sized crowd.

"If Caroline had her way," Ruby teased, grinning at her, "we'd be diagramming Shakespearean sonnets."

The woman—Caroline, I guessed—broke into a wistful smile.

"Excuse my sister. She's an English literature PhD

dropout," another woman added. "I'm Linda. That's Caroline."

"You must come to the spa," Caroline added.

Ah, the spa. Chloe had mentioned it. According to her, it was located inside a beautiful inn in town, which also housed a fancy restaurant.

"Oh my God," Evie groaned. "Frankie and Stella took me for my birthday this summer. It was blissful. Better than any I've been to in New York."

Linda snorted. "We're nationally ranked for a reason."

"And we host literature themed weekends," Caroline added, her face alight.

Though a trip to the Thistle Inn spa was not in my budget, it sounded heavenly. I hadn't looked at prices, but I'd heard how luxurious the place was, and the emerald on Linda's cocktail ring was probably worth more than my car.

But for now, this was enough. Or maybe too much. I was being folded into Maplewood at an alarming speed, welcoming handshakes and hugs from everyone I crossed, like I'd always been here.

Too much or not, strange or not, it was nice. The people of my hometown in Maine were prickly toward outsiders, so this was all foreign to me.

"Before we were innkeepers, we were academics. French philosophy." Linda was lithe and tiny with a platinum pixie cut. Caroline was taller, with ballerina posture and deep red lips. Her look was finished off with an Hermes scarf wrapped chicly around her shoulders.

Mrs. Fitzgerald returned with onion rings and dropped into the seat across from me, bullying me into trying one.

I folded quickly, and damn, it was stupidly delicious.

"Have another, dear. You look like you could use a little comfort food," she said with a smile.

Without much fight, I took another and let the salty greasiness ease some of my anxiety.

For years, I'd dreamed about having a night like this. The chance to go out and meet people. To make adult friends and be part of a community.

Donny never allowed it. We didn't have friends.

That's not true. He did; I wasn't allowed to leave the house. He'd manipulate me, reminding me that Julian needed me and convincing me that a good mom would want to stay home and keep the kids comfortable.

But Stella had texted a photo a few minutes ago, an image of my kids decorating cookies together, and they looked pretty damn comfortable right now.

"We've got to step it up on the Harvest Festival," Callie said.

Ruby laughed. "Is that why you said the onion rings were on you? Is this bribery?"

"The Maple Street Mafia is breathing down my neck," my boss complained. "You know how relentless they are." She craned her neck, scanning the bar like a real-life mafia don might be lurking nearby. "I cannot with Bitsy Bramble right now. Tourism numbers are down, so she's out for blood."

With a nod, Ruby said, "We've got to get the tourists back."

"Agreed," a woman farther down the table chimed in. "The arrest helped."

With that simple remark, a blanket of unease settled over the crowd.

"Okay." Callie clapped, pasting on a bright smile. "Scott, we need more vendors. You know everyone. Can you start reaching out? And I was thinking a food tent. Something a little fancier than usual."

"Opal could do it," Linda said.

Evie rubbed her hands together, eyes glimmering. "What about a spa tent? Mini services to highlight what the inn offers? You could offer some of the products and sell candles."

The sisters looked at one another, having a telepathic conversation, and Caroline nodded.

"And Ruby," Callie said, "we need merch. Come up with a catchy slogan and print it on T-shirts, hoodies, hats. All of that."

Ruby bounced in her seat. "I'll dust off my graphic design skills."

"Atta girl."

The table came alive, one person after another shouting out suggestions while Evie took notes on the back of a paper menu.

"We need better entertainment," Stacy, the florist, said. "Any way we can convince Naomi to play on the main stage on Saturday night?"

"What if we brought back the art walk?"

"Didn't Birch Hollow poach all our usual artists?"

"Nothing's stopping us from poaching them right back."

"What's Birch Hollow?" I asked.

Several heads snapped in my direction.

"A town," Ruby said, her expression suddenly going stony. "Thirty minutes north-west of here."

"We hate them," Marty added.

"The place is filled with assholes," Tony piped in from the far end.

Nora clenched her fists. "They try to sabotage us. Every year."

"Do you think they put a hit out on Will so they could steal our tourists?" someone else asked.

"Birch Hollow has spent the past hundred years wishing it was Maplewood. And the second that tragedy started, they jumped in and took advantage," Mrs. Fitzgerald said to me.

"Been ripping us off since the Revolution," Marty added.

Huh. A small-town-Vermont blood feud? That certainly made the town even more interesting.

All around me, the brainstorming continued, the people here all rallying together. It was sweet and only slightly terrifying.

"And the hayrides." Callie, who was now standing at the head of the table, in full principal mode, clasped her hands. "They were always so popular, especially when they were themed each year."

"But now that Mr. Watkins is retired, he's sold off his tractors."

Callie tapped her chin, looking straight at me. "Hmm. Who do we know around here with a big tractor?"

I slumped in my seat. Everyone had gone quiet, and every eye was on me.

"Your landlord does." Evie broke into a devious smile. "Grumpy farmer Josh. If you ask, I bet he'll agree to help out."

Panic rose up inside me. They wanted *me* to ask? I barely knew Josh.

"Excellent." Callie beamed. "Celine, you are captain of hayrides. Be sure to plan the route first. The rides should last at least twenty minutes but not much more than that. And look for varied terrain. Then coordinate with the residents on the route in regard to themed decorations."

"Wait," I said, blinking rapidly, racking my brain for a way to gracefully get myself out of this.

I locked eyes with Callie, the person responsible for bringing me here. And Ruby, whose sister was currently delighting my kids, nudged me gently. The rest of the crowd watched me with such hopeful looks. And they had all been so warm and welcoming to me.

"Talk to Josh," Callie suggested. "You can work together."

"But—"

She shook her head. "It's the Harvest Festival."

"The way you said that makes it sound like the Superbowl," I joked.

Rather than laughs, all I garnered were blank stares.

"We've got to get the tourists back," Marty said.

"This is our Superbowl. The small-town-Vermont Superbowl. We've got two major festivals each year. The Maple Festival in April, which kicks off tourist season and helps us all get over our seasonal depression," Linda explained. "And the Harvest Festival in October."

"There are several others as well," Caroline interjected, adjusting her scarf.

"But these are the big ones" her sister continued. "We pull out all the stops. And this year the necessity to go above and beyond is even more important."

"This town needs tourists, press, and lots of excitement."

As I scanned all the hopeful faces, my stomach twisted. Could I convince Josh to help? I had no experience with hayrides or small-town festivals, but the warmth and affection I'd received from this town made me want to try.

Chapter 11

JOSH

I hadn't planned on staying.

I'd swung by after catching Betsy on the north side cameras and wanted to give them a heads-up.

When I found Stella Stone here moments after being hit by the smell of snickerdoodles, confusion took over.

"Get in here. We've got cookies," she said.

Wayne, traitor that he was, ran inside the house before I could collect myself and decline.

The kids were scattered across the living room floor, Julian working with Legos and Ellie with a book. Maggie was currently scratching Wayne's belly.

"You came to visit," Julian chirped.

"Do you know how to play chess?" Maggie asked.

Lips pressed together, I nodded, answering both questions at once.

"Good, because I'm learning, and I need someone to play with."

Discomfort crept through me. I should get out of here. "I'm not very good."

"That's okay," she said. "It's annoying when people are super good at everything."

"Did you come to see Mom?" Ellie asked, peering at me over her paperback, her eyes narrowed. "Because she's not here."

"No, actually," I said, stuffing my hands into my pockets, unnerved by her scrutiny. "I just wanted to warn you all to stay inside. Betsy Ross popped up on a couple of my cameras."

Stella perked up and took a step toward me. "Betsy's here? Have you kids seen her yet? She's a town celebrity."

"Actually," I corrected, "she's a black bear. And very dangerous." Though I'd mentioned her the day I showed them the blackberry bramble, we hadn't actually discussed her.

By the way the kids looked at me, all wide-eyed and pale, this fact was lost on them.

"Betsy Ross is not a very scary name," Ellie said in that bored teenager way.

"She's a bear. She doesn't care."

Stella shrugged. "She sort of named herself."

Julian scooted closer to me, still seated on the floor. "How big is she?"

"She's small for a bear," I told him. "But still a big scary wild animal."

"Is it true bears are fast runners and can climb trees?" Maggie asked, pushing her glasses up.

"Yes." I nodded once. "They are also excellent swimmers."

"Is she a mean bear?" Julian's voice quivered.

My stomach sank a little at the fear there. "Um. No. Not really. She's ..." I looked over at Stella, considering the best way to explain her to a child without terrifying him.

"Opportunistic," Stella explained.

A sigh of relief escaped me. "Yes. She gets herself into trouble."

Ellie folded her arms, her lips turned down. "Is she going to eat us?"

That nearly got a laugh from me, but I tamped it down before I could embarrass her. "No."

"Are you sure?" Maggie quipped. "You just told us how strong and fast bears are."

"Yeah," her sister piled on, "what if she's hungry?"

"She wouldn't eat a person." Dammit, I'd been here for three minutes, and already, I'd given these kids a year's worth of nightmare fuel. "Bears like easy food. Trash, apples, chicken feed."

"Does she know where we live?"

I shook my head. "Nope. She knows where the blackberries are. Remember? I planted them there to keep her far away from my chickens and my garden. She never comes down here. But I just want you to always be aware and stay safe."

Ellie stood with a huff and paced. "This feels personal."

Stella snorted. "Betsy is always sort of... around. She's a pain in the butt. But we've all learned to live with her. The best way to stay safe is to stay away."

"Can we see the video?"

"No," I replied.

"Why not?"

"Because I'm worried that if I showed you, you'd go out and try to find her."

"Hey," Maggie protested.

"I'd go find her," Julian said.

I admired his blunt honesty, even if the statement put all my nerves on edge. Because I believed him.

"But I'd take Wayne," he added.

Wayne lifted his head off the carpet.

"Don't even think about it," I said to my dog. "You'd lose that fight."

He lay back down with a sigh, his head on his paws.

"Ooh." Maggie clapped. "Does she have baby bears? OMG, baby bears are *so* cute."

"As far as we know, she's never had any cubs."

"That's depressing," Ellie said. "Is she lonely?"

I blinked at her. I'd never contemplated the emotional health of the damn bear and I never thought I would. "Possibly?"

"There must be no emotionally available boy bears around here," Ellie mused.

Stella snorted. "Relatable, Betsy. *So* relatable."

I tried to make myself scarce, but the kids insisted I stay for cookies and milk, so we migrated to the kitchen table and snacked while Stella and I shared several of Betsy Ross's greatest hits.

"She was just relaxing in the hot tub?" Maggie squealed.

"Yup," Stella said. "Ruby stepped outside in her bathing suit with a bottle of champagne in her hand, and a second later, she was screaming and darting back into the house. That was an anniversary Paul will never forget."

"She's been known to take naps in the canoes folks leave

on the bank of the river," I added, my storytelling not quite so entertaining. "And one time, she walked into Reed's garage and opened his beer fridge."

"Nothing but fancy stuff in there." Stella laughed.

Stella put Julian to bed shortly after, and the girls wandered back to the living room. Though I was tempted to head for the door, I stayed and loaded the dishwasher, waiting for Stella to return.

When she came down the stairs, she crossed her arms. "You're great with them." Despite her posture, she wore a soft, observant look. The teacher look that made me feel like she was clocking my every move.

I shrugged. "They're good kids."

"That's not what I said." She stuck her tongue out at me.

I'd known Stella since we were kids. And in my mind, she still was a little girl. While she was probably over thirty now, all my memories of her involved her tagging along with the big kids, cheering at hockey games, and coming to the farm to sell Girl Scout cookies to my dad.

She was cute and curvy, with a bright smile, big brown doe eyes and wavy blond hair. And she was smart. She was exactly the kind of woman who should fascinate me.

But I'd never seen her that way. She lived firmly in little sister territory.

And I imagined Stella hadn't ever thought of me romantically either. As far as I knew, she'd been in love with Gabe since junior high.

While we cleaned up in silence, my thoughts were occupied by someone else. A woman I should absolutely not be thinking about. Ever.

Blessedly, before my mind wandered even farther down

this very inappropriate lane, Maggie called me from the living room.

"You gonna play me chess with me or what?"

She'd already set up the board, so we dove right in. It was more fun than I'd anticipated. She was hilarious, and while I was a bit rusty, I found myself getting back into it.

"Why does the king only move one space at a time? That's so boring," she complained, dropping her chin into her hand with a sigh.

"Sorry, kid. That's because the queen"—I picked the piece up—"holds all the real power. She can go anywhere, anytime."

"Because women are superior to men," Ellie said, not looking up from her book.

Giggling, Maggie made her next move.

I won the first game, but Maggie caught on quickly and was dominating the second.

"My rook is going to end you," she chirped.

She may have only been getting the basics of chess, but her trash talk was excellent already.

While we played, Stella and Ellie got into a spirited debate about *The Hunger Games*, so when Celine walked in, none of us noticed, until she cleared her throat.

My focus snapped to her immediately. She frowned at me, her face awash with confusion, but as she surveyed the room, her shoulders lowered.

Damn. I was beginning to think she'd lived her entire life on edge.

"Did you have fun?" Stella asked, doing some kind of ornate braid in Ellie's hair.

Celine nodded. "It was nice. But a bit overwhelming. I

met your sister," she said to Stella. "And," she turned to me, "your... sister-in-law?"

"I wish," I said. "But Evie is family regardless. With any luck, she'll make an honest man out of my brother at some point."

Jasper and Evie were madly in love. With each other and with their son Vincent. Jas was the baby of the family, and he'd always been the wild child.

Now he was a devoted father and husband. The kid had changed in so many ways, yet he was still the same fun-loving little brother he'd always been.

He was a natural with his son, diving into fatherhood and learning the ropes with rapid speed.

And he'd fallen hard for Evie, who wouldn't even give him the time of day for a long time. She was so far out of his league, yet he'd won her over. I still couldn't wrap my head around it.

But I didn't have to. It was reality, and it made me happy.

He was growing into the man Dad had always raised him to become.

Who loved and protected. Who could be vulnerable when needed.

I was prouder of him than I'd ever been.

But as he'd grown, my own stagnation had become more and more evident. I'd given up hope a long time ago, committing myself fully to the farm and to my parents' legacy.

I stood, the back of my neck prickling. That was the reminder I needed. There was no place for me in this cozy family scene.

"Sorry." I nodded at Celine. "Came over to check on everyone."

"Mom!" Maggie jumped out of her seat. "We've got a bear!"

Eyes widening, Celine turned to me. "Explain, please."

"Spotted her at the blackberry bramble. She seemed happy to stay there and snack, but I wanted to make sure the kids weren't out riding bikes."

"Mom, it's fine. She's just a single lady looking for a good time," Ellie said.

When Celine didn't crack, I choked back my laugh.

"Sorry. You said she didn't go past the blackberries. Why were you worried about the kids being outside. Are you telling me she'll attack my children?"

"No, no," I said. Shit. Here I was stirring up fear again. "Betsy's a runt and not much of a threat."

"A bear? Not much of a threat? Ha." She let out a humorless laugh. "I'd say a bear is always a threat."

"She's only got one eye, Mom. She's so cool," Maggie said, bouncing on her toes. "Josh taught us all about bear safety. We're not allowed to pet her. But we can wave from far away."

"Anyway." I shoved my hands into my pockets, my shoulders rising. What was it about this pint-sized woman that put me on the defensive? "I should get going."

"*No,*" Maggie complained. "We've got to finish our game."

Celine gave her daughter that mom look that said she meant business. "It's a school night."

Ellie scoffed, her head tilted back while Stella worked on her braid. "It's not even nine."

"Is your homework done?"

"I didn't mean to intrude," I said, taking a step back.

She ran her hands through her hair. It was down now, gathering in soft waves around her collarbones. I'd never seen it like this. Only pulled back tightly. It was nice. Made her look softer somehow.

"It's fine," she gritted out. "Thank you for the bear warning. And for the new nightmare material."

"I've got cameras," I explained. "If she shows up, I'll text you."

"I know it sounds scary," Stella said. "But Betsy is part of this town. She's always around, always getting into things. And she's just in search of food. A nuisance, really, but a cute one."

Whistling for Wayne, I headed toward the door. I'd overstayed my welcome, my skin suddenly itchy. My dog followed, though his steps were slow and his head hung.

I'd stepped off the porch when Celine called my name.

I turned, finding her framed in the porch light. She was undeniably beautiful. In a scary way, actually. But my brain didn't have the capability of registering fear as I drank her in.

She wore a twirly dress that hit at her knees. Very different from the usual uniform of leggings and Crocs.

She looked girlish and pretty. Like someone I'd like to take on a date.

Somewhere nice with candles and fancy food. I'd treat her. Pull out all the stops. Based on our interactions so far, I got the sense no one had ever taken care of her before.

"Thank you," she said, "for looking out for us. And for playing chess."

"No problem." It wasn't. I'd had fun. They were good kids, and spending time with them was easy. They asked a lot of questions, but most were harmless and lots were funny, and the chatter was surprisingly comforting after a long, quiet day.

She stood in the doorway, her face in shadow, scrutinizing me.

"You look nice," I said awkwardly.

She looked down at her pink dress. "Thanks. It's nice to remember I own clothing besides leggings."

"And Crocs," I added.

Her eyes flashed. "Do not criticize the Crocs."

I held my hands up in defense. "Wouldn't dare. Plastic shoes are the height of fashion."

She glared at me. "Your ignorance is showing. Crocs are God's gift to moms. They're easy to put on. Kids step into them. Washable and waterproof. Kids are filthy. You can hose them down."

I crossed my arms, amused at her rant.

"And the shape makes it so sizing doesn't really matter. A little big or small makes no difference. Ellie wears mine, Julian gets whatever color he's currently hyperfixated on, and everyone is happy."

"Sounds great."

Her eyes flashed. I liked this side of her, playful and confident. "So if you come for Crocs, you're coming for moms. And I will not stand for that disrespect."

She put her hands on her hips.

Suddenly I had the strange urge to kiss that smirk right off her face.

"Don't look at me like that. Don't judge me because I've ascended to a higher plane of functional living."

I nodded. "Understood. I will never malign your footwear choices again." I gave her a curt wave and turned to walk home. To process this weird, fun evening and all the strange feelings it was inspiring within me.

"Actually." Her voice was soft. "Josh."

I turned back. "You okay Matchstick?"

She looked hesitant, and she tensed further when I used the nickname. But I couldn't help it. She had this energy about her. A riot of emotions always brewing below the surface. Sparks igniting, ready to set her off.

"Since you asked," she said, lowering her focus to her feet. "Tonight I got, um, persuaded to help with the Harvest Festival."

I crossed my arms. "Who got to you?"

"Callie." Her shoulders drooped.

It was surprising, really, that it had taken this long for Callie to broach the subject with her.

"Yeah, she's hard to avoid. Just be grateful you've got the younger generation of townsfolk on your case. It could be the mafia, and they don't make requests."

"So I got off easy?" the corner of her mouth quirked.

"Probably. What job did she give you?"

She shifted, grimacing, then padded down the steps, leaving only a couple of feet between us.

"I'm in charge of organizing and overseeing the hayrides."

My heart thudded heavily.

"Decor, route planning, and, um..."

I held my breath, knowing where this was going.

"Persuading you to donate your time and the use of your tractors." She forced her face into something resembling a smile.

I smirked. "Are you trying to charm me right now, Matchstick?"

Her expression vanished quickly. "No. I know you're too smart to fall for that. I'm just." She shrugged. "Asking."

I took a step forward, closing the distance between us.

"So ask," I said, my voice thick. "Nicely."

She tilted her head up to meet my gaze. She was so tiny and yet so strong, her chest rising and falling rapidly.

I stood for a moment, shoving my hands into my pockets for something to do. There was no time. I was short-staffed and dealing with the most volatile season I'd ever experienced on this farm. Also, I did not volunteer. I didn't do town events unless everyone showed up and forced me to, like Chainsaw Day. There simply wasn't time.

But I didn't actually give a shit.

Every instinct told me to gather her in my arms. To tell her she could rest. That she didn't have to hold the weight of the world on her shoulders all the time. That I'd help carry the load. Do whatever she needed.

She pursed her lips, attention roaming over my face.

I clenched my fists to keep from reaching for her.

"Please," she said, her voice softer than I'd ever heard it.

With my teeth sunken into my lip, I nodded. I couldn't trust myself to respond with words.

Then I did the only safe thing I could think to do.

I turned and walked back to my house.

Chapter 12

JOSH

The engines were rolling up the hill before I'd taken my first sip of coffee.

Sighing, I looked down at Wayne. "You ready, buddy? It's gonna be one of those days."

Jasper's Bronco appeared first, and Gabe's Jeep followed.

As they got closer, I sipped my coffee, already resigning myself to being disappointed. With any luck, we'd have five or six show up. That would at least allow us to get the high priority stuff done before sundown.

"Happy Chainsaw Day," Jasper hollered as he climbed out of his vehicle.

Another car pulled up, then another, followed by Nolan's police cruiser.

Shit. In the past, he'd come out to help on Chainsaw Day, and the two of us had been friends all our lives, but since the murder, he'd pulled back, and not just from me but from everyone in town. Over the last several months, there'd been a strange distance between him and the rest of us, meaning his presence was only going to make things awkward.

"What is happening?" I asked as more and more people showed up. With the stress we'd all been under and the scrutiny that had been put on the farm, I really hadn't thought many people from town would come.

"Chainsaw Day." Gabe opened his tailgate and plucked a piece of yellow fabric out of a cardboard box, then threw it at me.

I caught it and shook it out, surveying it. It was a T-shirt, and it read *Lawrence Farm Chainsaw Day 2026* on one line, and below it was printed *Safety Third.*

"Orange," Gabe said. "For safety."

"All we're doing is clearing tree limbs," I groused. "This isn't open heart surgery."

With a chuckle, my cousin shook his head.

Logan, who'd just parked, climbed out of his own truck with a smile. "Shirts? Sweet." He stripped off his tee and dug an orange monstrosity out of the box, beaming brightly when he'd tugged it on.

"Why are there so many cars?" I grumbled to the three of them. "I wanted help, not to host a town meeting."

Gabe wandered to the porch. "Can't it be both?"

"You always fight it," Jasper said. "But it's a Maplewood tradition."

"It's not a tradition," I groused, the lie tasting bitter on my tongue.

"You sure about that?" Logan stroked his unruly beard. "It's the last Saturday in September, and like every year, we all showed up with axes and chainsaws to clear branches, take out the dead trees, and clean up the trails before the winter." He strode up beside Gabe. "We've been doing this for years, and that's called a tradition." He clapped me on the shoulder.

"And you know how much this town loves a tradition," my brother added.

I pinched the bridge of my nose, trying to tune out the sound of engines. It was no use. When I opened my eyes, several more vehicles had parked and men and women, young and old, many of whom had brought their own chainsaws and safety chaps, emerged.

"Mrs. Moore," I said to the octogenarian who'd just popped her trunk. "What are you doing here?"

"Helping." She held up a chainsaw that looked like it hadn't been used since the eighties. "I've been cutting down trees since I was a girl. This belonged to my Merle."

An image of Mrs. Moore covered in blood spatter flashed through my mind, making my heart race. I shoved it down hard. Panic wouldn't help right now.

"Don't worry. I changed the chain last night. And lubed her up." Smiling, she hobbled over to Gabe, who handed her a small T-shirt.

"Good work, Mrs. Morris." Logan beamed. "Lubrication is essential."

Giggling, the woman wandered over to a small group of elderly people who were pulling the bright orange shirts over their clothing.

Nolan eventually sauntered over, wearing his usual serious expression.

"Don't worry, Sheriff." Gabe held up a manilla envelope. "I brought liability waivers."

"That doesn't actually make me feel better," I said.

"As your legal counsel," he retorted, "it makes me feel much better."

"And I've got a spreadsheet." Paul held up his laptop. He was the local accountant, a smaller guy usually dressed in Oxford shirts, but he handled a chainsaw like a pro. "I'll inventory the firewood and make sure it's distributed."

Paul could always be counted on to have a system. He treated chaos like a solvable equation. If only we could clone him. I needed more Pauls and fewer Logans if I was going to make it through this day.

Summer thunderstorms always left us with dead limbs and trees that needed clearing, so my dad had started doing this years ago.

We cleared it all, hauled it out with the ATVs, and then cut and chopped the wood. Everyone who helped out took home a portion of the firewood for the winter.

It had started with a handful of us, but like all things in this town, it had grown to wild proportions.

"I've got donuts," Stella said.

Donuts? This was officially out of hand.

The bakery box was stamped with the Bean There, Done That logo, confirming that Jenn had her mischievous hands all over this.

Stella always showed up too. She'd never miss an opportunity to watch Gabe wield and axe. She and Ruby climbed out of Paul's car, Stella wearing her usual sunny smile and her sister in a vibrant pink dress.

"Hello, boys. We brought sustenance." Ruby ducked into

the back seat and hauled a car seat out, putting the bucket over her arm. Her little guy was tiny, born a few months after Vincent.

"Jenn will be here at lunchtime with sandwiches," Stella called out. "Now grab some chow before you get to work."

Saturdays were the shop's busiest day, especially now, during leaf peeping season. But Jenn and Mel would be over later. My sister was a farm girl who never missed a chance to wield an axe.

"Will you be chopping wood, Gabe?" Stella asked.

"I'll go wherever Josh needs me," he responded, eternally clueless and completely unaware of her attempts to flirt with him.

I cringed internally. Stella's crush got more and more obvious every year, yet he still couldn't see it. But he was the only one with that problem.

"People," Paul said. "Let's circulate the sign-in sheet and get organized."

Reed Ashburn had pulled up with a trailer and a large ATV, and probably several kegs of beer.

"I brought extra gas," Vince said, holding up two canisters.

I gave him a thumbs-up, then turned, searching for my coffee mug.

"Why the fuck is Badge Boy here?" a loud voice called.

Frankie Dunne strolled up, wearing work overalls and carrying an orange chainsaw case that probably weighed more than she did.

"Behave," I said.

She stomped right up to me and elbowed me hard in the ribs. "I need to work out some aggression," she said. "And I don't care if it's on dead trees or Nolan fucking Foster. Either way, I'll clean up my mess." The smile that broke across her face was terrifying.

Nolan turned and pinned her with a glare, his nostrils flaring. He was an intimidating guy, stoic and large. He served in the Marine Corps for many years before coming home and joining the police department. That man had seen some things.

"Fuck off" she growled.

Jaw tight, he abruptly turned and walked away. The dude was scared of her. She was barely five foot, but she had a sharp tongue and even sharper claws. I didn't necessarily blame him, but it took a lot to scare our sheriff.

"If they fight I've got twenty dollars on Frankie," Logan said, handing her a T-shirt.

She gave him a smile.

"How's Muffin?" he asked, switching immediately to caring vet mode.

"So much better," she gushed, her demeanor doing a total one-eighty. "He's eating again. Thank you again for the house call."

"You make house calls for cats?" I asked.

"For Frankie, who fixed my Jeep last winter and had it back to me in two days so I could drive to Boston for that continuing education clinic during a snowstorm? Yes. I make house calls."

The two of them wandered toward the bakery boxes, and as what looked like the last of the crew gathered, I whistled loudly and climbed up into the bed of my truck. I had to put at least a few rules in place, and this was the part where I had to pretend to be in charge.

"Thank you all for coming."

"Chainsaw Fest 2026!" Jasper cheered.

At his side, Evie beamed at him.

"Safety is our top priority. And we've got to be organized. Make sure you sign in with Paul, then you must provide Gabe with your signed waiver. And everyone wears an orange T-shirt." They remained quiet, most of them still stuffing their faces. "If you don't know what you're doing, you're on hauling duty, no exceptions." I eyed Mrs. Moore, wondering if I could convince her to leave the chainsaw in her trunk. "Jasper and I will each lead a team, one into the tree stands to the east and one to the west. Every branch that needs to come down is marked with orange spray paint. We will direct you in the field. Clear the limbs, and any debris and load it into the ATVs."

I'd spent weeks marking trees that needed to be downed or trimmed. It was essential if I wanted to keep overly excited volunteers from going wild with their chainsaws and it limited damage to my production.

"Gabe will be leading the clear team. You'll be collecting downed limbs and branches, keeping the trails cleared. Take photos of any other damage you find and text them to him. We've got a trailer for big pieces and another for sticks and kindling."

A few of the kids gravitated toward my cousin. He'd keep them busy, as well as most of the older-timers. It was much safer that way.

"Logan and Paul will be here overseeing the log cutting and splitting," I explained.

Some of the firefighters cheered, clearly having chosen that station for themselves.

I scanned the crowd, annoyed yet also grateful for the turnout. This town was full of helpers, whether I needed the help was irrelevant.

Preparing to dismiss the group, I took a deep breath. That's when I spotted Julian, sitting on the ground next to Wayne, happily listening to my chainsaw safety briefing. He was more focused than half the adults.

Half impressed and half terrified he'd left his house without telling his mom again, I froze. But after a heartbeat, I saw her.

Celine.

She stood behind him, next to Stella, holding a coffee mug with both hands.

Dammit. I hadn't thought to warn her about all the commotion on the farm today or considered that Julian might be bothered by the noise. I'd been too wrapped up in preparations.

She didn't look mad. No, she looked comfortable. Maybe more comfortable than I'd ever seen her. She was smiling and chatting, her red hair piled on top of her head and an oversized fleece wrapped around her, her cheeks pink with the cool morning air.

"Remember the rules of Chainsaw Day," I yelled, ready to get started. "Chaps and safety gear are mandatory. No drinking, no smoking, no heroics. Jasper, Gabe, and I are in charge of the zone. You do not cut without our permission first."

Satisfied with the nods and affirmative responses, I climbed down. For a moment, I stood in place, surveying the chaos as the group disbanded. People took off in all directions, chatting and laughing and carrying equipment.

Damn. Would it even be possible to keep everyone safe today? The enthusiasm for chainsaws in this damn town was far too prevalent.

"Um. Josh. Mr. Josh?"

Julian appeared at my side, Wayne dutifully trotting along with him. The little boy had his bright blue noise canceling headphones around his neck like a collar and was wearing the fuzzy blue hoodie I'd often seen him in.

"Morning, Julian."

"Can I help?" he asked, his blue eyes shining bright. "I don't have a chainsaw. But I can carry wood."

Celine jogged over, putting her arm around his shoulders. "Julian, let's not bother Josh. He's super busy."

"It's okay," I said. "Julian offered to help. Which is very generous of him."

I crouched so we were face to face. "Only the grown-ups can cut down the trees. But you can ride along and watch if you'd like. And I could use your help counting up the logs later. But only if it's okay with your mom."

He turned and looked up at her. "Can I watch? I won't touch anything. I promise."

She studied him, then me, her expression wary. "Just for a little bit."

We got everyone assigned and organized, then set off into the woods, and Julian remained at my side the whole time. Jasper was a firefighter and paramedic, so I was confident he could handle his crew. But I had the honor of leading a ragtag team of Marty from the diner, Vince and Mrs. Morris and her vintage chainsaw.

The trouble started mid-day, the way it always did. Quietly.

We had cleared out the first sector when the sound of one chainsaw caught my attention. It revved too loudly and too quickly rather than steadily like I'd drilled into my group.

The sound could only mean someone inexperienced was overcompensating on the throttle.

I turned, but before I could head toward the noise, a dead limb cracked loose far higher up the trunk than it should have.

"Heads-up!" a man yelled.

The branch wasn't fully cut, so instead of dropping clean, it sheared sideways, swinging and hitting another limb. Only then did it finally crack, and that sent it bouncing wide toward the edge of the clearing where a crowd had congregated.

"*Move,*" I shouted.

As folks scattered and yelled and stumbled, I darted for the overeager kid with the chainsaw.

Grabbing Marty by the back of his jacket, I yanked him clear an instant before the branch slammed to the ground in an explosion of bark, making the earth beneath us shake.

Silence followed as I hauled in breath after breath.

When I could see clearly, I took his saw and turned it off.

His face was white, his eyes huge.

"Never cut above shoulder height," I said flatly. "Ever."

"I-I thought—"

"Wrong," I said, pointing at the road. "Hauling duty. Now."

He nodded, swallowing hard, and trudged away.

Heart still pounding, I scanned the group. "Everyone back toward the road unless you've been assigned to cut. There are still several flagged trees here. I will confirm with each of you where you need to be. Please wait for my instructions."

No one argued. No one made a sound.

Squeezing the bill of my hat, I slammed my eyes shut, collecting myself. When I opened them again, I noticed Julian.

He stood next to Wayne, inspecting the massive fallen tree limb. I'd need to slice this with my chainsaw just to get it out of here. God, it could have crushed Marty. Dumbass.

But the boy hadn't run. He hadn't hidden.

Celine was moving toward him, panic etched in every line on her face.

I held my hand up and approached him slowly so I wouldn't spook him.

"Julian," I said calmly. "You okay?"

He nodded, still staring at the tree limb. "It didn't fall where it was supposed to."

"Good eye," I said.

I crouched in front of him, keeping my voice steady. "I could really use your help right now, bud. Do you want a job?"

His eyes widened, roving over me.

Behind him, Celine stopped, watching me just as intently.

"What kind of job?" he asked.

"The most important one." I rested my elbows on my knees and clasped my hands. "I need you to be my spotter."

"What's a spotter?"

"You stand here." I patted the bed of the ATV. "Then you watch and listen. If you see limbs falling or people cutting branches too close to one another. You wave this flag and yell." I handed him an orange safety flag. "If you see anything that looks unsafe at all, wave it and yell." I snapped my fingers, signaling for Wayne to sit. "I'll leave Wayne here with you. He can bark to get my attention."

Wayne wagged his tail proudly, like he'd just been promoted.

Julian pressed his lips together, his focus on my hands for a moment before reaching for the flag. "I can do it," he said in a serious tone.

"You do not leave the ATV," I warned, my words absolute.

He searched my face, determination in his expression.

"You do not touch any tools," I added. "You are my eyes and ears, and I'm depending on you."

"Julian." Celine took a hesitant step closer, her teeth pressing into her bottom lip.

"Mom. I've got an important job to do." He turned and climbed up onto the bed, then shaded his eyes with one hand and assessed the area. "Gotta keep everyone safe."

Wayne's tail thumped furiously against the ground next to me.

"He's doing great," I said, standing. "Kid's got great instincts."

"I'm good at spotting patterns," he boasted, never taking his eyes off the trees.

"Can I stand here with you?" she asked him gently.

"Sure," he murmured, still on high alert, "but only if you promise not to distract me."

She cracked a smile at him, then turned to me, the look on her face morphing into one of deep gratitude. Like she'd noticed my efforts not to touch or grab him. How I had given him space and autonomy and boundaries.

"Thank you," she said quietly.

"He's a good kid." I took a step back, then another. "And a great farm hand. He'll keep us all in line."

And for the rest of the afternoon. He did.

Chapter 15

CELINE

"Welcome to the testosterone buffet." Ruby stepped up beside me, handing me a can of seltzer.

Her infant son was laid out on a blanket in the grass next to Evie's son while down the hill, various townsfolk sawed tree limbs and chopped logs. Her little boy, Brooks, was so much tinier than Vincent, though they were only a couple of months apart in age.

"I'm still not sure what's happening here," I admitted.

It had been a long and thoroughly confusing day, and I'd spent most of it in the woods, supervising Julian while he "helped" Josh saw off tree limbs and collect branches.

I'd seen more chainsaws today than I had in the rest of my thirty-six years combined. I'd woken to the sounds of engines, voices, and cars filling the farm. Naturally, panic had hit me, but after the initial anxiety spike, a peek outside, and a cup of coffee, I realized some kind of town event was beginning.

Men and women had been milling around in Josh's yard, holding thermoses full of coffee, sporting various flannel fashions, and toting around the accessory of the day—chainsaws. Every person I met greeted me warmly, like it was business as usual as I stumbled around trying and failing to make sense of it all.

Eventually, Ruby had arrived, positively giddy, and explained Chainsaw Day and its traditions. It was heartwarming, really, the entire town pitching in to help. We'd been here for a month already, and I still hadn't wrapped my mind around the vastness of Josh's farm. We were surrounded by thousands of trees, all of which had to be inspected and maintained and tapped.

The place was both wild and tamed. Kind of like Josh. He was careful and precise and serious, yet I'd seen flashes of a wicked sense of humor here and there, like more lurked beneath the surface.

The girls had wanted to stay at home, Maggie absorbed in a book and Ellie texting photos of her nails as she painted them bright blue. So I'd come outside to chase Julian around. There was no way he was missing this. It was all ATVs and chainsaws, and he was fascinated.

Josh had been efficient and commanding, yet so kind to Julian, involving him in the action and keeping him safe.

As grateful as I was, he hadn't given me a chance to say so. He'd barely looked at me all day. And that was fine. He was working hard to keep everyone safe while he simultaneously chopped wood, ran saws, and directed crews. Some folks from the No Book Club were here, and Evie had pointed out the small group of firefighters who worked with

Jasper. Then there was the handsome mayor that Stella was always talking about.

This was an all-out event, yet despite the commotion and all the working parts, Josh had made time for Julian. He'd been kind and direct. He'd set boundaries and given him clear guidelines.

And Julian responded beautifully. Working hard to be the lookout and taking pride in his work.

"It's a Maplewood thing," Ruby said.

"They really all pretend to just 'show up' to help?" Evie asked.

"Yep," Ruby confirmed. "When in reality, Paul's had this date blocked off on his calendar since last year. And he went to Staples last week and upgraded his clipboard for the occasion."

"Bless his accountant heart," Stella said.

"It might sound cute, but you weren't the one stuck listening to him go on last night about the model he built to estimate firewood yields," Ruby grumbled. "It's a good thing he looks so hot swinging an axe right now."

I snorted, watching the men work. "Are they competing with one another?"

Evie laughed. "Yes and no. From what Jasper told me, the idea is that they chop all the wood so that everyone can take some home for the winter. But a few of them, Jasper included, seem to think this is some kind of manly challenge." Licking her lips, she surveyed the scene. "Not that I'm complaining."

"Hear-hear," Ruby said. "My husband is a beast in the spreadsheets, so I enjoy seeing this side of him."

"I'm especially impressed by Josh," Evie said. "Jasper

and I took bets on how quickly he'd melt down after the old people started messing around with their chainsaws."

"Nah. I'm not surprised. He's nicer when he's got his tools," Stella explained.

"Yes," Ruby added. "He doesn't have to talk. Or feel."

Evie sighed. "Trust me, that man feels deeply."

I studied my fingernails, pretending I wasn't fascinated by this conversation.

"He just hides all those feelings under the beard and flannel," she mused.

Half the group was chopping wood and several high school kids were stacking it. A third faction, led by Jasper, had broken off to build a bonfire.

"But Frankie's kicking all of their asses," Stella said, her lips twitching.

"She always does," Ruby said. "That woman has enough rage to power the entire state of Vermont."

"I'm surprised Nolan hasn't gotten in his car and driven away," Evie added. "She's got a blade in her hands."

I'd heard Frankie mentioned a few times and gathered she was a close friend of these women, and according to Callie, she was an excellent mechanic, but I hadn't yet met her.

As if she could hear my thoughts, Evie looked up at me. "She's one of our best friends, so we can say this. But she's been in a bad place since the arrest."

Ruby nodded, her face falling. "I'm worried about her. She still won't talk about it, and she spends every minute she isn't under the hood of a car contacting lawyers and reading legal articles."

Frowning, I looked from one woman to another. I wasn't following.

"Her little brother," Stella explained, lowering her voice. "He was arrested...um." She trailed off, looking at Evie and Ruby for help.

"He was arrested for murder," Ruby whispered, covering her mouth with her hand.

My eyes shot to Julian. He was throwing a stick to Wayne, who dutifully returned it each and every time. I blew out a breath. There was no way he'd overheard that from where he stood.

"And arson," she added. "But she swears he's innocent and that Nolan botched the investigation."

"But then he went and confessed," Stella said, watching Frankie with a sympathetic look on her face.

"She's been on a crusade for justice ever since. Going down to Boston to find him the best lawyers, visiting him in jail. Hounding the FBI, demanding they investigate Nolan. She's grieving."

My stomach twisted painfully. I knew what that felt like. The grief of realizing a person I loved had the capacity to hurt. I'd rarely been as devastated as I was the moment I realized my trust had been broken completely.

Evie checked her watch. "Shoot. Jenn and Mel should be here with dinner soon. Can you help me get the folding tables out of my trunk?"

"I hope they get here quick," Ruby said, scooping up her son. "Food as a distraction would be great right about now. We're probably twenty minutes from someone lighting something on fire."

Stella giggled. "Ten if Logan is involved."

A bit dazed, I called Julian over and trudged down the hill toward the packed driveway. A big crowd was still chopping wood, but several others were pulling camp chairs and coolers out of their vehicles.

"This is going to turn into a party very quickly," Stella warned me.

I held Julian's hand as he scanned the scene. By now I was sure he'd be overstimulated, but with Wayne by his side, he was calmly taking in the sights.

"Do you want to go back to our house?" I asked him. "We should probably check on the girls."

He looked up at me, his eyes swimming with contentment. "I like it here."

I squeezed his hand. Okay, then. I guess we were staying.

As I helped Evie with a folding table, I marveled at how naturally the whole crowd was coming together. Someone had set up a speaker and music was now playing. Another person had produced cornhole boards from the back of a pickup.

"Is that...?" I frowned at the man standing at his open trunk.

"Yup. Nate is rolling a keg out of his car."

"I'm glad I brought Vincent's jammies," Evie mused. "I may have to put him in the baby wrap and hope he sleeps."

"The cool air will probably knock him right out," Ruby said, looking down at her own cooing son in his offroad stroller.

"Is Josh okay with all this?" I asked.

Ruby laughed. "It's Chainsaw Day. He doesn't have a choice. He'll make a half-assed effort to kick us all out, but he'll quickly relent. This is what happens every year. People will eat and drink all that beer, and we'll be here all night."

"That's why all those hay bales are stacked up. For seating." Evie lifted her chin, signaling to the makeshift rows. "Jasper brought them down from the big barn last night without Josh noticing."

"And I've got blankets in my car for when it gets chillier," Stella added.

Julian and I hiked back to our house with Wayne in tow to grab layers and the girls. Unsurprisingly, Maggie was reading on the couch and more than ready to join the party. Ellie was nowhere to be seen, so I sent the other two upstairs to find her.

Alone for the first time all day, a familiar sense of panic built in my chest, and suddenly, my mind was taking off without my permission. If I'd known there would be a town potluck in my backyard tonight, I would have made a dish or two.

Generally, I hated spontaneity. I liked to know precisely what was expected of me. And now my nervous system was spiraling. Because I'd done something wrong. I'd fucked up. I was stupid.

Those thoughts were cut off, thankfully, by three sets of feet thundering down the stairs. I pushed away the negative emotions and cleared my throat while I waited for the kids.

There were dozens of people here. No one was going to judge me. I'd had no clue this was even happening, and even if I had, with the chaos going on, no one would notice that we'd come empty-handed. Right?

Even so, that feeling, that I was wrong, or I'd done

wrong, stuck with me, niggling at the back of my mind like it always did.

By the time we rejoined the party, it was in full swing. Jenn and Mel were serving chili and cornbread while Josh grilled hot dogs.

"Celine!" Evie shouted. "Come say hi to Basil and Etienne."

With a small smile, I pushed away my instinct to shy away and shook the hands of both men.

"They brought that magazine-worthy charcuterie board and the champagne." Evie giggled.

The folding table covered in a cute yellow gingham tablecloth now held what could only be described as a work of art.

And as if he'd teleported from my side, Julian was in front of it, reaching for what was probably a forty-dollar block of cheese.

I intercepted him quickly, my face heating.

"Sorry," I said to the Etienne and Basil.

Etienne only smiled. "You've got great mom reflexes."

I helped Julian choose a piece of cheese and several cherry tomatoes, his favorite, and then turned back to properly greet these new faces.

"It's great to see you again," Basil said.

"I never thanked you," I said, keeping one eye on Julian to ensure he didn't touch every piece of food on the table. "For sending cheese when I first moved in."

He broke into a big smile. "Yes."

"Thank you. I ate all of it. The bread you sent with it was the best I've ever eaten," I admitted. "I had to hide it so my kids couldn't find it. There was no way I was sharing."

Pink dots appeared on his full cheeks. "I'll deliver more."

Etienne smiled warmly. "You just made his year. He is deeply devoted to his sourdough craft."

"How do you feel about Brie?" my new best friend Basil asked.

"You're welcome for the cheese hookup," Evie said, nudging me. "Just make sure to remain loyal, No defecting to Lola."

"Even though her cheddar is better," Ruby whispered. "I didn't say that. You heard wrong."

They'd lost me, but I smiled anyway and scanned the area, needing to lay eyes on my kids.

Thankfully, I found them easily. Julian was captivated by the bonfire that Josh and Jasper were building and Maggie and Ellie were helping pour lemonade for the other kids that had shown up.

By the time Callie arrived with her twins I'd been introduced to everyone at least once—some that I'd already met at No Book Club, but many I hadn't—not that I remembered many of their names.

"Having fun?" Josh appeared beside me. He was dirty from a long day's work and the knit hat he'd traded his ball cap for made him look even more like a lumberjack.

I nodded. "This turned into quite a day."

"Yeah. Sometimes this town annoys the ever-loving shit out of me, but on days like this, I can't help but appreciate the place." He sighed, stuffing his hands into his pockets. "My parents started this tradition a long time ago. Feels good to keep it going even if they're not here to take part."

He looked tired in the firelight, his face sagging, his shoulders drooping.

The strangest urge to hug him took over, but I held strong. I wasn't one for spontaneous touching. But I felt for him. I didn't know what had happened to his parents, but I did understand how it felt to walk around every day feeling the weight of a loved one's absence.

"I lost my mom when I was thirteen," I said softly, staring at the fire.

My kids now sat on a hay bale, roasting marshmallows on sticks. Julian was wrapped up in a blanket and his hands were coated with sticky mess, but he was beaming. Even Ellie and Maggie had gotten into the fun. And they were safe. I was safe.

"I'm sorry," he said.

I remained facing forward, relishing the way the fire's warmth spread through my body.

It was more than warmth, really. Even surrounded by so many people, most of whom I had only just met, I felt safe.

Closing my eyes, I let out a breath.

One I'd been holding for a very long time.

He belonged here.

We belonged here.

Chapter 14

CELINE

I'd woken up with an extra spring in my step. I typically spent my weekends doing endless chores and desperately searching for a way to feel "caught up."

But the impromptu town bonfire party had interrupted my weekend, resulting in a lot more hanging around than usual. Yesterday had been rainy, so we'd had a family Monopoly battle before making fancy grilled cheese sandwiches for dinner and watching *Lilo & Stitch*, Julian's favorite movie.

I woke at five, slipped out of bed without disturbing Julian, who had come in around two, and threw on a pair of leggings and a sports bra.

As I headed out into the cool fall morning, a new determination hit me. We were okay. The kids were healthy and happy. I'd made friends. Actual friends.

And it was fall, my favorite time of year.

After a twenty-minute run up and down my favorite hill, I determined I was badass enough to treat myself to coffee.

Maybe I'd get really wild and defrost a croissant I'd stashed in the freezer.

Propped up against the counter, I watched the sun rise over the tree line and sipped my coffee. After that first taste, I took a second to breathe. I was doing it more than usual. Just letting myself exist.

The moments were small, but their effects infiltrated my whole body. Carrying so much tension and the anxiety all the time was exhausting. I'd gone years without sleeping a full night or taking a full breath.

But my instincts, the same instincts I'd spent years questioning and doubting, had served me well this time.

Maplewood was good for us.

Our future was looking brighter.

Coffee in one hand, phone in the other, I opened my email app and scanned one of the newsletters I'd subscribed to.

I clicked out of it, then scrolled, quickly reading subject lines until I discovered one that made my stomach plummet.

Oh fuck.

I steadied myself on the counter. Shit. Shit. Shit.

Don't read it. Don't do it.

My finger took over, tapping on it, even though I was certain I wouldn't like what I found inside.

Phyllis.

She'd created yet another Gmail account to use to harass me. Just fucking great.

I skimmed the multi-paragraph email, noting all the usual rhetoric my former mother-in-law typically stuck with.

You're ungrateful and cruel.

How could you do this to my son? You drove him to depression and alcoholism.

I always knew you were a trashy whore.

I will take away those children. They deserve better than a mother like you.

How could you destroy my family?

You deserve to rot in hell.

Phyllis was not particularly creative or articulate. But over the years, her hatred of me hadn't waned.

Back when I'd been a doormat who let my ex-husband terrorize me and my kids, she'd adored me. Of course she had. I'd provided her with grandkids, always chipped in with the dishes on Thanksgiving, and never complained.

But her true colors had begun to shine through when Donny was arrested.

She'd even hired a lawyer and petitioned the court for grandparent custody rights.

Lucky for me, those rights didn't actually exist. Regardless, she argued that I was an abusive mother and that she should be given sole custody of my children.

Her suit had no merit. But it had cost me tens of thousands of dollars in legal fees and many, many months of worry and stress.

That, I assumed, had been her plan from the beginning anyway. Donny learned the abusive tactics from someone, right?

I set the phone on the kitchen counter, stepped away, and closed my eyes and counted to ten. Then I did exactly what I'd done the dozen or so times this had happened before. I forwarded the email to my sister and my lawyer and then blocked the email address.

"Mommy," Julian yelled from upstairs.

Heart lurching, I wiped the tears out of my eyes.

Fuck Phyllis for ruining my day. She'd done it deliberately, choosing a Monday morning to ruin as much as she could.

"Coming." I scraped my hair back, trying to school my expression.

The last thing Julian needed was more anxiety about his mean grandma stealing him from me.

Upstairs, I helped him get dressed and brush his teeth, then I distracted him with cartoons while I jumped in the shower. For the entire five-minute speed shower, my thoughts tumbled through my head. I told my lawyer. The logical thing to do now was ignore it. Ignore Phyllis. But I was so sick and tired of living my life scared. Scared that Donny or one of his toxic family members would drop a grenade into my day.

I was half dressed when Ellie groaned. "*Mom.*"

I darted into the girls' room, only finding Maggie, who was fast asleep in the top bunk.

"Ellie?"

A retching sound echoed off the tile walls in the bathroom.

"Sweetie." I peeked in, my chest already aching.

"I don't feel good." She peered up at me, looking so young, her skin sallow.

Shuffling closer, I held the back of my hand to her forehead.

Instantly, my stomach sank. She was burning up.

"When did this start?"

"Just a minute ago. I felt terrible when I woke up, and then I threw up."

"Okay, sweetie. Let's get you back to bed. Then I'll get you water and some Tylenol."

"No," she groaned. "I'll be fine once I brush my teeth."

I brushed her hair away from her sweaty face. "You're not fine."

"I am. I'll take a shower and be ready to go on time."

My oldest baby was pale, glassy-eyed, and shivering.

When she was healthy, she acted like she was thirty-five, like she was completely independent, but like this, it was clear she needed me.

I pressed the back of my hand to her forehead again. "It's probably a virus. But you need to stay home and rest, and you need fluids."

Ellie never got sick, and when she did, she hid the signs and soldiered on. My poor kid put so much pressure on herself.

But to my surprise, she gave up the fight easily, nodding, a look of relief taking over.

For me, though, I was hit with another wave of concern.

Because I couldn't stay home with her. I needed to get Maggie and Julian to school, plus I had my first curriculum meeting today.

Standing in the doorway, I flipped through all the worst-case scenarios like I always did. The thought of leaving my baby alone paralyzed me. What if she needed me?

"Mom," she rasped. "It's okay. I have my phone."

My throat closed up. Dammit. "Is it charged?" When we'd move, I'd relented and given Ellie a "dumb" phone. The kind she could only use to contact preapproved numbers. She complained that it was worse than having no phone at all and rarely used it. Hence why it was never charged.

"Yes. I plugged it in last night."

I took her in, noting the dark circles around her eyes. If she'd thought ahead like that, then she must have felt sick but hadn't told me.

Sighing, I backed out of the room. I didn't have a choice. I was on my own, so I'd do the best I could.

After confirming the phone was charged, leaving her with water, crackers, and my laptop, I got Julian and Maggie out the door.

Only to be met by Wayne, who was once again standing behind my van.

"Wayne's here for his good-morning hugs." Julian darted for him, scratching his ears and wrapping his little arms around the dog's bulk.

Maggie followed, petting his head and chatting with him about the book she'd been reading.

"Okay, Wayne," I said, stroking his floppy ears. "Time to go."

Rather than wander away, he stared at the door, tail thumping.

"Ellie's sick," Maggie told him.

The dog didn't move.

"Come on." I grasped his collar, trying to move him along.

Again, he sat, perfectly still behind my car.

God, this dog.

I patted my pockets for my phone, then dove into my purse in search of it.

Luckily, he picked up after one ring.

"Can you come get your dog? He won't let me pull out of the driveway."

"Did you say good morning?" Josh asked, his tone light.

"Yes," I snapped, "and I'm really not in the mood."

"I'll be there in two minutes. I'm in my truck."

It didn't even take him that long. When he pulled up, he hopped out, bringing a bag of dog treats with him.

At the sight, Wayne's tail thumped even louder.

"Where's Ellie?" he asked, peering inside the van.

My shoulders sank. "She's sick."

His face softened. "Where is she? What does she need?"

"She frew up," Julian said.

Josh looked at me, concern written all over his face. The expression was kind. So kind it momentarily threw me off guard.

"I'll keep an eye on her," he said.

My breath caught, and I snapped back to my senses. "There's no need."

"It's fine. I planned to work on this side of the farm today anyway. Does she have a phone in case of emergency?"

I nodded.

"Is it charged?"

A huff escaped me. How he anticipated my tweens inability to keep her phone charged, I didn't know.

"Yes," I said.

I unlocked my phone and navigated to the parental control app so I could add him as an approved caller. "It's really okay—"

He held a hand up. "I'll check in on her. Bring her

snacks if necessary. Don't worry, I won't give her a chainsaw or anything."

I shot him a glare over my phone while Julian laughed like the man had told the most hilarious joke he'd ever heard.

"Does she need medicine? I can run to the pharmacy."

I shook my head. "I gave her Tylenol, and she's going to try eating a few crackers, then let me know."

Once I'd finished adding him to the approved list, I locked my phone and stuck it in my purse.

"It's okay," he said, eyes roving over me. "I know you feel guilty, but you've got to get to school."

"I can try to run home during lunch," I said.

"I've got it." He patted my shoulder gently.

On instinct, I flinched.

Eyes widening, he took a step back.

"Sorry," I said, my face flaming. God, why was I such a weirdo? It was a friendly pat, for God's sake. He wasn't pointing a gun at my head.

Without another word, I loaded the kids up, and Josh got back in his truck, taking his dog with him.

As I walked Julian to his classroom, he clung to me more than usual, and Maggie hadn't said a word the entire ride to school.

With each step I took deeper into the school, my chest tightened. I wanted nothing more than to grab my kids and run home.

We'd just put all the backpacks away and finished morning circle time when my phone buzzed on my desk.

. . .

It was a photo of Wayne lying on my front porch, blocking the door.

JOSH

Wayne's on guard duty. He's taking it very seriously.

While my students got settled in their designated centers, I quickly responded.

CELINE

I'll make him fresh bacon tomorrow.

JOSH

Already got a text from Ellie asking me to share my Netflix password and not to tell you.

I laughed. Okay, she was definitely feeling better. I'd cut all nonessentials a while back and Ellie was dying to watch a show all the kids at school had been talking about. I'd disappointed her when I told her I couldn't waste money on Netflix and I didn't want her watching something I hadn't vetted yet. It figured that she'd seen Josh as a potential patsy who'd let her watch *The Summer I Turned Pretty* without Mom's approval.

CELINE

Thanks to you both.

. . .

AND JUST LIKE THAT, I BREATHED A BIT EASIER.

My kindergarten classroom could be described as controlled chaos on a good day. On a day when my oldest child was home alone sick and I'd heard from my evil ex-mother-in-law, it was an exercise in compartmentalization. One I should have earned a medal for.

I sang songs, tied shoes, and mediated a dramatic dispute over a purple crayon. I praised good listening and redirected big feelings.

By lunch. I had texts from both Ellie and Josh.

JOSH

She's requested soup and is watching
Family Feud.

I SIGHED. GOOD. ELLIE'S MESSAGE PUT ME EVEN MORE at ease.

ELLIE

I'm alive. Feel gross but not terrible. Wayne
is here and Josh is bringing me soup.

CELINE

Please rest.

ELLIE

I'd feel a lot more rested if we had Netflix.
Maybe you can make an account during
your lunch break?

CELINE

Not a chance.

NOT LONG AFTER LUNCH, THE EXHAUSTION HIT ME LIKE a tsunami.

When Callie walked into the teacher work room during my planning period, I realized I'd been staring blankly at the copier and that my stack of papers was waiting for me in the tray.

With a sympathetic frown, she steered me into her office.

The moment my butt hit the seat across from her desk, I burst into tears.

She slid a box of tissues at me. "You've got 21 minutes before music class ends. Start talking."

I blew my nose, trying to tamp down all the thoughts and feelings coursing through me.

"I can't do it all," I said, sniffling.

She laced her fingers on her desktop. "No one can."

"But I have to," I explained. "If I drop one ball, everything falls apart. I'm tired and cranky and anxious all the time." A hiccup escaped me. "I love them so much, but I'm a terrible mother. I'm destroying their childhood."

She stood abruptly and rounded her desk. Sitting next to me, she squeezed my hand like this wasn't the first time she'd seen a breakdown like this here. "You're doing too much."

"I don't have a choice."

"You do," she urged. "You just haven't learned to accept help yet. But you will."

I laughed, my nose still running. "Bullshit."

When I looked over at her, she was smiling, and that only made me laugh more. I was having an honest-to-God breakdown in my boss's office. Excellent work. A-fucking-plus, Celine.

She took a deep breath and squeezed my hand again. "You got yourself and three kids out. I don't know many details, but what I do know tells me how brave and capable you are."

I swallowed thickly, emotion clogging my throat. Yes, Callie knew some hazy details. My ex-husband's rap sheet was public record, and she knew I'd taken many years off from teaching. I'd filled in a few blanks as vaguely as I could when I interviewed, and she hadn't pushed much.

But like most teachers, she was perceptive. Maybe more perceptive than I'd realized.

"You moved states. You went back to work and got a job so you could provide for your kids. You've kept everyone alive while also meeting their complex needs. That's not failure. That's hero-level exhaustion."

I wiped my face. "Ellie's sick, and I left her home alone."

Head tilted, she remained silent, like she knew that wasn't the full story.

"Josh has been checking on her," I admitted. "She's making him run around for soup and trying to blackmail him into sharing his Netflix password."

She broke into a wide smile. "Then she's on the mend." With a chuckle, she shook her head.

I sniffled, blotting my nose with a clean tissue. "I feel so guilty."

"Don't. Kids get sick, and she's old enough to take care of herself in these situations. On top of that, you've got a trustworthy person checking on her. That's called problem-solving."

My phone buzzed, on cue, and a notification appeared, alerting me to a new text from Josh.

This time it was a photo of Ellie, sprawled out on my couch, a bottle of red Gatorade next to her that Josh must have given her, and Wayne snuggled into her side.

Damn, the dog was as long as she was. I couldn't help but giggle at the image.

Callie leaned over. "See? That's community. That's help. Ask for it. Come in here and vent. I'll help. Ask Josh to bring your kid soup," she commanded. "Come in late or take your PTO, hire a babysitter and give yourself breaks. This town is filled with people willing to help. But you've got to be willing to ask."

Later that afternoon, as I herded small humans toward backpacks and bus lines, I caught myself smiling. The day had brightened considerably since my meltdown.

I'd accepted help. It hadn't cost me anything, and I wouldn't be punished or shamed.

Phyllis had tried to ruin my day. But she hadn't.

It was okay.

I was okay.

And that felt like progress.

Chapter 15

JOSH

The last thing I needed was more bullshit to deal with today. My list was a mile long and growing, thanks to the raccoons that had caused damage to one of the tubing junctions.

I could feel it. This day was already going off the rails.

The tricked-out, spotless white truck driving up my road only solidified that.

It was equipped with tinted windows, a logo too polished for a Vermont fall, and the fancy trim package. My dad had taught me at a young age, never trust a person with a brand-new gleaming truck.

It parked right inside the gate like it had every right to be there.

I walked towards it, with Wayne on my heels, annoyed, undercaffeinated, and too busy to put up with any more shit today.

The driver's door swung open and the man who stepped out looked like he'd never held a shovel in his life. Pressed khakis, clean boots, branded fleece vest with a distinctive green and gold logo stitched over the chest.

"Josh Lawrence?" his tone implied we were old friends who shared a friendly round of golf once a year. He smoothed his short blond hair and unfolded a pair of Ray-Bans that he'd tucked into the collar of his shirt.

I slowly removed my work gloves. "Depends," I said. "You lost?"

He laughed like I'd made a funny joke and reached out. "Tristan McDevitt. Regional development for AgriNova."

Of course.

I crossed my arms. "When we last spoke on the phone, I told you I was all set."

His smile got wider. "I was in the neighborhood and thought I'd stop by. As you know, I'm deeply committed to supporting independent producers." With his hands in his pockets, he wandered up the driveway, surveying my land like he owned it. "You've got quite an operation. Family-run, organic certified, one of the highest yields per tap in the region. Well done."

His knowledge of my business made my hackles rise. "What do you need, Tristan?" I asked. Wayne stared him down like he was an annoying squirrel.

The man stepped closer, lowering his voice like this was a friendly chat. "BGX-9."

My jaw muscles clenched involuntarily.

"It's not a fertilizer," he said quickly. "We're past that. Twenty-first century innovations. It's a bio-organic enhancement agent. Improves flow efficiency and cellular response during freeze-thaw cycles."

I'd heard this sales pitch half a dozen times. Every few

years some giant agro-chemical company came out with a *revolutionary* product that was going to make us all rich. Investors and scientists were always trying to hack nature. But maple syrup wasn't like that. We needed healthy trees, the right weather, and appropriate expectations. Maple trees weren't faucets that could be turned on and off. The tree gave what it gave, when it wanted to give it. But these assholes could not accept the reality that maple sap was a finite resource. No, they wanted bigger and better and more.

"It's already being piloted across the state. And it's having major success in Canada. We've seen a 12-percent increase in yield due to high flow efficiency and increased Brix percentages."

That was the pitch, the sentence designed to hook me and make me see dollar signs.

"Which producers?" I asked.

He hesitated a beat too long, and when he spoke, his eyes shifted to one side. "Several in Addison County. And even more in the north. This upcoming season will be the best ever."

"You talk to the Fitzgeralds?" I asked.

He'd likely been chased off their farm with a shotgun. They were one of the biggest operations in the state, and I had no doubt they wouldn't touch this shit with a ten-foot pole.

Another flicker. "We're in conversation with the family," he said diplomatically.

"Not interested," I said, already bored of this conversation. "I don't chase yields." I also did not take risks with my trees. A maple tree had to be around thirty years old before it could be tapped. Each tree was a long-term investment, and some of my best producers had been planted by my grandfather. I didn't fuck around with them.

"I get it." He held his hands up in surrender. "You're a steward of the land, which is why we are aligned environmentally."

I'd spent five years on Wall Street trading agricultural commodities. I knew the buzzwords and all the corporate bullshit that came along with them.

"You're pushing this really hard."

"Our company is committed to—"

"Your company," I interrupted, "is owned by one of the largest agro-chemical manufacturers in the world. Filling our soil and our crops with all kinds of genetically enhanced and synthetic shit."

His eye narrowed, but the creepy smile remained. "BGX-9 is EPA compliant. But I only stopped by to have a conversation. Independent farms like yours are under pressure these days."

His tone only set me further on edge.

"Things happen," he went on. "Bad weather. Dwindling tourism. Supply chain disruptions. Farms like yours..." He trailed off, turning and surveying my land. "Run lean margins, any season could be your last."

There it was.

The pressure. The hard sell.

"We're good," I said firmly. "But you mentioned Addison County, and that got me thinking. Funny thing about all those beehive collapses. More failures this year than ever. No mites. No disease markers. Just failure."

Logan had been going on about the bees and what he'd heard from colleagues near the New York border. I had no idea whether they were connected, but I was sick of this guy's shit.

He froze for a second, his face falling before he recovered his salesman's smile. "Unrelated."

We stood, staring at one another. I refused to look away. This guy needed to go. Wayne trotted to my side, and Tristan's eyes widened. Wayne was a sweet boy, but he looked like the progeny of a pony and a wolf.

"I'll just leave some pamphlets." Tristan strode to his truck, then returned with a green folder. "Call me when you want to talk."

I took it from his hand. "I don't need to talk."

"You will." With that, he hauled himself into the driver's seat of that too clean truck. Then he was gone, turning around and rolling down the driveway.

As I watched him disappear, my stomach tightened. I'd spent too many years watching markets spike because of so-called innovation, only to crash on buried data and junk science.

"No shortcuts," I muttered to Wayne as we walked back towards the barn.

"Excuse me?"

I lifted my head up from the front-end loader I was working on. I was cranky and had skipped lunch to finish this.

Celine stood in the barn doorway with a clipboard clasped to her chest like armor.

"Hey," I said, standing up and dusting the dirt off my jeans.

She continued to hover there, with the posture of someone bracing for impact, standing at the edge of the building, scanning everything around her, taking inventory, looking for exit paths.

The more time I spent with Celine, the more I clocked these behaviors. And I desperately wanted to ask her *Who hurt you?* But I knew that would be a massive overstep.

"You lost?"

"No," she said. "I mean, yes, but intentionally lost."

I waited and crossed my arms.

She exhaled and lifted the clipboard. "I was hoping we could talk about hayrides." She gave me a forced smile.

I shoved my hands into my pockets. "Okay. What do you need?"

"Um... I thought that since I'm not familiar with the area and you are, that maybe you could help me plan the route and..." She sighed, her jaw tightening. "I know this is a lot."

"Of course I'll help," I said, admitting the inevitable. "And I've done it before. So no need to worry."

"You have?"

"Unfortunately. Well, I've helped. My dad used to do it." Just the mention of him made me thaw a bit more.

"The committee told me to ask Charlie at Whittaker Farm, that he usually plans the route, but I don't know them, and I'm not good with new people."

I nodded. Glad that she hadn't asked Charlie, pleased that she'd asked me instead. Why? I had no clue, but I wasn't in a position to be particularly reflective at the moment.

Instead I was mesmerized by her sad eyes and her bravery. In coming here and asking me.

"I'm glad you asked me," I said softly. "I can help."

Her shoulders dropped an inch. It was a small change, but it was real.

"I've been outside all day, and I'm cold," I said. "Wanna work on this plan over a cup of coffee?"

With the smallest of smiles, she nodded, so Wayne and I led her from the barn to my house.

The moment she stepped inside, she gasped.

I followed her in and smiled, toeing off my boots. I'd forgotten that she'd never been inside my home before.

"This isn't fair," she said, turning to me, all the traces of fear gone from her face.

Wayne cozied up next to her, and she immediately scratched his ears, taking in the space. I was proud of my home. I'd updated and modernized my parents' old farmhouse, but I'd kept some of the rustic qualities.

I'd opened up some walls, adding a breakfast nook and mudroom and creating a massive living dining area with large wooden beams. The five-bedroom house was too big for just me, but I'd grown up here, and my mom had always dreamed of one of us living here and taking over the farm. So when she passed, I moved in. Jasper had lived with me for years, sleeping in his childhood bedroom, which he had not allowed me to touch. But these days it was just Wayne and me.

She walked through the open-plan living room, running her hand along the honey brown leather couch. "Look at those light fixtures."

As she examined every detail, pride filled me. People

were often complimentary about my house, and I always appreciated the remarks, but seeing it through Celine's eyes felt special.

"You've got to be fucking kidding me."

She stood in the entryway of the kitchen, hands on her hips. "Quartz? An AGA? That farmhouse sink is the size of a bathtub." Spinning, she tapped her chin. "No wife... oh." She nodded, a smile playing at her lips. "You're gay. That must be it."

Head back, I laughed. "I am absolutely not gay." Though I was amused by her theories. "Also, that's a bit of a tired stereotype."

She hung her head. "Fair. Sorry. I'm just confused. How do you have this house? And *why?*"

"I grew up here. When I moved in, it was very much stuck in the seventies. So I renovated it to suit my taste but also to keep it true to its farmhouse roots."

Teeth pressed to her bottom lip, she scanned the cabinets. "You did an incredible job."

I puffed up a bit with her praise. "Thank you."

"And here I thought our cottage was amazing. Josh, you're wasted as a maple farmer. You should be a designer."

Heat crawled up my neck. "Nah, it's just a hobby. I like projects."

She shot me an incredulous look.

But before she could snap back, I strode to the coffeepot. "So you've got that map?"

We spread the town map out on top of the island and walked around it, noting hayride routes that would ensure maximum safety and, in her words, "autumnal charm."

"The routes haven't included the Falls in years." I tapped

the spot on the map. "But it's been pretty dry lately, so the logging road should be in good condition. We could loop around the town center and head down Maple Street toward the falls. Then we could swing by the brewery on the way back. Nate and Reed would probably love to decorate the place."

Nodding, she scribbled notes in her pad. "This is ambitious."

"Nobody wants to waste time on a lame hayride. Let's make it a true event. An experience. I'll see if Jenn and Mel will set up a little stop for hot cider at the midpoint. Or maybe we could do music inspired by the different spots on the tour."

Her face lit up and she wrote faster, and when she bit the end of her pen when she was thinking, it was actually pretty cute.

"How many rides can we run at once?"

I took off my hat and stretched, relishing the ache in my muscles. "Two. I can drive and so can Jasper. We've got to confirm he's not on duty, though. I'll check in with Uncle Ed. He and my aunt live in Florida now, but they visit often. If he's in town, he'd probably help. And we'll need volunteers at various spots and to manage the line."

We talked through schedules, safety checks, and the budget, and every time she asked a question, she apologized.

But I didn't mind. She was smart and detail-oriented, and it was clear that she cared. I could respect that. She'd only lived in Maplewood for a couple of weeks, but she was already invested.

"What's the theme this year?"

"The debate over that has been intense." She tapped her

pen against the quartz countertop. "Bitsy Bramble insisted we do Maplewood Throughout History, but people fought back hard. Thank God. That would be a logistical nightmare."

I grimaced. Shit. She was right.

"Olive suggested Romantic Rural Autumn, but all of us single people vetoed. We can't combine fall with Valentine's Day. It's just... wrong." She shuddered.

She was single. That confirmation brought to life a small pang in my chest. I'd assumed she was, given that she lived on my property and I'd never seen anyone coming or going but her and the kids. It shouldn't, but knowing comforted me.

"Eventually we settled on Cozy Harvest Haunt but family friendly, but only after Mavis presented her Power-Point, focusing on why she was certain that a sexy scarecrows theme would bring back all the tourists."

I laughed. Of course Mavis would go there.

"So it's just harvest themed for the Harvest Festival?" I chuckled.

"Yes."

I rubbed my hands together, fighting a smile. "I can work with that. We've got straw bales, and we can talk to other local farmers about donating corn stalks and pumpkins. But I may need some help decorating the wagons we'll tow behind the tractors."

"I'll help. And I can bring the kids."

"Great."

She rested her forearms on my countertop, studying me.

I let her, scanning the kitchen to give her a second. I didn't mind. She was so much softer and easier to talk to than she'd been an hour ago when she'd come into the barn. So far, this version of her was my favorite, and I didn't want her to disappear. This woman laughed and came up with ideas and bantered. She wasn't the scared, closed-off woman who always looked like she was ready to fight.

"You good?" I asked eventually, desperate to know what she was thinking.

"Yeah. You've been..." With a breath out, she examined my face. "Super helpful."

"I aim to please."

She ducked, trying to hide the pink stain on her cheeks. "There's one more thing."

Hands on the countertop, I leaned forward. "Hit me."

"Route decorations. Apparently I have to convince the people and businesses along the route to decorate. Which means knocking on doors." She swallowed audibly, her attention still lowered.

"I can go with you."

Her eyes snapped up and she inhaled. "You don't have to."

"I know."

For a moment, silence stretched between us. Not uncomfortable, just weighty.

"I'm not great with new people." She licked her lips. "Or surprises. Or being told I'm doing things wrong."

There it was. Not a confession. Not a story. But the information I'd been missing.

I took a risk, placing my hand next to hers so that our pinkies barely brushed.

Rather than recoil like I thought she might, she left her hand there, keeping her focus on me.

"We'll make a schedule, plan out the conversations, and I can update you on who's who in town so you aren't met with any surprises."

"Thank you." She looked away, frowning. "It's not that I can't handle it. I just—"

"I know you can handle it," I said calmly. "You wouldn't be here if you couldn't."

She blinked at me, unmoving.

For a moment, I could see through her tough exterior. The walls she'd built up to keep herself and her kids safe.

And I respected the hell out of it.

But it killed me that she felt they were necessary, that someone had probably caused her to hide behind them.

"I know what you must think," she said, staring at the tiniest sliver of space between her pinky and mine. "That I was weak. And maybe I was. I didn't see the signs until it was too late."

I grasped her hand and squeezed it. "You are not weak," I growled. "Don't ever say that."

She nodded, her eyes filling with tears.

"You don't owe me anything. You don't have to tell me anything," I added. Even if I wanted to know everything.

She'd never said it outright, but I had to assume the man she had those children with was a piece of shit. But I wouldn't force her to share what she wasn't ready to.

She squeezed my hand back and closed her eyes, blowing out a shaky breath. "Okay."

She gently pulled away, and I immediately missed the warmth of her skin.

"Cozy hayrides." She swallowed thickly and pulled her shoulders back. "I think we can do this."

"You're already doing it. I'm just supplying the tractors."

The smile that spread across her face made my chest tight. This woman's smiles undid me. They had to be earned, worked for. And when she finally rewarded me, they felt like the best kind of gift.

"Oh shoot." She picked up her phone and frowned at it. "I've got to run. Julian has a birthday party."

Adjusting my hat, I took a step back. "Fun."

It was my lucky day, because she broke into another smile, though this one was a little more sardonic. "On the one hand, I'm thrilled he's getting invited to these things. After so many years of being on the outside..." She sighed, her body deflating. "But I can't say I'm looking forward to spending two solid hours in a room full of screaming seven years olds hopped up on sugar."

We said our goodbyes and I walked her out. As she walked back up the road toward her cottage, clipboard and map clutched against her chest, it hit me. Our dynamic had shifted.

She'd asked me for help. She'd let me touch her. And she'd opened up.

She'd trusted me. And despite how little I knew about her, I trusted her too.

Chapter 16

CELINE

This neighborhood had to be the number one trick-or-treat destination in this town.

The street was lined with impeccably maintained homes, each with a large, shiny SUV in the driveway.

And the party was impossible to miss.

The moment I turned onto the road, the pirate flags strung between the trees and the black and white sails fluttering cheerfully were visible. A hand-painted sign on the mailbox read *Ahoy! Jacob's 7th Birthday*, with an arrow pointing to the backyard.

The house was enormous, with white siding and a wraparound porch. Like all the homes around it, the plump shrubs and flowering bushes in the yard were perfectly manicured. It was the kind of house that was built for big family Christmases and tearful graduation photos.

The backyard was huge and had been transformed into a full-blown pirate fantasy. Cardboard ships, rope nets, kiddie pools, and a bounce house.

As we approached, a lump formed in my throat.

Julian tugged my hand. "Look!" He pointed, practically vibrating with excitement. "This is the coolest."

"I see it, buddy," I croaked.

Kids ran wild in costumes, dressed as tiny pirates with foam swords and eye patches. Vests and tricorner hats. One kid had a full captain's coat that looked expensive.

Julian was wearing jeans and a sweatshirt. Despite the details on the invitation suggesting guests dress in pirate theme, our dress-up box was in storage, and I wasn't in a position to buy a costume.

The familiar creeping nausea hit me instantly, accompanied by the quiet voice that was so good at reminding me that I should have done more. That I wasn't enough. I should have planned better, found a costume, hired a sitter. Figured out a way to be two people at once.

A cheerful woman in a pirate hat waved us over. "You must be Julian." Assuming she was Jacob's mom, I strode toward her. She was a smiling, bubbly blond woman, her demeanor kind and effortless, like she'd been dressed by tiny birds this morning.

"Yes," I said quickly, sticking out my hand. "I'm Celine."

"Sara."

"And, um, I'm so sorry." Heart in my throat, I gestured to the girls behind me. "I had to bring my two big kids. Single mom." The words tumbled out of my mouth before I could stop them. As always, I was offering an apology no one had asked for.

"Of course," Sara said, her smile only growing. "Join the party, girls. We've got plenty of pizza, and if you're up for a challenge, I could use help keeping these kids in line during the scavenger hunt."

Maggie lit up. Ellie, on the other hand, only nodded, her hands stuffed into the front pocket of her hoodie, scanning the yard for the best escape route.

Jacob, a boy I'd met a few times at school, ran over, grinning as widely as his mother had been. "Julian!"

Julian beamed, looking happier than I'd ever seen him.

And relief hit me. This was why we were here. Because my baby deserved friends. Deserved belonging and birthday parties.

He peeked up at me, seeking permission, and when I nodded, he took off after his friend, an eager golden retriever hot on their heels. I clutched the bag that contained Julian's headphones and snacks, since he was unlikely to eat novel food at a party, mentally psyching myself up.

Parents, mostly couples and most I'd seen in the carpool line yet had never met, were clustered in small groups near the picnic tables, coffee cups in hand, laughing and chatting. As a few glanced over, smiling and waving, a kernel of anticipation joined the unease that wouldn't die down completely.

"We're fine, Mom." Ellie leaned in, her arm brushing mine. With a concerned look on her face, she pried the gift bag out of my hand and took it to the folding table already overflowing with presents.

My chest was still tight, but I soldiered on. Julian was on cloud nine, the girls were doing okay. And no one here had even given me an unkind look.

Yet it still felt like I was standing outside the circle. Realizing these people were living lives I no longer had.

Or maybe never had in the first place, which was an even more depressing thought.

Exhaling, I pushed the negativity away. Then I forced a smile, straightened my shoulders, and followed Julian into the chaos. I would make this the best possible experience for him.

Because that's all I could do. Show up.

Sara and her husband Will sure knew how to throw a great party. They'd set up craft stations, a pirate-themed ice cream bar, and a scavenger hunt that had probably taken weeks to plan. Despite my reservations, I found myself having a nice time pretty quickly. I met several of the parents, chatted about school, and learned way more than I'd ever want to know about youth sports in this town.

While the kids sat at a long table for cake and juice boxes, Julian joined them. He may have been eating the sliced cucumbers I'd packed instead of cake, but this was still a major milestone, and no one even mentioned the choice in snack.

Both girls had jumped in to help distribute cake and refill drinks, and Maggie had guided the kids at the treasure-chest decorating station with enthusiasm and kindness.

Every time I sought them out, my eyes would heat. I was proud of them and the love they had for their little brother.

"We're gonna win this year," a little voice said.

"Nope," Jacob responded. "Me and my dad are. We've got a plan. I'm finally big enough to canoe with him, so we're gonna win."

He beamed at his father, who gave him a thumbs-up.

Julian's lips turned down in confusion.

"Are you talking about the pumpkin race?" a little girl across from him asked.

"Yeah. You're supposed to do it with your dad," Jacob said.

Julian's face fell, and not far behind him, Ellie shot me a look.

Sara leaned in, probably sensing my confusion. "The Harvest Festival is in two weeks."

That I knew. Josh and I were still finishing the hayride plan.

"The big event is a canoe race," she added. "But the canoes have to be built out of a giant pumpkin or gourd."

"Oh." I pressed my lips together. That was so fucking Maplewood.

"It's a big to-do every year. Will always goes way over-board, and this year Jacob is going to paddle with him. It will be so cute."

I nodded, keeping my face neutral, my focus fixed on Julian.

With a look of distress, he glanced at one kid after another as they talked about the boats they were building.

On our way home, I ran through scenarios that might allow me to acquire a giant pumpkin, make it seaworthy, and train my scrawny arms to paddle fast enough to win that race for him. None of them were rational. But at moments like these, all I wanted was to make my kids happy. Be two parents at once so they never had to feel like they were missing anything.

As I lay in bed next to Julian that night, stroking his hair after we reread his favorite book, *The Day The Crayons Quit* three times, he looked up at me, his little face drawn.

"Mama," he said softly.

My eyelids were heavy, but I still needed to move the laundry from the washer to the dryer and run the dishwasher before I could close them.

"I wish I had a dad."

The words were a gut punch. I'd known they were coming, but that didn't make it hurt any less.

"Not my dad," he whispered, fiddling with the collar of my T-shirt, his attention fixed there. "I don't miss him."

I opened my mouth, then snapped it shut again, deciding to let him say whatever he needed to say.

"I'm sposed to." He curled up against my chest. "But I don't miss him. He was mean and scared me, and I like it here without him."

Gently rubbing his back, I kissed his forehead, my heart cracking. "That's okay, buddy. You can feel however you want. Your dad made some bad choices. And you don't have to miss someone who hurt you and let you down."

He pursed his lips, thoughtful, then added, "But I want a real dad. Like Jacob has."

"They seem like a very nice family," I said diplomatically, even as my eyes welled.

Though it only took five seconds to lose composure, the tears falling freely. God, I wasn't supposed to do this in front of my kids.

Julian hugged me tight. I held him just as firmly as footsteps sounded down the hall.

Then both girls were jumping into the bed next Julian.

"Mama's sad," he said.

Two more sets of arms surrounded me.

"Mom, you're amazing," Maggie said.

I inhaled, trying to compose myself, not willing to drag my kids into my shame spiral.

Ellie hummed. "And we can be both sad that Dad turned out to be terrible and also really happy that we have each other."

"Yeah," Maggie added. "And we can be happy that because he sucked, we get to live in a cool house in a cool town."

"On a farm!" Julian added.

Warmth bloomed inside me at their positivity.

"You taught us that we can feel multiple feelings at once. Don't forget that," Ellie said, wise beyond her years. "And our family may look different, but we're super awesome."

I hugged them all, my little hive, and took a few deep breaths. A strange mix of pride, grief, and uncertainty mingled inside me. Things were looking up.

Even so, forward progress was never linear, and my kids deserved to grieve their dad.

I'd done the right thing.

Now I had to keep going. Even when my heart was breaking for all they'd lost.

Chapter 17

JOSH

By the third house, Celine's façade cracked a little. She still knocked confidently, with her trusty clipboard tucked under her arm and her shoulders squared. But she couldn't quite hide her nerves.

She'd take a step back after knocking, then she'd angle herself so she could see past the person who opened the door. And she always kept her hands busy and her head on a swivel.

I should have been on the farm, working. Instead I was door knocking with Celine, finalizing decoration plans for the hayride route.

Each time I recognized another sign of her unease, I felt a little more protective of her. Doing this had forced her to push through some serious discomfort, and I couldn't help but be impressed.

So here I was, following her lead, though being sure I introduced her to each person we met, all of them people I'd known my entire life.

Mrs. Glover met us at the door with a wide smile. "Are you here to ask me to decorate? I've been hoping you would," she said with a grin. "Do you want a cup of tea?"

"The house looks great," I said, diverting the woman's attention away from Celine.

Mr. Glover appeared behind her, his movements slow, his cane in hand. "We can never thank you enough for helping us, son," he said. "Truly, if you need anything, all you have to do is ask."

Lips tugging down, Celine looked from the elderly couple to me.

"We had a chimney fire early this spring," Mrs. Glover said. "And Joshua insisted we stay at the cottage on his farm."

"Free of charge," Mr. Glover added. "It's quite a fancy house."

My face heated, but I was too off-kilter to come up with a way to change the subject.

Celine smiled, connecting the dots.

"At least take some banana bread," Mrs. Glover said. "I baked a dozen loaves this morning for my bridge group tonight. Please come in for a moment."

"And I'm ready to decorate." Mr. Glover shuffled back, his feet barely lifting off the floor as he moved. "I've got a tall ladder."

I cringed. He had no business getting on a ladder. Not at his age. So I made a mental note to come over and decorate for him.

We relented easily, joining the Glovers for a cup of tea and banana bread while Mrs. Glover *ooh*ed over photos of

Celine's kids. Then she sent Mr. Glover to the basement to pull out their scarecrows and lanterns.

By the time we returned to the sidewalk, Celine was smiling. "Is everyone in this town like that?"

"Nope." Lips twitching, I led her to Dr. Peters's house next door. The man—who had been practicing since well before he delivered me and all my siblings—answered the door in his white coat with a stethoscope around his neck.

"No clowns this year," he groused before either of us could speak.

"The theme is Cozy Harvest Haunt," Celine explained. "Nothing scary. Just autumnal vibes with spooky fun."

Doc crossed his arms, humming. "Okay. But the clown last year gave me nightmares."

"It was a mime," I corrected.

"Exactly. Everyone knows they're just silent clowns," he mumbled.

We got Doc to agree to decorating with pumpkins and ghosts and moved on, hitting most of the houses on the town green, leaving fliers and chatting with the folks who were home. Unsurprisingly, the majority of Maplewood citizens were excited about getting into the festival spirit. We needed a win after the challenges of the last year.

And house by house, as Celine made notes on her clipboard, her posture softened a little. She grew more confident too, perfecting her elevator pitch for the Cozy Harvest Haunt theme.

"Lanterns over jump scares. Think hay bales and ghosts instead of gore," she explained to the Whittakers. "The Millers are recreating the Lover's Leap Falls stories with skeletons dressed in replica Revolutionary War uniforms."

People listened.

Because she was good at this.

"Can we do autumn-themed vampires?" Nora Hatch asked. "Like they wear cozy sweaters and drink maple blood lattes?"

After agreeing, we moved on.

By the end of our route, the page attached to the pink clipboard was full of notes. Most everyone we came across committed, and many had lots of fun ideas. Including a four-foot-tall paper mâché raven that sounded like a bad idea but wasn't my problem.

In front of my sister's coffee shop, where Celine had parked her minivan, we stopped. She leaned against the hood, staring off into space for a moment, some of her hair having escaped her ponytail and curling around her neck. Her dangly earrings had drawn my attention to the curve of her neck at least a hundred times today, mesmerizing me. She was precious and delicate, despite her strength and fierce demeanor.

"You okay?"

She nodded, but hesitation flashed in her eyes.

"Tell me," I said softly.

"I've got to pick up my kids soon," she muttered. "They're at the after-school program today. Julian has never been able to do that kind of thing before, but they play gaga ball for hours, and he begged me. So—"

"Celine," I said softly, cutting off her spiraling.

"Sorry." She turned away, facing the van. "I'm just in a weird place emotionally."

I thought about walking away, giving her space. But a tiny voice inside me was saying "show up." So I did.

"I can listen." I rounded the front of the vehicle and opened the passenger door. "I probably can't help or fix anything. But I can listen."

She opened her own door, frowning at me. "I don't want to bother you."

"I'm your friend," I said firmly.

Her expression only darkened further at my choice of words. But it was true. Despite my initial reservations about her, I liked her. I cared about her. Sure, occasionally those thoughts went a little beyond friendly, but I wasn't going to say that part out loud.

I climbed in and shifted, facing her.

Lips pursed, she surveyed me, then the driver's seat before she finally slid into it.

Instead of starting the car, she put both hands on the steering wheel and stared straight ahead, pulling in a deep breath. "We went to a birthday party last weekend. Julian had so much fun. And he finally has friends. There were days when I didn't think that was possible."

Hands in my lap, I stayed silent, letting her work it all out.

"But the other families..."

My fists clenched instinctively. Had they been unkind to her?

"They were all so kind and welcoming," she explained, unknowingly allaying my fear. "Loving and supportive. Perfect, really. We were surrounded by families with two parents and bounce house birthday parties and big yards. We'd stepped into the kind of tranquil childhood my kids deserve but that I can't provide." Head lowered, she traced a seam on her steering wheel. "My ex-husband is in jail," she admitted.

I schooled my features. I had so many questions, but it was none of my business.

"I put him there."

Eyes closing, I mentally pumped my fist. Fuck yeah, she did. I didn't know why or how, but I was proud of this strong woman anyway.

Licking my lips, I reined myself in. "You're very brave."

She looked at me, tears running down her face. "Thank you. But brave doesn't give my kids a dad. And it doesn't erase the abuse they witnessed."

That admission was like a knife to the heart.

Abuse.

The word I'd assumed but had never outright heard from her lips.

A red curtain shrouded my vision and anger coursed through my veins. Why the hell was this man still alive?

But as a sob escaped her, I came back to my senses. My feelings were irrelevant.

"The kids and their dads," she hiccuped.

I opened the console and dug out a small stack of napkins.

"At the party." She blew her nose loudly.

"Celine?" I said softly. "Can I give you a hug? Would that help?" I didn't dare move a muscle. I didn't want to make her uncomfortable.

She nodded, blinking at me. "You don't mind?"

"Not at all." I leaned over, the console digging into my ribs, and embraced her.

While she buried her head in my chest, softly crying, I closed my eyes and focused on giving her as much comfort as I could. Trying like hell to ignore just how good she felt in my arms. How she smelled and how soft her hair was.

"He was so sad about the pumpkins," she said, her voice muffled.

"What pumpkins?"

She pulled back and blew her nose again. "At the party." She ducked, tears once again welling. "Some of the kids were talking about making pumpkin boats with their dads. Some special tradition. And he was so sad. So left out."

Frowning, I replayed her words. "The gourd race? At the Harvest Festival?"

"I think so."

I sighed. "It's not just for dads."

"I know. I found a blurb about it on the town web page. Then I went on Facebook and watched videos of previous years."

It was an honored part of the Harvest Festival. Townsfolk hollowed out massive pumpkins and gourds and built wacky boats, then they raced down part of the river. Many of the participants teamed up and wore costumes and did all sorts of fun stuff.

I'd done it many times with my dad, and the memories I had of building the boats were some of my best. For a good week, we'd design our watercraft, then mess around with power tools after dinner. I missed him every day, but moments like this reminded me of how lucky I was. What a gift loving parents could be and how not everyone was as fortunate as I was.

"It's stuff like this that makes me feel like I'm failing them." Sadness radiated from her. "That they will suffer forever because I was an idiot and married their shithead father."

"Hey." I resisted the urge to grasp her wrist for emphasis. "I'm going to give you another hug just to shut you up, okay?" I wrap my arms around her. "Do not speak like that. I don't doubt he's a piece of shit, and someday, if you find you trust me enough, I'll be here if you want to tell me about him. But for now, know one thing: Your children are amazing. And I say that with authority. They are smart and kind and curious."

"You actually give amazing hugs. You're like a big, strong teddy bear," she said.

I smiled, though inwardly I was cringing. God, was there anything less sexy than a teddy bear? Not that I should even be thinking in those terms.

Sweeping that thought aside, I pulled her in for another hug an held her until her body relaxed.

And I made a plan.

When Wayne and I approached the front door later that night, my shoulders were tense and I was second-guessing myself. Was I overstepping? Was this inappropriate?

Maybe, but I'd try anyway, because there was a chance this would do some good.

A few seconds after I knocked, Ellie opened the door and made a beeline for Wayne who licked her face in greeting.

Celine immediately came to the door, always on alert, but when she saw me, her face softened.

The memory of holding her today hit me hard, and my

neck heated. It had felt right. Like I was supposed to be doing it.

"I was wondering if I could talk to Julian," I said.

Her eyebrows shot up. "Sure."

She gestured for me to come inside. In the kitchen, Maggie, who was hunched over her math homework, gave me a big smile.

Julian sat next to her with his headphones on, building a Lego structure.

"Bud." Celine squeezed his shoulder.

He looked up, and when his attention drifted to me, he took off his headphones.

"Hey, Julian," I said, pulling out a chair. "I was wondering if you could help me with something."

In response, his eyes widened.

"I don't know if you heard, but at the Harvest Festival coming up. There's this race."

"The pumpkin race?" he blurted.

"Yes. It's technically any gourd, but yes. See, my dad and I always competed in it when I was a kid. I miss doing it now that I'm an adult, so I was thinking I should get back into it."

"It sounds so fun. Jacob is doing it with his dad," he said, but then his shoulders slumped. "But I can't because my dad's in jail."

"Julian," Ellie screeched, her face blanching.

"*Stop*," Maggie told her. "It's the truth. Who cares if Josh knows?"

Ellie crossed her arms, huffing in answer.

"And while I could do it alone," I said. "It's not as much fun without a partner. And I don't have any kids of my own."

Julian's eyes sparkled with hope, the simple expression making my chest ache.

"So I was thinking, do you want to do it with me? Be my race buddy?"

He jumped out of his chair, knocking the Lego creation to the ground. "Mama. Mama." He pulled on the hem of Celine's shirt. "Can I?"

She was peering down at him, her eyes glassy.

"It's a lot of work," I explained. "But if you're up to it and your mom says okay, I brought paper so we could start drawing out our ideas."

He jumped up and down, his auburn hair flopping.

"Okay," Celine said softly, her eyes now locked on mine. "You can do the race."

Chaos erupted, all three kids cheering and throwing out ideas. So we all sat at the table, brainstorming. Maggie thought we should make our gourd look like a horse, while Julian obsessed about finding a big enough pumpkin.

"My buddy has a farm about an hour from here," I said. "He grows the really big ones. Maybe we could take a ride up there this weekend and pick one out. Then this week, we'll hollow it out, design the boat, and make sure it floats."

All three kids looked at Celine.

"Sure." She shrugged. "But only if you all behave. Your beds need to be made every day, and the trash needs to go out before it's overflowing. And"—she zeroed in on Ellie—"you've got to finish your algebra homework."

With a scoff, her oldest daughter went back to her binder on the couch, clearly motivated now.

We spent an hour planning, and Julian even built a

model out of Legos, but when Celine told him it was time for bed, Wayne and I headed out.

I'd just hit the bottom step when Celine stopped me.

"Thank you," she said.

I dipped my chin. "You're welcome."

"Not just for the race. For all of it." She wrung her hands, her head bowed. "Today was weird and sad but also somehow good. And just—thank you."

"You did good. You're *doing* good. Please don't doubt yourself."

She looked up, and when her eyes met mine, a flame ignited in my chest. I wanted to close the gap between us and pull her into my arms again. Give her the comfort she needed. Be quiet and strong for as long as she needed me.

"I didn't think people would just... say yes," she whispered.

"We haven't won America's Most Charming Small Town every year for the past two decades by not being good to one another." I paused, holding her gaze. "People here show up when you ask."

We weren't just talking about festival decorations and we both knew it.

"I see it." She sighed. "Even though I struggle to under-stand it."

My heart clenched. I'd grown up here. I didn't know another way of life, yet she couldn't understand the simple kindness the people of Maplewood always led with? Clearly Celine hadn't had the kind of support system she deserved. But the joke was on her, because this tiny town had fully adopted her and her kids.

"You need to get used to it. You're one of us now."

The doubt on her face faded as she studied me, searching for the lie and coming up empty, and she broke into her true smile.

It only made me more determined to help. Because our little project wasn't about hayrides or decorations. It was about showing her that not every knock ended badly. And sometimes, when a person asked for something, the door actually opened.

Chapter 18

CELINE

It was barely seven, yet we were up and dressed and ready for a pumpkin acquisition road trip. The morning had gone far smoother than any this week. The kids had been up since six, completely overwhelmed with excitement about securing a giant gourd.

Julian had been so excited last night that he'd struggled to sleep. All week he'd talked about nothing else. It filled me with warmth seeing him lit up like this, excited and using his special talents to figure out a problem.

And while I doubted my daughters had much interest in the buoyancy of pumpkins, they had thrown themselves into the process, encouraging him and helping him draw pictures. I'd never been more proud.

When Josh pulled up and hopped out of his truck, his hair was still damp from his shower. I nearly staggered back as he sauntered closer. Damn, he was good-looking. All jeans and work boots and flannel, a gruff smile beneath that beard. He'd been like a little kid the other night, brainstorming with

Julian. Initially, I assumed he'd offered to do this to be kind to Julian, but after the way his eyes lit up any time they talked about the project, I was beginning to wonder if it was Julian doing him the favor.

"I've got to get Julian's booster." I turned toward the van, sticking a hand in my purse and rummaging for my keys.

"No need. I got one."

Lips pursed, I turned back to him.

"Here." He opened the back door, and sure enough there was a booster.

I strode to the door and examined it. "That's the same."

"Yes. The same one you have. I saw it while I was at Costmart and grabbed it, figured it would be easier."

Blinking, I turned to him, my brain not quite understanding.

"Got snacks too."

Julian wandered to Josh's side. "Is Wayne coming?"

Ducking, he shook his head. "He's keeping Jasper and Vincent company while we're gone. Since we need my truck to haul the pumpkin back, there isn't enough room."

Julian's whole body sagged with disappointment.

"But he'll help us build our boat. Don't worry."

The truck was equipped with snacks, water, blankets, and a few extra hoodies. Well-worn hoodies that looked so cozy I wished I could slip one on now, then take it home with me.

"Why do you have so many snacks?" Maggie asked.

"Cause kids eat a lot," he replied, eyeing her in the mirror.

Ellie shrugged. "Accurate."

We hadn't even driven outside town limits before they were digging in.

"Mom," Julian shouted far louder than necessary. "He has cucumbers. Cut in circles, not sticks."

I turned in my seat, and sure enough, Josh had procured cucumbers, Julian's favorite, and had cut them with precision.

"He got my crackers too."

Heart thudding, I eyed the man beside me. "How did you know which foods were Julian's safe foods?"

His focus was on the road, his fingers tapping the steering wheel. "I noticed and took a photo of the box with my phone. Didn't want to mess it up for him."

I ducked, lacing my fingers in my lap, hiding my shock, then pulled my sunglasses down over my eyes, determined to enjoy the ride.

"What should we listen to?" Josh asked, interrupting the girls, who were fighting over granola he'd brought from Jenn's shop.

"K-Pop!" Maggie shouted.

"No, put on Lake Paige!" Ellie countered.

"Queen," Julian declared, crossing his arms in his booster.

"Okay. I can get behind Queen," Josh said, handing me his phone. "Will you pull up Spotify?"

His phone was unlocked and protected in a black case. One of those super tough unbreakable kinds. And unlike mine, the screen had no cracks.

"You each get a turn to choose songs," I said, opening Spotify. "But I also vote Queen first."

Julian giggled. "Mama, put on 'Don't Stop Me Now.'"

The kid was only six, but he had an encyclopedia worth of knowledge of Freddie Mercury's discography in his brain, and I wasn't mad about it.

We sang along, mixing in some K-pop and other hits, the kids being silly and loud.

Every couple of minutes, I'd steal a look at Josh, checking for signs of discomfort or anger. But his expression remained easy, and he didn't even flinch or say a word when Julian kicked the back of his seat to the beat of "We are the Champions."

Once we'd exited the highway, we turned onto a dusty country road and crested a large hill. On the other side sat a massive farm surrounded by mountains and painted with the foliage. The view was stunning.

Josh pulled up next to a big red barn with peeling paint, and a woman wearing denim overalls strode out.

The kids scrambled out of the truck, but I couldn't help but be struck by the woman walking toward us.

She was tall, easily six foot. She was willowy, with her waist-length blond hair in a braid. She looked like she was here for a farm core photoshoot.

"Josh." She broke into a jog, running into his arms, giving him a huge hug.

The warmth and familiarity in her smile made my stomach clench.

Were they lovers? It made sense. They probably had a lot in common.

Stepping back, she patted his bearded cheeks. "It's been way too long."

He turned and waved us over.

"Annie, this is Celine, Maggie, Ellie, and Julian."

I had to crane my neck to meet her eye as I shook her hand. She was so pretty and wholesome, with skin tanned from outdoor work.

"Excuse me," Julian said, looking away. "We would like your largest pumpkin, please."

Annie smiled and kneeled down to his level.

Jeez, did she have to be good with kids too?

"I have some really big ones. How big do you want?"

Julian hummed, still avoiding eye contact. "The race rules say that in order for Josh and me to do it together, it has to be at least 1000 pounds."

She tapped her chin and stood. "Then I've got some ideas. Did you bring a forklift?"

Josh shook his head.

She waved easily. "No worries. I've got you covered."

We hiked around Annie's farm, which was just as charming as it had looked from afar.

When Maggie got sidetracked by the herd of goats, Annie sidled up next to her. "I'll send you home with some of our cheese."

How was it possible to be simultaneously annoyed by the unnervingly friendly woman and impressed by the respect and kindness she was showing my kids?

The field she led us to was full of what looked like orange and green boulders but were actually gourds. I'd never seen anything like it.

The kids went wild, running around and yelling, assessing and climbing on top of them. They ranged in size, but some were the size of small cars.

"These," Annie said, gesturing to a few of the biggest

pumpkins I'd ever seen, "are Atlantic Giants. They're big and have thick walls. They're great for racing on a river."

Julian's eyes lit up.

"Remember," Josh cautioned, "shape doesn't matter. We're looking for size and character."

One by one, the kids considered them.

"This one looks like a giant potato," Ellie observed of the eighth or ninth they'd inspected.

Josh stroked his beard. "Potatoes have great buoyancy."

Eyes rolling, she scoffed. "You made that up."

"Oh, I absolutely did."

She dissolved into a fit of giggles while Maggie used her arms to measure the width of one just ahead.

Julian was careful and serious, assessing every one. "This one looks brave." He declared after at least three rounds of inspections.

Josh wandered up to him, standing close but not touching. Always respectful of Julian's boundaries.

"I think you're right," Josh said, his tone deferential. "You've got a great eye."

"It's wide," Julian observed, "but not too tall. I think we can win with this one."

Eyes flashing with what might have been affection, Josh slowly held out his fist.

Still examining the pumpkin, Julian reached out and bumped it.

Getting the gourd into the bed of the truck took twice as long as it took the kids to choose it.

When Annie rolled up with her forklift, I couldn't help but sigh. Of course this woman could confidently operate heavy machinery. Jesus. She probably knew the Karma Sutra and did particle physics in her spare time.

Once it was loaded in the bed of the truck, padded with moving blankets and straw bales, then secured with about a dozen rachet straps, we were ready to head back.

If the ride there was rowdy, it had nothing on the ride home.

"We can't hollow it out today," Josh told them halfway home. "I've got to get it out and up on a platform in the barn. If I put it on the ground, it will rot. I'm going to spray it with a sealant tonight, but we can start scooping it out tomorrow."

"How much will we scoop out?" Maggie asked.

"Not sure, but I'm bringing a dumpster over. You'd be shocked by how much we'll end up with."

"Do we get to use power tools?"

Smirking, Josh slid his arm across the console and gently brushed my arm.

I froze, keeping my gaze forward, not wanting to move but also a bit frightened by how much I enjoyed the contact.

Had I spent more than a normal amount of time thinking about last week's hug? Yes, I had.

I was hardly touch starved; I had three kids hanging off me most days, and Wayne was quite needy as well.

But being held like that? In his strong arms. I wasn't sure I'd ever felt so safe. So secure. It felt like, for once, someone else was carrying the load with me.

It only lasted for a moment, but the sensation was one I'd known a long time ago. One I hadn't felt since I was a kid and I'd wake up to my mom gently stroking my hair.

For a few moments, Josh had helped me feel like I could do this. Helped me believe that I'd be okay.

And as a result, I was barreling at top speed towards a full-blown crush on the man.

He was kind and decent, which shouldn't have been out of the ordinary but was novel in my experience. Each time I thought about him, I felt like a teenage girl. Even Ellie would be disgusted by me.

So I'd sit here and enjoy the feel of his forearm brushing against mine, and then I'd go back to reality and do all the stuff that had to be done. Because there was no room in my life for crushes. Though was it possible there was room for a kind friend? Someone who was good to my kids and cared enough to pack the right snacks? I'd never had one of those before, and more and more, I wanted to be his friend. To hear his jokes and listen to his stories and figure out what the hell the machines he used on the farm were for.

Crushes were silly. But friendship? That was the kind of relationship that I'd begun to think I could handle.

After pizza and a reunion with Wayne, we stood back and watched Josh operate his own forklift, which was strangely hot.

The kids crashed hard shortly after, but I was still buzzing. It had been a good day. Minimal disagreements and a new project. Plus Julian had done really well with the car ride and the pumpkin. He hadn't had one meltdown, and honestly, was more animated than I'd ever seen him.

I had to savor days like this. Reflect and wring out every good moment. Because there would be hard days, and when they came, I'd need these memories to keep myself going.

The best way to get rid of this kind of nervous energy was to work out, so I stepped into my sneakers and banged out three sets of pushups on the porch, followed by planks and lunges.

I was considering which workouts would exhaust me the quickest when I realized I hadn't gotten the mail today. Our mailbox was down at the end of the drive, about a quarter mile from our cottage, and I usually stopped when I drove into the farm after work or running errands, but we'd been in Josh's truck today and out of our routine.

Surveying the house where all three kids slept, I reassured myself that it was okay to jog there and back. I could see the cottage the whole way, though not as well as I could from the hill where I typically ran.

So I took off, jogging down the gravel drive, smiling and laughing to myself about how incredible and hilarious my kids had been today.

Julian's serious calculations, Maggie's decoration ideas, and Ellie's eye rolls. It had been a while since I'd seen them let loose and be themselves. If we stayed here, maybe it would happen more frequently. Maybe they'd eventually get comfortable and let their guard down.

I picked up the pace, and almost instantly, my lungs burned. I loved the sensation. It had been at least a decade since I'd run a race, but I'd recently started thinking about entering one. Having an event to train for was good motivation, and I'd like the kids to see me racing. I wanted to show them that a person could still set goals and do things even when they were, as Ellie constantly called me, elderly.

At the mailbox, I stopped, my breaths heaving in and out of my lungs, and pulled out a stack of what looked mostly like junk.

On the way back, I stuck to walking briskly as I sorted

through it. It was dark, but the moon was bright enough that if I squinted, I could make out the print on the envelopes. Fliers and ads, my car insurance bill, a catalog, and a lime green envelope.

The scrolly, loopy handwriting caught my attention, and I came to a quick stop. It wasn't printed. No, the words were in ink.

And it was addressed to me. At this address.

My chest tightened. No. It couldn't be.

Heart thudding, I opened the envelope.

Inside was a cheery greeting card with cartoon animals on the front. Written inside, in a scratchy scrawl I'd never forget, it read *Found You*.

Vision tunneling, I dropped all the mail to the ground.

Every part of my body shook with panic. Nausea rolled through me, and I dropped to my knees, vomiting on the side of the driveway. I stayed there, head down, palms pressed to the gravel, for several minutes.

My mind spiraled, and only when a dog barked in the distance did I come back to the moment.

"Wayne," a deep voice bellowed. "What are you doing?"

Wayne ran toward me, his paws hitting the driveway quickly and his tags gently clinking against his collar.

Then he was next to me, panting and whining.

I couldn't move my head to look at him. Couldn't lift a hand to pet him.

"Celine?" Another set of footsteps. "Are you okay? Should I call an ambulance?"

Josh appeared in front of me, wearing a pair of plaid pajama pants. He was shirtless and barefoot, but I barely registered his presence.

"Are you sick?"

I nodded.

Wayne spun in a circle, barking, then sat beside me like a sentry.

"Sorry," I croaked, finally forcing myself up onto my knees.

"Can I help you?" He held out a hand.

Shame washed over me, but I accepted the offer, and when I was standing, I breathed in deeply, trying to get my bearings.

"I can take you to the hospital."

I shook my head, swallowing against a fresh wave of nausea.

"I'm not sick. Just give me a second."

He gripped my elbow and stood silently while I attempted to compose myself.

"Breathe," I said out loud, forcing air into my lungs.

A warm hand landed on my back. "Is this okay?"

Eyes closed, I nodded.

"Do you need water?"

I shook my head. "Could you just walk with me back to the house?"

"Of course."

Slowly, Josh and Wayne accompanied me down the driveway, Josh holding the mail I'd dropped on the ground and Wayne looking up at me every couple of seconds.

Josh had threaded my arm through his, and I couldn't resist the temptation to lean against his warm, solid torso. If he was cold, he didn't show it, and he didn't seem to mind slow walking me toward my house in the middle of the night.

He was warm and steady and strong. And although I couldn't say it out loud, I was grateful he was there with me.

When we reached the house, I let go of his arm and walked away. It would have been polite to turn around and thank him or maybe give him an explanation, but I was too overwhelmed to speak.

But I couldn't do this to him. I couldn't burden this earnest, kind man with this ugliness. Not after today.

He'd look at my kids differently. He'd look at me differently.

And I couldn't live with that.

"Pushed myself too hard," I said as I stepped onto the porch. "Not as young as I used to be."

"I respect your privacy." He strode closer and squeezed my hand. "And when you're ready to tell me, I'll listen."

I nodded, trying to not look like a complete train wreck. I took the mail from him, then shuffled toward the door.

"If you need anything, call me."

Without responding, I closed the door and leaned against it. I took a deep breath, then another. How had he found us?

I poured a glass of water and sat on the couch, willing my heart rate to slow. Eventually, when the terror had dulled, I could focus again.

And what I focused on was memories. Memories of my kids laughing. Julian's wonder at the giant pumpkin. Singing along with the radio on our road trip. Morning snuggles before school. Stella and Callie and the lovely community we were building here.

And Josh. The gentleness hiding behind his giant masculine exterior. The care with which he treated me and the kids, the thoughtfulness, knowing almost instinctively what Julian needed from him, right down to the brand of crackers.

I was sick of this shit. Sick of Donny and all he'd put us through.

The fear I'd experienced when I opened that envelope had now been replaced by burning hot rage. I balled my hands into fists and closed my eyes.

He doesn't get to touch this life.

He doesn't get to ruin what I've worked so hard to build.

Rolling my shoulders, I got up, checked all the door locks, and headed upstairs. I lingered in doorways, watching each of my kids sleep for several minutes, and made myself a promise.

I was done hiding.

Donny would be in prison for another year. He had no power over me anymore.

He might have found me.

But the joke was on him, because I was no longer lost.

Chapter 19

♥

CELINE

I loved my sister.

Truly. Deeply.

But she was a drill sergeant in Lululemon and Louboutins.

She was the eldest daughter stereotype on steroids. The kind of woman who didn't so much arrive as deploy.

Within hours of stepping through my front door, she had done loads of laundry and was cooking freezer meals to leave for us. She even had Gus under the hood of my car. If I blinked wrong, she'd probably do my taxes and color my hair.

Her protective instincts knew no bounds. Or chill, for that matter.

"You look good." She stepped into my space, tucking a lock of hair behind my shoulder like she was checking for injuries.

"I am good." I batted her hand away and took a step back. Personal growth, apparently, looked like asserting my bodily autonomy with my sister.

She narrowed her eyes, assessing, like she wasn't totally convinced by my declaration.

My kids were running around with Simone, Chloe's three-year-old daughter, who was obsessed with her older cousins in that special way a tiny person can be. She had arrived in a tutu and work boots, a combination that was aggressively on brand for my niece. She was an absolute force of nature, much like her mom.

Who was currently assessing me a little too closely. They'd arrived yesterday, gladly accepting our invitation to join us for the Harvest Festival, and had checked into the Thistle Inn and Spa.

But I suspected that this visit would also include an inspection.

"You sleeping?" she asked.

"Yes."

"Eating enough?"

Not really. But I wouldn't admit that out loud. "Yes."

"Locking the doors?"

I crossed my arms. "Did you create a spreadsheet to keep yourself organized for this interrogation, officer?"

"Don't get cute." Her lips quirked.

The situation with Donny had brought us closer, but in many ways, I still felt like the little sister, trailing behind her as she collected straight A's, trophies, promotions, and every gold star in existence.

She was a CEO, for God's sake, and she had a devoted husband who followed her around like she was the sun. She'd gotten pregnant unexpectedly in her forties and had delivered a healthy, joyful child like it was no big deal. She'd always been a goddamn superhero.

And I was just ... me.

Though as I surveyed her, our kids playing around us and the whole town buzzing all week about the festival I was helping organize, it hit me.

I wasn't waiting for her approval anymore.

I was good. Not perfect, but doing pretty damn good.

"I'm okay," I said, holding her eye. "I'm not falling apart. The kids are thriving. I love my job. Life here is pretty good."

She studied me for a long moment and sighed. "That's inconvenient. Because I miss you guys so much. I want to kidnap you all and take you home to Maine."

Warmth unfurled in my chest. "I miss you too. But I'm good here. I promise."

Once Chloe had folded another load of laundry and started the dishwasher, we headed into town so we could show her and Gus around. The festival preparations were underway, the town green full of tents, stages, straw bales, and lots of electrical wiring. I had no idea how this would all transform in twenty-four hours, but I knew better than to doubt Maplewood.

Jasper gave me a big smile when we walked past where he and a few guys dressed in blue with MFD printed on their shirts were hanging lanterns. Several people greeted us as we meandered, including a handful of kids who waved to Julian.

"Did you run for mayor and not tell me?" Chloe asked.

I huffed. "We live here. And I teach at the school."

"And people are super nice," Maggie added.

When we reached Pie in the Sky, Gus held the door open, and the kids scrambled in, headed for the large booth in the corner.

The pizzeria smelled like yeast and garlic, the vibe warm and comforting. The twinkle lights and red checkered table-cloths made the place cozy, and the old leather booths and mismatched tables that had seen years of spilled sodas, homework assignments, and long conversations that outlasted the food told a story of just how treasured this place was. It wasn't fancy, but it wasn't trying to be. The food was amazing, and Tony, the owner, was one of the kindest folks in town.

Restaurants weren't part of our normal routine due to cost and Julian's eating challenges, but even he loved Tony and his pizza, or the crust, at least.

Tony and Marco waved from the open kitchen while Ellie procured a stack of menus and Maggie snagged a pitcher of water.

After much debate about garlic knots and garlic bread, we went with the knots, and the kids spent the next several minutes talking over one another about school, the farm, and the upcoming festival.

"Aunt Chloe, we hollowed out a giant pumpkin," Maggie announced, pouring water for everyone.

Ellie shook her head. "No, not just giant. Like, a massive pumpkin. The size of a hot tub."

Julian pushed up to his knees in the booth, holding his arms out as far as he could. "Even bigger than this. It was wet inside. And stringy."

"Kind of smelled dirty, but also sweet," Maggie said.

"I'd say it smelled like a compost heap," Ellie added.

"Josh gave us shovels." Maggie dropped into her seat, her chin lifted. "Real ones, not kiddie ones."

Brows jumping, Chloe looked at me.

I shrugged, helpless and amused. "They were supervised."

"We dug and dug, and we had a big dumpster for all the pumpkin guts."

Julian, who was practically vibrating with excitement now, knocked over a saltshaker. "But we had to be careful. The walls have to be thick. For secular integrity."

"Structural integrity," Ellie corrected.

He shook his head a little wildly. "It's important to be integrated."

Angling forward, Chloe giggled. "Why?"

Julian frowned, looking at his aunt like that was a silly question. "For racing down the river."

"Time out." Gus, dressed in flannel like always, shifted Simone on his lap and put his elbow on the table. "You're racing a pumpkin in a river?"

Hands splayed on the table, Julian beamed. "I'm the captain."

"He picked the pumpkin too," Ellie said, looking at him with genuine affection that made my heart expand.

"I had to find a brave one," Julian explained. "It had scars. And I could feel it."

"That's on brand," Gus muttered.

"We used power tools," Ellie added casually. "And I got to hold the hack saw."

Brow furrowed, Chloe looked at me.

"Josh used them," Maggie corrected. "Ellie got to hold if for like a second while Josh showed her how he was going to cut the top off. She's exaggerating."

Ellie stuck her tongue out at her sister.

"We were safe," Julian said. "Josh loves safety rules."

Lips pursed, Chloe sat straighter. "Josh? The landlord?"

I ignored her raised eyebrows and played with the striped straw in my water glass. "He's... thorough."

"And funny," Maggie gushed. "But not like ha-ha joke funny. More..."

"Dry funny," Ellie chimed in.

"He pretends not to smile," Julian said. "But he does. And he's listens really good."

"His dog Wayne is the best," Ellie added.

"And he packs great snacks."

"He bought my special crackers for our trip."

As they continued blurting out praises, my face flushed.

"He remembers that I don't like loud noises," Julian said. "He warns me before anything noisy happens."

My chest tightened with an unfamiliar ache. It was strange the way they chatted about Josh so casually. Like he was just this safe, dependable presence in their lives. Yet at the same time, it felt natural.

Chloe caught my eye, and my face flamed again. Thankfully, Marco and Tony stepped out from the back, bringing our meals and rescuing me from my sister's scrutiny.

It took several minutes to get the kids situated with slices and refill drinks, so by the time I set a slice of pizza on my plate, I was confident that I was off the hook.

I was wrong.

"I didn't realize you were such good friends with your landlord," Chloe said, picking up a piece of her fig and prosciutto pizza.

I chomped down on a too-big bite to delay my response and shrugged. "He and I are planning the hayrides for the festival. That's all."

"Sure." Ellie snorted, studying her pepperoni.

"And he and I are going to win the pumpkin race," Julian declared.

"With the giant pumpkin you hollowed out?" Gus asked.

Julian nodded. "The kids here race with their dads. But since my dad's in jail and Josh's dad died, we're doing it together."

"He's super cool," Maggie said. "I'm trying to talk him into getting goats for the farm. I think I'll wear him down soon."

Chloe's lips twitched as she took us in. It wasn't just the new town, the new school, or the farm. My kids were talking and laughing in a way they hadn't in years, in a way that showed that we were no longer just surviving.

Maybe, just maybe, we'd worked our way out of survival mode and into living. Into thriving and succeeding.

On the walk back to the parking lot, the kids, who'd inhaled too much pizza, groaned, their feet dragging, and I prayed to every known deity that they'd go to bed early tonight so I could crash.

The town green was buzzing now, lanterns glowing and townsfolk darting around with extension cords, full of last-minute chaos. Pride filled me as I watched, because Josh and I weren't rushing around, stressing like the rest of the town. We had gotten ahead of it. The tractors and trailers were all decorated and ready. The route was cleared and, miracle of miracles, all the places along the way were ready. Despite

Josh's insistence otherwise, I assumed he had something to do with how efficiently all the decorations went up.

Even Mr. Fletcher had put out a skeleton kicked back in a recliner with a remote in hand. And for him, I was told, that constituted festive enthusiasm.

"Josh," Julian shouted, taking off down the sidewalk at a high speed.

My heart leaped, and Ellie lunged for him. But Josh intercepted him easily, picking him up and swinging him around before setting him back on his feet.

He kneeled and leaned in close, murmuring something that made Julian giggle as we caught up.

"Maggie," he said next, "you were right about the chickens."

She crossed her arms and held her head high. "Told you."

"Ellie. How was the astronomy test?"

She gave him her patented bored tween stare. "Easy."

"Good thing you studied then."

If I'd told her that, she'd have rolled her eyes and argued, but for Josh, all she did was dip her chin.

He stood, wiping his hands on his work pants, and turned my way. When he noticed my sister and her husband, he froze.

"Oh, hi," he said, his attention drifting to me.

"This is my sister Chloe, my brother-in-law Gus, and my niece Simone," I said, finally remembering my manners.

Josh shook Gus's hand and waved at Simone, who was riding on her dad's shoulders, then turned to Chloe. "I've heard a lot about you. The scary one."

She glared at him, looking him up and down, then turned to me and nodded once. "I like him. Seems smart."

Wow. That was high praise from Chloe.

Her family headed back to the inn shortly after dinner, and I got the kids into bed. Tomorrow would be a long day.

I was exhausted. And happy.

I'd just finished brushing my teeth when my phone buzzed.

CHLOE: WE WILL BE DISCUSSING YOUR LANDLORD. VERY soon.

Celine: I have no idea what you mean.

Chloe: Don't be cute. We LeBlanc women have a type.

Celine: We do not.

Chloe: Really? So we haven't both gravitated toward bearded grumps built like linebackers?

I GIGGLED DESPITE MYSELF. OKAY, JOSH DID BEAR MORE than a passing resemblance to Gus. But Josh was younger and taller and objectively hotter. With lighter hair, a shorter beard, and a wardrobe that occasionally extended beyond flannel.

CHLOE: AND HE COULDN'T STOP STARING AT YOU.

Celine: I'm tired. Got to go to bed.

Chloe: Denial is not growth.

· · ·

I CLIMBED INTO BED AND PUT MY PHONE DOWN, STILL smiling.

My sister was relentless. I had no doubt she would wear me down.

But I wasn't ready to answer her questions about Josh.

Not yet.

Chapter 20

JOSH

The scents of cider, wood smoke, and kettle corn hit me before I even parked the truck a couple of hours ago. Now, lanterns swung gently and hay particles floated in the chilly air, kicked up consistently by the crowds of people. They were everywhere, playing games, enjoying the music on the town green, and eating all the delicious food.

Opal Lin had stopped by the hayride station earlier with a takeout container of butternut squash soup that may have actually changed my life. I had to promise her a special bottle of the late season Grade-D syrup from my personal stash, but I got a second bowl.

Year after year, I'd provided supplies for the maple festival, just like my dad did and his dad before him. But I hadn't actively participated in a town event since my mom died. I'd thought it was best to keep my distance, that being here would only make her loss more painful, but I was beginning to see the benefits of active participation.

Mainly being in the proximity of the smiling redhead who was bundled up and controlling the chaos with me.

Celine was in her element, energized and laughing while keeping everyone in line. She loaded the riders, checked wristbands, managed the kids, and chatted easily with parents.

We each had a radio, allowing us to communicate easily over the tractor engine.

Once she gave me the go-ahead, I pulled out with a fresh wagon full of shrieking kids and parents sipping hot cider spiked with maple whiskey.

"Tractor One," Celine said less than a minute later. "This group is heavy on tourists."

"Copy Tractor Command," I replied. "Any special instructions?"

"Don't scare them. Maybe attempt a smile?"

I huffed. "I don't scare people."

"Debatable. Do your best."

"Copy," I said, struggling to suppress a laugh. "Will attempt friendly."

"Don't injure yourself. We still need you to drive. Over."

The wagons were lit up with string lights, and Celine had created a family-friendly spooky soundtrack that played through a Bluetooth speaker as we made the twenty-five-minute loop around the town square and out toward the falls. Along the way, kids *oohed* and *aahed* at the decorations and the teens snapped selfies. Driving the tractor was an easy gig. The festival shut down most of the main roads, and Nolan had his officers set up barricades to keep any rogue vehicles from ending up on the route.

I'd have to wait for Gabe's report, but the festival seemed

busy, with tourists everywhere, wait times at all the restaurants, and vast crowds at the concert this afternoon. With any luck, this would be the economic boost the town had been looking for since Will's murder.

After unloading this set of riders, I spotted Celine and gave myself a moment to take her in. She wore layers to keep warm, and her navy blue knit hat made her eyes sparkle.

"Tractor One," she hollered like she was trying to get my attention.

She already had it, but if she didn't know that, then at least I was doing a semi decent job of hiding the way I couldn't stop watching her.

"Got you a present." She strode over and held up a cardboard cup. "Cider."

I reached out a gloved hand. "It's not spiked, is it? I've got to drive."

She shook her head. "Nope. Virgin cider for you Tractor One."

When I took it from her and our hands brushed, my body fizzled with the contact, regardless of the gloves. "Thank you, Tractor Command."

With a bright smile, she headed for the next group of riders, redirecting anxious kids and anticipating issues. She adjusted the blankets and pulled out the stepstool to help people into the wagon. She moved with purpose, threading through the chaos and managing the mayhem with calm and kindness.

She had to be one hell of a teacher.

"You missed your calling," I told her when she stepped away from the group.

She looked at me over her clipboard. "What? festival planning?"

I shook my head. "No. Command. Logistics. You're great at being in charge."

Her face flushed, a tell I was beginning to both recognize and enjoy. Quickly, she looked away, busying herself with wristbands.

"Josh," a voice called, snagging my attention.

Logan was waiting in line, beanie askew and his Carhartt jacket zipped all the way up to his chin suspiciously. His five-year-old niece stood next to him, arms crossed and unimpressed.

"Hey, Rosie."

In greeting, she said, "My uncle brought a raccoon."

More than one person nearby gasped and Logan glared at her.

"No wildlife on the hayride," I said.

He sighed, like he really thought he'd get away with it. Next to him, Rosie caught sight of Celine and waved frantically, making me wonder if she was in her class at school.

"Please tell me you didn't bring a raccoon," I said.

Logan slowly unzipped his jacket, and a tiny masked face poked out.

"Ew, gross," Celine said, suddenly beside us, her clipboard still at the ready. "Absolutely not. No. Get that thing out of here. It probably has rabies."

He gasped and covered the raccoon's ears, his brow furrowing. "How dare you. He can hear you, you know?"

"Miss LeBlanc," Rosie said primly, hands clasped. "This is my Uncle Logan. He always carries animals around. My mom says that's why he can't get a girlfriend."

With his head tipped back, my buddy groaned.

"Can we please just ride?" she pleaded. "We've been waiting forever."

Celine looked at me, indecision in her expression, likely fighting the instincts that came with being a teacher, the organizer of this activity, and just a plain old responsible adult.

With a shrug, I wandered to the tractor. I was cold and tired, and honestly, a raccoon on a hayride was fairly tame by Maplewood standards.

"Fine," Celine muttered. "But if he bites anyone, I'm calling animal control."

Logan beamed.

"It's okay," Rosie said solemnly. "Uncle Logan almost never bites."

As I climbed up into the tractor, a laugh burst out of me with so much force I nearly lost my footing and tumbled to the ground.

The night wound down a little after nine. Most of the families had gone home, so with any luck, we could call it a night. Getting the equipment home and put away would take hours.

"One more ride," Celine said, gesturing to a group waiting.

"I thought we closed at nine." I walked toward them, squinting. With the lights behind them, it was difficult to make out their faces.

I was about ten feet away when I realized who they were. The Maple Street Mafia. Bundled up and in high spirits, probably after hitting the maple whiskey.

They piled into the hayride like they owned it, Bitsy

claiming the bench directly behind me immediately. Olive Foster followed, giving me a saucy wink. Mavis came next, along with Gail, Lorna, and finally Marigold, with her walker, which was decorated with colorful fall foliage.

"Do you mind if I ride too?" Celine asked them. "Since we're done for the night?"

She sat near the front of the wagon with the ladies, near the small space heater. When the music started, Bitsy fussed, saying she couldn't keep up with the conversation, so Celine clicked it off.

"Now Celine, dear," the woman said as I pulled out onto Main Street. The tractor was loud, but I could make out most of her words. "We've all been talking, and we want to help you."

My spine went rigid. Favors from the Maple Street Mafia always came with strings.

"Help with what?" Celine asked, her tone friendly but guarded.

I glanced over my shoulder and caught her eye.

"Why, with your romantic prospects," Olive shrieked.

Okay, she had definitely been hitting the maple whiskey.

When her words registered, I missed the clutch. And the tractor lurched, stalling out.

Shit.

Everyone bounced.

"Joshua Lawrence," Bitsy hissed. "Do you mind?"

"Sorry," I said, my muscles locking up. "Big stick in the road."

There was no stick, but it was the best I could come up with.

I started the engine again and got back to my route.

"We thought we'd set you up with Tom Walters."

"No," Celine said firmly.

My jaw clenched.

"Why not?" Mavis prodded. "He's got a boat."

"I don't want a boat," Celine said.

I peeked back, noting the pink in her cheeks. God, their meddling was out of control. This was why I stayed away.

"He's emotionally available too," Olive said. "And has all his hair."

I hit the brake too hard, and we all jolted forward.

"Joshua," Bitsy barked. "I'm too old to be rattled like this."

"Bumpy road," I muttered.

"It's paved," Mavis groused.

"You okay up there, Tractor One?" Celine asked.

"Peachy, Tractor Command."

"Anyway," Bitsy went on. "Tom is divorced and he composts. Did we tell you that?"

I turned around in my seat and glared. "Hayrides are not for matchmaking."

A massive grin spread across Olive's wrinkled face. "Did you hear that, girls? Joshua, sweetheart, are you feeling territorial?"

As the women burst into a fit of giggles, I turned back, gripping the steering wheel until my knuckles were white.

"Just responsible," I said lamely. "For the tractor and the hayride."

"I am not interested," Celine said firmly.

Bitsy sniffed. "Well, if not Tom, there's always—"

"No," Celine and I said at the same time.

Silence.

Then the old ladies fell into laughter again.

"Please," Celine said, her tone pleading. "Stop match-making. I do not want to date anyone."

"Fine." Olive snorted. "But only because I worry if we don't stop this, Josh will drive us over the Falls."

"I will not," I snapped.

"Sure," Mavis said. "And thank you for confirming our suspicions."

She cackled, the sound making me wince, and the others joined in. Shit. I'd just made things so much worse.

I managed to dispatch the Mafia without too much more trouble and was getting the tractor onto its trailer when Celine appeared. Her scarf was pulled up over her neck and mouth, and her cheeks were pink from the cold.

"Did you have fun?"

She nodded, her eyes fixed on mine.

"You did this," I said quietly. "You made this magic happen."

Her smile was small but real. "So did you."

I assessed her for a moment too long. I hadn't looked at a woman like this in years. And I wasn't sure I'd ever had such strong feelings. It was too much.

This day had been long and busy and emotionally over-loading. Memories of my parents popped up randomly, slicing into my heart while also making me smile. The friendly faces were all so familiar and the Maplewood traditions were just as important as they were years ago. My parents loved this place and these people.

But I hadn't come here today for my parents. And I hadn't done it for the town.

I'd done it for her.

The realization hit me hard. Attraction, I could handle. But this, whatever it was, was big and unwieldy and hard to define. Care and curiosity and an ache inside the deepest parts of me.

I'd left my life in New York to live quietly on the farm. To take care of the land and provide my family with financial security. And for years, I'd done it. I'd mostly kept to myself, keeping my heart safe in the process.

But Celine had broken me out. She'd forced me to physically and emotionally leave the farm. To be a part of something again.

And I wasn't sure I could ever go back.

Chapter 21

♥

CELINE

My hands shook as I pulled Maggie's hair back into a messy ponytail. By the time I'd wound the hair tie around it three times, pieces were already trying to escape. It was windier than I'd anticipated, the chilly air snapping at our coats and scarves. It was that deceptive kind of cold that went far deeper than the weather in fall ever should.

Chloe had sent Gus in search of hot chocolate, and the rest of us watched as massive pumpkin boats of every size and shape were lowered into the water and tied to a long line strung across the river like a festive clothesline. Some were painted like pirate ships, others sporting googly eyes and costumes.

The water was slow and shallow, but I was still doing what I did best. Worrying. Going through mental safety checks, watching and calculating and studying Julian's body language.

He was calm.

Alarmingly calm.

It didn't add up. If history were to be trusted, this experience would conclude with complete sensory overload. It was cold and windy and noisy, with far too many visual distractions and an occasional strange smell. Not to mention the risk of getting wet. Normally this kind of thing would send us home overstimulated and exhausted before it even really got started.

Instead of struggling, my son was studying the other pumpkin boats and giving me a confident thumbs-up every few minutes.

I wanted to trust it. But I couldn't help but wait for him to melt down. Trying new things was virtually impossible for him. Novel experiences terrified him and never turned out well.

But we were here. And he was holding up better than I was.

Crowds lined the riverbank, and the people prepared with cowbells and homemade signs. The family race was first, kids of all ages with their parents, looking equal parts thrilled and unhinged.

"Remind me why this is a thing?" Chloe asked, shifting a sleepy Simone on her hip.

"It's only one hundred yards long." I pointed downriver to the inflatable finish line that had been set up. "And the fire department is here, ready to help if any of the boats capsize."

"This seems like a lot of work for bragging rights."

She wasn't wrong. The engineering that went into hollowing out the pumpkin had gone beyond my comprehension. And the time and energy and heavy machinery required to make the pumpkins seaworthy for a few minutes seemed a little absurd.

"I think it's the kind of thing that only works if you don't think too hard about it," Ellie said in her bored twelve-going-on-thirty-five drawl.

I snorted.

As ridiculous as all of this was, I couldn't help but be excited. For Julian and for Josh, who despite the early hour and the cold looked happy to be here.

The man with us this morning was far removed from the grump we all knew. He kept fist bumping Julian and squatting down to chat. Gesturing in ways that made me think they were talking strategy.

As they lined up to begin, I panicked and darted for Julian so I could check his life jacket one more time.

"Everything okay, bud?"

He nodded, the movement making his helmet slip low on his forehead.

Josh, who'd donned waders, squatted next to him. "Remember how this is going to go?"

"First you get in. Then Jasper will pick me up and put me inside." Julian said. "Then we hold onto the rope and float until it's time to start." He went through the checklist they'd reviewed.

"And then we paddle as fast as we can," Josh added. "You sure you're okay with that?"

"Yes. We're gonna win."

"We might win. We might not. But I want to make sure you feel comfortable and have fun. You can just watch if you want."

My chest tightened, making it hard to breathe. I wanted

to jump in, overexplain, and tell Julian he should hold my hand and just watch from the sidelines.

But I held myself back, giving him this moment. If he ended up melting down, I was prepared for it.

Julian turned slowly, his little face hard. "I made this boat with you, and I'm gonna paddle it with you. We're gonna win and then I'm gonna take the trophy to school to show everyone."

"Good man." Josh stood again, patting his helmeted head. "Ready to get in our boat?"

"Mama." Julian spun, looking up at me. "Will you be at the end?"

"Yes. We're going to walk to the finish line." I pointed at the girls. "You okay with that?"

"Yup. Go, Mama. I want you to see me win."

Forcing a smile, I took a step back.

I wrung my hands as Josh picked him up to carry him to the edge of the water. Holding my sixty-pound child like this only highlighted just how thick his arms were.

They were like the rest of him. Sturdy. Strong. Thick and manly. Capable. He could fix things and build things and probably wrestle a bear if necessary.

And the way his biceps flexed and the sleeves of his T-shirt clung to him made my heart thud heavily. Or maybe that was terror, because he was about to put my sweet boy in a fucking floating pumpkin.

He ducked, talking to Julian, then handed him to Jasper, who was volunteering. Then he pulled himself into the pumpkin.

Jasper helped Julian in, and my little guy slid in front of Josh, then the two of them grabbed their paddles. Julian was wide-eyed and focused, but there wasn't an ounce of panic on his face. He wasn't overwhelmed. He was alive.

Tears filled my eyes, making my vision blurry.

"Come on, Mom. We gotta go." Maggie tugged on my arm.

The two of us jogged to catch up with Chloe and Ellie, who were headed to the viewing area by the finish line, but I turned back halfway there to check on Julian.

The massive man was shoved into a lumpy pumpkin, carefully protecting my overjoyed son whose smile was so big, it looked like he'd already won.

A buzzer sounded, and the pumpkins were cut loose, paddles flying and colorful gourds wobbling in the water.

One painted with black and white stripes capsized almost immediately, and the firefighters pulled its occupants out quickly.

The crowd was cheering, and Maggie, Ellie, and Simone were screaming "Jul-i-an. Jul-i-an" over and over.

Water splashed up around the pumpkin, making it hard to see his face, but they were paddling hard, Julian's tiny arms to Josh's huge ones, and they were moving pretty quickly.

I inched closer to the water's edge, not caring if my sneakers got soaked. "Come on," I shouted. "You can do it."

Another boat capsized, and one near them wobbled, slowing them down. Within seconds, three boats had made it out of the fray and were ahead, and Josh and Julian were in control of one of them.

The first boat listed, then tipped, the adult paddling on one side making it worse.

It gave Josh and Julian the opportunity to pull ahead.

Ellie grabbed my hand and squeezed, screaming her lungs out for her brother, whose little face was soaking wet but smiling.

My heart soared at the expression. God, I was so damn proud of him.

"*Go,*" we called as Josh's muscular arms powered them forward, so close to the finish.

Moments later, they were crossing the finish line in second place.

Josh immediately handed his paddle to a volunteer who'd approached to steady the pumpkin while the firefighters helped them out of their boats.

He scooped Julian up, the two of them blurry as tears filled my eyes and spilled over my lashes. It was a strange sensation, being so happy while also being this tired and overwhelmed.

As Josh waded out of the water, holding a cheering Julian in his arms, my emotions took over completely, and I ran to them, throwing my arms around them.

"You were both amazing," I cried, barely feeling the freezing water seeping through my clothing. "I am so proud."

Julian beamed. "We came in second."

"I saw, and you worked so hard."

He threw his arms around Josh's neck and snuggled against him, a sight that almost made my heart burst.

This big, quiet, intimidating man had done so much for my little boy. He'd given him an opportunity to grow. One with clear rules and a defined goal. Then he'd been at his side, a trusted partner, the whole way. Rather than chaos, he'd created structure and adventure that allowed Julian to thrive.

Stepping back, I wiped at my tearstained cheeks.

Autism made Julian cautious, made him hide his talents away. But Josh had helped him find something new and build his confidence.

And Josh. He wasn't performing or seeking recognition. He did it all to help my little boy feel a little less lonely and a little less afraid.

And in the process, he'd sparked to life the emotions I'd been avoiding for a long time.

Once the boys were dry and Julian assured me he wanted to stay at the festival, we spent the day playing games, eating junk food, and taking silly selfies all over town. Ellie and Maggie took turns with Julian and Simone on the merry-go-round and Chloe bought us all matching maple-leaf-shaped lockets from the artisan jeweler.

Julian conked out the moment his head hit the pillow, and the girls begged to watch a movie, so once they were set up and I ensured that Ellie's phone was plugged in, I slipped a hoodie over my head.

"I'm going to run down to the barn and help Josh clean up." When we rolled down the driveway tonight, all the lights in the big barn were on, and after he'd donated so much of his time and equipment, I felt guilty for not helping more. I didn't have a clue how I could help, but surely there were small tasks that didn't involve heavy machinery that I could complete.

I owed him so much and didn't have the words to

adequately thank him, so I hoped I could show him by pitching in.

At the front door, I slipped into my fuzzy Crocs, then I headed out into the night.

Josh was dressed in a thick flannel, working inside the barn. The air was chilly and the smell of hay and earth blanketed the air. A single work light cast soft shadows to one side of the space where he was shelving items that looked like tools.

As I stepped into the barn, my shoulders didn't tense up, and my breathing didn't quicken. For once I wasn't bracing, preparing for pain. I didn't search for exits or excuses. Instead, I was present. All my focus was zeroed in on this moment. On this barn and this man. They demanded nothing from me, and the relief that brought was incredible.

When he looked up, his attention landing on me, my stomach flipped. I opened my mouth and start babbling without thought.

"I wanted to say thank you."

His brows jumped into his hairline, like the praise had caught him off guard. "For what? I didn't do anything special."

I almost laughed. The man didn't have any idea just how special this day had been.

"You did," I said, moving closer to him.

He plucked a rag off a shelf and wiped his hands, studying me as I walked toward him.

"It's hard sometimes. Raising Julian in a world that doesn't understand or accept him. A world that ignores his gifts."

He dropped the rag. "Celine—"

"Wait." I held up a hand. "Because of, um, past experiences, I am overcautious and overprotective. I wish I could keep him covered in a layer of bubble wrap to keep him from getting hurt. I know how cruel the world can be. And time and again, I've witnessed how easily people misunderstand him and mistreat him."

Tears welled in my eyes. My sweet boy was so gifted and special, and yet some days he walked through this world being told he was anything but.

"What you did for him…" I wiped at my eyes with the sleeve of my hoodie. "You made him feel capable. You gave him a complex problem to solve. And you helped him be brave."

"It was nothing."

"No," I said, frustration flowing through me. "It's not nothing. What you did was actually quite significant. This kid struggles to try new things, and novel situations usually send him spiraling. He struggles to regulate when met with too much sensory input. But today, he grew. So much. He tried new things and worked through problems. And that wouldn't have been possible without the help of a very special adult. Someone he trusts unconditionally. Someone who really gets him and helps him push through his challenges."

Josh shuffled closer, taking his hat off and smoothing down his hair, his eyes filled with emotion. "He did the hard part," he said softly. "I was just there for support."

He stood close enough that I could feel his warmth, yet he didn't encroach on my personal space.

"You can take the credit," I said.

"Nah." He ducked, shaking his head. "Because none of

this would be possible without the foundation you've built for Julian and the girls. Yeah, I helped, but today was not about the pumpkin. Today was the result of all the work you've done with him. Building him up and supporting him during the hard moments. All the love you pour into him."

I was fully crying now. I'd never needed to hear those words. Never needed anyone to see what I did every day. The care with which I parented and rebuilt my life. The progress Julian had made was reward enough.

Yet I couldn't deny the way my chest expanded now. Because Josh saw me.

He looked at me with respect. Admiration. Reverence. Not a hint of pity.

He looked at me not like I was a prize or a conquest but a precious gift. There was heat in his eyes. But it was quiet.

His thick chest rose and fell rapidly. He felt it too. And the steady desire in his eyes made it clear he wasn't going anywhere.

He looked down at his hands like they held the answer to an unasked question.

I studied them too, those large, strong hands calloused from hard work.

And desire pooled deep within me.

Not fear. Not apprehension.

Because I wasn't afraid of Josh.

But I was afraid of wanting him. Of how natural this felt. Of how quickly my trust and attraction had grown.

"I want to be brave." I took another step, my toes inches from his, my head tipped back so I could continue looking him in the eye. I was consumed by his scent and his heat. My body ached to be wrapped in his arms. To be held the way he'd held me a few weeks back.

"Then do it," he said, his voice a low growl. "Be brave for me."

I gripped his shirt and pulled him in until our bodies were flush. Then I pushed up onto my tiptoes and wrapped my arms around his neck, pulling his lips down to meet mine.

He tasted like whiskey, his lips warm and tentative. The kiss was gentle. Slow and luxurious and maddening. I wanted more. Hell, I needed more.

"Celine," he said, pulling back a fraction. "What do you want?"

I bit my bottom lip, my brain temporarily scrambled. "I... I don't know."

He put space between us, his hands at his sides. They'd never left that position.

My heart sank.

"Let me be clear," he murmured. "I have no expectations. There is no pressure. I'm here now, but say the word and I'm gone." Ducking, he ran his hands through his hair again. "Fuck, the last thing I ever want to do is make you feel unsafe."

His words unlocked a strange sensation inside me. A deeply buried desire that ignited and began to burn bright.

I reached out, needing to touch him. To anchor myself in this moment. Was this what safety felt like? To feel desire freely?

I trailed my fingers down his chest, the fabric of his shirt rough beneath them.

"I want to kiss you again."

The corner of his lip quirked. "I'm all yours."

I cupped his neck and pulled him in again, smashing my mouth to his. The kiss was sloppy and hungry and thrilling.

A kiss I'd initiated. One I controlled. I ran my hands up his chest and over his shoulders, acquainting myself with the bulk of him under my fingertips. Anchoring myself to him while devouring his mouth.

When my lungs burned, I pulled back.

His chest heaved, his eyes wild. "Are you okay?"

I nodded. "Yes. I'm great."

I clutched his neck again, but before I could make contact with his lips, he asked, "Can I touch you?"

It hit me then that his hands were still at his sides, his fists clenched like he was restraining himself.

My heart melted. He'd kept his hands off me, ensuring he didn't push past my boundaries.

"Please," I begged. "Please touch me everywhere."

Immediately, one of those large hands was wrapped around my waist, pulling me against him.

"You can tell me to stop any time." He stroked my jawline with a thumb, then tilted my face up. "You're in charge."

Chapter 23

CELINE

I thought I understood kissing.

Lips and tongue. Maybe some hands.

But what Celine and I were doing went far beyond that.

We devoured one another, our hands roaming and caressing and squeezing. With her in my arms, the fear and apprehension that had haunted me for years weakened.

I would do anything this woman asked me.

Anything.

Anywhere.

Anytime.

"You are so beautiful." I kissed my way down the column of her neck. "God, I've wanted to taste you right here." I licked behind her ear. "Since the first time I saw you."

She slipped her hands up under my shirt, gripping my belt to keep me close.

It was hot as fuck.

"Really? My Crocs and sports bra combo did it for you?"

A chuckle escaped me, and I buried my face in her neck. I had no words to describe what this woman did to me. Physically or emotionally. So instead, I picked her up and guided her legs around my waist, reveling in the way heat radiated from her core. Then I set her on my workbench, giving myself more access.

I was hard as goddamn stone, not that it mattered.

She'd kissed me. She wanted me. But I wouldn't allow myself to get carried away.

This was about her.

"Tell me what you want," I rasped, basking in the softness of her skin as I cupped her neck.

She let out a small moan.

Pulling back, I took a moment to admire the look of pure want on her face. Her skin was flushed and her hair wild. It was unbearably sexy.

"Josh."

I bit my lip to keep from throwing her over my shoulder and marching her straight to my bed.

"I will give you anything. But I won't touch you again until you tell me you want it."

"Touch me," she said softly. "Your hands. They're so strong. They feel so good."

My cock surged in my pants, desperate for attention, but I kept all my focus on her.

She took my hand, running her fingers over the calluses on my palm. Her touch was featherlight, yet it set my skin on fire.

With her fingers circled around my wrist, she guided my hand to her stomach, then slowly inched upward to her breast.

"Yes," I hissed, taking her mouth again. Our tongues tangled while my hands roamed freely. Cupping and squeezing her perfect breasts over her shirt.

"They're small," she said softly.

"Fucking perfect," I growled into her mouth, my erection straining against her thigh. "You're fucking perfect."

I could die here. Just like this. With this sexy, strong woman wrapped around me. And it would be the happiest of endings.

Moaning, she slid her hand down my chest, and when she continued past my belt and stroked my cock over the fabric of my pants, I saw stars.

"Jesus." She gasped, cupping me. "You could hurt me."

"I would never hurt you," I said, both hands on her face.

"I mean hurt in the good way." She gave me a saucy wink.

Unable to control myself, I dove in for another kiss, then worked my way lower, nipping and sucking at her neck, one of my hands up under her sweatshirt, pulling her sports bra down.

She clutched my wrist and pushed until my hand rested on the waistband of her leggings. Then she shifted closer, rubbing herself against my erection, panting, radiating heat, pulse fluttering against my fingers.

"Fuck," I breathed out. There was a very real chance I would come in my pants like a teenager tonight. "Can I?"

"Yes." She dropped her head back. "I need you to touch me everywhere."

With a groan, I slipped my fingers down beneath her waistband, and when all I found was warm skin, a beast was awoken inside me. "No panties?"

"Nope," she said, her hands in my hair, her mouth on mine.

Lower and lower, I explored the heat of her, caressing her inner thighs and memorizing the feel of her skin, then focusing on her clit, caressing gently.

"Please." She gasped and shuddered in my arms.

A thrill shot through me in response. Fuck. I avoided her pussy, knowing she'd be wet and ready but also knowing I was too worked up to do more than make her feel good.

I pulled my hand away, but before I could slip it out of her pants, she let out a feral growl.

"Don't you fucking dare."

Her tone sent a lightning bolt straight to my cock.

"You're in charge," I said against her mouth, finding her clit again, this time with my thumb. "You call the shots. I'll walk away right now if you want me to."

"I want." She gasped, pushing against me. "I don't want you to stop. I want your fingers inside me."

"Spread for me," I commanded.

Quickly, she shifted on the workbench, spreading her legs wide.

"You're soaked." I teased her opening with one finger, then pushed inside her.

She moaned, her body welcoming me, warm and wet and so ready.

"How's that?" I asked. "Okay?"

She responded by tugging on my hair and biting my neck.

"Do you need to come?"

She nodded against me, whimpering, so I got to work,

gently fucking her with one finger while circling her clit with my thumb.

She gasped and shook, clutching my shirt and my hair.

My body hummed with pleasure. Fuck. I'd never felt anything as good as this, and my pants were still buttoned, my belt still on. I didn't need more. All I wanted was to make this woman feel good.

"Still okay?"

"Yes." She gasped. "More. Need more."

I slipped a second finger inside her, and her inner walls clamped down hard, the sensation making my vision go dark.

"That's it. Take it." I focused on working her clit while she bucked and rode my hand, setting her own rhythm. "So fucking sexy. You're in charge. You tell me what you need."

"Don't stop." She gasped. "I'm close."

Her channel clamped around me even tighter, proving her point. Her body was tightly wound on a good day, but in this moment, she was ready to combust.

"You are perfection," I said. "I've never seen anything so beautiful."

"Josh." She clutched my hair, her pussy pulsating around me. She threw her head back and cried out as she came.

Watching her let go, releasing all the tension she carried around with her, was exquisite.

She rode out her release, still in complete control.

Shit. I'd never been so grateful to be used in my life.

When she collapsed against my chest, breathing hard, I withdrew my hand, then adjusted the waistband of her leggings.

Head tipped back, she watched me with heat in her gaze.

"You are so sexy when you come." I brought my fingers to my mouth and sucked on one, then the other.

Her eyes widened, and her breath caught.

"And fuck, you taste incredible."

I couldn't help but swell with pride.

She'd come undone. Because of me.

With trembling hands, she reached for my belt and palmed my cock again.

But I put both my hands on top of hers, stopping her. As much as I loved the attention, I needed to slow things down.

"You should get home," I said gently. "I can walk you."

A look of shock registered on her face. "But—"

"I like you," I said softly. "And what just happened. Kissing you, touching you. Making you come?" I shook my head. I didn't have the right words, and I was sure I'd fuck this up. "It means something," I finally said. "To me."

"You mean you don't just go around kissing girls?" Her tone was teasing, but genuine curiosity swam in her eyes.

Grunting, I gripped her waist. "I do not. Before I met you, I hadn't looked at a woman in years. I thought that part of me had died."

"But?"

"But you woke me up, Matchstick. With your fiery energy and your strength and your kindness."

She blinked, as if she didn't know what to say, or maybe she didn't know if she believed me.

"You've got me thinking things and feeling things." Fuck, I really was making a mess of this, but I soldiered on. "And I want to take it slow. Build trust."

She trailed her fingers up my chest, then dragged them back to my belt buckle. "Can't we—"

I shook my head. "I'd love to take you home and fuck you right now," I said. "But I'm not a casual sex kind of guy. I like you. And I like your kids. I don't want to mess things up with you by doing anything rash."

She swallowed and tilted her head. "I get it. And I don't do that either."

"Casual sex?" I offered.

She laughed. "Any sex. Ever."

That sent a thrill through me. The woman didn't have sex, yet she'd let me bring her to orgasm tonight. That had to be a good sign. "How about..." I wrapped my arms around her and pulled her close.

She put her head on my chest and hugged me, the simple move making my heart stutter.

"How about we just see how things go? I want you to trust me."

"I'm starting to." Her tone was soft but sure.

"Then I'll keep showing up and earning it. I will never push you. But I will be honest."

"I can do that. Honesty."

"Good. Because when you're ready. I'd like to know what happened. Why you came here. What you've been running from."

She tensed in my arms like her body was considering fleeing.

I stroked her hair and kept my tone low and soothing. "I'm not entitled to anything. You can tell me to fuck off. But I'm invested. In you. In your kids. And one day, I'd like to earn the right to know your history."

"I'm not there yet."

"That's okay. But I'll be here, ready when you are."

Chapter 23

CELINE

I woke up smiling. Despite the mountain of tasks I had to complete today, I felt good. Rested.

With one eye cracked open, I reached out for Julian on the far side of the bed.

When all I found were cold sheets, I blinked and scanned the room.

Huh. It was much brighter in here than usual, so I reached for my phone on the nightstand to check the time.

And when I realized it was just after nine, I jumped up, my heart racing and panic flooding me. I should have been awake three hours ago.

Snagging a hoodie off the floor, I darted out the door. As I tore down the stairs, fear gripped every inch of my body.

I launched myself off the third step from the bottom and landed with a thud.

"Mom, are you okay?" Maggie said as I spun in a circle.

Ellie giggled. "Did you just legit fly?"

All three of my kids were sitting at the kitchen table with Chloe, Gus, Simone, and a massive box of donuts.

"Your mom needs coffee." Chloe pushed her chair back and stood.

"Why is it nine a.m.?" I asked, looking from face to face, still trying to make sense of reality.

"Well, Mom, it's because the earth makes one full rotation on its axis every twenty-four hours," Ellie snarked.

"We got here early, and the kids said you were still sleeping," Chloe explained. "Simone wanted to see you all before we head home."

I nodded, though my heart still raced.

"I've never slept this late before," I said

"Shocker." Chloe chuckled. "Most people find sleeping in restful. I didn't realize it would make you more anxious."

"No. Sorry. Thank you." I turned to Gus, who was wiping melted chocolate off Simone's face, including him in that sentiment too.

"I just." I deflated. "Sorry."

Chloe handed me a coffee cup. "How about you drink this and get dressed? I want to chat a bit before we take off."

Her tone was too calm, too nice. It made the hair on the back of my neck stand up.

She pushed me toward the stairs. "Go."

After a quick shower and clean clothes, I came back down. Chloe was alone, the kids having gone outside to play something called Infection Tag, Gus tagging along, helping Simone keep up with her older cousins.

Chloe took my coffee cup and refilled it. When she handed it back to me, she said, "We need to talk."

My heart lurched. Was the guilt plaguing me that obvious? Did she know I'd snuck out of my home last night? That I'd fooled around with Josh? Did I have that orgasm blush that makeup companies were always trying to package and sell?

"I had a missed call yesterday," she said. "From Ava."

My throat tightened, making it difficult to breathe.

"I called her back this morning. She had news."

I clutched my coffee cup to my chest, wishing I could disappear. I didn't know what she'd say, but I knew I didn't want to hear it.

"Donny is up for parole," she said gently. "His hearing is next month."

My knees nearly gave out on me, but she caught me before I sank to the floor.

"Listen," she said, guiding me toward the couch. "Parole isn't guaranteed. Hopefully they won't grant it. But if they do, there will be conditions, and Ava will file a petition for maximum monitoring. And obviously the restraining orders are still in place."

I thought we had nearly a year of freedom left. Enough time for us to heal and get our fresh start. We'd just gotten here. We were still acclimating. He couldn't just get out.

"Breathe," Chloe commanded, and I did, having been conditioned long ago to obey her. "He was going to get out eventually. And all my sources tell me he's been a model prisoner. Going to AA meetings and anger management. He's not going to bother you."

I shook my head. He would. I knew Donny Whittier better than I knew myself. I'd spent more than a decade walking on eggshells and trying to predict his moods, and all that work had made me an expert.

And I felt it in my bones that he wasn't ready to let go of me yet.

"Shouldn't I get official notice? Of the parole?" I squeaked.

"Yes. You'll likely get it this week. But I wanted to warn you. And make a plan."

I wanted to cry. I wanted to scream. But not with my kids right outside. So instead I froze.

"Celine," my sister urged. "We will get through this. Whatever you need."

I got up and made a beeline for the junk drawer in the kitchen, then handed her the card.

"Shit." She gasped. "When did you get this? Who delivered it? Why didn't you tell me?" she asked without giving me time to respond. "We need to go to the police right now. What the fuck, Celine?"

A numb sensation crept through me, my fingers and toes tingling as they lost feeling.

It figured that the moment I experienced a fucking second of happiness and peace, Donny would ruin it.

"I planned to tell you. I just wanted to enjoy the weekend first," I admitted. "And not feel like a charity case or some fragile soul you and Gus have to protect."

"You are not fragile," she snapped. "You're doing amazingly well. And we had a wonderful visit. But if you receive threatening mail from your violent ex-husband in prison, I need to know about it."

"The handwriting on the envelope." I pointed to it. "That's Phyllis."

"Fucking Phyllis." Chloe rolled her shoulders. "I will murder her. I own several commercial-grade woodchippers.

It's actually quite easy."

Not even her dark sense of humor could lighten my mood. "Chloe."

"No. I should have done it when she filed that bullshit grandparent lawsuit. Fuck her and her entitled asshole son." She pulled her phone from her pocket and tapped the screen furiously. "I'm reaching out to Parker Gagnon. She's Chief of Police in Lovewell, but she has connections with the staties too. See what we can to do keep Phyllis quiet."

"It's not worth it," I said softly.

"Yes it is. You are worth it. Your safety is worth it. Those kids are worth it." She clutched my shoulders and shook hard. "You've got to fight this."

"Of course I'll fight it." I scoffed. Did she really think I'd slip back into defeated victim mode so quickly? "But I need a minute to process. This card is evidence I can submit to the parole board, yes?"

She nodded.

"And the lawyers will handle most of it. I know I'm not alone in this."

"Have you thought about security?"

"There is a system here. I've got the app on my phone. And Josh has cameras all over the farm for wildlife," I told her. "I can talk to him. Learn more about it."

Chloe's lips quirked, her expression holding a hint of humor for the first time today.

"What?"

"I'm not sure the guy who's blatantly in love with you should be the one doing an objective security sweep."

"Please be serious," I begged.

"He's seriously in love with you. And I suspect you're into him as well."

Unease threaded through me. "It's not like that."

"Did you see the way he looked at Julian after they crossed the finish line yesterday?" she asked.

I'd pretended not to, but of course I had. He'd been bursting with pride and affection, swinging a gleeful Julian—who hated to be touched—around and carrying him on those broad shoulders. Standing by his side as he tried new things and faced his fears.

She flopped onto my couch dramatically. "We LeBlanc girls really do have a type, don't we?"

Ignoring her, I sat at the other end of the couch.

"Burly lumberjacks," she said with a wistful sigh.

She'd said that before. I still didn't want to think about it too much.

"You know," she elbowed me, "giant protectors with teddy bear personalities who secretly want us to dominate them."

"Ew." I hit her with a throw pillow. "Chloe, I did not need to hear that."

She shrugged. "Regardless, I get it. You've been through hell. He seems like a good guy. But Celine, this is not the time to be getting distracted."

Her words hit me hard. As usual, my big sister was right. She was the practical one and I was the one with my head in the clouds.

"Of course."

"Let me schedule a call with the lawyers this week. And I'll talk to my friend at the state house. There's a good chance we can get this parole denied or, at the very least, delayed."

I nodded, a plan already forming in my mind. I'd have to take a few days off, probably drop the kids with Chloe and Gus, and head to court in Bangor. I'd say whatever the lawyers told me to say to make sure he wasn't released. To ensure he served the rest of his time and couldn't hurt us anymore.

Chapter 24

CELINE

pple picking was serious business. At least the way my kids approached it was.

I'd avoided Josh all week, at a loss for where to go from here. It wasn't all that difficult, actually. Between teaching, momming, and calls with my lawyer, who was preparing an objection statement for me to send to the Maine parole board, I'd barely had time to breathe.

After our incredible weekend, the kids were more at ease than ever, so I'd worked hard not to burst that bubble. But keeping all that anxiety to myself, not letting them experience even a hint of fear, was draining every ounce of energy I had.

Staying away from Josh like I had hurt. Warm, flannel-clad Josh, with his thick beard and kind eyes. So when he'd sent a group text last night, asking for help picking the last of the apples in his orchard, I couldn't say no.

All around, the maple trees were exploding with color—

burnt orange, crimson, and gold. The air was chilly but clean, recharging some of the energy I'd lost this week.

We trudged through the spongy grass of the orchard to the sound of laughter and the thudding of apples falling into crates. My hands were cold, but the sun warmed my face. It was the perfect October day. There had been a time in my life when this was my favorite month. It always felt different from the rest. An invitation to slow down, to linger. The last buffer of color and sun before the long winter.

"You've been busy." Josh approached, his hands shoved into the pockets of his worn jeans. It was a good thing, since with one reminder of what those thick, strong hands could do, I'd probably spontaneous combust.

I nodded, scanning the area, noting Callie and Evie nearby, along with Jasper and Vincent, the little guy content in his dad's arms, gumming on a giant red apple.

My kids were having a blast, Ellie currently lifting Julian so he could reach apples higher up one tree.

Jenn and Mel were here with their boys, and a few other folks from town joined in as well.

Including Stella, who was pretty heavily made up for nine a.m. on a Saturday. She was constantly looking around, probably hoping Gabe would show up.

I, on the other hand, was drinking cold coffee out of my mug and wearing yesterday's clothes.

"Fun footwear," Josh said, looking down at my feet.

Bristling, I followed his line of sight.

Shit. I was wearing two different Crocs. One blue, one pink glitter. Damn Ellie. Now that her feet were the same size as mine, my shoes disappeared randomly, sometimes only one at a time.

I'd been tearing the house apart looking for my left pink sparkle Croc but had just given up.

"Don't hate the Crocs." I stuck my tongue out. "So you invited us for the free labor, I assume?"

"Mostly for the company," he said, his voice low.

I looked away, unable to meet his eye. Was he flirting with me again? God. Why couldn't he just be an unapproachable grump all the time?

He wanted to talk. I could sense it, but I wasn't ready. Not after the week I'd had. I was too wound up, too anxious, and I had too much on my mind. I'd say the wrong thing and destroy this lovely little thing between us.

Though maybe that would be a blessing. Chloe was right. I didn't have the luxury of distraction right now. I couldn't. But I wanted to sit with the warm memory of last weekend for a little longer. The tiny glimmer of that good, real, fun moment was keeping me going while the world caught fire around me.

A series of wild screams and shouts stole our attention before he could say more.

I whipped around, searching for danger.

But it wasn't danger. At least the kind I'd been concerned about.

It was Logan, the veterinarian who looked like a Viking, striding toward us with two small goats on leashes.

"Logan," Josh growled as the kids sprinted toward him.

"I brought goats," he said cheerfully.

I didn't know him well, but between the man bun, the multiple earrings, the height, and the hoodie with a picture of a raccoon on it that said *I choose violence*, he certainly had, as Ellie would say, a vibe.

Wayne harumphed beside me like he was already over it.

Maggie pushed everyone out of the way, squealing with delight. "Can I pet them?"

"Sure," Logan said. "Hold your hand out like you would for a dog."

"Why did you bring baby goats?" Josh asked.

His friend gave him an unbothered smile. "They're not babies. They're dwarf Nigerian goats. Huge personalities in tiny bodies."

"What are their names?" one of the other kids asked.

"This one's Calvin." Logan lifted the leash connected to the harness clipped around one goat's body, then did the same with the other. "And this one's Hobbes."

Josh crossed his arms and glared at him. "You still haven't explained why Calvin and Hobbes are here."

"Oh. Yeah." He crouched, showing the kids how to scratch the goats' ears. From what little I knew about him, he was some kind of animal whisperer. A revered veterinarian with a quirky personality. "They're recovering from stress. Rescued them a few days ago from a place up north. They need environmental enrichment."

The big, burly man beside me grunted. "That doesn't sound promising."

"They need socialization and they're super chill. Just don't scream or startle them."

Josh's eye twitched, making me giggle. This was objectively funny. Especially because they were wearing colorful leashes and harnesses, like tiny, stocky dogs.

Wayne, who remained by my side, huffed, unimpressed.

With a smile, I patted his head. "It's okay, boy. You're still my favorite."

He responded by tipping his head up and giving me a soulful look.

"Mama," Julian said without looking away from the goats. "They have rectangle-shaped pupils."

Logan held out a fist for a bump. "Very observant."

My heart exploded just a little. Julian touching an animal he'd never encountered before, one that smelled and probably felt strange? His therapists would be impressed by this exposure exercise. Not that I could take any credit.

"Josh has a lot of space," Maggie said. "And I'll do all the necessary research for their care. We can adopt them." She finished off the statement with a winning smile.

"No," Josh said.

She spun around, a flash of fury on her face that reminded me of Ellie. "I will walk them every day."

"Can't keep goats."

Arms crossed, she looked him up and down. "I will eventually persuade you."

"Is that a threat?"

"Yup." She popped the *P*, then whipped around again and went back to asking Logan questions about goat physiology and behavior.

Ellie said nothing, but by the way she was letting one of the animals chew on the string of her hoodie, she seemed on board with the new friends.

Eventually we got back to picking, but the kids all took turns walking the goats, who loved eating apples, tree branches, and also the apple crates. It turned out Calvin and Hobbes, like most goats, did not have discerning palates.

"You could offer an orchard experience," Jenn said,

mirth flashing in her eyes. "Apple picking with goats. Then maybe pressing cider like grandpa used to do."

"I don't provide experiences," he said, bristling. "I run a damn farm."

"Just saying." She elbowed him in the ribs. "We're trying to win back the tourists who have migrated to Birch Hollow. Goat yoga is huge. Maybe goat maple sugaring could be next."

"They'd eat all the plastic tubing," Josh groused.

"Oh, they definitely would." Logan jogged up beside us. "They ate part of the water bucket I put out for them last night."

The kids sorted the apples into two categories: those suitable for eating and those that would be better used for cider, with plans to take home several dozen. It had been a fun adventure, and Julian was already working to convince Josh to plant peach trees, since peaches were his favorite fruit.

"Hey," Josh said, pulling me aside while the kids chattered about what they were going to make with all the apples. "Can you take a walk for a bit?"

Frowning, I waved at my kids. He knew better than that. I couldn't just leave them unaccompanied.

Stella, the traitor, jumped in and immediately. "Who wants to make an apple pie with me?" she asked.

Naturally, all three of my kids cheered.

"Perfect. But we've got to make it here. I don't have any butter at my house."

"We have lots of butter," Julian chirped.

"I'll hang with them for a while," Stella said, her eyes dancing with mischief. "Take a break. You deserve it."

Despite my annoyance with her, she was a responsible

adult and my kids were dancing around her like she was a goddamn fairy princess, so I'd let them have their fun.

As they wandered away, Josh held out an elbow.

"A walk?" I asked.

He nodded. "Want to show you something."

We took off down the hill toward the big barn, but before we made it there, we headed off the road toward the far side of the farm I was mostly unfamiliar with.

"Seems like you've been having a tough week," he said.

I didn't respond. I didn't know how to, and I didn't know how he'd know that. We'd barely spoken, and I hadn't mentioned anything to anyone.

"You didn't have to say it," he said, apparently a mind reader. "I could see the tension in your jaw, the way you hurried off to school every day. And even this morning."

A knot formed in my stomach. I did not want to talk. I wasn't ready for that. Couldn't I just live in that little happy moment for a bit longer?

He pulled me by the arm toward a small shed. "But I want to help. And I've got an idea." He stopped in front of the shed, and all I could see behind it was a bunch of debris. Wooden pallets and old crates and barrels. "You seem like you need to get a few things off your chest."

A tired huff escaped me. "I'm not in the mood to talk, Josh."

He crossed his thick arms and raised an eyebrow.

Dammit, why did he have to be so damn handsome?

"I figured," he said. "But are you in the mood to break shit?" He grinned.

The effervescent expression from this usually stoic man made my stomach flip.

I had no idea what he was talking about, but the gleam in his eye made my core clench.

"Come on." He opened the shed and produced a box. "A present for you."

Rather than take it, I stared at the large package with *Timberland* printed on the side.

"Open."

I lifted the lid, finding a pair of pink work boots nestled inside. Fancy ones with steel toes.

"They're pink."

"It's your favorite color."

I peered up at him, frowning. How did he know that? I'd never told him, and while I had a lot of pink stuff, I wasn't exactly walking around looking like Barbie.

"Turns out they make them in doll sizes for your tiny feet."

"How did you know my size?" I pulled one out and inspected it.

"I texted Ellie and she told me."

"She has your number for emergencies," I scolded.

He put his arm around me, pulling me in for a half hug.

It was less than half of what I needed, but it helped a little.

"Lack of proper footwear *is* an emergency," he corrected. "You know how much I care about safety."

Timberlands. A wave of self-consciousness hit me. This was an expensive gift. Was this a charity thing?

"Just because no one has ever treated you like you matter doesn't mean you don't," he went on, making me really think he had direct access to my thoughts. "You matter. To me and to a lot of other people. So put the damn boots on. You need proper footwear. Can't be dancing around the farm in mismatched Crocs all the time."

With a sigh, I sat on the ground and put them on. They were a bit stiff, but Josh said they needed to be broken in, and they were warm and supportive, so I didn't argue.

"Now follow me. You'll need these." He handed me a pair of protective glasses.

Behind the shed, close to one of the maple tree stands, was a clearing. And it was filled with... junk? Old buckets, crates, wooden pallets and other scraps.

The items were evenly spread out, confusing me further.

"What is this?"

"A rage room." He held out an arm, gesturing to the random collection of things. "I know you don't like enclosed spaces, so it's more of a rage yard, but you get the idea." With a step forward, he handed me a new pair of pink work gloves.

I continued perusing the area. Was that an old printer? What was this?

I looked down at the gloves in my hands and the boots on my feet, at an absolute loss.

"Sorry. I'm confused."

He walked over to the back wall of the shed, where a few sledgehammers had been propped up.

"This one's light and well-balanced." He grasped it by the neck and held the handle out to me.

Tentatively, I took it in both hands, feeling the weight of it.

"You're carrying a lot around," he said gently. "And I wanted to help. But I can't imagine a bubble bath is enough to do the trick, so I set this up. You can let it all out here. There's no judgment. No pressure."

My eyes heated and gratefulness washed over me. I opened my mouth, my instinct to minimize, to make a joke, or to say this was unnecessary kicking in, but I quickly snapped it shut again.

But maybe it was necessary. I was drowning. And he'd noticed.

And he'd tossed me a life preserver.

He didn't ask me to explain, to tell him what had been eating at me. He didn't expect me to package my emotions up for him to consume.

He just noticed and did something about it.

"So I just..." I looked up at him, emotion clogging my throat.

"Swing it and break shit," he said, crossing those thick arms again.

"But I'll make a mess."

"I've got a dumpster." He lifted one shoulder easily. "I'll clean it up later."

"But—"

"Get swinging, Matchstick." He took a step back, then another. "I promise it will help."

He was so strong and calm. I'd never say it out loud, but his presence helped soothe my anxiety. Josh couldn't solve my problems, but when he was nearby, I felt a little tougher.

Hefting the sledgehammer, I studied it. "I don't know if I can."

He stepped in again and took it, holding it out at a different angle for me. "We both know you can smash the shit out of anything. Now be a good girl and break something. It's cathartic."

Self-conscious, I put on the safety glasses, repositioned

the sledgehammer in my hold, and surveyed the clearing. The sledgehammer was heavy but not too heavy. And he'd gone to all this trouble.

So I walked tentatively toward a stack of wooden crates and swung.

Wood splintered, flying everywhere, and the loud crash made me jump.

My heart rate kicked up, but not in a bad way. Okay, this might be fun after all.

I swung again and again, cracking plastic containers, bending metal, and shattering wood. I laughed, cried, and got one hell of a workout.

My fingers stung, signaling that blisters were forming, but I didn't slow. This was the most fun I'd had in a very long time.

Most days it felt impossible to shed the person I'd once been. The woman who had slowly unraveled. Who'd lost herself and was too dumb to even realize until every recognizable trait was gone.

It started in little ways, skipping plans with friends because he didn't like it. Going to his mother's when I knew she wouldn't be kind or sitting through one dumb action movie after another, all of which I hated. At the time, it had felt like compromise. Like maturity.

I convinced myself that I was bad at laundry when he'd complained one too many times.

Maybe the turkey meatloaf I made for dinner did taste like shit and my tastebuds were just messed up.

I wasn't perfect, and I'd grown up so alone and isolated and without my mom. So I convinced myself that maybe I actually was a shitty person.

And I loved my kids so much. Would do anything for them. So working a little harder to please their father seemed like the least I could do.

So I folded towels differently.

I took over all the holiday gift giving and sent his mom flowers on Mother's Day.

I attended every school meeting and function alone because he was either busy working or needed to decompress by playing golf with his friends.

When I discovered that he was spending most evenings at strip clubs, getting drunk and high with his friends, I blamed myself.

I was boring. I was ugly. My world had become so small. Of course I wasn't interesting.

But when it became clear that Julian's mind worked differently from either of his sisters', when I realized he wouldn't grow out of his quirks, a deeper, stronger loyalty inside me woke up. My desire to understand him, to support him, pushed out many of my insecurities.

Only then did I begin to understand just how much power I had given away.

And I wanted it back.

All that I had given him. Donny hadn't stolen it from me. I'd given it away. And I'd never forgive myself for that.

"Use your whole body," Josh coached. "Not just your arms."

I swung the sledgehammer again, driving down with my legs, and the faded bucket cracked in two. Fuck, this was addictive.

He clapped, the sound echoing off the trees. "Awesome."

I studied him, so large and intimidating and quiet.

I'd written him off as an asshole.

But I couldn't have been more wrong. This man saw me. The dark cracks and corners and places where I had shoddily patched myself up. And he wasn't scared of any of it.

And he was one hell of a kisser.

"Having fun?"

I nodded, adjusting my safety goggles. "When do I get a chainsaw?"

He chuckled, his lips tipping up, his eyes shadowed by his ball cap. "We'll work up to that."

"You sure you don't mind?" I worried my bottom lip. "That I'm making a mess and breaking things?"

"Giving you this moment is my absolute pleasure," he said, and damn it, that stupid dimple popped, making his lopsided grin even sexier.

How was it that he could be so scary on the outside—his size, his attitude, his general sneer—yet put me at ease so easily? With him, I never felt the need to remain on alert or walk on eggshells. I could just be me.

My arms ached and my lungs burned, but I couldn't stop. I moved on, bashing an old chair, its legs and back splintering. My hands, that had once held so many crumbling pieces together, were breaking these items into their most basic components. Years of swallowed words poured out of me silently. Years of fear and grief, and the bone-deep exhaustion that came with living in survival mode.

I dropped the sledgehammer to the ground scattered with splintered wood, bent metal, and the remains of things that had once been useful.

Josh stood a few feet away, leaning against the shed, his

hands loose at his sides. He was there. Steady and unflinching. No judgment, no concern, and no pity.

And like before, I realized that I wasn't bracing.

My shoulders weren't locked up around my ears and my jaw was unclenched. I wasn't subconsciously making an exit plan, replaying conversations or preparing to explain and defend myself.

The constant hum of vigilance that had buzzed around me for years had finally gone quiet.

And in that quiet, I saw him.

Not the gruff farmer. Not the careful landlord. Not the man who kept his distance and pretended not to pay attention. He didn't tell me to calm down or soften my anger or placate me with empty assurances.

He'd given me space to be who I needed to be and do what I needed to do.

My next thought hit me harder than a sledgehammer.

I wanted Josh.

Not just wanted. Needed.

The pull toward him was a strong, steady kind of gravity.

I swallowed, my throat tight. "I don't know how to say thank you."

"You don't have to."

My nose stung, tears threatening. "Thank you for not trying to fix me."

His brow furrowed, like the idea hadn't occurred to him. "I would never."

With Josh, there were no conditions. No expectations. He stood near the shed, his eyes dark and locked on mine. Not moving, not initiating, but making himself available if I needed him.

"I feel safe with you." I padded to him.

"I'll keep it that way," he promised, his expression solemn.

That was it. The last string holding my reservations together. I could no longer contain my desire. And I was done letting the bad stuff consume all my thoughts.

Because Josh made me brave.

I closed the distance between us, pressing my body to his. His warmth met me before his hands did. Like the other night, he was letting me take the lead. He made me feel more seen than I ever had in my life.

Only when I threw myself into his arms did he touch me, and he lifted me effortlessly as our mouths found one another in a desperate kiss, our teeth clinking ridiculously, the elation bubbling inside me making me weightless in his arms.

"Fuck." He turned and pushed me up against the shed, taking my mouth. My knees wobbled. Nothing had every felt as good as his lips on mine or the grip of his strong hands on my thighs.

He pinned me with his bulk, his erection digging into me.

"God," he growled, nipping at my neck. "I could fuck you like this."

Face buried in my hair, he slowly lowered me to my feet.

"But I won't."

A protest clawed its way up my throat. Because at the moment, being fucked like this sounded like an excellent idea.

The wistful smile he directed at me signaled that he was under the impression that the kissing had concluded.

But I had not consented to that.

"I enjoyed the hell out of that." His dimple was just visible beneath his thick beard. It was adorable. "But I get it. And I'm not asking for anything."

Annoyance flashed through me. "What If I'm asking?"

"Then I'll give you anything you want," he said firmly.

"I want you to fuck me," I said, a newfound courage overtaking me.

His pupils blew wide. "Celine—"

I shook my head. "I want you. I want this. The kids are with Stella. Who knows when we'll get another chance?"

He studied me, his chest rising and falling with labored breaths. Good. He wanted this as badly as I did.

Then he scooped me up and took off toward his house.

Giggling, I curled into his chest and relished the security his arms gave me. And I reveled in the haze of lust that had fallen over us.

For the first time, wanting someone didn't feel like danger.

It felt like safety.

Chapter 25

JOSH

This could only be a dream.

Celine was in my bed, straddling me, her mouth fused to mine like I was the oxygen she needed to breathe. Having her had become a fantasy, and after our encounter in the barn last weekend, that fantasy had begun to run wild.

I wanted days, weeks, *months* to explore her body. But we were already on borrowed time. Watching her swing the sledgehammer, witnessing the way her face lit up and her muscles loosened when she was finished, had been the most powerful aphrodisiac.

Now that her weight was settled on top of me, keeping a lid on my desire for her was impossible. With my hands on her ass, I kissed her back with as much passion as she was showing me.

When she moaned into my neck, I knew that this was heaven.

I'd asked her what she wanted, and she'd asked me to fuck her.

I could have come in my pants right there and then. It was officially the hottest phrase I'd ever heard.

Sitting upright, she took off her T-shirt, revealing a pink sports bra that did little to hide her pebbled nipples.

"All of it," I growled.

Without hesitation, she ripped the undergarment off and tossed it over her head.

With one hand on her breast, teasing her rosy nipple, I took the other into my mouth. "You're in charge," I said, trailing kisses along her chest as she ground her hips against me. "Anything you want."

"You know what I want." She squeezed my cock through my pants, whimpering.

"You'll get it," I gritted out. "But first, please let me taste you."

Her already flushed face went crimson. "No... you don't have to."

I clutched her hips, clocking the uncertainty in her expression.

"Um, I desperately want to. But obviously only if it's okay with you."

"It's just." She let out a shuddering breath. "I'm all sweaty. Maybe I should shower—"

I grasped her wrist and brought it to my lips, kissing her pulse point.

"Fuck, that just makes you taste even better. Please."

"I mean, I guess." Though there was hesitation there, desire burned in her eyes. "For a minute?"

I rolled over and pushed up on my knees, making sure

not to cage her in or make her feel trapped. "Can I take off your leggings?"

She nodded, her hair fanning out on my pillows, her hard nipples still wet and glistening from my mouth. She looked like a sexy goddess, and my God, I wanted to do the filthiest things to her.

Slowly I inched her pants down, relishing every inch of her soft skin. I tossed them to the floor and eased her legs open wider, then locked eyes with her, waiting for permission.

When she gave me a slight nod, I dove in.

I considered teasing her, but we didn't have time to waste, and I'd already waited so damn long for this.

I was starving.

And she was wet and warm and tasted like heaven on my tongue.

Despite her initial reservation, it took less than thirty seconds for her to start bucking against my face.

"You worked up?" I nipped at her inner thigh and slipped a finger inside her. Immediately, she clenched around me, just like she had the other night. This woman had loved riding my hand, there was no way she could deny it.

I focused on her clit, licking and sucking and searching for a rhythm that made her squirm and moan. I found it quickly, and I was just settling in when she convulsed beneath me.

"Yes. Josh. Yes," she cried. Lifting her hips.

I kept my pace, licking and sucking and nipping, then repeating. I was barely holding on. Fuck, I was so wound up I was tempted to hump the mattress for relief. Because

Celine coming on my tongue was too much for me to handle. It was perfection.

She pushed me away, then threw her arms out to her sides, panting heavily. "Holy shit. How did you do that?"

I sat up, cataloging every detail of her naked body.

"I'll do it again," I said, reaching for her thighs.

"No." She put her hand on her chest, giving me a saucy smile. "Get naked."

"We don't have to," I said, even as I tugged my shirt off.

She bit her lip, her lashes fluttering. "Didn't you say I was in charge?"

"Yes, ma'am." I stood and shucked my jeans.

She pointed to my boxer briefs and commanded, "Off."

What could I do but obey? And when my cock sprung free, her eyes went wide.

"Jesus, Josh."

I stood in front of her, fully naked, heart hammering. "You're in charge. Where do you want me?"

She sat up and scooted to one side. "Lay down."

I did, sprawling out on my back and grabbing a handful of her ass along the way.

She straddled me again, kissing down my chest, deliberately ignoring my cock and driving me absolutely wild.

"Condom?"

I reached for the nightstand, knocking over the lamp in my haste, and plucked one out, then handed it to her.

She tore it open with her teeth, her eyes locked with mine, and a zap of electricity worked its way up my spine. Fuck, that was hot.

As she covered me, my eyes rolled into the back of my head. Goddamn.

She hovered over me, teasing me with her heat, dragging my tip through her wetness.

"I don't know," she said, between sloppy kisses. "It might not fit."

"It will fit." I slid a hand between us and found her core, confirming that she was still drenched. "You want it so badly, don't you?"

Cheeks flushing, she lined me up with her entrance and sank down an inch. Fuck. Already my vision was darkening. There was no way I would last long.

She took me little by little, looking like a wild fucking goddess.

"You're so big," she whimpered. "Keep those hands up."

I grabbed the headboard to keep myself from reaching for her. This was her show and I wanted her to know it.

She bit her lip and rolled her hips once, then again. When she was fully seated, she let out a sigh. "God, this feels so fucking good."

She rolled her hips again, grinding her clit against me.

"I'm so full."

"That's it," I gritted out, my heart pounding. "Take whatever you want. Use me."

She rode me gently, tentatively as first, testing until she found the spot that had her groaning and picking up the pace. It didn't take long before her head was thrown back and she was riding me, moaning and shaking.

It was the hottest moment of my life. Just the sight of her threatened to unravel me.

"Look at you," I said, clutching the headboard tighter. "You're so sexy. You were made for me, Celine. Made to drive me crazy and fulfill all my fantasies."

She loomed over me, her eyes full of heat. "Touch me," she begged. "I'm close."

Without second-guessing the directive, I pulled her down. I cupped one breast while I found her clit, applying steady pressure right where she needed it.

I was rewarded instantly, her walls tightening around me.

Oh fuck. Muscles clenched, I fought the urge to spill myself inside her.

"That's it," I said as she closed her eyes and threw her head back again. "Come on my cock."

"I don't know if I can," she squeaked out, her chest flushed, her hands splayed over my pecs.

"I can feel you. You're so close. Let go." I rubbed circles around her clit once, twice. When I did it a third time, she detonated. Riding me hard and fast as she spasmed around me.

A stronger man would have held on. Would have made her come at least one more time.

But in this moment, I was weak. My orgasm ripped through me violently, black dots dancing in my vision. I thrust up, surging deeper, and she clutched me tighter, holding on while I rode out my own release.

When I'd stopped pulsing inside her, I dropped my head back.

She collapsed on my chest, out of breath and sweating. "That was..." She didn't even finish her sentence.

"Incredible," I groaned, wrapping my arms around her and pulling her close so her heart beat against mine. "Truly incredible."

Chapter 26

CELINE

So warm and so safe like this, I was tempted to let my heavy eyelids close and fade into blissful rest in Josh's lavender scented sheets.

But I had to get back to the kids. Stella had been with them long enough. It felt wrong to just lounge in Josh's bed, knowing she was corralling all three of them on her own. Even if it was the biggest, most comfortable bed on earth.

My world had been rocked in several ways today, and I when I got up, when I climbed out from beneath this fluffy duvet, I'd be a different woman.

And I was pretty fucking proud of her.

With a sigh, I pushed off his chest.

"Don't go." He looped his arms around me, pulling me close and burying his face in my hair.

"I need a shower," I said

"You're perfect."

Propped up on an elbow, I assessed him, his hair wild and the lines on his face soft in the afternoon light filtering through the blinds. "Should we..." I let out a long breath. "Should we talk?"

He ran his hand gently down by back. "Whatever you want."

"I just." A wave of panic rose up inside me. Now that the haze of my orgasm had faded, it hit me just how big the step we'd taken today was.

I liked Josh.

I more than liked him.

But I was a thirty-six-year-old single mom of three trying to prevent my ex-husband from making parole. I wasn't exactly datable, even if I had the time.

"I think I like you," I blurted.

Rather than panic, he broke into a lazy smile. "That's a relief. Because I think I love you."

That should have worried me. We should have both been panicking. Instead, his words sent a warm feeling buzzing through my limbs.

"I owe you so many details—"

"You don't owe me anything," he said, his voice firm.

"I do," I replied. "Because I come with a lot of baggage. And I can't do this or anything or—"

He sat up and put an arm around me. "It's okay."

I let out a long breath. I had two choices.

I could get dressed and go back to my house and my kids and pretend this day never happened. Avoid Josh and chalk this up to a fun, sexy time and nothing more.

Or I could put on my big girl pants and have the difficult conversation.

And when I thought about it like that, there was no question which I'd choose. Because he was worth it.

Scratch that. Because I was worth it.

"My mom died when I was thirteen. Cancer," I said, the familiar sense of grief creeping through me. Like a weighted blanket keeping me pinned down even on the best days.

"My dad," I went on. "He just checked out. He'd loved her so much, and all of a sudden he had four kids to raise on his own while keeping the family business going. Chloe was only eighteen, but she jumped in to help. Though a year later, she took off to the West Coast and didn't come back for twenty years."

His lips turned down. "I'm so sorry."

I shook my head. "Not her fault. The burden my dad placed on her was unbearable."

Beneath me, his muscles tensed. "Was he abusive?"

"No. He loves us in his own way, he just didn't know how to take care of us. If we wanted to eat, we went to the grocery store ourselves. I went to my brothers' games, otherwise there wouldn't have been a single person in the stands to cheer for them. But Dad paid for everything. I asked to take an SAT prep course, and he happily gave me a check, but I had to arrange rides back and forth."

"So you lost both your parents."

I nodded, thankful he could see it.

"But I was determined to make it work. To be the loving glue that kept our family together the way my mom had been. Chloe was in the wind, and my brothers were kids. So I bent over backward trying to be perfect. To please everyone and be the best at everything.

"Got a full scholarship to U Maine. Got my bachelor's in three years and went straight into earning a master's in elementary education."

"Impressive."

"But after college, Dad expected me to move back home. To Heartsborough, Maine. The town has been struggling for years, and opportunities are limited. The idea wasn't appealing. But Donny was there. His dad owned the last surviving privately owned sawmill in Maine. Our fathers did a ton of business together, and their family was a big deal."

"And Donny? Did you fall for him?"

I laughed. No. I absolutely didn't. I was naïve and flattered by his attention, nothing more. "I was twenty-two. My brain was not fully developed," I explained. "He swept me off my feet, and before I knew it, I was planning a wedding. It made my dad so happy that I was marrying Donny. And at the time, I believed he was a good man. He was funny and kind and he looked at me like I was a prize."

"You are a prize," he growled, his lips brushing my bare shoulder.

"Then I had three kids by the time I was thirty. I gave up teaching because working full time while raising my babies almost completely alone wasn't easy. And that was before Donny's constant criticism. I never did enough around the house. He wanted me to be a full-time nanny and maid and somehow magically make six figures at the same time."

"What an asshole."

I shrugged. Stupidly, I thought it was mostly reasonable. "I never fought back or questioned him. My kids gave me a purpose. A place to put all the love I'd been storing up since my mom died. But marriage..." I closed my eyes and dug deep for the little strength I had left after this long day.

Only a few people knew this story, and while I'd told it

to police and lawyers and therapists, getting the words out was still a challenge.

"Marriage to Donny was the price I had to pay for my kids. He'd rage and scream at me. Nitpick and criticize incessantly. I was always walking on eggshells, and at some point, I decided that I must have been a fuck-up who did everything wrong."

Amazingly, I wasn't crying, and saying it out loud made me feel lighter.

"I chafe every time I hear the word lazy. It sends me into a spiral. Because he called me lazy every day."

"You? Lazy that is literally the last word I would ever use to describe you."

"Logically, I know I'm not," I said. "My therapist had me keep a list of my accomplishments on my phone and look at it every day for a year. I've done the work, but when someone so young and vulnerable is manipulated the way I was, the negative self-talk and self-image are hard to shake. Year after year, things got worse. He drank more. Stayed out all night more often. Got angrier about little things. Started taking it out on the kids. And then things escalated."

A low rumble worked its way up his chest. "What did he do?"

"He'd push me once in a while. Shove me. Shake me sometimes. With the girls, it was mostly just moving them out of the way a little too aggressively or yelling. It didn't take them long to figure out that they were better off out of sight of him. But Julian was so little." Emotion welled up inside me, making my eyes water. "And he was struggling so badly. We didn't get the diagnosis until he was four and a half. Before that, I didn't know how to help him. And then—"

The words clogged in my throat. The tears were streaming down my cheeks in earnest. I could heal from a lot of this, and logically, I knew it wasn't my fault. But I would never forgive myself for letting it go so far.

"Donny hit him. Smacked him in the head because he was acting 'weird.'"

Josh's body went rigid, his usually kind eyes murderous. "What the fuck?"

"That's when a switch flipped inside me. I started fighting back. But that just made him madder. I told him to get out. I threw things at him and threatened to call the police."

"Good for you."

"No." I could see that day so clearly, and each time the memories came to me, it was like being stabbed in the heart. "It wasn't. I should have left the house with the kids and gotten a restraining order. Instead I was a massive, naïve idiot."

"Celine. You can't blame your—"

"He came back angrier," I interrupted. "Showed up at the house, dragged the kids out of bed. Threw Julian down the stairs and then—" A sob got caught in my throat, my entire body shaking.

"He tried to strangle me," I whispered. "He had his hands around my neck. Left terrible bruises."

His face crumpled. "Jesus. I'm so sorry."

"Ellie hit him with her hockey stick, and when he let go of me, she and I rushed to the bathroom, where Maggie was already holding Julian tight. I called my sister, and she's the one who had to tell me to call the police."

He wrapped his warm arms around me and held me as I

sobbed against his bare chest. The familiar worthlessness and fear rolled through me at a high speed.

"I was so dumb I didn't even think to call the police," I hiccuped. "His shitty behavior had become so normalized that it didn't even register that this was a crime."

"This is not your fault." He pressed his mouth to my crown. "You did nothing wrong."

"I did this to my kids," I said into his neck. "Donny was a shit father, but if I had been a better mother, I would have seen the signs and gotten them out before it got so bad."

"You cannot blame yourself." He brushed my hair back from my face. "You were a victim too."

Breath catching sharply, I pulled back and glared. "Fuck you. Don't use that word."

The thought was too much to bear. That word, victim, implied helplessness. Weakness. Every time I heard it, I wanted to crawl out of my skin.

"Sorry," he said. "But you were in a difficult position. You didn't know then what you know now. And carrying that guilt around with you every day? Does that help your kids, does it serve them?"

"Fuck you." I slumped against him. He was being annoyingly logical.

"You can't change the past," he murmured. "Trust me. I, of all people, know that. And I'm not a professional, but they are pretty stellar kids. You've done an amazing job."

"Anyway." I swiped the back of my wrist across my face, clearing away tears. "That's my story. And the best part? After the months it took to get him prosecuted and sentenced, he's already up for parole."

"So soon?"

I nodded, my chest tightening. "Yeah. I'm going to fight it. Give testimony and present evidence. Chloe hired the best lawyers, but it's just so much."

"That's why you've been off this week."

He was so damn perceptive. I considered telling him about the card, about Phyllis's emails and the lawsuit, but I'd laid enough on this man today. And ultimately it wouldn't make a difference. I wasn't available. Not for something real.

"Yes," I admitted, head bowed. "And that's why, as much as I like you, this cannot be anything more."

"I disagree."

With a deep breath in, I studied his face, taking in his honest vulnerability and the kindness in those dark eyes.

"I have feelings for you, Josh. And acting on those feelings today felt incredible. But you deserve someone who is all in. Who wants the same things."

"You don't get to tell me what I want," he said softly. "I want you, Celine."

I almost threw myself back into his arms. Into his safety and his strength, where nothing bad ever happened. But that wasn't real life.

"I want you too," I said softly. "But the timing—"

"Timing doesn't matter. I'm not going anywhere."

"This town is filled with so many lovely women. You deserve to meet a great person, do the dating things, fall in love, and have your own kids."

He bristled, though he swallowed audibly and kept his tone even. "I adore your kids," he said. "And I'd do anything for them."

I believed him. Hell, I'd seen it with my own eyes.

"What about Annie? She's pretty, and you have so much in common."

Glaring, he roughed a hand through his hair. "Are you seriously trying to set me up with another woman while we're both naked in my bed? You were screaming my name and coming on my cock twenty minutes ago."

I bit my lip, face heating. God, that had been incredible. But I shook the thought free. "You know what I mean."

"No. I don't."

I got up and spun in a circle, searching for my clothes. I'd left my kids with a friend so I could get laid. I was officially the worst mom ever.

"Josh," I pleaded, pulling on my sports bra.

He lay back, putting his hands behind his head, watching me as I struggled into my leggings. The combination of biceps and chest hair almost had me crawling back into the bed.

Almost.

"I'll wait," he said firmly. "As long as it takes."

Chapter 27

JOSH

I'd wait. I'd waited this long. And now that I knew what I could have, how incredible it could be? I'd never settle for anything less.

Celine could keep me waiting for decades, the memories of our encounters could sustain me for years.

And what she had told me about her ex-husband? Rage flared in my chest every time I thought about it. How could anyone be so cruel?

And while I was glad the asshole was in jail, I would have been much happier if he was in the ground, where he could never hurt Celine or her kids again.

I got out of the truck at Logan's place, taking it in. He was chaos personified, and his home-slash-farm-slash-animal-sanctuary followed suit. He had been saving to buy the place, and with any luck, that would happen. It fit him perfectly. Cats and dogs running all over, a pen of goats, dozens of chickens, and a potbellied pig who ran and slept with the dogs.

He emerged from the barn wearing rubber boots and a big grin, rubbing his hands together. "The surprise is ready. Wanna see?"

Nervousness coursed through me, but it wasn't due to the usual fear or stress. No, this felt more like hope. I'd moved mountains for trees, for land, for the family legacy. Yet this felt bigger.

The barn smelled like hay and leather, soft light filtering in through the large door and the windows. Halfway back, we stopped at a stall where a calm quarter horse stood, ears flicking, her tail swishing lazily. "This is Daisy. She's a bay," he said. "She's funny and friendly."

I surveyed her, noting the white star on her forehead.

"How old?"

"Ten, so she's past the wild stage, and she's not hotheaded. Rescued her from a neglect situation in upstate New York."

The horse had calm, kind eyes, and by the way she shifted her weight and swished her tail again, she was unfazed by our presence.

"And she's safe?"

"For grooming, snuggles, and walking? Yes. No riding yet."

I nodded, easing a hand out to stroke her head.

She pushed into me, craving affection.

"She's perfect," I said.

"You gonna tell me about the girl?" He stretched, grabbing the rafter above him. The move caused his shirt to ride up, putting his lower abs on display.

I had no clue how he cared for all these animals, kept up his practice, stayed in good shape, and found time to eat.

"Maggie? Sure, she's nine and obsessed with horses."

"No." He let go of the rafter and crossed his arms. "I know Maggie. She asked me five dozen goat questions last weekend. I'm talking about her mom. You know, the woman you're madly in love with?"

I didn't deny it. I was a shit liar.

"It's complicated," I replied, ducking. "And I'm not rushing anything."

He shook his head. "That's the most Josh response I've ever heard. But if you're happy, I'm happy for you, man."

A sigh escaped me. "Making these kids happy makes me happy."

"Then I hope she doesn't keep you waiting too long."

"I'm in no rush."

Before he could grill me any further, Celine pulled up in her minivan, the damn thing making noises that probably weren't good. I needed to get it over to Frankie for a full tune-up sooner rather than later.

Heading toward the commotion, I dug my phone out of my pocket and prepared for the big moment.

"Is this the rescue?" Maggie shouted. "Can we see our friends Calvin and Hobbes?"

"Actually," I said, giving her a nonchalant wave, "there's someone we want you to meet."

She peered up at her mom, pushing her glasses up her nose, and when Celine smiled at her, she ran toward me.

I hadn't told Celine about Daisy yet. I'd only asked her to meet me here after school. But I was certain she would love the surprise as much as Maggie did.

"Oh my God." Maggie squealed when she caught sight of Daisy. "Is she real? *I'm dying.*"

I put a hand on her shaking shoulder and bent at the waist. "Breathe."

She was silent, but her body remained trembling with excitement, her eyes huge behind the lenses of her glasses.

"This is Daisy," I said, nodding at the horse. "And Daisy, this is Maggie Whittier."

Maggie reached out with shaking fingers, and the mare lowered her head, meeting her halfway. They froze like that, the two of them perfectly still, connected.

Shit. My heart squeezed. I looked over at Celine, who was wiping a tear from her cheek.

"She's the most beautiful thing I've ever seen," Maggie breathed. "Mom, do you see this? Get your phone. Take pictures of me with Daisy, my best friend."

Logan cleared his throat. "Let's talk a little bit about how we can care for Daisy."

Maggie, always excited to learn, snapped to attention.

"Would you like to brush her?" he asked

"It would be my great honor."

My lips twitched, and beside me, Celine let out the tiniest giggle.

"Here." Logan held the brush in his hand and showed her how to do it. "Long strokes, shoulder to flank."

Maggie took the brush and mimicked his motion, a look of fierce concentration on her face.

"The most important signal she can give us is with her ears. If they're facing forward, that means she's happy. But if they're pinned back, that lets us know she's scared or unhappy, and if we don't pay attention, she could accidentally hurt someone."

Maggie nodded, blissfully brushing Daisy, who had lowered her head and was sniffing the ground near her feet.

"Ellie? Julian?" Logan said. "Would you take this bag of dried crickets over to the chicken coop and give them some treats while I teach your sister a few more things?"

Julian rushed up to him and snatched the plastic bag from his hand. "Crickets are gross, but Josh's chickens love them,"

With a small smile, Ellie led him across the barn, where the chickens were already gathering for their snack.

"Getting to know a horse takes time," Logan said. "They are big feelings trapped in big bodies. We can't rush them, and you've got to do the work to earn their trust."

I snuck a glance at Celine, who was staring at me, her eyes teary.

"Daisy has some recovery to do before she can be ridden," he told Maggie. "But would you like to take her for a walk?"

Her face lit up. "Yes. Please, yes."

He leaned over the stall, and when he straightened, he held out an apple to Maggie. "Offer it with a flat palm. See if she takes it from you."

I winced, praying this horse wouldn't bite off her fingers. But Maggie did as she was told, radiating calm energy, and Daisy snapped the apple up, crunching it happily.

"Okay, then. Let's take you for a walk around the paddock. Always walk on a horse's left side and keep your hand halfway down the lead."

He stayed close but gave Maggie freedom to do the work. Daisy plodded along next to her, matching her pace.

"Doing great," Logan called. "Walk a bit faster and see if she knows to change her pace."

Maggie was beaming, her shoulders pulled back, her confidence blooming more with each step.

She immediately fell into a one-sided conversation with the horse, telling her about her day at school, her siblings, and how she'd been dreaming of having a horse best friend for years.

Celine followed, giving them a wide berth and snapping photos. She was doing her best to stay composed, but she was failing beautifully.

"You did this," she said softly, her eyes still on her daughter as I approached.

"Logan did," I lied.

She huffed. "I don't believe that."

I crossed my arms, sidling up close enough to feel her warmth, but without touching.

Celine looked over her shoulder, checking on Julian and Ellie, who were playing with the chickens and filling a wire basket with eggs. "I've dreamed of this for so long," she said. "Giving her a moment of pure joy like this." She wiped at a rogue tear. "Thank you."

I squeezed her hand in response.

"Mom," Maggie said, leading the horse toward us. "Logan says he needs help taking care of Daisy. Can I come by after school and help?"

Lips pressed together, Celine nodded. "We'll have to speak to Logan and find out his schedule."

"I can learn so much. It's educational," Maggie begged.

Logan raised a brow. He didn't plan to keep this horse

once she'd been fully rehabbed, but he didn't mention that detail.

"We could find room. We've actually got a horse barn. It's on the piece of adjacent land I bought from my aunt and uncle—"

Maggie shrieked.

Logan gently but quickly moved in, grabbing the horse's lead. "Don't spook Daisy."

Maggie quieted immediately, wincing, then eyed her mom.

"My aunt was actually quite a horsewoman when I was a kid. She could probably give you a few tips."

Uncle Ed and Aunt Suzie had retired in Florida, although they came for extended visits in the summer, staying at the old farmhouse on the property they'd sold to me a few years back and sticking around to help out with harvests.

But back in the day, they had housed several draft horses, so the barn wouldn't need much work to be habitable again.

"Mom, can I keep her?"

"Let's start with visiting and learning how all this works." She shot me a scolding look, but the joy in her eyes took the sting out of it. "We can see how things go from there."

Maggie beamed, pulling a sugar cube out of her pocket for Daisy. The two of them wandered off for another lap around the paddock with Logan trailing closely.

Dust hung in the air, glowing in the late afternoon light, making Celine's features look softer.

She lingered at the fence, watching her daughter, breathing in the moment.

"You don't have to adopt a damn horse," she whispered.

"I know," I said. "But I like seeing her so happy, and Logan can't keep her here forever."

With a quiet laugh, she turned to face me.

When her eyes locked with mine, I forgot how to speak. They were bright and full of joy and tears. Like her heart had stretched in a way that both hurt and healed at the same time.

She opened her mouth and then closed it. Like she wanted to say a hundred things but didn't trust any of them to come out right.

"You made her dream come true."

I took a step back and stuffed my hands into my pockets, suppressing the urge to pull her into my arms.

"I don't know how to hold on to all of this," she admitted, looking away. "The joy. The excitement. The..." She sighed. "The ache of wanting more."

I understood the sentiment. I felt that ache too. But I had no idea how to reassure her. How to survive the riot of emotions she caused inside me.

"I did this for Maggie," I told her. "You don't owe me anything in return, okay?"

Frowning, she dipped her chin.

"Logan told me he was going to see about a horse, and it felt like the perfect opportunity."

Her gaze softened. "You're a good man. Too good. So good I don't deserve you."

"Hey—"

She held up a hand. "Let me finish. The way I feel? It scares me."

The space between us was charged, a deep, complex pull making it impossible to stay away from her.

"I can live with scared," I said.

She sniffled. "You shouldn't have to."

"I'm not in a hurry. I'm waiting for you." That was the truth of it. The real offering. Right out in the open. I would wait forever. And I'd be damn happy to do it.

She stepped closer, making it so damn tempting to reach out and touch her.

"Thank you," she said, looking at me from beneath wet lashes. "Not just for the horse, but for everything. What you've done and who you are."

Warmth bloomed in my chest as I smiled at her. "Anytime."

We stood there a moment longer, the barn breathing around us, the unspoken words hanging heavy and tender between us.

It was only interrupted when Julian and Ellie came running, talking over one another and asking for a turn brushing Daisy.

Celine followed them to where Maggie and the horse were bonding.

I couldn't stop smiling.

Because this wasn't nothing.

We would get there.

Chapter 28

♥

CELINE

I'd never been a farmers' market kind of girl. Between the chaos and the forced chitchat, I'd never seen the appeal. Especially with curious kids bound to touch things they shouldn't and get into trouble.

But in the few short months we'd been here, it had become clear that attendance at the Maplewood farmers' market was mandatory. The entire town and surrounding communities came out, not only to shop, but to catch up and learn.

The kids loved the snacks and the opportunities to see their friends, and I'd discovered that if I didn't show my face, the Maplewood Mafia would stop by to check on me. So the market, it was. The chaos was far less painful than Bitsy Bramble's presence at my home.

As the smell of cider and fresh donuts flooded my nostrils, Ellie stomped up to my side. "I'm hungry."

That comment was followed by echoing sentiments from her siblings.

Promising that we would get snacks in a bit, I led them over to a complex display of honeycombs that fascinated Julian.

"The bees built all of this," a friendly looking woman with gray hair and jeweled glasses explained.

Julian nodded, still transfixed. "Oh, I know. Every bee in the hive has a job," he explained. "Some are builders. They build these combs, and each cell will be filled with honey from the other bees."

I smiled with pride as he chatted with this stranger about beekeeping. It had been so long since he'd been this open to new experiences.

"There's Paige," Ellie said, waving at a friend. She gave me a quick questioning look, and when I nodded, she wandered toward a group of bored-looking tweens. I kept an eye on her while Julian asked more bee-related questions and Maggie scanned our surroundings furiously, probably searching for any animals that may have come along.

She had not stopped talking about her new best friend, Daisy, in days.

"Mom." She tugged on my sleeve. "He's here."

I turned, following her line of sight, and found Josh standing next to the town mayor. He was holding a cardboard coffee cup from his sister's shop and sporting a green flannel shirt and his usual grumpy expression.

Annoyingly, my stomach did a little flip. As much as I tried to ignore it, my body reacted every time I saw him. My pulse quickened and I couldn't help but stare.

He said he loved me. It didn't make sense. This was too fast and too messy.

But I couldn't stop my mind from racing, from getting

ahead of me and thinking about what could be. When things calmed down, when I got through this parole hearing, when the kids and I were more settled. Could this be something real?

Because my body thought it was very real. So real I'd been having some very, ahem, explicit dreams about him.

The situation was so messy. He was my landlord. My neighbor. My... lover?

I shook my head. No, we'd had sex. Very hot sexy sex. And we'd said things. Heartfelt, intense things. But only that single time.

Yet I found myself constantly walking around in a daze, trying to bump into him while convincing myself it could never happen again. Clearly I was a paragon of mental health.

Before I could stop her, Maggie was running toward him, shouting his name.

He turned, and his face lit up in a way only reserved for my kids.

She threw her arms around him in a big hug. He was her hero, after all, introducing her to her new best friend. She'd ruminated for days about how to thank him, eventually settling on baking cookies and making him a thank-you card. But so far, she'd spent all her free time researching horses and horse care.

He caught her, wrapping her in those comforting arms.

"Hello, superstar," he said, meeting my eyes.

My face heated instantly. It was ridiculous. It was damn cold outside, yet suddenly I had the urge to fan myself.

"Hello. I'm Gabe," the mayor said to my daughter.

She looked up at him, her glasses askew. "Do you know

Josh? He's amazing. He found me a horse named Daisy and —hold on. Mom, can I have your phone? I wanna show this guy the pictures I took."

Gabe smiled at her, his eyes dancing. "Sure, I know Josh. He's my cousin."

"Do you have a horse?" she asked.

"Sadly, no." He pressed his lips together. "But I like horses."

Maggie looked him up and down, as if making up her mind about him. "Okay, that's cool. I'll vote for you."

He chuckled. "You may be a little young for voting."

Unbothered, she flipped through photo after photo of her new equine friend. Before long, she clutched Josh's hand and tugged. "We're going to get cherries. Come on."

He smiled at me and offered Julian a fist bump, then walked with us toward the Hogans' farm stand where the kids started picking out more produce than they would actually eat.

Several people said hello to Josh, but he only sipped his coffee quietly, giving them small nods.

"You're popular," I said, elbowing him gently. It wasn't nearly the kind of contact my body craved, but it was the best I could get out in public like this.

"I've been working on my brand."

I gave him a once-over, wearing a teasing smile. "Farm-dad chic?"

He stared down at me, intensity radiating off him. "I make it look good."

Face heating again, I lowered my attention to my feet. Thankfully I was wearing matching Crocs today. The Fuzzy kind for cold weather. My left pink glitter was still missing, but it would surface soon. Sometimes looking for my stuff felt like an archaeological dig.

"You look beautiful," he said.

My instinct was to brush off the compliment. Make a comment about how I'd just rolled out of bed. If I had, I'd have been lying. This morning I was wearing new leggings and had put on mascara just in case I ran into him.

Rather than fight it, I looked him dead in the eye and said, "Thank you."

We'd just stepped into the cider donut line when a familiar voice set my nerves on edge.

"Well, well, well." Bitsy Bramble stepped into view, wearing a long purple coat and a knit hat.

"Certainly took them long enough," Olive Foster added.

Mavis held up her phone with a boney, shaky hand. "Need a photo of the happy couple for the town Instagram page."

"No." I threw a hand up. "We're not a couple."

The three of them looked between Josh and me, all wearing knowing expressions. The two of us probably looked like kids who'd been sent to the principal's office—at least that's how I felt—rather than actual adults who'd recently had (excellent) sex.

"Why not?"

A wave of panic hit me. Screaming "none of your business" probably wouldn't be well received, but no other explanation came to mind.

"Ladies," Josh said, his tone cool. "Can you give me some time?" He raised an eyebrow, and they exchanged a knowing look.

"Sorry," Olive said. "Forgot what a slow poke you are.

Would you mind making a move before I croak? I want to win the betting pool."

Josh gave them a stern look, crossing his arms.

That was enough to send them scampering off to terrorize other innocent folks.

We stayed for another hour, sampling cheeses and several types of maple candy, then listening to a folk band cover nineties hip-hop hits. Maggie must have told at least a dozen people about her horse, and I wouldn't be surprised if she told a dozen more before we left.

I was cold, but just existing with josh like this kept me from feeling the discomfort of my frozen toes and fingers while we wandered, snacking on cherries and drinking coffee. Josh was patient and present with my kids, as he always was, buying treats and stopping them before they tried the chili pepper jelly and the stinky cheese.

"Do you need to get right home?" he asked as the kids ran wild on the town green.

Julian had found Jacob, and they'd roped Ellie and Maggie into a game of tag with really convoluted rules.

"No. We've got nothing today."

"Great." He gave me an awkward grin that instantly made me suspicious. "Give me one second."

Before I could question him, he strode away. When he returned, Frankie Dunne was at his side.

I'd seen her once or twice but had never spoken to the woman. She was terrifying. Tiny and muscular with colorful tattoos, big doll eyes, and a "don't fuck with me" air that I heeded with extreme caution.

She was my polar opposite. I couldn't imagine her

twisting herself into a pretzel to please others the way I'd done far too much in my life.

"Frankie, do you know my friend Celine? She and her kids live in the cottage on my property."

She gave me a nod. "Teacher, right?"

Smiling, I shook her hand. "Yes. Kindergarten."

"Celine's minivan is not gonna survive the Vermont winter. You mind taking a look?"

Hackles rising, I took a step back. "Excuse me?" I wouldn't hear any trash talk about my van. Not from anyone. We'd been through a lot together. I'd bought it used with my own damn money; it was mine. It was big and boxy and slow, but it had enough room for my whole family and all the gear we'd need for road trips. I used to drive a luxury SUV. One Donny chose because it "sent the right message." The damn thing was uncomfortable, and a simple oil change cost several hundred dollars. I'd hated it. So when the time had come, I'd found my baby blue Honda Odessey and instantly fallen in love.

It was all mine, stow-and go-seats and all.

Arms crossed, I glared at him. "It will be fine."

He adjusted the bill of his hat. "Our winters are harsh."

I scoffed. "I'm a Mainer. I know how to drive in snow. I can operate heavy machinery in the snow. Hell, I could bake a cake in the snow. So thanks for the concern, but I'm good." Suddenly, I was sweating, the anger running through me raising my body temperature. How dare he insinuate that my car wasn't safe?

"I like her." Frankie sipped casually from her travel mug, surveying me over the top of it.

Josh pinched the bridge of his nose. "I just want to help.

We've got a lot of unpaved roads and hills here. Uneven terrain, lots of ice. You need better tires, at least."

I had zero dollars for new tires and mine weren't bald. I'd make it another year, at least.

Frankie turned slowly and looked at Josh. While I was twitchy and quick, Frankie took her time, her unhurried movements making her even more scary.

"Are you trying to mansplain winter driving to this nice woman?"

A laugh threatened to escape me. Suddenly, I wanted to hug her. She'd probably hate that, so I focused on scowling at Josh.

"If she doesn't want me to look at her car," Frankie told him, "don't waste my time. I've got shit to do."

Yikes. I was definitely not going to hug her. But maybe she'd like a batch of homemade cookies instead. Maggie had perfected brown butter chocolate chip this fall.

Or maybe she'd want to be my friend.

Should I get tattoos? Hers were incredible.

"I'm sorry." She eyed me, her lip curled on one side. "His Y chromosome makes him stupid. But while I'm here. I could take a look at it for you. No charge."

I cringed internally, feeling like a child backed into a corner. Though I supposed I'd rather a qualified woman look at my car than Josh, who was being an overprotective ass at the moment.

So I told Ellie I'd be right back, then guided Frankie to the side street where I'd parked.

"Can you pop the hood?"

Once she'd propped it up, she took a flashlight from her pocket and examined the engine.

Josh leaned against the fender, giving me a smug look.

I glared back at him, hoping the look communicated something like "We might have had sex, but that does not give you the right to get all territorial and force me to buy tires."

Clearly not getting the message, he broke into a smile, that damn dimple popping.

After a few minutes, Frankie closed the hood and dusted her hands off. "She's in good shape. I'd need to take it in and run some diagnostics to be sure. But at a minimum?"

I held my breath.

She kicked the front tire. "These are not in great shape. Our roads suck in winter. I'd like to do a tune-up, new wiper blades, and at least a tire rotation before the first snowfall."

I nodded, mentally scrambling for a way to pay for all of that.

"The good news is that I know a very qualified person who can help."

I smiled at her, avoiding Josh's eye. There was absolutely no way I'd admit that he may have been right.

"I'm not going to force anything on you. It's your car and I love telling Josh to fuck off. But..." She trailed off, lifting her brows.

A sigh escaped me. It looked like my credit card would have to take the hit.

"Come here." She nodded, lifted her chin, then waved a hand, shooing Josh away.

Once he was out of earshot, she put an arm around my shoulders. "Drop it off tomorrow before school. I'll work up an estimate."

"I—"

"Also," she went on before I could even figure out whether to agree or argue. "I've heard rumors. Is it true you put your piece-of-shit ex-husband in jail?"

My heart sank. Wow, the small-town rumor mill was no joke. "Um. Yes."

She pulled me into her side. She was ridiculously strong for someone so tiny. "Fuck yeah, you did. Okay, then you get the friends and family discount. I was raised by a single mom and have a piece of shit dad. I'll take good care of you."

"No," I protested. "I can't accept that."

"Yes you can. You're one of us now. And in this town, we take care of each other."

She turned, eyeing Josh. "Which is what this dufus was trying to do, in his own annoying, controlling way."

I let out a sigh. Despite the happiness that had hit me at the potential of a new friend and discount tires, I was deeply annoyed with Josh.

"He's actually one of the good ones," she said quietly so he couldn't hear. "Granted, the bar's low."

I laughed. "It's in hell."

"Don't I know it. But he's a decent guy. He just wants you to be safe on the road. Don't kick his ass too hard."

"Thanks."

Chapter 29

♥

CELINE

By the time I got Julian to bed and Ellie and Maggie washed up and tucked in with books, my annoyance had turned into legitimate anger.

"Do you mind if I take a quick walk?" I asked the girls.

"Sure. My phone's plugged in," Ellie said, frowning. "You okay?"

"Yes." I nodded. "I borrowed some tools from Josh. I'm just going to return them before I forget."

She studied me, lips pursed skeptically.

"Lights out in fifteen minutes," I said. "I can see your window from the road, so I'll know."

"*Fine*," they grumbled.

I dropped a kiss on each of their foreheads, then jogged downstairs and slipped on my Crocs and coat before I could change my mind.

I found him on his porch, in a rocking chair.

"Were you waiting for me?" I asked as I climbed the steps.

"I'd sit here and wait for you every night," he said with the kind of cocky grin that made my knees weak.

And my body's reaction only made me more annoyed.

"This isn't—" I paused, grasping for courage I didn't actually possess. "We had sex."

In response, he only continued smirking.

I put my hands on my hips, scowling. "It does not mean you need to protect me. I can protect myself and my kids."

He dipped his chin. "I know."

"And you don't get to force me into car maintenance."

"I was just trying to help."

I stepped up close, my knees nearly brushing his, and loomed over him. "I don't need help."

He reached out and tugged my arm firmly, pulling me into his lap.

"There," he said, tucking a strand of hair behind my ear. "Better. Now what were you saying?"

A wave of heat coursed through me, part anger, part attraction. "Don't do that."

"Do what?"

"Be all helpful and protective and thoughtful."

"You're so sexy when you're pouting." He picked up one of my hands and kissed my knuckles. The move was sweet and gentle but also surprisingly erotic.

"And I can't help myself," he said. "Please forgive me for overstepping. You're strong and capable and amazing."

He kissed the knuckles on my other hand, his lips lingering longer, causing goose bumps to erupt all over my body.

"I have feelings for you, Celine. The deep desire to

protect you and the kids. I'll try harder to tamp it down. But it's part of who I am."

Fuck. I deflated, because it was impossible to deny how hot that sentiment was.

Beneath me, he hardened, his hot length pressing against my thigh.

"We can't do it again," I said, more to convince myself than him.

"Okay. I respect your boundaries. But just know that I'm here for you and the kids. For anything. Anytime."

Had a sexier sentence ever been uttered? Probably not, which was why my brain stupidly decided it would be a great idea to kiss him.

Not because I was weak or needed help, but because I was strong, and for too long, I'd denied myself what I wanted. And in this moment, I really wanted him.

"Goddamn," he said into my mouth, wrapping those strong arms around me as I threaded my fingers through my hair.

"Shut up and kiss me." I dove back in, my teeth clacking against his. I couldn't be bothered to care. The connection was hot and heavy, and I needed more of it. I wanted to feel cared for yet independent. Delicate yet strong.

I straddled him, gripping his hair as he kissed a trail down my neck. When he found a spot that lit me up inside, I rolled my hips.

The moan he let out was feral. Pure need. So I did it again, nerve endings I didn't even know existed sparking to life. It had been so long and I was so turned on.

"Celine." He pulled back, breathless. "Can I fuck you?"

I stared into his eyes, my body swamped with want and need.

"Yes." I kissed him again. "Yes, please."

He carried me into the house, his grip on my ass keeping me in place.

"You sure?" he asked again.

"Yes."

We landed on the couch, and he snagged a small remote control from the end table, using it to turn on the gas fireplace.

The space lit up with a dim, sexy light and glowing warmth.

"I can't stop thinking about you," he said, unzipping my fleece slowly. "Fuck, Celine, I've tried."

"Same." I kissed him back, unable to put into words just how needy he made me. "But I don't have a lot of time."

He stopped and sat back, cupping my face.

"You're in control," he said. "This is about you. We can stop now. Or—"

"Don't. Fucking. Stop," I hissed, lifting my hips and pushing my leggings down my thighs.

With a wicked grin, he dragged them the rest of the way down my legs, peppering my skin with kisses.

When I was down to my bra and undies and he was still fully clothed, I pushed him away.

"Get naked."

A slow, sexy smile spread across his face.

"And get a condom," I added firmly.

"Yes, ma'am." He hopped up and dashed up the stairs.

Thirty seconds later, he returned, yanking his shirt off as

he approached, his movements frantic and silly and so, so sexy.

I patted the couch cushion. "Sit down." This was reckless and selfish, but I couldn't think beyond my need to have him inside me.

He obeyed, and I pulled down his boxers, making his thick cock spring to attention.

A tiny bead of moisture pooled at the tip, taunting me, so I bent over him and licked it away.

The growl that left him made his chest vibrate. "My God."

I pushed his legs farther apart and knelt between them, gripping him with my hand and licking up the underside of his hard length. It was intoxicating, the feel of him in my hand, the sound of his gasps and groans.

"Celine," he said, his breathing ragged. "Please. You've got to stop."

Glaring up at him, I slowly enveloped him just to torture him. Then I released him with a pop.

Shaking with need, I stood and stripped off my bra and panties.

"I, um," I said, suddenly self-conscious on display in front of him. "I need to be on top."

Josh was warm and gentle. But I needed to be in control. I wasn't sure I could handle the weight of him on top of me. Not when I was just figuring all of this out.

"Anything you want," he said, his lids heavy. "Anything."

I snatched the condom off the couch, tore the wrapper open, and slid the latex over his length, a thrill coursing through me when his thighs shook.

Straddling his thick thighs, I hovered over him, nearly preening as he hungrily devoured my body with his eyes.

"I could stare at you naked for the rest of my life," he said quietly.

While I questioned the sentiment—I wasn't sure my boobs and stretch marks were that special—it was hard not to feel invincible in this moment.

With my hands on his shoulders, I eased onto his shaft. Slowly and deliberately, I lowered myself, letting my eyes close and my head fall back as my body stretched to accommodate his size. It was delicious, these sensations. And between his hands and lips and the heat of his body, I was dizzy with lust.

Slowly, I moved, rocking and shifting until I found a rhythm that sent arcs of electricity through me.

He pinched my nipples and kissed my breasts, looking so rugged and strong in the firelight, yet contained.

He was holding back. For me.

He was letting me take the lead.

"You okay with this?" he asked, his arms stretched out on the back of the couch.

"Yes," I cried out, riding him harder, clenching around him.

"That's it," he said. "You're so tight. God, you're squeezing the life out of me, but I love it."

I tossed my head back, leaning into the familiar tightening in my core. I angled forward until my breasts were in his face and ground against him, hitting all those spots that made my eyes cross.

"Fuck. Celine," he gritted out. "I don't know if I can hold on."

I kissed him hard, chasing the tension still building inside me. Being with him felt so good, so right, and so perfect. Everything about this moment was perfect.

In his arms, I was safe.

And so I let go.

Wild and moaning and messy and sexy, I came. Hard. Wave after wave of pleasure crashed over me, making me gasp and shudder.

Josh was right there with me. Holding me down to earth with those strong hands on my hips, surging up into me as his own release overcame him.

This gentle, kind man was unraveling me, piece by piece, and there was nothing I could do but give into it. Let myself have it.

Josh made me feel like more.

More than a mom.

More than my past.

More than a woman who needed saving.

Chapter 30

JOSH

I spent more time in the store than I intended to, obsessing and considering. Checking reviews on my phone. I didn't want anything too flashy, but it still had to be solid. Something that would last and help her be a kid again. Which may have been too much to ask from a piece of composite wood.

But this time, I wasn't buying equipment for the farm or a tool I'd use until it fell apart in my hands. I was considering hockey sticks and trying to remember the last time I'd worried so much about getting something right.

Thirteen was a big birthday. Ellie was no longer a kid, but she wasn't yet an adult. That age was scary and over-whelming but exhilarating at the same time. She was also old enough to smell bullshit from a mile away. And the last thing this kid needed was an adult making promises they couldn't keep.

I hefted the stick, assessing the weight. It was solid. The

kind that could be used a lot and thrown around. I'd cut it to fit her height and grab a roll of tape on the way out.

There was no pretending I wasn't nervous about this.

I wanted to show up for her. To be a part of things. In whatever way they'd let me. I wasn't trying to win points with Celine, and I'd never use her kids to get closer to her. I just wanted to be another supportive adult for Ellie.

Because somewhere between the pumpkin race and the horse and the way Ellie hovered, always alert, I'd started to see it. How observant she was. How careful. The way she held herself like she was bracing for impact. Like if she stayed sharp enough, she could keep the ground from shifting again.

I knew the feeling.

The house looked warm, the balloons tied haphazardly to the porch railing telling me Julian was involved with decorating.

"Josh," Maggie called, darting out the front door. "Come in. We have cake. Does Daisy eat cake? Can I bring her a piece tomorrow?"

Celine and Julian followed, and finally Ellie, who was wearing her usual black hoodie but also a sparkly birthday crown.

"Happy birthday," I said, handing her the stick without ceremony.

She looked at it for a minute, her lips tugged down, before taking it out of my hand.

She examined it closely, felt the weight of it, but she remained silent.

"If you don't want it, I can take it back," I said. "You shoot righty, correct?"

She nodded, now studying the blade, her fingers lingering like she didn't trust it not to disappear.

Celine was quiet, her focus fixed firmly on Ellie's face, probably to gauge her reaction.

"You didn't have to get me anything," Ellie said.

"I know." I lifted one shoulder. "But I figured you could use it. I heard you used to play."

She nodded.

"I was a hockey player when I was your age. I wasn't very good. But I loved it. I still play a lot with my friends."

"Friends?" She arched a disbelieving brow.

"Logan and Gabe," I admitted. "We play street hockey in the summer when the rink is closed."

"Does Logan bring animals to hockey?" Maggie asked.

I chuckled, stuffing my hands into my pockets. "Sometimes."

Hockey had been great for me as a kid. It had given me an outlet for my emotions and frustration, as well as some lifelong friends. But it was also an activity I shared with my dad. My sisters never had any interest, and Jasper preferred running wild in the woods. But Dad taught me and coached me and always cheered at my games. We'd even driven down to Boston a couple of times to watch the Bolts play. I always figured that one day, I'd have kids, and I'd teach them to skate and play with them out on Carver Pond the way he did.

Ellie gave me one of those tween glares, full of suspicion.

"I have nets and gear in my garage. If you ever want to play in the driveway."

She only scrutinized me further. When the silence was almost unbearable, she finally said, "I'm rusty."

My lips twitched. "So am I."

That admission was enough to break through the wall she'd put up between us. With an almost hopeful look, she turned to her mom.

"Go play. Dinner isn't ready yet. I'll yell when it's time."

Ellie and I played in my driveway as the sun dipped low and the air turned sharp. Wayne watched, retrieving errant street hockey balls.

We didn't attempt anything serious, just passing and shooting. Laughing when one of us missed the net entirely.

She loosened up as the minutes passed, her movements instinctive, muscle memory kicking in. Her laugher and smiles hit me hard. I'd never seen her like this.

Celine and Julian walked down eventually, watching for a bit and giving us a thirty-minute warning. I avoided Celine's eyes, not wanting to take away from Ellie's moment and not wanting to cross any of the invisible boundaries Celine kept putting up.

"We should get you home for dinner," I said.

"You're invited too."

My heart clenched. "I don't want to impose."

"It's my birthday." She harrumphed. "I'm a firstborn daughter and a Scorpio, so I'd do what I say if I were you."

"Yes, ma'am." I gave her a mock salute.

We cleaned up the nets and the gloves and the balls, Ellie clutching her stick the whole time, like she wasn't ready to let go of it.

"You can use this gear whenever you want to play," I said as we wandered toward the cottage.

"I don't play hockey anymore."

"That's cool. But if you want to just mess around in the driveway, it's there."

She hit me with another glare.

"The code to the garage keypad is 1991. So you can go in and borrow stuff whenever."

"1991?"

"It's the year I was born."

She scoffed. "Oh my God, that's, like, so long ago."

I winced.

"It was last century."

"Wow." I smirked. "You make me sound ancient." I ran my hands through my hair, knowing that I already had a healthy number of grays.

"You sure you can you still pay hockey?" she joked, her eyes dancing. "Wouldn't want you to break a hip."

I shook my head as we climbed the hill. She was funny, I'd give her that. "You're kinda mean," I teased.

"I'm just playing," she said. "But." She stopped walking. "I know you're in love with my mom."

I couldn't lie to the kid. She was too smart. And I cared about her. I wanted to earn her trust. After she'd been so let down. I knew I had to tell the truth.

"I'm going to talk to you like you're an adult for a minute," I said.

Her face lit up.

"Yes, I am in love with your mom. She is amazing."

Eyes narrowing, she clutched her stick with both hands. "So you want to marry her? She's already been married."

"I know. And no, I don't want to marry her."

Shit, that hadn't come out quite right. I was making a complete mess out of this conversation already. But I hadn't exactly been prepared for the teen girl interrogation squad today.

"Listen," I said, figuring she probably assumed everyone had an ulterior motive. "I love your mom. I want her to be happy and healthy and safe. That's all."

She tightened her grip on her hockey stick. "I don't want anything from her. And I would never pressure her to do anything she doesn't want to do."

"She doesn't need a husband."

I dipped my chin. "I can see that. You four are doing so great on your own."

"She's strong now, but she wasn't always," she admitted, her voice suddenly much quieter.

Despite her best efforts, she couldn't hide the fear or the anxiety that came with having to grow up too fast and too soon.

My heart broke for this scrappy girl. The girl who'd had her childhood taken away by the person who was supposed to love and protect her at all costs.

"I may love your mom, but I respect her even more. And I respect you," I said slowly. "So if you want me to stay away," I said, even as I cursed myself for making this promise, "I will."

"No." She shook her head, frowning. "My mom gets to make her own decisions. I like you. My brother and sister like you. So if Mom likes you, then that's okay."

Huh. A sense of relief washed over me. I hadn't expected such a thought-out response.

"You're very mature," I said.

"But," she went on, "just because I say it's okay doesn't mean I'm not watching you."

I nodded once. "Of course."

"And if you hurt my mom—"

"I won't."

"If you hurt my mom, my siblings and I will hurt you. You think I'm the scary one?" she asked, passion in every word. "Julian's super intense and Maggie's the wildcard. She may get distracted by books and baby animals, but she can be ruthless." She heaved out a breath, ducking. "Everyone is finally doing better. It took a long time, but it finally happened."

I wanted to wrap her in my arms and tell her that nothing bad would ever happen again. But I knew better than to promise the impossible.

"You did a great job," I said. "I see how protective you are. How you anticipate Julian's needs. How you help your mom and step in when your siblings need you." I rocked back on my heels. "You had to take on a role no kid should have to. And if you need to vent. I'll always listen."

We walked the rest of the way in silence.

"Josh?" Ellie said as we approached the porch.

"Yes."

"Thanks for the stick. I've missed playing hockey."

"Anytime, kiddo."

Chapter 31

CELINE

"Oh my goodness, I'm so thrilled you're here!" Suzie pulled me into a warm hug. "And thank you for coming," she said to my kids as she released me. "The boys are out back getting into trouble."

Ellie and Maggie greeted her, then wandered toward the back door. Julian, on the other hand, stayed tucked into my side. We'd been in Josh's house several times, but never when it was filled with noise and people and delicious smells like it was today. Josh had insisted we come over, saying his family "forced" him into Sunday dinners a couple times a month, but I was already having second thoughts.

The kitchen, which seemed so vast the first time I saw it, was crowded. Mel gave me a wave as she slid a pan into the oven. Gabe was standing in the corner in a suit, his head down, texting furiously.

"Hi." Josh shuffled up to me with a dishtowel slung over his shoulder. He was dressed in a blue polo shirt, a style I'd never seen on him, and he looked particularly delicious.

"Did you dress up for me?" I asked, tugging on his collar.

He smirked. "My mom trained me well. Julian," he said, focusing on my son. "Do you want some apple cider?"

The two of them took off toward the fridge, leaving me on my own to marvel at the chopping, talking, and cooking that was going on all around me.

The house smelled of roast chicken and fresh bread, and the windows were cracked, letting in the chilly fall air.

Mel held up a wine bottle from across the island and raised her eyebrows at me.

I shook my head. "No thanks."

"I brought a deck of cards," Ed said, grinning at Julian. "Care to challenge me in go fish?"

"Can we play here so I can see my mom?" Julian asked.

"Sure thing, kiddo." With an easy nod, Ed dealt the cards, using one corner of the crowded island.

I'd never witnessed a family gathering like this. One where no one was performing and no one was being tested. And for the first time, I understood why people did this willingly.

The farmhouse table was large, and Josh and Gabe had added a leaf, but elbows still bumped as plates were passed around.

I sat between Maggie and Julian, who had begged Josh to sit on his other side. Ellie sat across from us, talking to Mel about baking.

Typically, loud, crowded situations like this put me on edge, yet with them, I didn't feel like I needed to brace myself.

I hunched over, bringing my mouth close to Julian's ear. "Do you need your headphones?"

He shook his head, digging into his artfully arranged plate of cucumber slices, strawberries, his preferred brand of crackers, and four cubes of orange cheddar cheese. Foods he'd eat without negotiation or overwhelm.

"Josh remembered," he said, shoving a cucumber into his mouth.

"I can see that." My heart expanded as I noted how content he was.

But then my mind quickly betrayed me, dragging me back to Phyllis's house without my permission.

Thanksgiving with Donny's family had been painful. The long table, the china, the scrutiny and expectation that Julian would behave, which in her mind meant that he'd sit still and eat whatever he was served. That he wouldn't fidget. That he wouldn't be himself. The way she'd snapped at me for daring to bring along food for him.

She'd cackled, insisting that he'd eat when he was "hungry enough." As if starving a neurodiverse child was somehow a crack parenting strategy.

Julian leaned closer to Josh, holding up a ripe strawberry. "These are my favorite."

With a simple nod, Josh said, "I know."

He didn't say "I remembered" or "I guessed." No. He *knew*.

Warmth and affection rushed through me as I watched the two of them.

Gabe sat at the head of the table, as if by accident and tradition at the same time, fielding questions and answering emails while trying to eat.

"How many crises have you solved today, Mr. Mayor?" Suzie asked.

Shoulders lowering, he sighed. "Define crisis."

Nate, his younger brother, who I'd learned co-owned a brewery on the outskirts of town, joined in. "She means how many times have you been cornered in the grocery store and forced to listen to complaints about parking spaces?"

"Or tree trimming ordinances," Mel added.

"Three," he groused. "I didn't even make it to the frozen food aisle before I'd had enough and checked out, and I really wanted to pick up a few of those frozen acai bowls I like to eat for breakfast."

"Then you saved a cat, right?" Jenn teased. "And finished off the day by balancing the budget and fixing the broken stop light?"

"You'll have to excuse my oldest son," Suzie said to me. "He skipped childhood and went straight to responsibility."

"It's just the job," Gabe muttered, stabbing a roasted potato with his fork. "And you don't get to make fun of me." He pointed the utensil at his brother. "Not all of us get to sit around making beer all day."

"It's a valuable public service," Nate quipped.

Ed cleared his throat. "You didn't have to run for mayor."

Gabe huffed. "You raised me to be like this."

"We warned you." Ed chuckled. "You didn't listen."

Laughter ripped across the table, easy and warm. The kind that didn't require checking the room first to make sure it was safe. This was so different from what I was used to. After Mom died, we never had family dinner, and Phyllis made every family gathering miserable with her demands and constant judgment.

It felt like I'd wandered into the wrong house and been offered a seat and a plate anyway.

Midway through the meal, Josh cleared his throat. He was different today. His movements were unhurried, practiced. He listened and asked questions and teased his sister and his cousins.

"I'd like to um, propose a toast," he said, raising his glass.

Everyone followed suit, Julian even holding up his mostly empty cup of cider.

"At Sunday dinners, we raise a glass to my parents. James and Louise. Dad used to say that Sundays were for football and Mom said that they were actually for feeding people." He swallowed heavily. "I miss them both so much. But I know they'd be happy to see us gathered around their table today."

My heart swelled as we all clinked glasses. My kids were so comfortable here. Maggie was siphoning as much of Suzie's horse knowledge as her little brain could handle while Julian chatted with Josh.

Ellie was quiet as usual, though when Gabe mentioned Lover's Leap Park, she perked right up.

"I've got the zoning board screaming at me to expand the parking lot. And a whole group of people threatening revolt if we don't replace the metal slides."

"That park is pointless," my oldest daughter said, meeting Gabe's eye.

The table quieted.

"Ellie," I said gently, my stomach sinking.

"No. Listen." She put her fork down and sat straighter. "It's not close to the elementary school and the playground is outdated and not handicap assessable."

Gabe leaned forward, his eyes bright with curiosity.

"But it's within walking distance of the junior high and

high schools. Don't add more parking. Older kids need outdoor space too."

He hummed. "What would you suggest?"

"Get rid of the old dangerous playground, add another basketball court closer to main street. Add lights. Benches. Maybe one of those outdoor fitness courses."

"It's true." He nodded, his lips turned down like he was impressed. "Little kids have lots of options, and the park is an eyesore."

"Exactly. Maybe put in a skate ramp, or just a walking trail. It could be awesome. Bigger kids need safe community spaces too."

The confidence in her tone filled me with pride.

And my chest tightened as I realized every person at the table was listening to her. They were showing her respect. No one was minimizing her or brushing her off.

A warm hand squeezed my shoulder, Josh's steady presence only settling me further.

Nate rubbed his hands together, his lips kicked up on one side. "You're pretty smart, kid. And my brother the mayor is outsourcing to a child."

"I'm thirteen," she said, her voice dripping with teen condescension.

"My apologies," Nate muttered into his chicken, his eyes widening.

Gabe laughed. "You've got good ideas. I'm hiring you."

"Absolutely not," I said. "She's in seventh grade."

"I can work remote," Ellie quipped.

The entire table burst into laughter.

Dessert consisted of three types of pie for the crowd and

a popsicle for Julian, who had eaten all his dinner and had even tried a few bites of green beans. As I shoveled a chunk of apple pie into my mouth, Josh tapped my shoulder subtly and lifted a brow, silently checking in.

I responded with a smile. For the first time in years, being involved in a family gathering didn't make me tense. It made me feel alive. I was stuffed and warm and more relaxed than I'd ever felt in a crowd of people.

The adults cleaned up while the kids sprawled out on the couches watching a movie and Julian played go fish with Ed.

"Hey." Josh cupped my elbow and pulled me toward the back hall before Suzie and Mel, who were debating about who was going to brine the turkey for Thanksgiving, noticed.

He guided me into the laundry room and shut the door.

"You okay?" he asked. "Was that too much?"

I shook my head, my cheeks warming. "It was really nice. Thank you."

He tipped my chin up and gave me a light kiss.

"Sorry." He gave me a sheepish smile. "Been waiting all day to do that."

With my hands on his cheeks, I pulled his face down to meet mine and really kissed him. When he groaned, I snaked my arms around his neck and tugged at his hair.

Kissing Josh was a gateway drug. And soon I was light-headed and achy. Desperate to feel his skin against mine.

"We should probably get out there," he said gently, grasping my hips and putting a little space between us.

I closed my eyes, my face flaming. "Sorry. I got carried away."

He kissed the top of my head. "Matchstick, I don't mind."

"Later," I said firmly, my brain still short circuiting.

He raised his eyebrows. "Are you sure?"

With a grin, I palmed his hard cock, giving it a squeeze. "I'm sure."

Chapter 32

CELINE

Sneaking out to see Josh made me giddy. I was a grown-ass woman, and after such a long day, the kids had crashed at a reasonable time. I sat in the living room, attempting to read a book on my Kindle and failing to comprehend a single word for another thirty minutes to make sure the girls were fully out. Then I left a note next to Ellie's bed saying I was going out for a late night run around the farm in case she woke up.

As I tiptoed out into the cold night air, guilt plagued me.

I should not be doing this.

I should be at home, in bed with a face mask on.

But Josh had woken me up. He'd stirred the kind of desire inside me that I'd only read about in books.

As embarrassing as it was, I was horny and letting my hormones control me.

I was also deeply infatuated with the man. Not only was there intense physical attraction, but I constantly longed for his company. Throw in muscle memory and my body's need for more of the orgasms he had given me, and I was power-less to stop myself.

Every time I closed my eyes to sleep, I saw his face when I was riding him. He looked at me like I was a wild goddess, like he was the luckiest man on earth.

He was waiting on the porch when I walked up to the house.

"Did you leave a note?" he asked before I could greet him.

"I nodded. That's why I'm in my running clothes."

Smirking, he stood and grasped my hand. "We better not waste any time, then."

We were kissing before the door shut behind us.

He lifted me easily and carried me up the stairs as I unbuttoned his shirt. I was desperate to get my hands on his skin. To feel all of him.

He gently set me on my feet inside his room, and I pulled his face down to meet mine. I couldn't stop kissing him. I needed to feel him everywhere. This feeling, it was like mania.

He snaked a hand up my back and unclasped my bra, then pulled my shirt over my head.

"What do you want?" he asked, cupping my breasts. "Tell me."

I wanted all the things. In all the ways. All night long. But my brain was too scrambled to even begin to articulate that.

"Do you think that maybe we could..." I winced. I never in my life thought I would ask this questions. "Could we get tested?"

"Of course," he responded immediately. "I'll do whatever you need."

I let out the breath I was holding. "Thanks. I know it's not sexy, but I was just thinking—"

"Shh. You don't explain," he assured me, his mouth on my neck. "I'll do anything if it means being with you, Matchstick. Safe and prepared is very sexy."

When he found the spot that made my knees weak and nipped, heat washed over me.

"I'll do anything to make you feel safe." He kissed across my collarbones, then dropped to his knees in front of me.

My head bumped the wall behind me as he pushed down my leggings.

I did feel safe. And exhilarated.

He bit my inner thighs, sending a strange mix of pleasure and pain through me. I liked this version of him. A little rougher. A little less gentle with me.

"Josh," I growled, burying a hand in his hair. "I need you."

He looked up, a wicked grin spreading across his lips, then spread my legs wide. With his thumb, he circled my clit, priming me, then he pushed one finger inside me.

I gasped. But it wasn't enough.

"More," I whimpered.

With lazy movements, he withdrew his finger and licked it clean. "Soaked." Then he threw my leg over his shoulder and licked me in all the right spots.

I shuddered. Leaning against the wall and closing my eyes. His enthusiasm and excitement only turned me on more.

Even so, there was always that insecurity...

"You don't need to," I said weakly.

"Shh," he said. "Don't interrupt me when I'm eating."

Giggling, I tugged harder on his silky hair.

Before long, he was slipping those fingers inside me again, filling me and making me cry out. I was close, so close, and he was expertly breaking down every defense I'd ever put up.

"Fuck," I cried out as I came, riding his face with abandon, pressing one hand to the wall to keep from falling over.

I should have known I didn't need to. Because Josh kept me steady with his arms even as his tongue teased out the last of my orgasm. I was still out of breath, my thoughts jumbled when he swept me up into his arms and deposited me on his bed gently.

"Get naked," I said. Pushing up onto my elbows.

Looking at me, rubbing at the back of his neck, he looked almost shy.

"Come on, Lawrence," I teased. "Take it off."

That shy smiled appeared, and then he was dragging his T-shirt over his head, giving me an unobstructed view of his broad chest, his dark chest hair, and the sheer width of his shoulders. He wasn't cut like an athlete, but he was thick and strong from hard work. And every inch of him was irresistible.

"Pants," I commanded, spreading my legs wide.

Eyes glassy and locked on my core, he pushed down his pants and underwear. When he stood straight again, his cock unabashedly alert, I licked my lips.

With a sigh, he stroked himself.

"Oh my God," I breathed, nearly fainting. "That's hot. Do it again."

He lowered his focus to the floor between us, looking self-conscious.

"Please," I begged, dragging my fingers down my chest and stomach, stopping at my hipbone.

That did it. His eyes were locked on mine again a heartbeat later as he stroked himself.

"You like this?"

I nodded, heat flooding me.

"Good. Now imagine me doing this every single morning while I think about you," he gritted out. "All night I dream about you, Celine. And then I wake up rock hard and shaking."

Moaning, I slid my hand lower and brushed my clit.

"Then I get in the shower and fuck my hand, wishing it was you."

"Condom," I gasped, slipping a finger inside myself.

He moved quickly, pulling me onto my knees on the bed. "Do you want to be on top?" he asked.

"No," I said, easing onto the mattress again, arching my back.

"Are you sure?"

My chest ached at his care. He never pushed me out of my comfort zone. He listened and asked questions, always cautious of my feelings. But I wanted this man on top of me. I wanted to feel his full power as he thrust inside me.

"Please."

That one word set him loose. Between one breath and the next, he was on me, kissing and licking my neck as he lined himself up.

"Don't be gentle," I said, digging my nails into the muscles of his back. "I'm not going to break."

He'd taken his time. He'd let me call the shots. But tonight I wanted something different. I wanted to feel all of him. I wanted to experience the power in his body and the force of his desire for me.

Kissing me hard, he pushed inside me. "Fuck," he growled in my ear. "You feel incredible."

I clutched at him, my body arching to meet his, kissing and biting his neck and moaning as he thrust. I wasn't scared. I didn't feel unsafe. This was perfect.

"Harder," I cried as the headboard beat against the wall.

"Can I go deeper?" he asked, pulling back.

When I nodded urgently, he pushed my knees up, using them as leverage, and thrust harder.

"Is this okay?" he asked.

"Yes," I moaned, already on the brink of losing control.

My mind went blank. All I could do was relish the sensation as he thrust harder and faster.

"I've been dreaming about this," he growled into my ear, the timbre of his voice making me clench around him. "About fucking you properly. Going so deep and hard."

It felt like I was flying. Wild and free, bucking my hips up to meet his. My body driven by something even greater than lust.

Safety.

Belonging.

It was so fucking sexy. To be able to fully feel for once instead of overthinking.

"Tell me," he demanded. "Tell me how good it feels."

"Perfect." I gasped. "So full and stretched."

"I can't hold on for much longer," he warned, all his muscles pulled taut. "Can you come for me?"

So close already, I shut my eyes and let the first flutters take over. As the glowing sensation spread through me, my muscles spasmed and my body exploded.

His movements went jerky, and then he was groaning.

"You are incredible," he said as he collapsed on top of me, his racing heart beating against mine.

"Why does it feel so good?" I wrapped my arms around his torso, my voice slightly muffled by his beard.

"I don't know," he said. "But I don't think I'll ever recover."

Chapter 33

JOSH

"Okay, I'll ask again. And this time I want a straight answer." She hitched the blanket up around her chest, depriving me of the most gorgeous view.

I leaned back and put my arms behind my head, desperate to enjoy this bliss a little longer. To pull her into my arms and demand she be mine forever.

But we needed boundaries, and Celine needed time. And I was hardly in a position to complain. She'd spent the day here with my family and then she'd snuck into my bed.

She opened her mouth to speak and then paused. "Wait a second." She held the comforter up to her face and took a sniff.

I was seized by panic. I'd just changed these sheets.

"Last time I was up here, the sheet smelled like lavender," she said suspiciously. "Did you change detergent?"

I pretended not to understand. She reached for a pillow, pulling it up to her face. "Yes. This is different."

"I got new stuff," I said nonchalantly.

She pinned me with a glare. "This isn't new stuff. This" —she took another sniff—"is unscented organic detergent. I know it because I use it."

I nodded, feeling even more naked than I had a few minutes ago.

"I noticed," I said slowly, "that you used it. And I did some googling and thought that harsh detergent smells may be tough for Julian."

Her eyes widened. "You did?"

"Yeah." I ran my hand through my hair, trying not to feel like a stalker. "Got it online. Not a big deal. I thought maybe, um..." I trailed off. "That if you guys ever came over to hang out, I didn't want him to have to deal with any challenging smells."

She looked at me, blinking a few times. "Not a big deal," she muttered to herself. "Why are you single?" she asked suddenly, poking me in the chest with one finger.

I laughed. "Because I've been waiting for you."

She only glared.

"Just because it's cheesy doesn't mean it isn't true." I pulled her down for a kiss.

"I'm serious," she said, snuggling into my side. "How are you still single? Sure, your lectures about sap lines and the Brix scale are kind of boring, but—"

I squeezed her ass, making her squeal.

"I'm bad at small talk."

"Nope. Not buying it. You're kind. You're steady. You show up. You've got a great dick. And yet you're still single. It's statistically unlikely."

I closed my eyes. This woman. "Maybe I'm doing it on purpose?"

"Why on earth would you deprive the female population of your charms?"

She was teasing. I could continue teasing back, hoping we moved on to another topic quickly. Or I could deflect.

But neither felt right. Maybe it was the post orgasmic glow or having the woman of my dreams in my arms, but my defense mechanisms were nowhere to be found.

I wanted Celine to know me.

"I was engaged," I said.

Her eyes widened and the hand she'd been dragging over my pecs stopped.

"Four years ago."

She nodded. "I'm sorry."

"Don't be. It wasn't a good relationship. And everyone involved is better off now."

Her lips parted like she was going to ask me to elaborate on that, but instead, she put her head on my chest and sighed.

"Doesn't matter," she whispered. "Ending a relationship is difficult every time."

"I lived in New York before I took over the farm," I explained. "Feels like a lifetime ago. But I worked in finance. Spreadsheets and projections, that kind of thing."

I brushed a hand down her rib cage, letting the softness of her skin soothe me.

"My ex-fiancée, Allie, she was restless. Unsatisfied. Our relationship struggled, but I thought we'd have time to work on things. Then she got pregnant."

Celine stiffened in my arms.

"I was so happy," I said, forcing myself to go on. "I'd always dreamed of being a dad."

A lump formed in my throat. Even after all these years, I still ached for it. For the thing I'd never had. I'd loved that baby so deeply, even when she was hypothetical.

I'd had the pregnancy tracker on my phone and kept track religiously. One week it was a poppy seed, the next a blueberry.

And I'd been ready. Sure, our relationship wasn't perfect, but this child was. This child would fix things and give me the purpose I'd been lacking.

"With a dad like mine, I grew up with very specific beliefs about fatherhood. About what it meant to raise children. And even though the pregnancy wasn't part of the plan, I was ready for the challenge." I'd never forget that first ultrasound. Seeing the tiny beating heart, listening to its rhythm. Even now, that heartbeat haunted my dreams. The steady drum of what I'd never have. What could never be mine.

"After her first ultrasound, Allie sat me down and told me that she'd cheated on me. That she was leaving me."

"Oh my God." Celine sat up and threw her arms around my neck, puling me close.

"I worked too much. I was too serious. I was no fun. We didn't go to clubs anymore." A humorless laugh escaped me. "I assumed that I didn't have to go to clubs after age thirty. Apparently I was wrong. I was boring."

"You are not boring."

"I didn't pay enough attention or make her feel special.

There was truth there. I saw that. I wasn't an emotional guy. I kept quiet, put my head down, and worked."

It still stung. I thought that I was enough for her. I thought what we had was flawed but real.

"We did genetic testing shortly after. Turns out I wasn't the child's father."

"Oh Josh. I'm so sorry."

At the time, the grief was unbearable. The loss of that child hit me harder than the loss of my fiancée. It felt like the cruelest blow, taking away the one thing that I'd wanted more than anything.

"She married the other guy. They had another child too. From what I've heard, they're happy and healthy. When she moved out, I decided it was time for a change. So I packed up my own stuff, sold the condo, and moved home. My dad had passed and my mom was struggling to manage the farm, even with the help of Jenn and Jasper. So I came back and took over. My siblings all had their own lives and dreams. And I had nothing."

"Not true."

My vision blurred with tears. "Though I was suffering a pain I wouldn't wish on anyone, if that hadn't happened, then I wouldn't have spent those last few years of Mom's life with her. I was here when she needed me. I took care of her when she was sick. Listened to her retell stories from my childhood. And it was a blessing."

This farm, this land, had given me purpose. It wasn't glamorous, but my financial experience had helped me turn the place around.

My siblings and nieces and nephews now had a financial cushion. Uncle Ed and Aunt Suzie retired. I contributed to the local economy, kept jobs local, and honored what my family had been doing for generations.

"I used to think love was an endurance event," I explained. "That even when it felt wrong, the best thing to do was hold on." I would have loved Allie and that baby forever if she'd wanted me to. Because that was how I was built.

And no matter what Jasper said, it wasn't so easy. To just try again.

"I've had no interest in anyone since," I explained. "The curiosity and attraction were just... gone. Gabe and Logan kept pushing me to date, to get on the apps, but I didn't want to."

Her hold on me tightened. I loved her in that moment. For helping me say things out loud I'd never said before. To give me space to lay out my shame and my shortcomings without judgment.

"Until you," I said softly. "You changed everything."

She sucked in a startled breath. "I can't give you—"

"I know. And I'll take whatever you're offering. There is no rush."

"It's just I've got to get through the parole hearing," she murmured. "I've got calls with my lawyer set up, and I have to be interviewed by a member of the parole board. I'll probably have to go back to Maine at some point."

She was spiraling, the weight of what she perceived were my expectations on her pulling her down.

"Celine," I said softly. Squeezing her hand. "I'm not asking for anything. You and the kids at family dinner today?

Incredible. Sneaking into my bed tonight? A dream come true. If that's all I get, then I'm okay with it."

Her eyes welled. "I'm sorry."

"Take care of yourself and take care of your kids," I said, my heart aching. "I'll wait forever if you want me to."

Chapter 34

CELINE

This house had settled around us like an embrace. The late afternoon sunlight slanted across the wooden table scattered with art supplies, Legos, and algebra homework.

Maggie was narrating her Halloween costume engineering while Ellie offered suggestions and pretended to do math homework.

Julian sat on the floor by my feet, arranging crayons in perfect rows, calm and comfortable. The cottage was messy, loud, and thriving these days. We ate dinners at this table and watched endless movies on the couch. Julian had lost a tooth last week and was so relieved when the Tooth Fairy had "found" him at his new house. After years of only surviving instead of living, this felt like a miracle, wonderous and special.

Beneath the warmth and calm, there was a knot in my stomach I couldn't shake. Part fear and part hope. The parole hearing loomed. A shadow that continuously tried to drag me back toward a life I refused to return to.

But even with the dread and the preparation, I couldn't ignore the dizzying awareness that I might be in love.

The most impossible thing at the most impossible time. But resisting Josh, with his quiet steadiness, his care for my children, and his unguarded honesty, was hopeless.

Especially when he'd opened up about his past. About the loss and grief and betrayal.

But was it possible to fit this joy and hope alongside all the terror I'd carried around for so long? How could I build a future while always looking over my shoulder?

I wanted Josh. I wanted this life and a future that wouldn't cost me the safety and independence I'd worked so hard to build.

I was lost in those ruminations when my phone pinged on the table in front of me.

CHLOE

You still haven't submitted your statement.
Do you need my help writing it?

STOMACH SINKING, I SQUEEZED MY EYES SHUT. I DID NOT want to go down that road and reopen all the wounds. But the parole hearing was next week, so I didn't have a choice. I'd do it not just for myself, but for my kids, who had never been as content as they were now.

CELINE

I'm working on it.

CHLOE

I know it's hard, but you can do hard things.

THAT WAS MY OLDER SISTER, A VERITABLE inspirational poster.

With a deep breath, I gave myself a pep talk. Then I picked up my laptop and headed to the couch. I'd just started typing out notes, hands shaking, when the kids all clambered to their feet.

"Josh," Maggie yelled as she darted for the door.

"Wow. Hi, guys."

He gave me a shy grin, and my stomach flipped. Dammit. The last thing I needed right now was a big, warm, sexy distraction.

With a box held out, he stepped inside, Wayne with him, demanding pets and cuddles. "Jenn sent me over with these. New donut flavors they're considering."

Ellie took the treats, and the three of them rushed into the kitchen.

"Come in." I pushed my messy hair behind my ears and cringed inwardly. I'd worn makeup to school this morning, but I had a feeling most of it had crusted under my eyes by now.

"You okay?" he asked, his head tilted.

I nodded.

He opened his arms and I stepped into them, accepting a

quick hug. I wanted to cling to him, to beg him to help me put Donny and all this nastiness behind me.

"So," he said as he released me. "Hypothetically, if you were a bit tense and needed a break..."

Stepping back, I looked up at him.

He held up his hands. "Hypothetically, of course."

That comment only made me suspicious of his motives here. So I crossed my arms and cocked a brow, readying to argue.

"Maybe I could take the kids outside to play street hockey for a while. Give you some quiet."

My body deflated. Oh. God, this man was so sweet. "That would be okay," I said. "But Maggie and Julian don't have sticks."

"Um." Ducking, he shuffled his feet. "I bought them some."

"Josh."

"So we can all play. You know, a big family game."

The word "family" snagged on something sharp inside me. Because it was easy to imagine how good things could be. What Josh and I could build over time. Love, trust, security.

I blinked back tears, quickly collecting myself. I was too busy to break down, and I didn't need him asking more question or looking at me with pity. Like a victim.

"Okay." I nodded. "That would be helpful. I just need an hour to..." I waved a hand at my laptop. "To finish something."

In a matter of minutes, he'd rounded up the kids, found Julian's blue fleece hoodie, and headed out for street hockey.

"You sure you don't need me?" Ellie asked through the open door. Her siblings were already halfway down the road.

"I'm good," I said, my heart panging with gratefulness as I shuffled onto the porch. "You go have fun."

She bounded down the porch steps, suddenly seeming so much more childlike than she had in years. There had been a time when Ellie was bubbly and outgoing. Silly and creative. But when things got bad with Donny, the light inside her had gone out.

It was flickering back to life now. Between new friends, robotics club, and playing hockey with Josh, she was finding herself again. I wiped away a tear. I couldn't backslide. We'd come so far.

My phone buzzed in my hand, so as I stepped back inside, I scrolled through the latest texts in the group chat. The girls were making Halloween plans, and Callie was checking in for my upcoming IEP meeting. Chloe had texted again too, with reminders and legal suggestions.

I sat on the couch, breathed in, breathed out, and just typed.

Yes, I was nauseous.

Yes, my hands shook.

But I had to get this out.

I started with the incident. The impact it had on me. On the kids. I dug around in my files to find the reports from the child psychologists and the court advocate.

Robotically, I laid it out from beginning to end. I wasn't a victim. I was someone with essential factual knowledge. I had a duty to share it.

The emails were next. Those from Phyllis and those

from an anonymous email account. The hang-up phone calls. The strange packages and notes in the mail.

A retelling of the time he sent one of his drinking buddies to "check on us" when we were living in Portland and the man had kicked in the door of our apartment.

Donny wasn't satisfied unless he was controlling and intimidating me. It had always been that way. It had just started off more subtly, and I'd been too dumb to see it at the time.

When he was out on bail, he'd driven by Chloe's house, blaring the car horn in the middle of the night. Or triggering our alarm system remotely when we were asleep just to be cruel.

I typed official, legal phrases like "Escalation, behavioral patterns, and ongoing risk." I attached all the emails and notes. The police reports from the prior incidents.

The idea of him being released early terrified me. Donny didn't care about restraining orders, and clearly, he knew where we were.

A thought I hadn't wanted to acknowledge plagued me. Should we leave? Move again?

The idea made me sick. Even from behind bars, even years later, Donny was still taking things away from me. Still punishing me.

I wiped at my tears with my sleeve and kept typing, focusing on remaining objective and organized. Eventually, I wandered over to the kitchen and plucked out what looked like a cranberry-flavored donut.

Then I went to the junk drawer and pulled out an envelope. I'd tucked notes, letters, and cards inside it as they showed up over the past couple of years.

On top was the latest card. I stared at the handwriting. *Found You* screamed at me from the yellow cardstock.

"Fuck you," I said to the pile of papers. "You're not getting out early, Donny." My hands no longer shook with fear, but with pure rage. "Fuck you," I shouted. "You terrorized us. You stole so many years from me. And I'll be absolutely damned if I let you steal from my children. If you take away their home and their happiness."

With renewed motivation, I sat back down and finished typing.

An hour or so later, the kids' laughter floated on the air, loud enough to hear inside the quiet house. Smiling, I looked out the front window. Josh was carrying Julian on his shoulders. It was a sight I'd never seen before. Julian did not like being touched and definitely did not want to be carried. He tolerated it for the pumpkin boat race, but he'd been clear that it was only because it was necessary.

They spilled through the door.

Julian darted for me, tugging on my shirt. "I scored a goal."

"Awesome."

"Mom." Maggie was talking a mile a minute, her face flushed and her cheeks rosy. "Ellie taught me how to do this move."

Ellie wandered to the sink and filled a water glass.

"Good game," she said to Josh, a hint of a smile on her lips.

"Can Josh stay so I can show him my Halloween costume?" Maggie asked.

"Me too!" Julian jumped up and down. "I wanna see if he's scared."

"Okay. If he wants to." I padded toward where he stood near my open lap top and clapped it shut. "Thanks," I said.

He inspected me, a worried look on his face. "If you need to talk—"

I shook my head. "All good." Not today. For now, I wanted to talk about Halloween and algebra and street hockey. He was so kind and so good. But his visceral reaction to what had happened, while not wrong, made me feel ashamed. Made me feel stupid. Like a woman who wasn't capable of protecting her kids.

And right now. I couldn't afford that.

Chapter 35

JOSH

It had been a very long time since I'd gone trick-or-treating. But when Julian asked if Wayne and I would come along, I'd jumped at the chance. His zombie costume was very creative, and he'd affected the perfect limp. The way he giggled and groaned "Braaains." At his sisters was adorable.

Celine wore a fairy costume, complete with gossamer wings. She was the most beautiful thing I'd ever seen.

"You missed an opportunity," I told her. "You'd make an amazing Little Mermaid."

She blushed, ducking. "Stop it. You do not want to see me in a shell bra."

I leaned in, my nose brushing her hair. "Um, I most certainly do. I think I may have a mermaid fantasy."

With a roll of her eyes, she slapped my arm. I liked seeing her like this. In her element.

We'd already run into several of her students. Every few

minutes, little witches and superheroes waved at her with sticky fingers.

"Julian," Callie said, eyes dancing. "I love the zombie commitment. Very scary." She handed him two candy bars.

His face lit up, and he was sure to thank her before he stepped back.

"Maggie, the costume is ambitious."

Celine laughed easily, a sound that made my heart clench, and when Callie hugged her without asking, like it was the most natural thing in the world, and Celine didn't hesitate, I had to fight the urge to pump a fist.

Logan passed us with Rosie, both dressed as astronauts, and from what I could tell, he hadn't brought along any wild animals. But it was getting dark, so maybe I'd missed one or two.

"Uncle Logan," Rosie said, "take a picture of me with Julian. His costume is super scary."

Julian beamed, completely at ease, even in this crowd, as Logan snapped some photos.

Jasper caught up to us, wearing Vincent in a carrier on his chest and looking proud of himself. They were both wearing Ghostbuster jumpsuits. Vincent gurgled with happiness as he grabbed at the Snickers bar Julian held out to him.

As the night went on, I was struck by the natural way the town expanded and contracted around us. People greeted the kids by name, no one flinched or stared when Julian put on his headphones, and many offered hugs to Celine.

She wasn't tolerated here. She was welcomed. She was wanted.

She belonged here. They all did. I just hoped she understood that. Maplewood had adopted her and her kids, and we didn't give up easily.

At her side now, I began to feel like I belonged too.

I sipped my cider, my thoughts drifting to my parents. How they'd always been in the mix, organizing, handing out candy, donating cider and decorations.

Yet I'd withdrawn. For so many years I had shut myself up on the farm, determined that my only value lay in making it profitable. That I had nothing to offer besides my labor.

That if I saved the farm, I'd be respecting and honoring their legacy.

But the legacy was a lot more than acres of trees.

It was this town. Belonging, volunteering. Showing up for neighbors.

And Celine had made me realize that.

She'd drawn me out. Forced me to confront what I'd let my grief turn me into.

And I was ready to take the next step.

But only with her. So I'd wait. For now, I'd just enjoy these moments.

Maplewood had shown up like it always did. Loud and over the top. Callie and Nora were dressed as witches with oversized hats and even a big broom. The two of them had stationed themselves at the corner of Main and Maple Streets with a folding table and a plastic cauldron the size of a small bathtub and handing out full-size candy bars.

Eventually everyone headed over to the town green, where the fire department had started a large bonfire. A local band played on a makeshift stage nearby, and Mel and Jenn handed out cider donuts.

While the kids ran off to trade candy and play with

friends, Celine and I stood close, so close our arms brushed, and chatted with Stella and Ruby. So badly, I wanted to take Celine's hand, claim her as mine, feel her skin against mine.

My thoughts were interrupted when Logan sidled up next to me and handed me another cup of hot cider, and a second later, Evie rushed over, her eyes wide.

"Did you see it?" she asked, panting.

Ruby turned to face her. "What?"

"The TikTok? It's going viral."

I wasn't following, but others in the crowd were murmuring as if they understood.

Gabe strode up in his Captain America costume, gritting his teeth. "Everyone's seen it," he said.

"According to this. Millions of people have," Evie added.

"It's just some influencer," he argued.

"She's WanderBetch," Evie explained. "She travels to small towns and highlights local traditions and businesses."

Okay. None of this sounded terrible to me. But I was still lost.

Gabe growled. "She shit all over the town."

"She called us Murderville, USA," Evie said. "Showed footage of the Harvest Festival that made this place look like a crime scene."

"None of it's true," Jasper said easily. "It will blow over."

"Tell that to the mafia," Gabe snapped. "They're trying to declare a state of emergency."

With a sigh, I looked over at Celine and vowed not to get sucked into the latest Maplewood drama.

This town had been through a lot, and I was finally beginning to feel like I could be a part of it again.

"We'll get through it," I said. "We always do."

Chapter 36

JOSH

By the number of cars parked along the street, it was obvious this wasn't going to be a normal town meeting.

Inside, voices were raised, hands waved, clusters of people formed and reformed, and there were lot of secretive glances.

There was no bake sale. There were no programs. No one lingering in the entryway, making small talk. Just urgency.

Celine walked the kids down to the basement where high school students had set up activities so that parents could attend the meeting, and when she returned, I followed her into the meeting room.

She scanned the room subtly, stretching her neck and adjusting her coat. Her eyes clocking the exits, her shoulders tightening. Most people wouldn't have caught the signs, but I noticed everything about her.

"You okay?" I asked quietly.

"Yeah. Can we sit on the end?" she said, gesturing to the chairs closest to the doors.

"Course." I shuffled to the second seat, letting her take the one on the end.

This morning, we'd all gotten the alert about an emergency town meeting. Immediately, I was on edge. We hadn't had one of those since the river had flooded when I was a kid, causing massive damage.

Gabe stood at the front, in his usual immaculate dark suit, running his hands though his hair. My cousin never looked ruffled. He was always calm and smiling when he was Mr. Mayor. But tonight he looked one step away from a nervous breakdown.

The air was thick and stale, and the folding chairs scraped loudly against the floor as people shuffled around for space and exchanged tense greetings. A long table had been set up in the front, with pitchers of water that no one touched. The harsh fluorescent lights hummed overhead, making the room feel even smaller.

Over the decades, this room had seen bake sales, retirement parties, festival planning, and preschool graduations.

Tonight it felt like a courtroom.

Phones were everywhere, screens glowing in hands and laps.

"Have you seen this one?" someone nearby whispered.

"No, the other one," came from a few rows up. "Scroll down."

"They tagged the inn."

"They tagged the school."

Though I was pretty isolated out on the farm, Ellie had filled me in on the ride into town. Celine too, who hadn't heard much at school. These days it seemed the middle schoolers were our most tech savvy citizens, and they had hunted down hundreds of videos about Maplewood.

Murderville, USA.

The moniker was absurd.

"They're canceling reservations," a woman standing in the back of the room murmured. "Three weddings."

"The Airbnbs too."

"Yelp's a disaster. One-star reviews from people who've never been here."

"Some claimed Tony's pizzeria has multiple health code violations."

"Someone said they were mugged at the festival."

"All the true crime folks are drumming up theories about the murder."

"They're calling us unsafe."

That word landed hard. *Unsafe.*

As if the town itself had done something wrong. As if the streets I'd learned to ride a bike on were suddenly hostile or the maple forest my grandfather had walked every morning had become violent.

Celine stiffened beside me, and my protective instincts kicked in. I was angry. And sad. Our town was being unfairly flattened into a headline.

Etienne Pelletier, the owner of the wine shop, stood up in the back, and Gabe passed the microphone to him.

"Can we talk about the damage this is doing?" He asked in his thick French accent. "This year has been hard enough. My business has been hurting for months, but this? I don't know if I can survive it."

"None of us can," someone shouted.

A ripple of agreement moved through the room.

Marv O'Brien took the mic next. He owned the barber shop, coached my little league team, and he and his wife had raised several foster children over the years. "They're digging up everything," he said, holding up his phone. "Stuff from the eighties. Fires, old police reports, random occurrences. It's all being framed like some kind of pattern."

"Because the internet runs on outrage," Callie shouted from the front row. "The worst thing we can do is overreact."

"Yes," Nora added. "No one cares if it's accurate or not. Only if it's clickable."

The chatter swelled again, voices overlapping, hands raising.

At the front of the room, Gabe stood, clipboard in hand, his tie perfectly knotted but his face red.

"Let's take this one day at a time," he said slowly. "I know many of you are upset. I am too. But shouting isn't going to—"

"It's already out there. You can't take it back," someone hollered.

"How did this get started?" another volleyed.

The earth shifted beneath us, the fear in the room palpable. The citizens of Maplewood had built their lives around this town. Its safety, its economic opportunity, and the strong community.

Celine leaned toward me, resting her head on my shoulder. Heart thudding, I took her hand and gave it a squeeze. I appreciated the contact. The reminder that she was here with me.

Bitsy Bramble stood next, but she waved away the microphone. We all knew she was loud enough to reach the next block.

"By next spring, we'll be ruined. If we don't get a handle on this, the state might be tempted to move the official Vermont Maple Festival to another town."

The room erupted in a collective gasp.

"Birch Hollow wants it," Tony said.

Chris, a firefighter, grunted. "Their syrup tastes like kerosene."

"What if Birch Hollow paid her off?"

"They're evil. They probably did. Probably hired a bot farm to amplify it and spread lies."

Shit. This was getting out of hand. While Birch Hollow had no love for Maplewood and would certainly celebrate our demise, it was a stretch to think they could be capable of a sophisticated online smear campaign like this.

"Bitsy. Please," Gabe said, trying to regain control of the room. "We can work through this. It's just a bit of bad publicity."

Rowan held up her phone. "WanderBetch has four million followers."

"People are canceling reservations."

Caroline from the spa stood up. "The inn has received several cancellations. Including several spring weddings."

My stomach dropped. Okay, that was bad. The inn was usually booked up a year in advance.

"And this woman said our sheets were scratchy and gave her a rash," Linda added.

Half the crowd roared with anger.

"We should sue for defamation," Mavis shouted.

Gabe huffed. "That's not a sound legal strategy."

"Should we film some rebuttal videos?" Nina asked. "Tell the world she's a filthy liar and those lips are fake?"

Gabe pinched the bridge of his nose. "We're not attacking anyone's lips."

"Why not?" she groused. "They're 90 percent filler."

"That's irrelevant."

"What's not irrelevant," Bitsy said, her hands on her hips, "is that this town is not the safe, beautiful place it used to be." She shuffled, turning to face Gabe. "We'll never be the same after the murder."

In the doorway, Nolan stood, one shoulder resting against the frame, his face blank.

"WanderBetch lit the fuse," Opal piped in, "and now there are conspiracy theories everywhere."

Movement to one side of the room caught my attention and that of the people around me, every one of us now watching Frankie Dunne trudge to the front of the room.

She held her hand out and with a grimace, Gabe handed her the microphone.

Despite her small stature, her presence took up a lot of space. Always had.

"Everyone," she said sharply. "We have got to focus."

The crowd hushed. She didn't speak loudly, but her tone was full of certainty.

"Yes, we've taken a hit financially and our town's reputation has been dragged through the mud since the murder. Trust me, I want to punch this bitch as much as the rest of you for what she's said. But..." She pulled her shoulders back, her head high. "There is some truth to some of these claims. This town was rocked by a brutal murder. And it wasn't properly investigated." She stared at the doorway where Nolan stood perfectly still.

"The details don't add up. We understand that the local authorities were under a lot of pressure"—she looked at Gabe —"to solve Will's murder and wrap things up neatly. But maybe the internet is right. Maybe it's a little too neat..."

All around the room, people shifted, but they were all focused intently on her.

"One young man is dead," she said softly. "And another is about to lose his life to prison. My brother is innocent. And as much as I hate WanderBetch, I'm thankful she's shining a light on this bullshit investigation."

She handed the microphone back to Gabe and stalked out of the room, brushing right past a stunned Nolan and out the door.

The exterior door slammed shut, and the room erupted into chaos.

Marty shook his head. "It was too rushed."

"Why was the FBI here?" Clem asked.

"We should still be looking at that Louisa up at Sugar Moon. She's dirty."

Ned, the postman, grunted. "I always thought there was something fishy about that story."

Dread washed over me. The doubt spreading through the room could be dangerous. Because once doubt took hold, it didn't stay contained, especially where public safety was concerned.

The kids' laughter on Halloween still echoed in my ears. We'd all fiercely embraced them. And now this welcoming, friendly community was trembling under the weight of scrutiny and judgment.

Sitting in this room, with Celine's warm hand in mine, as doubt and anger swirled around us, it hit me.

This wasn't about a TikTok video.

This was about fear and its ability to take over and change the fabric of this place.

My head spun. This town had been a powder keg for six months, and Frankie Dunne, with the help of some influencer on TikTok, had just lit a match.

Chapter 37

CELINE

My thoughts raced as I cleaned up the kitchen, sorting homework and mail and sweeping up half-built Lego structures that I'd absolutely step on if left on the floor. The kids were upstairs, asleep or reading. We'd reviewed the plan for tomorrow several times. I felt guilty, but I didn't have a choice. There was no way I'd drag them into a prison.

My throat tightened. I'd have to see him tomorrow. Come face-to-face with my ex-husband.

I was different now. I'd grown and healed. But I couldn't heal what he'd done. Not fully. Not ever. Especially for my kids.

Ellie was hypervigilant and wary.

Maggie threw herself into distractions to avoid reality.

And Julian. I'd just gotten him sleeping in his own room. He was starting to get comfortable here.

I wished there was a way to go back. To intervene before

all the hurt. Before the kids had to see what they saw and hear what they heard.

Nausea roiled in my gut.

I stared at my hands. Small and dainty, with a few scars. Short nails and raggedly cuticles.

I'd spotted a nail salon in town, but I had neither the time nor the funds for a manicure today. So rather than perseverating about tomorrow any longer, I snagged Ellie's nail supplies, which now took up a medium sized Rubbermaid bucket, from the bathroom. While she favored black and other dark colors, there was a decent selection, plus the lamp thing that dried them.

Sitting at the table, I got the supplies ready. Cut and filed.

It gave me something to focus on. Something small and manageable.

But when I tried to apply the base coat, my hand shook so badly that I got it all over my fingers.

I removed it and tried again, bracing my hand against the table. But the difference that made was minimal.

What was wrong with me? If I couldn't do something as simple as paint my nails, how on earth could I drive to Maine tomorrow and testify at a parole hearing?

Tears filled my eyes and I slammed the bottle down.

Half a second later, a knock sounded at the door.

Dragging myself from my chair, I wiped my tears on the sleeve of my T-shirt.

Josh was standing patiently under the porch light.

"I just wanted to see you," he said as I opened the door.

I nodded, unable to say anything in response.

"No need to talk. I was just walking Wayne. Wanted to wish you luck."

He'd wished me luck at the hearing no less than a dozen times. It was sweet.

His hands were shoved into his pockets.

I didn't want to talk, to be "on," to explain myself.

But I also didn't want him to leave. I wanted his strong, quiet presence.

"Do you want a cup of tea?" I asked.

He nodded, following me silently into the kitchen. Wayne walked right into the living room and curled up on the floor in front of the couch.

"What are you doing?" Josh asked as I put the kettle on.

He gestured to the table, where the bucket filled with polish, files and the light thing sat.

"I was trying to paint my nails," I said, looking down at my sad fingers. "Wanted to look professional, you know?"

"I'm sorry. I can get out of your way," he said as if nail care was some deeply personal ritual.

"No. It's fine. It was a dumb idea. Every time I try, I make a mess."

I held up a hand and his eyes widened as it trembled. He reached out and squeezed it between his warm palms. I stepped toward him, looping my arms around his chest and burrowing my face against him.

He said nothing, just gently held me while I clung to him.

"Can I help?" he asked into the top of my hair.

I tilted my head to look up at him. "You want to paint my nails?"

"Sure do."

"How much manicure experience do you have?"

"Absolutely none. But as a licensed operator of precision equipment, I think I can figure it out."

He was so kind. But I couldn't ask that of him.

"Will having your nails painted make you feel more confident?" he asked.

I paused for a moment, contemplating his question.

"Yes," I admitted. It always did. I felt put together and unstoppable when my nails were done.

"Okay, then. I'm on it."

He rubbed his big hands together and pulled out a chair at the table.

"Walk me through the process."

"I cut and filed them already. So now we start with base coat." I slid a bottle to him.

"Then two coats of polish and then top coat."

He squinted, reading the different bottles. Then, with a nod, he picked up the pink polish.

His eyes met mine, and I nodded, sitting across from him.

I placed my hand in his, and rather than grip it, he waited for me to relax into his touch. Our knees brushed under the table as he positioned my hand the way he wanted it.

A long breath escaped me. Just having him here eased my nerves.

As I watched him study the bottles, it occurred to me that he hadn't forced me to talk or offered any platitudes. It was as if he knew that the last thing I needed to hear was "it will all be fine."

Instead, he focused on his work, providing me with a warm, steady anchor as fears stormed inside my body.

The bottle of base coat looked tiny in his farm-worn hands.

"Here." He ran his fingertips over my palm before turning it over and placing it flat on top of a paper towel.

"How do we take it off if I mess up?"

I nodded at the bottle of remover. "I already tried twice tonight," I admitted.

Gently cradling my pinkie, he brushed the clear base coat on gently and slowly.

He leaned forward, his face almost against my arm.

"Sorry. Just want to make sure I get it right," he said.

"You're concentrating like you're defusing a bomb," I joked.

He looked up at me, his dark eyes intense. "You know I don't half-ass things, Matchstick."

I bit my lip and nodded, unable to look away as he continued working.

His touch was featherlight and the juxtaposition of the tiny brush in his large callused fingers made me giggle.

But he was so earnest as he, gently, stroke by stroke, applied the polish.

"Ugh. I got some on your skin."

"It's okay." I handed him the wooden stick thing Ellie used. "You use this to scrape it off."

He eyed it like it was a weapon.

"Here." I showed him, running the slanted wood over the side of my nail, "See? It comes off."

He nodded, focusing on the next finger. When he'd finished my left hand, he peered up at me. "Now what?"

"I stick it under this light." I flipped the switch to illuminate it and splayed my hand out beneath it.

"Did NASA design that thing?" he asked, eyeing the white dome-shaped LED light.

"Probably." I shrugged.

He took my other hand and began with the pinkie.

"It's getting cold," he mused, carefully painting. "Random cold snaps can cause a hell of a lot of damage. Did I ever tell you about the time the sap lines exploded?"

"No." I wasn't sure I'd heard him right. Exploded?

He nodded. "Yup. I was sixteen and Jas was twelve. Dad had us checking lines before a big storm. We forgot to relieve the pressure in one zone.

"The next day, we went out to collect the sap containers. Before long, we noticed that several of the lines had cracked and splintered. We were standing there, trying to figure out what happened at a large junction, and heard a loud snap."

He smiled, his eyes creasing as he focused on finishing my right hand.

"The junction and the lines connected to it blew like a champagne cork. We got sprayed with sap slush. Covered from head to toe, misted with maple sap."

He chuckled as I withdrew my left hand from the light and put my right under it.

"We smelled like pancakes for a week. Mom refused to let us go into town because she said we were attracting flies."

I giggled, thinking of how mortified teen Josh must have been.

"But it was a lesson I've never forgotten."

"I'm sure."

He was picking up on the task at hand, smoothly painting my nails pink, only leaving minor smudges.

"We got into a lot of trouble as kids." He shook his head. "My cousins were right next door, and we always managed to find trouble."

"You?" I teased. "But you seem so responsible."

"Not back then. We were good kids, but we always found a way to injure ourselves. One time, during a huge snowstorm, one of Uncle Ed's cows wandered off.

"Gabe and I decided we'd track it and rescue it. And of course Jas had to tag along. We spent hours tracking hoof-prints in the snow, around in circles, while Gabe muttered about how our rescue crew was going to need its own rescue.

"When we found the cow behind the old cider shed, Jasper got so excited he slipped on the ice and slid into the cow. She got spooked and kicked Gabe. Fractured one of his ribs."

"Oh my God."

He shook his head. "We still managed to rope her and bring her back. Mom made us hot chocolate and Dad was impressed. I felt like a superhero."

"Of course you did. You were the only one uninjured."

"Eh. Trust me, I've broken plenty of bones too." We swapped hands again. "I tried to build a jump for my bike and ended up crashing through an apple tree. Broke my collarbone. Then there's the time I tried to teach myself to drive and destroyed Mom's rose garden."

"Oh no."

"Yeah. Took out most of the plantings. Snapped the trellis clean in two. Dad didn't yell." He huffed a quiet laugh.

"What did he do?"

"Told me to get a pair of gloves and clean it up." He smiled at the memory. "I spent the entire summer replanting, pruning, digging out roots, and reading books about rose care and maintenance. Mom and I took several road trips to specialty nurseries to find the rare varieties I'd destroyed." He examined his hands thoughtfully. "Still have scars from those thorns."

"Wait a second," I said, recognition dawning on my face. "I've seen the roses. On the far side of the farmhouse?"

He nodded. "Yes. Sixteen varieties. Hybrids, teas and English. A few heirlooms she insisted on keeping alive even when they barely survived the winter. And those climbing fuckers on the big trellis? Took four years to train them properly." His face softened. "But Mom wanted her storybook garden, and we got there."

"And you maintain it?" I asked softly.

"Of course." He shrank in on himself a little. "With all the reading I did, I became an expert. No use in wasting the knowledge. They've got to be cut back at a forty-five-degree angle, above and outward, facing bud. Deadhead in June and fertilize twice. Always watch for black spot after heavy rains."

He paused, and I could see the tension in his jaw.

"When she got sick, we'd sit out there and enjoy the blooms. She'd quiz me about the species, about best care practices, all of that. About how to care for Mr. Lincoln or the Black Baccara while I pretended not to notice how much more drawn she looked every day."

My heart ached. I saw it on his face, the familiar grief. The same I'd carried with me since I was a kid.

"She knew you'd take good care of them," I whispered.

He dipped his chin. "She used to say roses were beautiful, but they'd cut you if you forgot how dangerous they could be."

I felt that deep in my gut.

"I think the thing that stuck with me," he said, smoothing a glob of pink across the nail of my ring finger, "was the feeling. The security and the comfort. My parents were good people. I knew it in my bones. They loved us. They loved this land and this town. And I woke up every single day of my life secure in that knowledge."

That took my breath away. It was the thing that kept me up at night, the fear that raged inside me when things got tough.

He reached out with his left hand and tipped my chin up. "Don't do that."

I blinked rapidly, worried I'd start to cry again.

"Don't get down on yourself. Your kids have that too. I see how they look at you. I see how deeply they are loved. They know that. Deep down on a cellular level. And someday, when they are well-adjusted adults, they will tell you that."

I sniffled. "I just worry—"

"It's okay to worry. It's human. But don't doubt yourself. Or what you've given these kids."

We sat in silence as he added the top coat and I put my hands under the lamp to dry.

My nails looked good. Pink and cheerful and bright.

I stared at them, processing all he'd shared with me.

"You maintain the roses for her," I said, thinking about his mom and my own.

He held my gaze. "Yes. It's the least I can do. She loved me so deeply I can still feel it."

The honesty made my breath catch.

"And I've grown to love those fussy-ass flowers." He leaned back in his seat. "They require patience, attention. You tend to them, even when they look dead."

He reached out and brushed his thumb across my jawline.

"And every spring, they come back to you."

I held his hand against my face, soaking up the sensation of his skin on mine. This touch said things my words could not.

"Roses look fragile," he said quietly. "But they're resilient."

The room went impossibly still as we stared at one another, our hands connected.

He wasn't just talking about roses anymore.

And my hands weren't shaking.

The pool of dread in my stomach was gone.

He looked up at me with a shy smile, and discomfort along with a strange sense of contentment fizzled inside me. This was intimate. It was intense.

This man had been inside me.

But somehow, this kitchen DIY manicure felt like a bigger moment.

A step forward toward a destination I didn't yet understand.

Chapter 38

CELINE

This was the last place I wanted to be.

I shifted on my uncomfortable heels and scratched at the hives already blooming on my arm. Fuck, I hated court.

Chloe squeezed my hand and shifted a little closer. Her presence brought a modicum of relief. I couldn't have done this without her.

I'd considered bringing the kids and asking her to keep them during the hearing but ultimately decided to take them to school, drive to Maine, and drive home later. Stella planned to take them back to our house after school to work on homework and have dinner. With any luck, I'd be home before Julian fell asleep.

It was a three-hour drive, but I'd spent the whole trip here in a fog. I had no idea what the podcast I'd listened to was even about. I just stared at the gray sky and the road ahead of me, my coffee untouched in the cupholder, trying and failing to prepare myself to see him again.

For the last few years, Maine had meant danger. But now it meant confrontation. And I had agency. I had power. Chloe had been sending me encouraging texts all week, and though I still struggled to believe them, I read them several times a day.

A part of me, one I'd locked away, still felt small and fragile and vulnerable. And what I was doing today, it was for her.

When Josh had come over last night, he hadn't pushed or prodded, and he hadn't forced me to talk.

He wanted more. He'd been clear about that. He wanted me to let him all the way in.

But I couldn't. Not yet. Not with so much still unsettled.

Chloe met me at the entrance to the prison so we could go through the security checkpoint together. Once our bags had been searched, we were given identification badges, then led to a damp waiting room with plastic chairs and fluorescent lighting. Other folks were waiting too, likely family members here for other hearings.

"You ready?" Chloe asked.

I nodded, though my stomach twisted painfully.

She squeezed my hand once more. "I'm proud of you."

Ava, my lawyer, arrived shortly after, phone in one hand, briefcase in the other. She whipped out a file and had me review several documents, one of which was my written statement.

She was efficient and cool, treating me like a collaborator, not a fragile woman who was at risk of falling apart at any moment.

I sat with the printed copy of my statement in my hands.

Rubbing the paper between my fingers and breathing, trying to ground myself in the words I'd written.

The option to appear via videocall had been appealing when Ava brought it up, but in the end, it felt important to be here. To stand up in person. I'd already said what I needed to say. The outcome was out of my hands. But good or bad, I was here to look that fucker in the eye and make sure he knew that he would not break me. That he would not intimidate me or terrorize me. That my kids weren't living in fear anymore.

Chloe put her arm around me. "You sure you don't want me to buy you a gun?"

"Jesus," I hissed. We were in a prison, for God's sake. "No. I do not want a gun."

Her lips twitched. "How about a taser?"

"Stop it. I don't need weapons."

"Pepper spray?"

I sighed. She was not going to stop. "Fine," I whispered. "I'll accept pepper spray."

She clapped, drawing the attention from several people sitting nearby. "Perfect. I'll order you my favorite brand."

Ava leaned over, joining the conversation. "You have a favorite brand of pepper spray?"

"Of course I do." Chloe scoffed. "What an absurd question."

Eventually, we were led into a long, narrow space with a drop-tile celling and no windows. Three people sat behind a large table at the front of the room, each with a nameplate. The members of the parole board. One woman sat between two men, and they all looked to be in their fifties.

Just after we'd taken our seats, the back door opened and

Donny walked in, wearing his prison uniform, with handcuffs on his wrists.

He was led to a table in front, and then the handcuffs were removed by the corrections officer.

One of the male parole board members read the rules and procedures, explaining the original charges, conviction, and sentence as well as the offered grounds for parole.

A representative from the board of prisons came forward and summarized a report regarding Donny's physical and mental health. His success in the substance abuse program and his record of conduct in prison.

Donny made a statement next, reading from a piece of paper. His hair was short, almost a buzz cut, and his face was clean shaven. He was thinner than I remembered. I'd always considered him this larger-than-life figure. A man who oozed power and dominance. But as I looked at him now, after years of healing, I saw him for what he was.

Pathetic.

Weak.

And cruel.

His words were empty and his voice monotone. When he talked about his children, I had to suppress a snort. He talked about his career with his family business and a list of other reasons he believed he should be allowed back into society.

When he finished and sat down, the board asked if I'd like to make a statement.

Ava stood up. "My client has already submitted her statement in writing."

"Wait," I said, standing. The plan had been not to speak

but to be a presence here. But suddenly I couldn't not speak. I needed to be heard. "May I?"

The woman sitting at the table nodded.

"I submitted a written statement," I said, though Ava had just told them that.

"Yes," she replied. "We have reviewed it along with the exhibits you provided."

"So I won't repeat myself." I shifted, feeling several sets of eyes on me. Donny's scrutiny was the heaviest, but I forced myself to make eye contact with him. And when I did, I knew for certain that I would never, ever let this man hurt me again.

"My ex-husband has engaged in a pattern of harassment and threats since his arrest three years ago. I have no reason to believe he has been rehabilitated. My statement and the exhibits provide the necessary details."

Eyes narrowing, he clenched his jaw. I used to look for those fine movements with surgical accuracy. I would obsessively study his moods, appealing and deflecting when he got angry.

But his mood was no longer my problem.

"You will not hurt me again," I said firmly. "You will not hurt my children."

I sat down, my hands shaking. But I kept my spine straight and looked directly at the parole board members. No tears, no theatrics. Just the facts.

My breathing had just steadied when a shout rang out from the back of the room.

"You evil bitch."

I whipped around in my seat, the familiar voice making my hackles rise.

Phyllis stood at the back of the room, shaking her fist at me. Even from here, I could see the fury in her eyes.

Even enraged, her blond hair was smooth and immaculate, and she had an expensive wool coat draped over her shoulders. She looked less like a grieving mother and more like someone attending a board meeting. Her gaze was sharp, nearly cutting me from across this crowded room. She was unhinged, bordering on delusional. As if she genuinely believed that this outcome belonged to her.

She was not a woman who accepted limits, and regardless of how things played out today, Phyllis was not finished.

"Ma'am, we have to ask you to please leave the room," the male board member on the left said.

A guard strode toward her and grasped her arm, leading her out the door.

After the panel left the room to conference, Chloe pulled me into the hall. When there was no sign of Phyllis, she wrapped her arms around me and squeezed. "You did good."

Thirty minutes later, we were called back into the room.

"We have reached our decision. The parole is denied," the woman said firmly. "We came to this decision based on the record of continued threats, the demonstrated lack of remorse, and a credible fear for the safety of his victims." She looked directly at Donny. "You will serve the remainder of your full sentence. A referral will be made to the district attorney to investigate and prosecute these documented violations of the protective order."

The words landed slowly in my brain.

Parole denied.

Not postponed.

Not reconsidered.

Denied.

Donny was led out of the room in handcuffs.

The system had worked. It had done what it was supposed to do.

Relief hit me first, then anger. Why was I even here? How come, after three years, I'd been dragged back into this mess?

At least it was done with.

I didn't owe him anything.

Not my future.

Not my past.

And definitely not my fear.

All I wanted to do was go home. I needed to hug my kids. Then I needed to talk to Josh.

Chloe and I walked out of the prison arm in arm, past the high walls and the barbed wire and toward the parking lot.

Where we found Phyllis waiting, a glare firmly fixed on her face.

I glared right back.

"You ruined his life," she said as we walked past her. "You ruined my son."

My heart took off, panic setting in. How was it that I could never get away from these horrible people?

"Eat shit, Phyllis," Chloe spat, dragging me to my car.

She opened the driver's door and stood beside it as I buckled my seat belt and started the engine.

"I love you," she said. "Now go back to Vermont."

Chapter 39

JOSH

I'd been waiting all day, my nerves fraying with every minute that passed. She'd texted back, but her responses had been quick, terse.

I'd barely gotten any farmwork done. Instead, I stressed and paced and stressed some more, Wayne following me the whole time.

When Stella's car pulled down the driveway, I'd headed to the cottage to greet the kids. I sat with the girls while they did homework, and then we'd played street hockey until it started to get dark.

Now that we were all back inside, I was waiting again. And I didn't bother trying to hide it.

It was dinnertime when the headlights of the minivan swept over the land.

Before she'd shut off the engine, I was down the porch steps, but I pulled up short when she got out, looking unfamiliar in formal clothes.

Bracing myself for who knew what kind of emotion, I walked toward her slowly.

With a sigh, she darted straight for my arms.

I held her close, closing my eyes and breathing in the scent of her shampoo. "You don't have to tell me anything—"

"Denied," she blurted. "Parole denied. He's in for another nine months. Maybe longer. The DA is going to charge him with the violations of the restraining order."

"You did it," I said, noting the way the tension uncoiled from her shoulders as I held her. "I'm so proud of you."

"Have you been here all afternoon?"

"No. Okay, yes," I admitted. "Hung out with the kids, played street hockey."

"Thank you."

I buried my face in her hair. "You could have asked me."

"Stella offered," she countered.

I ran my hands along her arms and shoulders, needing to touch her, needing to know she was real. "You can let me in."

Head tilted, she sighed. "I know. And I think I'd like to. Can we talk? After bedtime?"

"Of course," I said. "Go inside and see the kids."

"Thank you. For everything."

I HADN'T EXPECTED HER TO FIND ME SO EARLY. I HAD planned to head home and shower, but I figured I had time to inventory our tubing before winter, so when she showed up, I was in the barn.

"They can't be asleep yet," I said, looking at my watch.

"Stella's watching a movie with the girls and Julian

crashed early." She walked toward me, clad in her usual leggings and fleece. "And I wanted to see you."

"I'm right here."

She was so beautiful, and she looked more unburdened than I'd ever seen her.

"I need to thank you. Today was..." She trailed off, tucking her hair behind her ears. "It was a lot. And I couldn't have done what I needed to without you."

My chest constricted. "I didn't do anything, Celine. You did."

She shook her head, her hair an auburn color beneath the dim barn lights. "You don't get it, do you? You've done so much for me. You've encouraged me to be brave. You make me feel strong and sexy."

I pulled her against my chest. "You are all of those things."

"And you helped me get to a place where I could heal. Where I could finally move forward."

I angled in and gently kissed her. We lingered, our lips close, and just existed for a moment. This close, she was intoxicating.

"You're strong," I said, dragging my nose down her neck. "I'd love to take credit." I nipped at a sensitive spot. "But it's all you."

Sighing, she threaded her hands in my hair. "Can't you just take a damn compliment?"

"Careful there, Matchstick," I replied. "Or I'll bend you over that workbench."

Her eyes widened and heat instantly crept up her cheeks. "Is that a promise?"

Fuck. The way her teeth sank into her plush bottom lip

made my knees nearly give out.

I ran a finger across her jawline, tipping her chin up. "Anything. You. Want." Ducking, I captured her mouth.

She kissed me back hard, her hands running up my chest, then down to my belt buckle. "I need you."

"Let's go to the house."

"No," she said, tugging down my zipper. "Here and now."

She didn't have to ask me twice.

In seconds, my hand was down her pants and I had two fingers inside her. She was so fucking wet. The heat of her made me want to fuck her through the wall of this barn.

As I picked her up to find a spot, my eyes snagged on the crate of syrup.

"Here," I said, placing her on the massive worktable.

I reached for the crate, removing a glass bottle.

"Josh," she said, "what are you doing?"

I twisted the cap off the glass bottle. "Playing." I smirked. "You okay with this?"

She nodded, looking a little uncertain.

I stuck my finger into the bottle and brought it to her mouth. She wrapped her lips around me and sucked, the move making my eyes roll to the back of my head.

"Delicious," she said.

I leaned down and kissed her, tasting the sweetness on her tongue.

"It's from my trees," I said proudly. "I had a dream," I said, snagging the hem of her shirt and tugging. "Of licking my syrup off your tits while I fucked you."

Gasping, she quickly ripped her sports bra over her head. "Yes. I want that."

I smiled at her, though I couldn't temper the demand in my tone when I said, "Get naked."

Once she'd shucked her leggings, she was completely naked in my barn, on a worktable surrounded by tools.

She reclined back on her elbows, giving me full access to her body. "What are you waiting for?"

I wasted no time, tipping the bottle at her collarbones and letting a thin stream of syrup run down the length of her body. I watched, fascinated as it ran between her breasts, down her stomach toward her pussy. I should have taken my time. Should have catalogued every single second of this experience. But I couldn't hold back. With a groan, .I dove in and licked and sucked at her skin and clamped her nipple between my teeth.

"Josh." She moaned, tugging my hair.

I poured more. Started again.

I was the one still fully clothed, but Celine was in control.

I savored the sweet taste of her skin and the syrup my trees and hard work had produced, working my way to her clit. It turned me on more than I'd expected.

"Josh, I need you." She moaned. "I want you inside me."

"I don't have a condom." I looked up at her from between her legs. She was wet and sticky, and those pink nipples I loved so much were rock hard.

"I don't care. Just fuck me."

I froze. I couldn't. We couldn't.

"Just pull out. Please," she begged.

I shouldn't. I should get her off like a gentleman and ignore the base need inside me to fuck her senseless. To feel her come on my cock and then give her more.

She sat up and glared at me. "Joshua Lawrence. Get that fat cock out and fuck me now."

Without hesitation, I pulled my pants down far enough to free myself. Then I gripped her thighs and spread her wide.

"Now," she begged, shaking with need, her tits bouncing.

I bent down and licked her nipples again, savoring the maple taste.

As I slid inside her, I was certain I'd died. That this was heaven. She was so hot and wet and soft. Already gripping me hard. Every thrust felt more intense than the last.

I plunged into her, long and deep, pushing her thighs even wider.

"So good," I growled. "Take me deep."

"More syrup," she begged. "It makes me feel so dirty."

I held the bottle above her and haphazardly tipped it, coating her chest and abdomen. The liquid ran quickly, some of it soaking into my clothes.

I bit her nipples, licking and sucking, relishing the sticky mess.

"Yes," she cried. "It feels so good."

This was bliss. I'd lost all control. Fucking her fast and hard, playing with her tits and thanking every higher power for bringing this woman into my life.

"I want to taste some," she breathed.

I tipped the bottle back again, and it spilled across her lips, dripping down her chin.

She licked her lips and thew her head back, clenching around me. "Yes. I'm close."

Fuck. If I wasn't careful, I'd go off the deep end before her. But my resolve was lessening by the minute.

"Good," I gritted out. Focusing on her face. "I need you to come."

"It feels so good with nothing between us. I can feel every inch of you. Filling me up."

As if I needed another reminder. "Yes." Fuck, I couldn't control this. But I didn't want to disappoint her.

"Take it," I growled. "I can feel you gripping me. Come for me. Show me what a good girl you are. Getting fucked in the barn, covered in syrup."

She moaned and threw her head back, shaking as I fucked her. Her pussy squeezed the life out of me while I clenched every muscle in my body to keep from coming.

She whimpered and gasped as I begged my body to cooperate, to let her have this moment. She moaned and shook, her orgasm cresting.

I held on with every ounce of willpower I had, but I couldn't stop what was happening. "I'm going to come," I groaned. The sensation crept up the backs of my thighs, overtaking me despite my efforts to hold it back.

"Yes," she cried, still convulsing. "Come on me."

I withdrew and before I could even reach down to get control of the situation, I came hard and fast. My vision blurred as I spilled my release all over her stomach and the underside of her breasts.

"You marked me," she said, giggling. "With your syrup. And your"—she giggled—"semen."

I flushed bright red. Shit, I suddenly felt like a dirty deviant. And I loved it. More than loved it.

I would have never admitted that I was that kind of man. The type who wanted to possess and mark a woman. Fuck her and come all over to make her mine.

But here we were. And I had no regrets.

"Let me get you cleaned up." I pulled my jeans up and buckled my belt.

All I had was paper towels, and though I worried the paper would be harsh against her skin, she didn't complain as I wiped her down.

"I need a shower. To get rid of this evidence." She giggled again, lighter and happier than I'd ever seen her.

Once I'd helped her into her leggings and pulled her sweatshirt over her head, we stood face-to-face, staring at one another goofily, unable to form words.

"I want—" She snapped her mouth shut. "Sorry." She shook her head and sighed adorably. Eyes closed, she inhaled deeply. "I can't even talk. Whatever you just did to me? I think it altered my brain chemistry."

As if that didn't fill me with pride.

"I want to say things," she continued. "Serious things. Important things."

I leaned down and kissed her. "Tomorrow," I said. "Go home and shower. I'll walk you."

"Yes. Tomorrow. Come over in the morning. We can talk. And... I don't know. Plan."

Those words unlocked a hope that I'd long ago buried deep in my chest. Plans. Hope of a future. A deep and real and permanent one. One we'd earned together.

Chapter 40

JOSH

I had to keep myself from running to Celine's house this morning. As happy as I was, my nerves were on edge. It had nothing to do with her and everything to do with how much I had to lose. Because hope, as I was quickly learning, was its own kind of risk.

Things had changed yesterday. There was certainty now. The knowledge that this was real.

I gently knocked on the door and was met by a sleepy Celine holding a mug of coffee.

She offered it to me and I took a sip before handing it back.

"Morning," I said, unable to hide my smile.

"Morning. Kids are still sleeping. I'm going to let them stay home today."

"What about you? Do you have a sub?"

"Yes. I took today off as well in case things didn't go the way I hoped and I needed time to recover."

I wrapped my arms around her, anguish that it was even a possibility running through me.

"I'm so proud of you." I kissed the top of her head.

"Anyway. I'm going to call the school. Figured I would let the kids do whatever today. Maybe we'll bake or play games or build a Lego set. I just want to be with them. Soak this up."

"You deserve that. All of you. You've waited a long time for this."

Her smile was so broad and genuine it made my stomach ache. She'd spent so long in fear, yet now she was free.

She studied my face, her own still bright. "I'm just happy," she said with a small giggle. "And it all feels possible now. A future. And—ugh. Sorry, I'm babbling. I need to get myself under control."

I stroked her jawline, angling her face up to give her a gentle kiss. "You never have to be in control with me. You can say what you're feeling. I will never judge."

She kissed me again, slower this time, and rested her hand on my chest. "I'm so happy."

"Me too. I have something to show you."

I opened the security app on my phone and cued up the video.

She took the phone from me, squinting at the grainy night vision security footage. "Is that? The bear?"

"Yes." I waited for her to notice what was hanging out of her mouth.

On screen, Betsy Ross waddled across the porch confidently.

Celine gasped. "Oh my God."

I waited.

The bear paused under the motion light, turning her head toward the camera and staring at it with her lone eye.

"Wait." Celine paused it and zoomed in. "Is that my Croc? That bear stole my shoe! It's been missing for weeks."

"In her defense," I said, "it's a very bold color."

On the video, Betsy ambled off the porch with the bright pink Croc dangling from her mouth like a delicious salmon.

"I've been tearing my hair out trying to find that damn shoe. I blamed Ellie. I even suspected the dog."

Wayne, who was lying next to the table, lifted his head in protest.

"I suspect that shoe is property of Betsy Ross now," I said.

She handed me back the phone. "Unbelievable. She didn't even take the other one. The kids will never let me live this down."

"Sorry." I bent down and kissed her head.

"Coffee's in the pot. I'm going to shower before Julian wakes up. How do you feel about chocolate chip pancakes?" she asked.

She was gone a moment later, bounding up the stairs, so I wandered into the kitchen.

The space felt more warm and welcoming than it ever had. Julian's artwork was stuck to the fridge, along with a test or two from each of the girls, both proudly displaying good grades. The table was cluttered with stacks of papers and half-abandoned Lego projects. This wasn't chaos; it was life. Loud and imperfect. Held together with effort and care.

I poured myself a cup of coffee and looked out the window at the northern side of the farm. I'd wanted this. The farm. The trees. To work hard and lead a simple life.

But these days I wanted more. I wanted challenge and adventure, and I wanted this incredible woman by my side.

The relief of knowing she wanted it too? It was overwhelming.

As the shower turned on upstairs, I started tidying up, filling the dishwasher, wiping down the countertops, and clearing the table.

I managed to move Julian's creations to the living room without breaking them, then set to work stacking and sorting the papers on the table.

When a few items slipped from one of the folders, I gathered them into a pile, and as I was returning them, a colorful card caught my eye. Worried Celine might want to keep it, I put it on the top of the stack. Why I flipped it open, I don't know, but when I did, my stomach dropped.

Rage flooded me, but fear swamped me even faster. Hot, sharp, and completely irrational. My mind jumped ahead—locks, cameras, routes, and worst-case scenarios all mapped out before history could repeat itself.

There was more to this story, yet I didn't understand. Had she been threatened? While she lived here, on my property?

She came down the stairs smiling a few minutes later, her hair damp and loose, and padded to the coffee maker.

"You okay?" she asked, refilling her mug.

My mind warred with itself. What do I say? And how?

Rather than speaking, I just pushed the card across the table.

Her smile fell slowly. "Where'd you get that?"

"I wasn't snooping. I saw it on a stack of paperwork."

"It's not," she said, putting the mug down. "It's not what you think. It's old."

"It says *found you*, Celine. You've only lived here for a couple of months."

She snatched it from the table and shoved it into the folder it had fallen out of. "It doesn't mean anything anymore."

I gritted my teeth and exhaled loudly. "It means everything, Celine. I could have helped."

"I handled it." She lifted her chin, her tone defensive.

"You could have told me." I wanted to grab her and make her understand.

How much I cared. How much I worried. But I kept my hands to myself. The last thing I wanted was to scare her. The thought of that man coming here pummeled me, making it hard to see straight.

"Someone who hurt you, who hurt your kids, was still contacting you, threatening your safety and you just, what? Figured you'd handle it on your own?" I sounded unhinged, and it disgusted me, but I couldn't control myself.

Her spine straightened as she stared at me. "Yes." She was bracing, not listening, on the defense, protecting herself.

Fuck, I wanted to reach for her, to pull her into my arms and magically fix everything.

But since that was impossible, I worked on lowering my voice. "That's not okay," I said.

Her eyes flashed with anger. "You don't get to decide what's okay."

"I do when it puts you and the kids in danger."

She stiffened. "I was not in danger."

"Really?" I quipped. "Was this the only incident?"

She lowered her head, her focus dropping to the floor. "No," she said softly. "There was more."

I threw my hands up, my lungs so damn constricted I could barely breathe. "We could have taken steps, precautions, changed routines. Made sure—"

"How?" she cut in. "By locking the doors? Pulling the kids out of school? Hiding in the house constantly? I won't live like that."

"I'd have done whatever it took." There was nothing I wouldn't do to keep her safe. Why didn't she understand that?

"That's the problem," she said quietly. "You don't understand how that sounds to me."

I snapped my mouth shut, searching for the right words. I was trying to protect her, not erase her. Couldn't she see that?

"You kept something serious from me," I finally said.

"Because I knew the second you found out, you'd go straight into fixer mode, like I'm a fragile, helpless damsel in need of saving."

"I'm not saying that."

"It's not what you say, Josh," she ground out. "It's what you do. It's how you react."

I dragged my hand through my hair. Fuck. How could I get her to understand? "I love you. And when I saw that card, my brain went straight to worst-case scenarios. I can't just stand here and pretend it's all fine."

"I'm not asking you to pretend." Her voice wobbled, her eyes welling. "I'm asking you to trust me. To respect me. And stop with the pity. *Please.*"

Fuck. I was the world's biggest asshole.

"I don't want your pity," she said, a single tear rolling down her cheek.

I took a step closer and wiped it away with my thumb. "It's not pity. It's love."

She shook her head. "Doesn't feel like it. Feels like you've got a superhero complex. Like your mission is to help the pathetic single mom who can't get her shit together."

"Do you actually think that?" I asked, lifting her chin. "Have you met you? You have your shit together. You don't need me. You don't need anyone."

Her expression softened, but only for a moment. Then it was harder than ever, and she was stepping back, putting space between us. "I've spent years being scared," she said. "For years, someone else decided what was safe for me. What I could do, where I could go, who I could speak to." She swallowed thickly. "I won't live like that again. Not even for you."

"That's not fair."

"Neither is being pitied."

"I don't pity you."

"You do," she said, her lips tugging down. "Maybe not consciously, but I see it. The way you jump in to take care of my messes. The way you brace yourself like I'm a bomb that could go off at any time."

I stepped back, reeling. Her words were like a punch to the gut. "You're not a mess. You're a survivor."

"I know I am," she said. "Because I saved myself."

We stood, staring at one another, the kitchen suddenly too small for this conversation, for all the baggage we were carrying.

"I don't know how to love you without wanting to protect you," I said softly.

She closed her eyes, her body deflating. When she opened them, her voice was gentler. "Then you need to learn," she said. "Because I want you. I choose you. But I'm not going to shrink or change. I'm not giving up all my hard-won independence to make you feel useful."

Her words landed with a heavy thud.

"I hear you," I said. "I think I just need some air."

She nodded. "That's a good idea."

"I'll step out for now, but that doesn't mean I'm leaving," I said quickly. "This matters to me, and I don't want to mess it up even more."

With a nod, she picked up her coffee mug, her hands shaking.

So with one last look at her, I turned and headed for the front door.

Love wasn't the problem here. Fear was. Mine. Hers. And we had to find a way to live with both.

Chapter 41

CELINE

Despite the frustration that came along with my argument with Josh, I put on a smile and enjoyed the morning with the kids. We baked banana bread and ate it in our jammies while playing Monopoly on the living room floor. Then Ellie put on music, and we had a dance party.

I needed to mark this moment. Recognize what I'd been through. It was time to start living my life again. To be the mom my kids deserved.

Maplewood was home now, and I was ready to embrace it without fear.

After we'd cleaned up the game and the kitchen, I left the kids playing to go for a quick run. Muscle memory kicked in right away, and I headed for my usual hill. But halfway there, I stopped and scanned the property.

The farm was safe. The house was safe. This town was safe.

I didn't have to sprint up the hill behind my house. I didn't have to keep my eye on it every second that I ran.

So I turned and headed toward the maple trees, determined to enjoy the cool air and this beautiful pace. My life wasn't about danger and paranoia anymore, so it was time to retrain my nervous system.

I'd overreacted earlier, but Josh's overprotectiveness had triggered me, sending me into fight-or-flight mode.

Head down, watching the path in front of me, I pushed myself hard, relishing the burn of the cold air in my lungs.

Josh was a good man. And I was in love with him. I hadn't planned on this. I never could have imagined I'd fall head over heels for this quirky town and my grumpy landlord, but here I was, and I owed it to myself and my kids to explore the possibilities. I'd been given an opportunity to heal. To grow. And to become the version of myself that Donny never allowed me to be.

I headed back to the house at a slow jog. My breath was still coming quickly when a strange car came into sight. It was parked in front of the cottage, and it wasn't Stella's. I sped up, my mind racing. Who did I know in Maplewood with a car like that?

It was a silver Mercedes. And as I got closer, the plates were visible.

Maine plates.

My stomach dropped.

Heart in my throat, I sprinted into the house. As I threw the door open, I was met with the last person on earth I wanted to see.

Phyllis.

Standing in my kitchen.

She was taller than I remembered. Broader too. Built like a woman who'd spent her entire life believing that space would always be made for her. Her hair was swept back in a style that didn't move when she did, the color of it the same shade as Donny's.

She moved with the confidence of a woman used to being obeyed, her shoulders squared, chin lifted, gaze level and unblinking.

"This is certainly an upgrade for you," she sneered, taking in the kitchen.

She pointed to the clutter on the kitchen table, the diamonds on her fingers catching the light, sharp little flashes that felt like warnings. "Still a terrible housekeeper, though."

My instincts had taken over, my eyes searching for my kids. Ellie stood blocking the entrance to the living room, with Maggie and Julian hovering behind her.

"These children are terrible listeners. I told them I'm taking them on a trip, and they've been so ungrateful."

Ellie met my eye, panic rolling off her. The kids hadn't laid eyes on their grandmother in almost two years. Not after the bogus lawsuit and several incidents of harassment. Not since I'd gotten a restraining order against her.

Phyllis didn't pace, didn't fidget. She just eyed me with contempt.

"You need to leave," I said. My tone was calm and cool, despite the way I was falling apart inside.

She sighed, like I was a naughty child. "I just got here."

I stood a little taller. "You're not welcome."

With a wave of her hand, she dismissed my protests. "That's not your decision to make."

My chest tightened, the air in the room thinning. Dammit.

What made Phyllis dangerous wasn't her brute strength, it was her certainty.

The way she stood in my kitchen, lording over the place, disgusted by the drawings on the fridge and the kids' water bottles in the sink.

The way she looked at me like I was beneath her. Replaceable.

That was the threat. Not violence. Erasure.

The quiet conviction that she could show up in my home and take it apart simply because she felt like it.

"You always had a flair for the dramatic." She picked up Ellie's most recent science test and studied it before placing it back on the table.

Then she picked up one of Julian's Lego creations. A robot version of our van, complete with minifigs of the four of us inside.

"Put that down," I said. "And leave."

Lip curled, she locked eyes with me and dropped it on the floor, where it shattered into a hundred tiny pieces.

Julian gasped and then began to cry.

"I see you're still indulging him. It only fuels weakness."

My vision went red. Bringing the kids into this was a step too far. I had no idea why she was here, but I wouldn't tolerate it anymore.

"Leave." I took a step toward her, pulling my shoulders back.

She did the same, pushing me with both hands, sending me stumbling backward. "You think you're protecting the children," she said, her voice almost kind. "But you're isolating them. Keeping them from their real family."

"She is our family," Ellie protested, one arm around Julian, who had buried his head in her side, still weeping. "Keep your hands off her."

"She's your family for now." Phyllis opened her Chanel purse and pulled out a handgun, then placed it on top of the table with a steady hand.

My whole body trembled, a familiar sense of panic setting in. But I couldn't fall apart. I couldn't break down. I needed to be strong for my kids.

So with a deep breath in, I steadied myself.

"Kids," I said brightly. "Why don't you go get your suitcases?"

"Mom," Ellie protested, tears in her eyes, her focus on the table.

I silently willed her to look at me, and when she did, I prayed she understood me.

Take Maggie and Julian and hide, I told her silently. *Just like we practiced.*

I made eye contact with each of them, sending them assurances that it would be okay. "TTG," I said. "Go get them."

Ellie reached for Julian's hand. "Where did you put them?" Ellie asked in a calm tone that meant she got my silent messages. "I forgot."

"In the garage," I said.

Phyllis looked between us.

"We can go on a trip with Nana," I chirped. "But the luggage is out there."

Ellie nodded quickly. "Okay. We'll do that. Julian?" she asked brightly, "Do you want to get your dinosaur suitcase?"

She pushed her siblings toward the back door, keeping her body between them and Phyllis. She had recognized our phrase. We'd planned it out a long time ago, when her therapist suggested that having a plan in case of danger might help to ease her anxiety. So we had keywords.

This house didn't have a garage. None of our crappy rentals had. Not that Phyllis seemed to have noticed. I just needed to distract her long enough to get them out the door and away from here.

Ellie looked back at me as she closed the door, her face a mask of fear that made my heart clench. My sweet girl. So strong and brave. She had been asked to carry a far bigger burden than she should. I hated myself for it. That I couldn't keep her safe. That I'd failed to give her the childhood she deserved.

"You know you can't be here," I said to Phyllis, moving toward the sink so when she looked at me, her back was to the door the kids had just stepped out of. I filled a water glass just to keep her attention on me and draw this out.

"I've been very patient," she said, "I let the courts handle things. I let the system run its course. But look where that's gotten us." She scanned the house, her eyes hard. "You, living like a scared little mouse. Teaching your children to be afraid. To reject their real family."

"I'm not hiding," I growled, the water in my glass trembling along with my hand. "And don't say a word about my children."

"They are my blood."

And that fact pained me every damn day. "They are my kids."

"You are replaceable," she said softly, running her fingertips over the tabletop, reminding me that the gun was within her reach.

My heart slammed against my ribs, my mind racing, at a loss for how to handle this, how to get out of it unscathed.

"Women like you love to make yourselves the victim, weaponize your suffering."

My old instincts rose up. The persistent urge to explain, to justify, to prove myself.

Instead I crushed them. I owed this woman nothing.

"Leave." My hand was shaking hard enough to cause some of the water to spill over the rim of the glass.

"I don't think you understand what's going to happen," she said, her demeanor unnervingly calm. "My son may not be free today, but he will be soon enough. In a matter of months, he'll leave that godforsaken place."

"No," I said. "He's being prosecuted for violating the restraining order and for witness intimidation. He's going to get more time added to his sentence."

She waved me off. "He's getting out soon," she said, the only sign of her distress a slight flare of her nostrils. "And when he does, he will need his children. And a clean slate." She looked from the gun to me again. "You complicate that." The cruel smile that spread across her face made my blood chill. "You don't get to keep them, Celine. You don't get to win."

That thread was enough to lift the fog of fear shrouding me. My body hummed with fury, burning off the last of my hesitation. "You will leave this house and never come back."

"Oh, I will leave this house when I'm ready," she mused. "But you won't. You have to be punished. You destroyed a good man. You destroyed our family. Do you have any idea what I've been through?"

I gripped my glass and covertly scanned the area near me, weighing my options.

"We were demoted at the club. To a golf only membership." By the horror in her tone, one would think it was a war crime instead of a natural consequence for raising a sociopathic abuser. "Because of this... scandal!"

There was no reasoning with her, no calmly defusing the situation. And I was sick and tired of being the victim. She had walked in here, into my home, because she believed I was weak. She believed that I couldn't fight back.

The joke was on her.

Her hand was still on the table, lingering inches from the revolver.

I had to move fast. All the training I'd done had to be good for something.

So I snapped into action, throwing my water in her face, then lunging at her as she reached for the gun.

I made contact, the force almost knocking the wind out of me, and grabbed for the gun.

She got to it first, but I was half a second behind, clutching for the weapon, my hands on top of hers. I stomped on her ballet-flat-clad foot and she jerked, whipping the revolver upward.

I struggled to pull it out of her grasp. The woman was strong. I'd give her that. With all the strength I had, I yanked violently.

A sharp crack ripped through the air, making my body shudder and my blood run cold.

Plaster rained down from the ceiling, and when Phyllis looked up at it in shock, I took my chance and snatched the gun from her. It fell to the floor, and instinctively, I kicked it, sending it skittering across the kitchen floor toward Julian's broken Lego van.

"You little bitch." She swung at me, her fist connecting with my jaw. My head snapped back on impact, but I kept my footing. I'd attended too many self-defense classes to be taken out by an old lady punch.

I got low and led with my shoulder, tackling her and using my body weight to knock her down. On the floor, I grabbed at her arms, using every ounce of energy I had to stop her from thrashing and throwing her knee into my stomach.

"Celine." The deep voice lifted me out of the fog.

"Help me," Phyllis screamed. "This is elder abuse."

Josh stood in the doorway with his arms crossed. He looked warm and strong like he always did, but so, so angry.

"The police are on the way," he said, scanning the room for the gun.

"Over there." I nodded to where it had slid to, keeping Phyllis's arms pinned to the ground.

He picked it up, opened the chamber, and tipped it sideways, letting the bullets fall into his hand.

He pocketed them, then knelt next to us. Instantly, his warmth seeped into me, and a hint of relief worked its way through me.

"Ma'am," he said respectfully. "The police will be here any minute. You will be arrested."

"For trying to see my grandchildren!" she wailed

"For trespassing on my property and threatening the woman I love," he said. "Among other felonies."

The two of us kept our eye on her until Nolan appeared with one of his deputies by his side. I gave a quick statement, all the while itching to dart out of here and hug my children.

"The kids are safe?" I asked Josh.

He nodded. "In my house with Wayne. Ellie found me in the barn, told me to call the police."

Tears rolled down my cheeks and my legs almost gave out. That girl. Of course she did.

"I need to see them," I sobbed.

"Of course. We'll go now."

We'd only made it a few yards when Nolan jogged over. He was tall and intimidating, with shaggy hair and thick stubble. "I'm going to need a full statement," he said.

"I know." I gave him a shaky nod. "I just need to get my kids first."

Nolan dipped his chin. "Can you come by the station after? We'll need to talk to the kids too."

"Fine," I said, panic now setting in. I needed my kids. I needed to hold them and thank them and apologize a million times for this. To look at their little faces and make sure that they weren't broken by all this grief and sadness.

I took off, and as the house came into view, a strange sense of relief and fear washed over me.

Josh was by my side, unlocking the door and pushing it open.

"Mom," Maggie cried, running toward me.

I dropped to my knees and hugged her, and a second later, Ellie's arms were around me.

"I was so scared," Maggie cried.

"I know, baby," I said, soaking in their warmth, reminding myself that they were safe. "It's okay. It's all over now. We're safe."

Standing, I inhaled deeply and let the breath out slowly. Then I kissed each of their heads.

When the scent of Ellie's shampoo hit me, the tears came rushing back. I owed her more than I could ever explain. "I love you," I said, pulling her close. She let me hold her, but after a minute, she squirmed, so I let go and scanned the room. "Where's Julian?"

"He said he had to pee."

"Julian," I called.

There was no answer. Josh was suddenly at my side, putting a comforting hand on my back.

"He was really upset," Ellie said. "Maybe he went to lie down?"

"I'll look for him upstairs," Josh said, striding away.

His boots thudded up the steps while we continued searching the first floor. With every second that passed, my chest tightened. Where could he have gone?

"He was here a minute ago I promise," Ellie said, panic and fear swimming in her expression. "I didn't take my eyes off him."

"I know you didn't—"

"Mom," Maggie yelled from the mudroom.

I darted through the kitchen, and when I found her, she was standing at the back door. And it was wide open.

Chapter 42

CELINE

The world got blurry and fear surged through me with enough force to nearly knock me over.

"Julian," I cried, my heart lodged in my throat.

Josh was by my side, holding me up. Keeping me from swaying. One hand steady on my back, not restraining, but anchoring me.

"We'll find him," he said. "I sent the girls upstairs to look under every bed and in every closet, just in case he's hiding."

As he spoke, his tone remained calm and soothing. He didn't rush me and he didn't bark orders.

"He ran," I said, looking through the open door. "I should have known. He hasn't eloped in weeks, and today? Today terrified him. I should have protected him, and I didn't. And just—" The guilt came sharp and viscous, stabbing into me and drowning me at the same time, my instincts screaming at me that I'd failed him.

A sob overtook me, and I clung to Josh, my tears flowing. I was wasting time and breath crying when I should be searching. It was one more reason to berate myself, yet my body needed to release all this pent-up emotion before I could think clearly.

"He couldn't have gone too far," Josh murmured. "I'll get my coat. We'll find him. The farm is big but not that big." He whistled.

"I think Wayne left too," Maggie said when the dog didn't immediately appear.

I stumbled to the door, scanning the farm for sight of them, calling my little boy's name at the top of my lungs.

"I'll get Nolan," Josh said gently. "He can help."

"I've got to go." My baby was out there, alone and in the cold. I had to find him.

"Go," he said. "I'll follow your lead." His words cut through my panic, steadying me.

"I'll go to the main barn," I said. "Check the orchard and call me."

After telling the girls to stay in the house, I darted to the big barn, calling for Julian again, begging the universe for a sign of him.

He wouldn't run toward anything noisy. He wouldn't cross water. If he was overloaded, he would have been searching for quiet and familiar. A place he'd been before. I forced my brain to slow, to think like his. He didn't run randomly; he ran with purpose.

"Julian," I cried. "It's Mom. I'm safe. You're safe. Please come out."

I paced around the building, looking in every nook and cranny. It wasn't dark yet, but the sun would set in another hour or so.

"Please," I cried. Please, baby. "I'm so sorry. I know you're scared."

I did another lap, looking for footprints or any other sign.

An engine revved outside, so I scurried out, finding Josh approaching on one of the ATVs.

"The deputy is taking Phyllis in to book her." He was calm and serious, delivering the information carefully like he didn't want to add to the weight of fear that was already crushing me.

It made my heart clench. His support was keeping me standing, and the way he filled me in rather than telling me what I should do only gave me more strength.

"Nolan's going to check the orchard, garden, and sheds. I told him no loud noises, no sirens, and that if he finds him, to call us immediately so we can intervene."

A shaky breath escaped me. "Thank you."

"Jasper is on his way too. No sirens. And I figured we'd take this. We can cover more ground with it."

I nodded, still searching and scanning. It was getting cold enough to see my breath, though with the way the panic burned inside me, I was covered in sweat.

"Where would he want to go?" Josh asked gently.

"Somewhere familiar," I said. "Somewhere he has positive associations with."

"Let's go up the main road. We'll check the buildings one at a time."

I held on tight to Josh as he drove up the road, both of us calling Julian's name. My mind reeled the whole time. I should have seen this coming. I promised him safety. The thought of him cold and alone...

My stomach turned over.

For a moment, I thought I would vomit up the banana bread we'd made this morning. But I forced myself to sit up straighter and swallowed back the urge. I needed to stop obsessing about what I hadn't done and focus on what I could do now.

As we drove past the old sugar shack, a flash of bright green among all the muted browns and mossy hues caught my attention.

"Stop." I hopped off the ATV and ran to the item.

"It's his," I said, holding up a single Minecraft sock. The sight knocked the air out of my lungs. Bare feet. Cold ground. I imagined him wincing with every step and almost collapsed.

I clutched the sock, my despair growing. It had been at least an hour. Who knew where he could be. And I'd failed him.

"Celine." Josh ran his hands up and down my arms. "You can do this." The statement wasn't encouragement; he'd worded it like a fact.

Eyes closed, I looked at the farm through Julian's eyes. I borrowed his joy, his logic and his patterns. Where would I go when the world felt too loud?

I visualized the tractors in the barn, the tasty apples on the trees, running wild with Wayne. This place had become his home. I could see him asking Josh questions, playing with the tools, and his broad smile at the pumpkin race.

"The pumpkin race," I said. "The building where you and the kids hollowed out the pumpkin." My mind spun. "He had so much fun. And he still talks about it."

"The equipment barn." He nodded. "Let's go."

We raced down the road toward the outskirts of the farm,

closer to route eleven. The building was not a folksy barn, but more of a giant metal shed. Josh stored machinery and other big equipment that didn't get used a lot in here.

There was a hill leading to the large door for easy access, so he'd driven the forklift right up to it and we'd spent days working on the boat, listening to music, and eating snacks. Julian had loved every minute.

Josh stopped outside the barn, and I scrambled to the ground, then took off toward the nearest door.

Inside, the barn was dark, but I closed my eyes and prayed he was here. My heart lodged in my throat. If he wasn't, I didn't have a clue where to look next.

"Julian" I called, my voice bouncing off the walls. "It's Mom. Are you in here?"

I dug my phone out of my pocket and turned on the flashlight, then swung it from one side of the building to the other, searching. Josh came up behind me, flipping on the lights.

Was he here?

I ducked behind every trailer, every piece of equipment, and all the extra hay bales shrink wrapped in plastic to save for winter.

Rather than a little boy, I discovered a wagging tail and a dog trotting toward us.

"Wayne," I sobbed.

Josh crouched, taking his head in his hands. "Where is he?"

"Julian," I shouted, following Wayne as he weaved through storage shelves. My heart was hammering in my ears, so I almost missed the faint whimpering. But when I heard it, I stopped and held my breath. Another whimper, and I was calling out his name again, darting toward the sound.

Julian was crouched in a corner, next to a stack of lumber. He was curled up, his hands covering his ears, rocking softly and crying, his whole body shaking. Relief and grief collided, relief that he was alive and grief that he'd been so scared.

I dropped to my knees, wrapping my arms around him. "Julian, baby," I said softly. "I'm here. You're safe."

He didn't speak, just kept shivering.

Josh towered over us, shucking his coat and handing it to me.

I wrapped the huge, warm garment around my boy's tiny body. "Mama's here," I said softly. "I'm so sorry. I'm so sorry." I memorized the weight of him in my arms. The proof of his life.

"You're freezing," I said through my tears. "Can we take you home?"

He didn't say anything, but when I stood and picked him up, he didn't fight or argue. Keeping him wrapped in Josh's coat, I brushed his hair out of his face and squeezed him tight.

Josh reached out to take him, but I only held him tighter. Julian was overstimulated and probably in shock. He likely wouldn't do well with anyone but me.

But then Julian shifted, loosening the hold he had on me, and reached for Josh. It was the clearest signal I'd ever seen. Trust and safety.

As Josh cradled him in his arms, Julian rested his head on his chest. Josh went utterly still, like he understood the weight of what he'd just been given. He held my son like he was precious, not fragile.

My chest ached with gratitude for this man. I could see it now. He wasn't trying to control me; he was trying to earn his place in our lives. As I stared at this man holding my son. The dam inside me burst. The love for my children, the fear I'd been carrying around for years, and guilt and shame and anguish. It all came crashing down.

I shook as I cried, with relief, with exhaustion, and with yearning for the very thing I'd been denying myself for so long. Safety.

"Jasper's at the house," he said. "I'll have him examine him. Let's get back."

We left the barn, with Wayne dutifully following.

Josh started a fire in the hearth and Jasper got his medical kit out right away. After a quick examination, he determined that aside from a few cuts on his feet, Julian was healthy.

The girls wouldn't let go of him, so the three of them were now wrapped in a comforter on Josh's couch. They were tangled together like they were instinctively rebuilding their bond. Not perfect, but whole.

Josh sat with them, feeding them snacks and watching *Sponge Bob Square Pants* while I spoke to Nolan in the kitchen, giving him all the details about my encounter with Phyllis. I handed over the cards, notes, and emails, as well as the parole board statement.

"I'm going to have to speak to the kids," he said. He'd been kind and patient, tall and broad shouldered and dressed in his uniform, but carrying himself like the weight of protecting this town had begun to wear on him. His beard was neatly trimmed, and grays had started to creep in at his temples, and the lines around his eyes were deeper than I remembered.

"Tomorrow?" I asked.

"Of course. I can come here. Or you can come down."

"She'll call you in the morning." Josh put his arm around my shoulder. "They've been through hell, man."

Nolan nodded. "Just making sure I've got all the details." He rubbed a hand over his face. "I can't take another violent incident in Maplewood. We're supposed to be a foliage and farmers' market kind of place."

"It's been a rough year," Josh said, pulling me into his side.

"That's one way to put it." With a sigh, Nolan headed for the door. "Another would be cursed."

Chapter 43

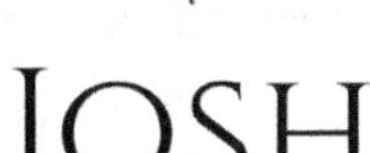

JOSH

"You did good today," I said, scratching Wayne's ears. "Tomorrow I'm buying you a steak. No arguments."

He thumped his tail once and trotted away happily. Once I'd confirmed that the door was locked, I wandered into the living room.

Just over the threshold, I stopped short, the scene nearly stealing my breath. The fire crackled low and steady, throwing warm light across the walls. Celine was carefully folding blankets, moving through the space like it belonged to her.

The house hadn't felt this full in years. Or this alive.

For the first time since my parents had passed, I didn't feel like I was trespassing in their house.

I took the blankets from her and headed upstairs. At the top, Wayne pushed past me and trotted into the guest room where Maggie and Julian were asleep on the queen-size bed.

He jumped up, circling twice before curling up at their feet. Like it had always been his job.

Something in my chest loosened at the sight.

Celine hovered over them, kissing both their heads, then lingering an extra second over Julian. For several seconds, she rested her hand on his back like she was counting his breaths. Then she stood and switched the bedside lamp off. They looked so innocent. Not on guard, not scared. Just tired. Tomorrow would bring questions, reports, and hard conversations. For now, I hoped they could rest undisturbed.

In my office, Ellie was lying on the couch, her feet slung over one arm, flipping through a book. "Do you have an extra phone charger?" she asked.

"We'll get it tomorrow," Celine said.

Ellie sighed dramatically. Teenage sass meant she was comfortable, so I'd take it.

"I have one downstairs. I'll grab it. Why don't you pick out a bedroom?"

"The couch is fine."

"Ellie. I've got five bedrooms. Take your pick. And Jasper's old room has a big screen TV, along with his gaming setup."

She was on her feet before I finished the sentence.

Smiling, Celine shuffled over to me. I wrapped my arms around her, and she leaned into me, resting her head on my chest. She wasn't fragile. She was fierce. And tonight she'd let herself lean on me, not because she had to, but because she could.

"You did everything right." I threaded my fingers through her hair. "You protected your kids. You trusted yourself."

She didn't answer, just breathed.

"You're an incredible mom."

"Thank you," she whispered. "For staying. For listening."

Wrapped around each other, my head resting on hers, we stood for several minutes, letting our hearts beat against each other. Just being still.

Loving Celine wasn't about fixing her. It was about standing close enough that she never had to look over her shoulder alone.

"I love you," she said.

The words settled into me. Into all the cracks and fissures in my heart. "I love you too."

"Can we go downstairs for a minute? To talk?" she asked.

I nodded and guided her out. We peeked in on Ellie, who was splayed out on Jasper's old bed, game controller in hand, then crept down the stairs.

In the living room, I watched the fire, giving Celine a moment to collect her thoughts.

She was pacing, her nervous energy apparent, and I didn't want to add to the stress.

"I don't know how to do this." She was wearing one of my shirts, the too-long sleeves pushed up, her hair piled on top of her head.

She looked wrecked. And impossibly beautiful.

"I don't know how to let my guard down. To trust you," she admitted in a quiet voice. "To make room for you in my life. It took me so long to get here. And I'm scared."

"Come sit down," I patted the couch.

She sat, and I pulled her against me, slow and deliberate, giving her time to pull away if she needed. When she settled in, her body molding to mine, I stroked her hair, grounding us both.

"We don't need all the answers today. All we need to know is that we want to do this."

"But how could you want me?" she whispered. "I'm a single mom. A mess. And I've got shipping containers full of baggage."

I tipped her chin up and kissed her forehead. "I want you because of those things, not in spite of them. And for the record, I own heavy machinery. I'm excellent with baggage."

A laugh escaped her. A real one. With a hand on my cheek, she pressed her lips to mine. "Can you be patient with me?"

"I'll never rush you. Never cage you. And I'll never leave you."

The most beautiful smile spread across her face, warming me like the first rays of the sun in the morning.

"And I'll never stop choosing you," she said. "My kids trust you." She sniffled. "And so do I. We're a team. You have been by my side, supporting me and helping me find my strength. And today, when I couldn't do it alone, you were with me."

"I'm always with you."

"Good," she said. "Because I'm not letting you go, Josh."

We held each other in front of the fire, soaking up its warmth. And for the first time in a long time, I believed forever was possible. Not as a promise, but as a practice.

Chapter 44

CELINE

One Month Later

The massive sectional was surrounded by wrapping paper. The tree Josh and the kids had cut down hit the ceiling of the living room and was crammed full of ornaments. Several of which were handmade by Maggie and were horse-shaped.

We hadn't meant to move in here. In fact, I'd tried very hard to avoid it. The bullet that had gone through the ceiling of the cottage had punctured a hot water pipe, and while it hadn't caused significant damage to the house, clean up and repairs had taken a few weeks.

So the kids and I had stayed here. Josh had a ton of space and went out of his way to make us feel welcome. The girls had their own rooms, and Julian got to hang with his best friend Wayne constantly. And pretty quickly, the five of us settled into an easy routine.

It was a temporary living situation. I often had to remind my kids of that. But they had other plans.

Julian took it upon himself to sneak back over to our cottage and bring his belongings over. He did it little by little, an armload or a box full each day. How I didn't notice is beyond me. When he finished his clothes and toys, he started on my stuff. It started small. One day, the *best mom* mug Ellie had made for me in kindergarten appeared in a cabinet in Josh's kitchen.

Not long after that, I came home from a meeting after school and found our framed family photos interspersed with Josh's along the fireplace mantel. When I'd asked how they migrated over here, Julian and Maggie giggled and ran upstairs.

Josh took a photo of my mom and placed it right next to one of his mom. "I think they'd have been friends," he said softly.

That moment was when my resolve—to move back to the cottage, to assert my independence, to get some distance from this man—crumbled into dust.

We hadn't made anything official yet. We were just sort of muddling through. Sleeping at the farmhouse and wandering back over to the cottage when it suited.

The aftermath of the Phyllis incident was difficult. But Josh's support made it more manageable. The kids had been interviewed by Nolan and advocates from the court system. I'd given my statements, and Phyllis had been formally charged.

Justice took time, but since the judge denied her bail due to the violent nature of her crimes, I slept easily.

After the incident, the town had really shown up for us, making sure we had food for months, volunteering to help out at the farm, and providing endless support.

"Mom," Julian said, crawling into my lap with a big smile, his eyes darting to the absurd pile of gifts. "Santa went overboard this year."

I shot Josh a look. He only shrugged. He looked extra delicious in the reindeer printed pajamas that Maggie had picked out for all of us. I worried that it was too much to ask, but he'd been honored to wear them. We'd already taken several goofy family photos, all five of us in our matching jammies.

Josh had not exercised restraint when it came to Christmas shopping. If the pile of Lego sets, books, and nail polish were any indication.

"There's more," he said, jumping up. He wandered around the massive tree and pulled out another stack of gifts. "These are from me," he said bashfully.

He sat down next to me, his eyes darting from kid to kid like he was nervous.

Maggie ripped hers open first.

"A riding helmet?" She squealed. "Wait. Does this mean —" She snapped her mouth closed, her eyes wide behind her glasses.

Josh nodded. "Logan says Daisy is doing so well in her training that you can start riding her soon."

My daughter burst into wild screeches, ripping the helmet out of the box and putting it on her head.

Excellent, she'd probably sleep in that thing for a week.

Julian took his time unwrapping his box. He tended to be more methodical, carefully removing the paper. Inside was another box with several items inside.

"Are these tools?" He held up a small screwdriver set, studying it.

Josh smiled. "You've been so helpful fixing things around the farm, I figured you needed your own set."

Face alight, Julian pulled out a tape measure, a child sized hammer, and a set of wrenches. "These aren't toys." Julian said excitedly. "They're real."

"Nothing dangerous," Josh whispered into my ear. "But he's gotta start somewhere."

"And Ellie," Josh said, handing her a very large box. "I didn't forget about you."

My oldest eyed him dubiously and then tore off the paper. "Bauers?" she said, her face brightening as she eyed the top-of the-line hockey skates.

Josh nodded. "After the holidays, we'll take them back to the shop. They have a special oven that will mold them to your feet."

She assessed him quietly, doubt swimming in her eyes. Fear and hesitance too. It killed me that this was her natural reaction. That her childhood had been so compromised.

But then she smiled, a real, genuine smile, and stood. Then she launched herself into Josh's arms. Maggie and Julian followed, piling on top of him in one massive bear hug.

"Get in here, Mom."

I wrapped my arms around the whole group as best as I could, soaking in this moment, relishing the feeling of togetherness.

Ellie broke away first, stepping away. "The skates are amazing, but I was hoping to ask you a favor as a Christmas present instead."

Josh pressed his lips together thoughtfully. "Ask away."

"*So.* You know how I joined the hockey team?"

Josh nodded. The season had already begun, but they'd

allowed Ellie to join. It had been a while since she'd been on a proper team and she was a bit rusty, but she was having so much fun.

"We don't have an assistant coach. And Olivia's mom is doing a great job, but she needs help. We need help"

My eyebrows shot up and Josh's cheeks turned pink.

"So I volunteered you."

I scoffed. "Excuse me?" She did what?

"I volunteered you for the position of assistant coach for Maplewood's peewee hockey team," she said. "Can you do it? I know it's a big deal and—"

Josh stood and opened his arms. "I'd be honored."

Ellie beamed at him. The sight made my heart clench. Her cool teen facade fell for a moment, and I took in every detail of it.

A weight lifted from my shoulders. She'd been missing this for so long. The safety and silliness.

Josh and my kids were making it very difficult to take this slow. I loved this man. I loved the idea of the family we could create together. But it would take time.

I'd had a plan. But my kids, as usual, were obliterating it.

"Josh, open this one. It's from us." Julian held the box out.

"It's Crocs," Julian blurted out before Josh could remove the wrapping paper. "I picked them out. They're blue. Just like mine."

With a big smile at him, Josh removed the paper. "You guys really are trying to convert me into your Croc cult, huh?"

"You'll eat those words when you experience Croc superiority," Ellie teased.

He slipped them onto his feet and bent over to study them, tapping his chin and acting suspicious. "Interesting," he admitted.

"You've gotta break them in before you make a decision about what you think," Maggie explained.

"How about I wear them while I make pancakes?" Josh suggested.

The kids cheered, and the four of them quickly migrated to the kitchen. I gathered up the wrapping paper, enjoying the moment to myself, and then made my way into the kitchen.

The room had been so large and stark before. Now it was filled with life. Wayne sat near the stove, thumping his tail, hoping for a scrap of bacon, and the kids were making funny-shaped pancakes while Josh supervised.

I refilled my coffee and stood silently to the side, watching. My heart was full of love and gratitude. Plenty of anxiety too, of course, but excitement for the future.

We belonged here.

In this town.

In this house.

And with this man.

While enjoying our Christmas breakfast feast, Josh prepped us for the afternoon. Jenn had invited us over to her home, and he made sure to explain everything carefully to Julian to help manage his expectations.

"We go there for a little while and eat food and open presents?" Julian asked.

"Yes," Josh replied with a dip of his chin. "And I've already packed special food for you."

Julian's shoulders lowered, his relief visible.

"And if it's too loud, we can take a walk into town and look at the Christmas lights again," Josh offered.

The warmth that had started in my chest grew. He was so patient and so accommodating with Julian, who was blossoming every day. My little guy had even asked Josh to teach him how to skate too.

"Do I have to wear fancy clothes?" Julian asked, his attention drifting to me.

I shook my head. "Nope, you can wear whatever you want. We'll stay for a little while, have some fun, and then come back to our house and play Mario Kart, okay?"

With an easy smile, he wandered off to play.

The girls took their plates to the sink and beelined for the living room too, no doubt anxious to play with their new stuff too.

When it was just the two of us, Josh pulled me into his lap for a kiss.

With a sigh, I closed my eyes and let myself enjoy the moment.

"You said our house." He kissed me again. "Not Josh's house."

I shrugged, going for chill, even as my stomach did backflips. That phrase had just slipped out.

"Is that okay?" I asked.

He stood, scooping me into his arms and spinning me around the kitchen. "It's the best Christmas gift ever."

With my arms around his neck, I held on tight and let out a giggle. "Good. Because you're stuck with us now. Forever."

Epilogue

JOSH

I stepped inside, chuckling at the sight of all the Crocs lined up by the door. The kids had given me my own pair for Christmas, but I still hadn't fully adjusted.

"Josh is back," Maggie yelled from the kitchen, where she was filling up a water bottle covered in horse stickers.

Muffled sounds floated down from upstairs. Then there were little feet running down the stairs.

"Hey, bud," I said, greeting Julian, who held his fist out for me to bump. He wasn't comfortable with hugs, so we'd worked out our greeting—a closed fist bump and a head nod.

"Are you coming with us to the fire?" he asked.

I nodded.

"Is it scary?"

"Not at all. The fire department just stacks up all the old Christmas trees."

"Why?"

I hummed, considering how to justify the bonfire to his hyper logical brain. "Because it's fun?" I suggested.

He thought about it, accepting my explanation. "Do I need my headphones?"

"Let's pack them just in case."

"Socks, Julian," Celine said, walking into the kitchen. "Thick socks, please."

He gave her an annoyed look and then headed back upstairs.

Celine reached up on her tiptoes to give me a kiss.

Officially, we'd been "taking it slow." Unofficially, there were no plans for them to move back to the cottage and Ellie and I had plans to paint her room next weekend.

I'd made one teeny tiny joke about "living in sin" and suggested maybe I should propose. But Celine shut it down.

Translation: she wasn't ready yet.

But I was.

Ready for all of it.

For everything.

I loved having them all in my house. We'd had so much fun at Christmas, baking cookies like I used to with my mom, cutting down a huge tree and decorating it in front of the fireplace. The house hadn't felt so alive in years, and I became more certain every day that I wanted this woman forever. Julian had asked me once if I was going to marry his mom and become his dad.

Every time I thought about it, I got choked up.

Because there was nothing I wanted more.

I looked down at Celine, her red hair pulled back in a ponytail, her eyes gleaming. And I thought about dropping to one knee right then and there.

It was a frequent urge that I was getting better at controlling.

"How was school today?" I asked instead.

"Nutty. Doing a unit on volcanoes, and the kids got a little too excited about mixing baking soda and vinegar."

I pulled her close and gave her ass a squeeze. "So that explains the smell."

She hip checked me and rolled her eyes. "I showered, though I think the sweater I was wearing needs to be incinerated."

"Are you gonna take me to practice this weekend?" Ellie asked, appearing in the doorway. She had recently started playing hockey again. The Maplewood peewee team was small and coed, but she was loving it. And I may have been forced into volunteering as an assistant coach.

"Course," I replied. "You gonna work on your grip for that slap shot?"

She looked up and rolled her eyes. "Fine."

"Find your fleece," Celine said, giving her a look. "And make sure Julian's got thick socks on."

"Missed you today," Celine said once Ellie had slunk off. I held my arm out, and she nestled up under it. "I'm worried."

"Don't be. It's just a quick town meeting and then the bonfire. It will be fun."

"People are so upset about that article."

I sighed. The article. We thought WanderBetch was bad for the town, but she had nothing on the *Boston Globe*, who sent up a team of reporters and published a multi-part article titled "The Fall of America's Most Charming Small Town." It made national news and set off a chain reaction. The internet was flooded with social media posts shaming Maplewood, and people, many who had never even been here, had been giving quotes left and right. Blaming all kinds of stuff on our "unsafe" town.

Nolan was under fire, led by all the conspiracy theories flying around social media and people were questioning why Gabe had hired him as police chief.

It was a mess. But we needed to put it behind us.

"Gabe has great instincts and he cares about the town. This meeting is a way to help people get things off their chests. The more transparent everything is, the better."

"I guess. The rumors have been getting out of control."

I rubbed her shoulders. "It's going to be a fun night." The Christmas tree bonfire had been a blast since I was a kid. "Once the meeting is over, everyone will come together. Nate is bringing kegs of the seasonal ale, and trust me, it will all blow over."

"Okay. I trust you. But I don't trust these kids to wear enough layers."

It was a long-time town tradition. The second Saturday in January, the entire town brought their Christmas trees to town hall, and the firefighters had the time of their lives building them into a bonfire and then lighting it up.

People brought camping chairs, food, and drinks, turning it into an outdoor tailgate in the freezing cold. After surviving endless festivals, leaf peeper season and the holidays, it was nice to be involved with a more laid-back event that was just for the town and its citizens.

But first, we had a town meeting to get through.

While Celine headed inside with the kids, I headed toward Gabe, who was standing at the edge of the parking lot. He was wearing a thick wool coat instead of layers of down like the rest of us, and a dark green scarf. He looked thinner, paler and more jittery than usual.

"You look like you lost a bar fight."

He was rocking several days of stubble and his hair was sticking up in all directions, like he'd been tugging on it.

As I got closer and noted the dark shadows under his eyes, my stomach sank. Shit. He was in worse shape than I'd realized.

"Really bad night," he replied.

"You okay?"

He smoothed the toe of his boot over a mound of snow on the sidewalk. "Blind date gone very wrong."

I almost laughed. "Blind date?" Gabe didn't date much and certainly wasn't one to allow friends to fix him up. I'd assumed his anguish was about town business.

"Never again. My mom is on my shit list for life. There were flying tacos."

"Sorry, what?"

He shook his head. "And a flat tire."

"Yours?"

He nodded. "Somehow, I found myself holding a jack in dress shoes trying to figure out when I'd lost the will to live."

I clapped him on the shoulder. He and I had literally known each other our entire lives, and I'd never seen this kind of cynicism from him. My cousin was all business. Effective and friendly all the time.

"It's gonna be okay, man," I said. "People are worked up,

but it's a quick meeting. And then we can watch the fire and drink Nate's new beer."

Rather than perk up like I thought he would, he shook his head. "No. I have some really bad news. It's only gonna get worse."

Before I could ask, someone called his name.

"Better get in there," Gabe said. "And face the firing squad."

Inside Celine had found seats next to Jasper and Evie. The kids were in the basement doing arts and crafts with high school kids again while parents attended the meeting.

"Gabe looks upset," Celine said. "I told you the pressure was getting to him."

I put my arm around her, unease making my stomach roll.

Gabe stood behind the podium, staring out at the assembled town. The place was packed. There wasn't an empty seat. Maplewood was a pretty engaged place, but this was an abnormally large crowd.

Before he could speak, Bitsy Bramble strode toward the center of the room. She pushed Gabe out of the way with shocking strength and gripped the microphone on the podium.

"This is a tragedy," she exclaimed. "After hundreds of years, Maplewood has fallen."

A gasp went through the crowd.

Gabe leaned in. "Now, Bitsy, let's discuss everything."

She threw a hand up to block him.

"The Maplewood Economic Development Committee received word today." She drew a breath, like she was purposely keeping us all hanging. "The state has decided we are no longer a suitable location for the Vermont State Maple Festival."

The room erupted into gasps and shouts.

Gabe pinched the bridge of his nose, his shoulders slumping.

"How could this happen?"

"It's because we're Murderville." Someone shouted

"That's what we get for trusting a child to run the town." Another added.

Gabe managed to wrestle the microphone from Bitsy.

"Ladies and gentlemen," he said, his voice deep and serious. "Please settle down and allow me to explain."

"The town is doomed," someone shouted.

"We're all going out of business," another added dramatically.

"After thirty-eight years, the state has awarded the maple festival and all the attendant grants and support to another town."

This was a disaster. Maplewood, Vermont, had been the official home of the Vermont State Maple Festival for generations. Thousands came to town, including press. Every person in this room depended on the income that festival brought in, and with only three months until that festival, everyone would be scrambling.

"Where is it being held?" Several people shouted.

"It doesn't matter. The decision has been made. We need to focus on the future," Gabe reasoned.

Bitsy stood next to him, arms crossed, her jeweled glasses on the bridge of her nose.

"Birch Hollow," she shouted.

Those two words were like an arrow to the heart.

The shouting resumed. Half the crowd was standing and moving and panicking.

"How will we survive?"

"We should all move."

"Can we sue?"

The panic made the walls feel like they were closing in on us. This wouldn't hit the farm too hard; I sold most of my sap to Sugar Moon, and they shipped to stores all over North America. As a producer, I'd survive.

But the inn? Jenn's coffee shop? All the restaurants and stores? The folks who owned rental properties? It would be catastrophic.

"As chair of the economic development committee, I want you to know we are not taking this lying down." Bitsy pounded her fist on the podium. "We will not stand for this."

The room quieted for a moment, all eyes on her.

"And I think I speak for all when I say that this is clearly a failure of our leadership. And for that reason, I move to recall Mayor Gabriel Harding."

My gut plummeted. Recall Gabe? What the hell was going on?

Gabe's eye twitched.

"On behalf of the citizens of this town, I have drafted a petition to recall the mayor."

"Bitsy," Gabe interjected.

"Too late," she snapped. "Check the bylaws. We the citizens have a right to recall the mayor with a town-wide election thirty days after a petition is certified. We need one hundred signatures."

She gestured to the back of the room where several Maplewood Mafia ladies stood behind a folding table. "You can line up to sign my petition in the back of the room after the meeting."

There was no waiting until after the meeting. Folks all over the room stood, gathering their things, and shuffled toward the ladies and their clipboards.

"You can't do this." Aunt Suzie stood and put her hands on her hips. "This is absurd."

"Yes we can." Bitsy glared, though between one blink and the next, her expression morphed into a fake smile. "Also, on behalf of the economic committee, I want you to know we are doing everything we can to fix this. We've hired a seasoned crisis manager to help us navigate the disaster caused by this complete failure of leadership."

She looked to the far corner of the room where a woman stood.

She wore high leather boots with an ice pick stiletto heel and a black trench coat. She looked like Carmen Sandiego if she had a side hustle as a hitwoman.

I squinted, surveying her. She looked vaguely familiar.

"Sabrina Monroe," Bitsy said with dramatic flair. "Here to save the town."

Heads turned and chatter erupted. The woman stood perfectly still, completely unfazed under the scrutiny of an entire town.

"I'm gonna go get the kids," Celine said, standing up.

"I'll come with you." I needed a break from the chaos to wrap my mind around the last five minutes.

"No. You should go talk to Gabe." She placed a hand on my shoulder. "He needs you."

My cousin, the usually unflappable mayor, had never looked so shaken. He loved this town more than anyone I'd ever met. More than Bitsy Bramble and her judgmental bull-shit. He prided himself on leading us in a way that served us all well.

I nodded. "I'll meet you guys outside." With that, I fought the exiting crowd, heading for Gabe.

His tie was crooked and his jaw was clenched tight. Gabe who'd talked us out of speeding tickets as kids, who could calm even the most irate old lady during a debate about parking permits.

"Mr. Mayor."

Sabrina strode up at the same time I did. That was when her identity hit me. I hadn't laid eye on her in probably twenty years, but it all came rushing back. Maplewood's prodigal daughter, the one who bested Gabe on every test. Their debates and science fair showdowns were legendary.

This version of her was all dark lipstick and venom.

She tilted her head, feigning concern. "Looks like you're having a bad night."

"Last night was a lot worse," he said, pinning her with a glare.

The two of them stood there, staring at one another, like bulls about to charge, for an uncomfortably long moment.

What the hell had happened last night?

"This isn't a game, Monroe," he said. "This is people's lives. You don't give a shit about this town."

"Of course it's not a game. This is a small town full of people who deserve better than a man who confuses being liked with being effective."

She leaned in slightly, her expensive perfume wafting around us. "You've always been protected. By the teachers, your parents, the voters. Sweet Gabriel could never do wrong. That was always the narrative."

She lifted her chin and arched a brow.

"And I'm so good at rewriting narratives."

Her words land with a thud.

Gabe was nearly vibrating with anger. "You'll only cause more damage."

She laughed. "Seems to me like you've done enough of that already. I came here for some rest and relaxation, yet now, because of your idiocy, this has become a working vacation. But don't worry, I'll save the day. I always do. And if it means getting to watch you suffer? If it means your blinding mediocrity will finally be exposed?" She clapped, her dark red nails gleaming in the fluorescent light. "Even better."

With a *humph*, she turned.

Before she could walk away, Gabe snapped, "Nothing's changed since high school, Monroe. You're still a nasty, ruthless opportunist."

She turned slowly, a smile spreading across her face. "And you still think I give a shit about your opinion."

With that, she strutted to the door, stopping to hug and greet townspeople as if she wasn't a viper in a Burberry coat.

"Take a breath," I said.

Gabe looked like his brain had been deprived of oxygen for several minutes.

"We'll get through this. The town will be okay."

He shook his head. "It's too late. I let everyone down."

I gripped his shoulder. "You did not. And we'll figure it out."

With a slap on his back I guided him out the door, where the bonfire was starting up and townspeople were grouped together, nervously chatting. Logan rushed over, took one look at Gabe's face, and handed him his beer.

After downing it in a few sips, Gabe pasted his usual smile on his face and smoothed his hair down. "I don't know what's gonna happen," he admitted. "But I hate her."

I frowned at him, surprised. My cousin didn't hate anyone. He wasn't capable. We'd shared a crib. I'd known him every day of my life. He was one of the good ones. He believed in people past the point of reason. He was a helper. A fixer.

"You don't hate anyone," I said carefully, shaken by this change in him.

He glowered as Sabrina walked by in the distance.

"Maybe she's the exception."

Bonus Chapter

♥

CELINE

Want more Celine, Josh, Ellie, Maggie & Julian?
Grab the Bonus Chapter HERE:

Acknowledgments

Thank you for visiting Maplewood! I hope you have had as much fun reading this book as I had writing it. I've been waiting years to write about Celine, Ellie, Maggie, and Julian. Thank you for your patience as I worked to give them the HEA they deserved.

First, I want to thank my son T. You keep me on my toes and push me to be a better version of myself every day. Because of you, I write books for a living and get to pick you up from school every day. You are brilliant and unique and hilarious. I am so lucky I get to be your mom.

Erica Walsh, I love you, appreciate you, and can't wait to finally meet you in person this year. From cover design to finding photos and editing blurbs, you are truly in my corner every single day. Your Instagram wizardry is incredible. We have cried and laughed and yelled together over the past four years, and I am a better person and writer because of you. Thank you from the bottom of my heart.

Morgan Leigh, I asked for help, and you jumped in with both feet, quickly becoming the MVP in my life and the person who keeps me organized and on track. I treasure your friendship and your positive attitude. No one is more willing or more capable of learning new things than you are, and I am pinching myself that I get to call you mine.

Beth, thank you for your thorough editing. I am amazed by your patience, professionalism, and kindness. Your careful work has helped bring these characters to life, and I am truly in your debt.

Summer, thank you for joining me on this wild ride. Your support means so much to me.

Daisy, thank you so much for your support over the years and for generously sharing your experiences to help make this book stronger.

To my oldest friend, the indomitable Caroline, thank you for igniting my love of romance by introducing me to Jane Austen (and Colin Firth in a wet shirt) at the tender age of fifteen. My entire romantic worldview has been shaped by our shared love of happy endings, and your friendship for these last twenty-eight (!!!) years is a true gift. You push me to grow and evolve and help me edit in airports. You are the best.

Linda, you are a badass. Thank you for your friendship, your book ideas, and your enthusiasm. You are a treasure.

Becca and Shauna, thank you for your professionalism and excitement about this series. You and the Author Agency have been such wonderful partners throughout this process.

Brittanee, thank you for your friendship over these past five years. I love watching you soar and am grateful for our morning chats.

To my content and hype teams, thank you from the bottom of my heart for loving these books and this crazy world I've created. Most days, I pinch myself, shocked that I've found myself surrounded by such an amazing group of positive, kick-ass people.

Thank you to my family for being hilarious, loving, and silly. To my children, G & T, you push me, challenge me, and surprise me every day. Being your mom is my life's greatest adventure. Thank you for never going easy on me. To G, my mini-me, you are my #1 fan, and I can't wait to share my author journey with you as you grow. And T, thank you for kicking ass in first grade so I had the mental and physical energy to write this book.

Thank you to my mother, who is my best friend, my confidant, and the person responsible for my work ethic. You've taught me how to love, to nurture, and to kick ass when necessary.

And finally, I'd like to thank Taylor Alison Swift for getting me through not only the production of this book, but through all of my life's challenges for the past decade. You have taught me, and countless others, how to harness my creativity and, most importantly, how to invest in my potential. Your work has made me a better mom, writer, entrepreneur, and person. Thank you.

Also by Daphne Elliot

MAPLEWOOD

Sap & Secrets

Maple & Moonlight

Sugar & Shadows

LOVEWELL

The Maine Lumberjacks Series

Caught In The Axe

Pain In The Axe

Axe-identally Married

Axe Backwards

Axe-ing for Trouble

The Lovewell Lumberjacks Series

Wood You Be Mine?

Wood You Marry Me?

Wood You Rather

Wood Riddance

THE MOM COMS

Mother Hater

THE DAD COMS

Bonus Daddy

HAVENPORT

The Quinn Brothers Series

Trusting You

Finding You

Keeping You

The Rossi Family Series

Resisting You

Holding You

Embracing You

About the Author

In High School, Daphne Elliot was voted "most likely to become a romance novelist." After spending the last decade as a corporate lawyer, she has finally embraced her destiny. Her small town steamy novels are filled with flirty banter, sexy hijinks, and lots and lots of heart.